Robert des noms propres

Amélie Nothomb

Robert
des noms propres

ROMAN

Albin Michel

IL A ÉTÉ TIRÉ DE CET OUVRAGE
VING-CINQ EXEMPLAIRES
SUR VÉLIN BOUFFANT DES PAPETERIES SALZER
DONT QUINZE EXEMPLAIRES NUMÉROTÉS DE 1 À 15
ET DIX HORS COMMERCE NUMÉROTÉS DE I À X

ISBN broché 2-226-13389-5
ISBN luxe 2-226-13449-2

Lucette en était à sa huitième heure d'insomnie. Dans son ventre, le bébé avait le hoquet depuis la veille. Toutes les quatre ou cinq secondes, un sursaut gigantesque secouait le corps de cette fillette de dix-neuf ans qui, un an plus tôt, avait décidé de devenir épouse et mère.

Le conte de fées avait commencé comme un rêve : Fabien était beau, il se disait prêt à tout pour elle, elle l'avait pris au mot. L'idée de jouer au mariage avait amusé ce garçon de son âge et la famille, perplexe et émue, avait vu ces deux enfants mettre leurs habits de noces.

Peu après, triomphante, Lucette avait annoncé qu'elle était enceinte.

Sa grande sœur lui avait demandé :

– Ce n'est pas un peu tôt ?

— Ce ne sera jamais assez tôt ! avait répondu la petite, exaltée.

Peu à peu, les choses étaient devenues moins féeriques. Fabien et Lucette se disputaient beaucoup. Lui qui avait été si heureux de sa grossesse lui disait à présent :

— Tu as intérêt à cesser d'être folle quand le petit sera là !

— Tu me menaces ?

Il s'en allait en claquant la porte.

Pourtant, elle était sûre de ne pas être folle. Elle voulait que la vie soit forte et dense. Ne fallait-il pas être folle pour vouloir autre chose ? Elle voulait que chaque jour, chaque année, lui apporte le maximum.

Maintenant, elle voyait que Fabien n'était pas à la hauteur. C'était un garçon normal. Il avait joué au mariage et, à présent, il jouait à l'homme marié. Il n'avait rien d'un prince charmant. Elle l'agaçait. Il disait :

– Ça y est, elle fait sa crise.

Parfois, il était gentil. Il lui caressait le ventre en disant :

– Si c'est un garçon, ce sera Tanguy. Si c'est une fille, ce sera Joëlle.

Lucette pensait qu'elle détestait ces prénoms.

Dans la bibliothèque du grand-père, elle avait pris une encyclopédie du siècle précédent. On y trouvait des prénoms fantasmagoriques qui présageaient des destins hirsutes. Lucette les notait consciencieusement sur des bouts de papier qu'elle perdait parfois. Plus tard, quelqu'un découvrait, çà et là, un lambeau chiffonné sur lequel était inscrit « Eleuthère » ou « Lutegarde », et personne ne comprenait le sens de ces cadavres exquis.

Très vite, le bébé s'était mis à bouger. Le gynécologue disait qu'il n'avait jamais eu affaire à un fœtus aussi remuant : « C'est un cas ! »

Lucette souriait. Son petit était déjà exceptionnel. C'était aux temps tout proches où il

9

n'était pas encore possible de connaître à l'avance le sexe de l'enfant. Peu importait à la fillette enceinte.

— Ce sera un danseur ou une danseuse, avait-elle décrété, la tête pleine de rêves.

— Non, disait Fabien. Ce sera un footballeur ou une emmerdeuse.

Elle le regardait avec des poignards dans les yeux. Il ne disait pas ça pour être méchant, rien que pour la taquiner. Mais elle voyait dans ces réflexions de grand gamin la marque d'une vulgarité rédhibitoire.

Quand elle était seule et que le fœtus bougeait comme un fou, elle lui parlait tendrement :

— Vas-y, danse, mon bébé. Je te protégerai, je ne te laisserai pas devenir un Tanguy footballeur ou une Joëlle emmerdeuse, tu seras libre de danser où tu voudras, à l'Opéra de Paris ou pour des bohémiens.

Peu à peu, Fabien avait pris le pli de disparaître des après-midi entiers. Il partait après le déjeuner et revenait vers dix heures du soir, sans explication. Epuisée par la grossesse, Lucette n'avait pas la force de l'attendre. Elle dormait déjà quand il revenait. Le matin, il restait au lit jusqu'à onze heures et demie. Il prenait un bol de café avec une cigarette qu'il fumait en regardant dans le vide.

– Ça va ? Tu ne te fatigues pas trop ? lui demanda-t-elle un jour.

– Et toi ? répondit-il.

– Moi, je fais un bébé. Tu es au courant ?

– Je pense bien. Tu ne parles que de ça.

– Eh bien c'est très fatigant, figure-toi, d'être enceinte.

– C'est pas ma faute. C'est toi qui l'as voulu. Je peux pas le porter à ta place.

– On peut savoir ce que tu fais, l'après-midi ?

– Non.

Elle éclata de rage :

– Je ne sais plus rien, moi ! Tu ne me dis plus rien !

– A part le bébé, rien ne t'intéresse.

– Tu n'as qu'à être intéressant. Alors, je m'intéresserai à toi.

— Je suis intéressant.

— Vas-y, intéresse-moi, si tu en es capable !

Il soupira et partit chercher un étui. Il en sortit un revolver. Elle ouvrit de grands yeux.

— C'est ça que je fais, l'après-midi. Je tire.

— Où ça ?

— Un club secret. Aucune importance.

— Il y a de vraies balles dedans ?

— Oui.

— Pour tuer les gens ?

— Par exemple.

Elle caressa l'arme avec fascination.

— Je deviens bon, tu sais. Je touche le cœur de la cible au premier coup. C'est une sensation que tu ne peux pas imaginer. J'adore. Quand je commence, je ne peux plus m'arrêter.

— Je comprends.

Cela ne leur arrivait pas souvent de se comprendre.

La grande sœur, qui avait déjà deux petits enfants, venait voir Lucette qu'elle adorait. Elle la trouvait si jolie, toute frêle avec son gros ventre. Un jour, elles se disputèrent :

— Tu devrais lui dire de chercher un boulot. Il va être père.

— Nous avons dix-neuf ans. C'est les parents qui paient.

— Ils ne vont pas payer éternellement.

— Pourquoi viens-tu m'embêter avec ces histoires ?

— C'est important, quand même.

— Il faut toujours que tu viennes gâcher mon bonheur !

— Qu'est-ce que tu racontes ?

— Et maintenant, tu vas me dire qu'il faut être raisonnable, et gnagnagna !

— Tu es folle ! Je n'ai pas dit ça !

— Ça y est ! Je suis folle ! Je l'attendais, celle-là ! Tu es jalouse de moi ! Tu veux me détruire !

— Enfin, Lucette...

— Sors ! hurla-t-elle.

La grande sœur s'en alla, atterrée. Elle avait toujours su que la petite dernière était fragile, mais là, cela prenait des proportions inquiétantes.

Désormais, quand elle lui téléphonait, Lucette raccrochait lorsqu'elle entendait sa voix.

« J'ai assez de problèmes comme ça », pensait la cadette.

En vérité, sans se l'avouer, elle sentait qu'elle était sur une voie de garage et que sa grande sœur le savait. Comment gagneraient-ils leur vie un jour ? Fabien ne s'intéressait qu'aux armes à feu et elle, elle n'était bonne à rien. Elle n'allait quand même pas devenir caissière dans un supermarché. D'ailleurs, elle n'en serait sûrement pas capable.

Elle enfonçait un oreiller sur sa tête pour ne plus y penser.

Cette nuit-là, donc, le bébé avait le hoquet dans le ventre de Lucette.

On n'imagine pas l'influence du hoquet d'un fœtus sur une fillette enceinte à fleur de peau.

Fabien, lui, dormait comme un bienheureux. Elle, elle en était à sa huitième heure d'insomnie, et à son huitième mois de grossesse. Son ventre énorme lui donnait l'impression de contenir une bombe à retardement.

Chaque hoquètement lui semblait correspondre au tic-tac qui la rapprochait du moment de l'explosion. Le fantasme devint réalité : il y eut bel et bien déflagration – dans la tête de Lucette.

Elle se leva, mue par une conviction soudaine qui lui ouvrit grands les yeux.

Elle alla chercher le revolver là où Fabien le cachait. Elle revint près du lit où le garçon dormait. Elle regarda son beau visage en visant sa tempe et murmura :

– Je t'aime, mais je dois protéger le bébé contre toi.

Elle approcha le canon et tira jusqu'à vider le chargeur.

Elle regarda le sang sur le mur. Ensuite, très calme, elle téléphona à la police :

– Je viens de tuer mon mari. Venez.

Quand les policiers arrivèrent, ils furent accueillis par une enfant enceinte jusqu'aux yeux qui tenait un revolver dans sa main droite.

— Posez cette arme ! dirent-ils en la mena-
çant.

— Oh, elle n'est plus chargée, répondit-elle
en obéissant.

Elle conduisit les policiers jusqu'au lit conjugal pour montrer son œuvre.

— On l'emmène au commissariat ou à l'hôpital ?

— Pourquoi à l'hôpital ? Je ne suis pas
malade.

— Nous ne savons pas. Mais vous êtes
enceinte.

— Je ne suis pas sur le point d'accoucher.
Emmenez-moi au commissariat, exigea-t-elle,
comme si c'était un droit.

Quand ce fut chose faite, on lui dit qu'elle
pouvait appeler un avocat. Elle dit que ce
n'était pas nécessaire. Un homme dans un
bureau lui posa des questions à n'en plus finir,
au nombre desquelles figurait :

— Pourquoi avez-vous tué votre mari ?

— Dans mon ventre, le petit avait le hoquet.

— Oui, et ensuite ?

— Rien. J'ai tué Fabien.

— Vous l'avez tué parce que le petit avait le hoquet ?

Elle parut interloquée avant de répondre :

— Non. Ce n'est pas si simple. Cela dit, le petit n'a plus le hoquet.

— Vous avez tué votre mari pour faire passer le hoquet du petit ?

Elle eut un rire déplacé :

— Non, enfin, c'est ridicule !

— Pourquoi avez-vous tué votre mari ?

— Pour protéger mon bébé, affirma-t-elle, cette fois avec un sérieux tragique.

— Ah. Votre mari l'avait menacé ?

— Oui.

— Il fallait le dire tout de suite.

— Oui.

— Et de quoi le menaçait-il ?

— Il voulait l'appeler Tanguy si c'était un garçon et Joëlle si c'était une fille.

— Et puis ?

— Rien.

— Vous avez tué votre mari parce que vous n'aimiez pas son choix de prénoms ?

Elle fronça les sourcils. Elle sentait bien qu'il

17

manquait quelque chose à son argumentation et, pourtant, elle était sûre d'avoir raison. Elle comprenait très bien son geste et trouvait d'autant plus frustrant de ne pas parvenir à l'expliquer. Elle décida alors de se taire.

— Vous êtes sûre que vous ne voulez pas un avocat ?

Elle en était sûre. Comment eût-elle expliqué cela à un avocat ? Il l'eût prise pour une folle, comme les autres. Plus elle parlait, plus on la prenait pour une folle. Donc, elle la bouclerait.

Elle fut incarcérée. Une infirmière venait la voir chaque jour.

Quand on lui annonçait une visite de sa mère ou de sa grande sœur, elle refusait.

Elle ne répondait qu'aux questions concernant sa grossesse. Sinon, elle restait muette.

Dans sa tête, elle se parlait : « J'ai eu raison de tuer Fabien. Il n'était pas mauvais, il était médiocre. La seule chose qui n'était pas médiocre en lui, c'était son revolver, mais il n'en aurait jamais fait qu'un usage médiocre, contre les petits voyous du voisinage, ou alors il aurait laissé le bébé jouer avec. J'ai eu raison de le retourner contre lui. Vouloir appeler son enfant Tanguy ou Joëlle, c'est vouloir lui offrir un monde médiocre, un horizon déjà fermé. Moi, je veux que mon bébé ait l'infini à sa portée. Je veux que mon enfant ne se sente limité par rien, je veux que son prénom lui suggère un destin hors norme. »

Lucette accoucha en prison d'une petite fille. Elle la prit dans ses bras et la regarda avec tout l'amour du monde. Jamais on ne vit jeune mère plus émerveillée.

– Tu es trop belle ! répétait-elle au bébé.

– Comment l'appellerez-vous ?

– Plectrude.

Une délégation de matonnes, de psychologues, de vagues juristes et de médecins plus vagues encore défila auprès de Lucette pour protester : elle ne pouvait pas appeler sa fille comme ça.

— Je le peux. Il y a eu une sainte Plectrude. Je ne sais plus ce qu'elle a fait mais elle a existé.

On consulta un spécialiste qui confirma.

— Pensez à l'enfant, Lucette.

— Je ne pense qu'à elle.

— Ça ne lui posera que des problèmes.

— Ça préviendra les gens qu'elle est exceptionnelle.

— On peut s'appeler Marie et être exceptionnelle.

— Marie, ça ne protège pas. Plectrude, ça protège : cette fin rude, ça sonne comme un bouclier.

— Appelez-la Gertrude, alors. C'est plus facile à porter.

— Non. Ce début de Plectrude, ça fait penser à un pectoral : ce prénom est un talisman.

— Ce prénom est grotesque et votre enfant sera la risée des gens.

— Non : il la rendra assez forte pour qu'elle se défende.

— Pourquoi lui donner d'emblée une raison de se défendre ? Elle aura assez d'obstacles comme ça !

— Vous dites ça pour moi ?

— Entre autres.

— Rassurez-vous, je ne la gênerai pas long-temps. Et maintenant, écoutez-moi : je suis en prison, je suis privée de mes droits. La seule liberté qui me reste consiste à appeler mon enfant comme je veux.

— C'est égoïste, Lucette.

— Au contraire. Et puis, ça ne vous regarde pas.

Elle fit baptiser le bébé en prison pour être sûre de contrôler l'affaire.

La nuit même, elle confectionna une corde avec ses draps déchirés et se pendit dans sa cellule. Au matin, on retrouva son cadavre léger. Elle n'avait laissé aucune lettre, aucune explication. Le prénom de sa fille, sur lequel elle avait tant insisté, lui tint lieu de testament.

Clémence, la grande sœur de Lucette, vint chercher le bébé à la prison. On ne fut que trop content de se débarrasser de cette petite née sous d'aussi effroyables auspices.

Clémence et son mari Denis avaient deux enfants de quatre et deux ans, Nicole et Béatrice. Ils décidèrent que Plectrude serait leur troisième.

Nicole et Béatrice vinrent regarder leur nouvelle sœur. Elles n'avaient aucune raison de penser qu'elle était la fille de Lucette, dont elles n'avaient d'ailleurs jamais vraiment enregistré l'existence.

Elles étaient trop petites pour se rendre compte qu'elle portait un prénom à coucher dehors et l'adoptèrent, malgré quelques problèmes de prononciation. Longtemps, elles l'appelèrent « Plecrude ».

Jamais on ne vit bébé plus doué pour se faire aimer. Sentait-elle que les circonstances de sa naissance avaient été tragiques ? Elle conjurait son entourage, à force de regards déchirants, de n'en tenir aucun compte. Il faut préciser qu'elle avait pour cela un atout : des yeux d'une beauté invraisemblable.

Cette nouvelle-née petite et maigre plantait

sur sa cible un regard énorme – énorme de dimension et de signification. Ses yeux immenses et magnifiques disaient à Clémence et à Denis : « Aimez-moi ! Votre destin est de m'aimer ! Je n'ai que huit semaines, mais je n'en suis pas moins un être grandiose ! Si vous saviez, si seulement vous saviez... »

Denis et Clémence avaient l'air de savoir. D'emblée, ils eurent pour Plectrude une sorte d'admiration. Elle était étrange jusque dans sa façon de boire son biberon à une lenteur insoutenable, de ne jamais pleurer, de dormir peu la nuit et beaucoup le jour, de montrer d'un doigt décidé les objets qu'elle convoitait.

Elle regardait gravement, profondément, quiconque la prenait dans ses bras, comme pour exprimer que c'était là le début d'une grande histoire d'amour et qu'il y avait de quoi être bouleversé.

Clémence, qui avait follement aimé sa sœur défunte, reporta sur Plectrude cette passion. Elle ne l'aima pas plus que ses deux enfants :

elle l'aima différemment. Nicole et Béatrice lui inspiraient une tendresse débordante ; Plectrude lui inspirait de la vénération.

Ses deux aînées étaient mignonnes, gentilles, intelligentes, agréables ; la petite dernière était hors norme – splendide, intense, énigmatique, loufoque.

Denis aussi fut fou d'elle dès le début et le resta. Mais rien jamais ne put égaler l'amour sacré que Clémence lui voua. Entre la sœur et la fille de Lucette, ce fut un ravage.

Plectrude n'avait aucun appétit et grandissait aussi lentement qu'elle mangeait. C'était désespérant. Nicole et Béatrice dévoraient et croissaient à vue d'œil. Elles avaient des joues rondes et roses qui réjouissaient leurs parents. Chez Plectrude, seuls les yeux grandissaient.

— Est-ce qu'on va vraiment l'appeler comme ça ? demanda un jour Denis.
— Bien sûr. Ma sœur a tenu à ce qu'elle porte ce prénom.
— Ta sœur était folle.

– Non. Ma sœur était fragile. De toute façon, c'est joli, Plectrude.

– Tu trouves ?

– Oui. Et puis ça lui va bien.

– Je ne suis pas d'accord. Elle a l'air d'une fée. Moi, je l'aurais appelée Aurore.

– C'est trop tard. Les petites l'ont déjà adoptée sous son vrai prénom. Et je t'assure que ça lui va bien : ça fait princesse gothique.

– Pauvre gosse ! A l'école, ça sera lourd à porter.

– Pas pour elle. Elle a assez de personnalité pour ça.

Plectrude prononça son premier mot à l'âge normal et ce fut : « Maman ! »

Clémence s'extasia. Hilare, Denis lui fit observer que le premier mot de chacun de ses enfants – et d'ailleurs de tous les enfants du monde – était Maman.

– Ce n'est pas pareil, dit Clémence.

Pendant très longtemps, « maman » fut le seul mot de Plectrude. Comme le cordon ombilical, ce mot lui était un lien suffisant avec le monde. D'emblée, elle l'avait voisé à la perfection, avec sa voyelle nasale à la fin, d'une voix sûre, au lieu du « mamamama » de la plupart des bébés.

Elle le prononçait rarement mais, quand elle le prononçait, c'était avec une clarté solennelle qui forçait l'attention. On eût juré qu'elle choisissait son moment pour ménager ses effets.

Clémence avait six ans quand Lucette était née : elle se souvenait très bien de sa sœur à la naissance, à un an, à deux ans, etc. Aucune confusion n'était possible :

– Lucette était ordinaire. Elle pleurait beaucoup, elle était tour à tour adorable et insupportable. Elle n'avait rien d'exceptionnel. Plectrude ne lui ressemble en rien : elle est silencieuse, sérieuse, réfléchie. On sent combien elle est intelligente.

Denis se moquait gentiment de sa femme :

– Cesse de parler d'elle comme du messie. C'est une charmante petite, voilà tout.

Il la hissait à bout de bras au-dessus de sa tête en s'attendrissant.

Beaucoup plus tard, Plectrude dit : « Papa. »

Le lendemain, par pure diplomatie, elle dit : « Nicole » et « Béatrice ».

Son élocution était impeccable.

Elle mettait à parler la même parcimonie philosophique qu'elle mettait à manger. Chaque nouveau mot lui demandait autant de concentration et de méditation que les nouveaux aliments qui apparaissaient dans son assiette.

Quand elle voyait un légume inconnu au sein de sa purée, elle le désignait à Clémence.

– Ça ? demandait-elle.

– Ça, c'est du poireau. Poi-reau. Essaie, c'est très bon.

Plectrude passait d'abord une demi-heure à contempler le morceau de poireau dans sa cuiller. Elle le portait à son nez pour en évaluer le parfum, puis elle l'observait encore et encore.

– C'est froid, maintenant ! disait Denis avec humeur.

Elle n'en avait cure. Quand elle estimait que

son examen était fini, elle prenait l'aliment en bouche et le goûtait longuement. Elle n'émettait pas de jugement : elle recommençait l'expérience avec un deuxième morceau, puis un troisième. Le plus étonnant était qu'elle procédait ainsi même quand son verdict ultime, après quatre tentatives, était :

– Je déteste.

Normalement, quand un enfant a horreur d'un aliment, il le sait dès qu'il l'a effleuré avec sa langue. Plectrude, elle, voulait être sûre de ses goûts.

Pour les mots, c'était pareil ; elle conservait en elle les nouveautés verbales et les examinait sous leurs coutures innombrables avant de les ressortir, le plus souvent hors de propos, à la surprise générale :

– Girafe !

Pourquoi disait-elle « girafe » alors qu'on était en train de se préparer pour la promenade ? On la soupçonnait de ne pas comprendre ce qu'elle clamait. Or, elle comprenait. C'était seulement que sa réflexion était indépendante des contingences extérieures. Soudain, au moment d'enfiler son manteau, l'esprit de Plectrude avait achevé de digérer l'immensité du cou et des pattes de la girafe : il fallait donc qu'elle prononce son nom, histoire d'avertir les gens du surgissement de la girafe dans son univers intérieur.

— As-tu remarqué combien sa voix est jolie ? disait Clémence.

— Tu as déjà entendu un enfant qui n'avait pas une voix mignonne ? remarquait Denis.

— Justement ! Elle a une voix jolie, pas une voix mignonne, répliquait-elle.

En septembre, on la mit à l'école maternelle.

— Elle aura trois ans dans un mois. C'est un peu tôt, peut-être.

Là ne fut pas le problème.

Après quelques jours, la maîtresse avertit Clémence qu'elle ne pouvait pas garder Plectrude.

— Elle est encore trop petite, n'est-ce pas ?

— Non, madame. J'ai des enfants plus petits qu'elle en classe.

— Alors ?

— C'est à cause de son regard.

— Quoi ?

— Elle fait pleurer les autres enfants rien qu'en les regardant fixement. Et je dois dire que je les comprends : quand c'est moi qu'elle regarde, je suis mal à l'aise.

Clémence, folle de fierté, annonça aux gens que sa fille avait été renvoyée de l'école maternelle à cause de ses yeux. Personne n'avait jamais entendu une pareille histoire.

Déjà, les gens marmonnaient :

— Vous avez connu des enfants qui s'étaient fait renvoyer de l'école maternelle, vous ?

— Et pour leurs yeux, en plus !

— C'est vrai qu'elle regarde bizarrement, cette gosse !

— Les deux aînées sont si sages, si gentilles. C'est un démon, la petite dernière !

Connaissait-on ou ne connaissait-on pas les circonstances de sa naissance ? Clémence se garda bien d'aller interroger les voisins là-dessus. Elle préféra considérer comme acquise la filiation directe qui la reliait à Plectrude.

Elle était ravie que son tête-à-tête avec la petite se prolongeât. Le matin, Denis partait au travail avec les deux aînées qu'il conduisait l'une à l'école, l'autre en maternelle. Clémence restait seule avec la petite dernière.

Dès que la porte se refermait sur son mari et ses enfants, elle se métamorphosait en une autre personne. Elle devenait le composé de fée et de sorcière que la présence exclusive de Plectrude révélait en elle.

– Nous avons le champ libre. Allons nous changer.

Elle se changeait au sens le plus profond du terme : non seulement elle enlevait ses vêtements ordinaires pour s'enrouler dans des étoffes luxueuses qui lui donnaient l'allure d'une reine indienne, mais elle troquait son âme de mère de famille contre celle d'une créature fantasmagorique dotée de pouvoirs exceptionnels.

Sous le regard fixe de l'enfant, la jeune femme de vingt-huit ans laissait sortir de son sein la fée de seize ans et la sorcière de dix mille ans qui y étaient contenues.

Elle déshabillait ensuite la petite et la revêtait de la robe de princesse qu'elle lui avait achetée en cachette. Elle la prenait par la main et la conduisait devant le grand miroir où elles se contemplaient.

— Tu as vu comme nous sommes belles ?

Plectrude soupirait de bonheur.

Puis elle dansait pour charmer sa petite de trois ans. Celle-ci jubilait et entrait dans la danse. Clémence lui tenait les mains, pour soudain empoigner sa taille et la faire voler dans les airs.

Plectrude poussait des cris de joie.

— Maintenant, regarder les choses, demandait l'enfant qui connaissait le rituel.

— Quelles choses ? feignait d'ignorer Clémence.

— Les choses de princesse.

Les choses de princesse étaient les objets qui, pour l'une ou l'autre raison, avaient été élus

comme nobles, magnifiques, insolites, rares
– dignes, enfin, d'être admirés par une aussi
auguste personne.

Clémence rassemblait, sur le tapis d'Orient
du salon, ses bijoux anciens, des mules en
velours carmin qu'elle avait portées un seul
soir, le petit face-à-main cerclé de dorures Art
nouveau, l'étui à cigarettes en argent, la fiasque
arabe en laiton incrusté de pierres fausses et
impressionnantes, une paire de gants en den-
telle blanche, les bagues moyenâgeuses en plas-
tique bariolé que Plectrude avait reçues d'un
distributeur automatique, la couronne en car-
ton doré de la fête des Rois.

On obtenait ainsi un monceau disparate que
chacune trouvait merveilleux : en clignant des
yeux, on eût dit un trésor véritable.

Bouche bée, la petite regardait ce butin de
pirates. Elle prenait en main chaque objet et le
contemplait avec un sérieux extatique.

Parfois, la grande lui mettait tous les bijoux
ainsi que les mules ; ensuite, elle lui tendait le
face-à-main et lui disait :

– Tu vas voir comme tu es belle.

Retenant son souffle, la petite regardait son reflet dans le miroir : au cœur du cerclage de dorures, elle découvrait une reine de trois ans, une prêtresse chamarrée, une fiancée persane le jour de ses noces, une sainte byzantine posant pour une icône. En cette image insensée d'elle-même, elle se reconnaissait.

N'importe qui eût éclaté de rire au spectacle de cette enfançonne parée comme une châsse délirante. Clémence souriait mais ne riait pas : ce qui la frappait, plus que le comique de la scène, c'était la beauté de la petite. Elle était belle comme les gravures que l'on trouvait dans les livres de contes de fées du temps jadis.

« Les enfants d'aujourd'hui ne sont plus beaux comme ça », pensait-elle absurdement – les enfants du passé n'étaient sûrement pas mieux.

Elle mettait de la « musique de princesse » (Tchaïkovski, Prokofiev) et préparait un goûter d'enfant en guise de déjeuner : pain d'épice, gâteaux au chocolat, chaussons aux pommes, biscuits aux amandes, flan à la vanille, avec pour boissons du cidre doux et du sirop d'orgeat.

Clémence disposait ces gâteries sur la table avec une honte amusée : jamais elle n'aurait autorisé ses deux aînées à se nourrir uniquement de sucreries. Elle se justifiait en pensant que le cas de Plectrude était différent :

– C'est un repas pour enfants de conte de fées.

Elle fermait les rideaux, allumait des bougies et appelait la petite. Celle-ci grignotait à peine, écoutant avec de grands yeux attentifs ce que lui racontait sa maman.

Vers quatorze heures, Clémence s'apercevait soudain que les aînées rentreraient dans à peine trois heures et qu'elle ne s'était acquittée d'aucune des tâches d'une mère de famille.

Elle sautait alors dans des vêtements ordinaires, courait au coin de la rue acheter des aliments sérieux, rentrait pour donner au logis une apparence possible, jetait le linge sale dans la machine puis partait à l'école chercher les enfants. Dans son empressement, elle n'avait pas toujours le temps ou la présence d'esprit d'enlever à Plectrude son déguisement – pour la simple raison qu'à ses yeux ce n'était pas un déguisement.

Ainsi, on voyait marcher dans la rue une jeune femme enjouée, tenant par la main une microscopique créature parée comme ne l'eussent pas osé les princesses des Mille et Une Nuits.

A la sortie de l'école, ce spectacle provoquait tour à tour la perplexité, le rire, l'émerveillement et la désapprobation.

Nicole et Béatrice poussaient toujours des cris de joie en voyant l'accoutrement de leur petite sœur, mais certaines mères disaient à haute et intelligible voix :

– On n'a pas idée d'habiller une enfant comme ça !

– Ce n'est pas un animal de cirque.

– Il ne faudra pas s'étonner si cette petite tourne mal, plus tard !

– Se servir de ses enfants pour faire son intéressante, c'est inqualifiable.

Il y avait aussi des adultes moins bêtes pour s'attendrir devant l'apparition. Cette dernière y éprouvait du plaisir, tout en trouvant normal, au fond, d'être ainsi contemplée, car elle avait remarqué, dans le miroir, qu'elle était très belle – et en avait ressenti un émoi voluptueux.

Il importe ici d'ouvrir une parenthèse afin de clore une fois pour toutes un début oiseux qui dure depuis beaucoup trop longtemps. Ceci pourrait s'appeler l'encyclique aux Arsinoé.

Dans *Le Misanthrope* de Molière, la jeune, jolie et coquette Célimène se voit tancer par la vieille et amère Arsinoé qui, verte de jalousie, vient lui signifier qu'elle ne devrait pas tant jouir de sa beauté. Célimène lui répond de façon absolument délectable. Hélas, le génie de Molière n'aura servi à rien, puisqu'on continue, près de quatre siècles plus tard, à tenir des propos moralisateurs, austères et pisse-vinaigre quand un être a le malheur de sourire à son reflet.

L'auteur de ces lignes n'a jamais éprouvé de plaisir à se voir dans un miroir, mais si cette grâce lui avait été accordée, elle ne se serait rien refusé de cet innocent plaisir.

C'est surtout aux Arsinoé du monde entier

que ce discours s'adresse : en vérité, qu'avez-vous à y redire ? A qui ces bienheureuses nuisent-elles en jouissant de leur beauté ? Ne sont-elles pas plutôt les bienfaitrices de notre triste condition, en nous offrant à contempler d'aussi admirables visages ?

L'auteur ne parle pas ici de ceux qui ont fait d'une fausse joliesse un principe de mépris et d'exclusion, mais de ceux qui, simplement ravis par leur image, veulent associer les autres à leur joie naturelle.

Si les Arsinoé déployaient, à tâcher de tirer meilleur parti de leur propre physique, l'énergie qu'elles consacrent à déblatérer contre les Célimène, elles seraient deux fois moins laides.

Déjà, à la sortie de l'école, des Arsinoé de tous les âges s'en prenaient à Plectrude. Celle-ci, en bonne Célimène, n'en avait cure et ne se souciait que de ses admirateurs, sur le visage desquels elle guettait la surprise enchantée. La petite y éprouvait un plaisir ingénu qui la rendait encore plus belle.

Clémence ramenait au logis les trois enfants. Tandis que les aînées s'affairaient aux devoirs ou aux dessins, elle préparait des repas sérieux – du jambon, de la purée – et souriait parfois de la différence de traitement alimentaire de sa progéniture.

Pourtant, on n'eût pas pu l'accuser de favoritisme : elle aimait autant ses trois enfants. C'était pour chacune un amour à l'image de celle qui l'inspirait : sage et solide pour Nicole et Béatrice, fou et féerique pour Plectrude. Elle n'en était pas moins une bonne mère.

Quand on demanda à la petite ce qu'elle voulait comme cadeau d'anniversaire pour ses quatre ans, elle répondit sans l'ombre d'une hésitation :

– Des chaussons de ballerine.

Manière subtile de signifier à ses parents ce qu'elle voulait devenir. Rien n'eût pu donner plus de joie à Clémence : elle avait été refusée, à quinze ans, à l'examen d'entrée des petits rats de l'Opéra, et ne s'en était jamais consolée.

On inscrivit Plectrude à un cours de ballet pour débutantes de quatre ans. Non seulement elle n'en fut pas renvoyée pour cause de regard intense, mais elle y fut aussitôt distinguée.

— Cette petite a des yeux de danseuse, dit la professeur.

— Comment peut-on avoir des yeux de danseuse ? s'étonna Clémence. N'a-t-elle pas plutôt un corps de danseuse, une grâce de danseuse ?

— Oui, elle a tout cela. Mais elle a aussi des yeux de danseuse et, croyez-moi, c'est le plus important et le plus rare. Si une ballerine n'a pas de regard, elle ne sera jamais présente à sa danse.

Ce qui était certain, c'était que les yeux de Plectrude atteignaient, quand elle dansait, une intensité extraordinaire. « Elle s'est trouvée », pensait Clémence.

A cinq ans, la petite n'allait toujours pas à l'école maternelle. Sa mère estimait qu'aller quatre fois par semaine au cours de ballet suffisait à lui apprendre l'art de vivre avec d'autres enfants.

– On n'enseigne pas que ça en maternelle, protestait Denis.

– A-t-elle vraiment besoin de savoir comment coller des gommettes, faire des colliers de nouilles et du macramé ? disait son épouse, les yeux au ciel.

En vérité, Clémence voulait prolonger autant que possible son tête-à-tête avec la fillette. Elle adorait les journées qu'elle passait en sa compagnie. Et les leçons de danse avaient sur l'école maternelle une supériorité indéniable : la maman avait le droit d'y assister.

Elle regardait virevolter l'enfant avec une fierté extatique : « Elle a un don, cette gosse ! » En comparaison, les autres petites filles semblaient des canetonnes.

Après les cours, la professeur ne manquait pas de venir lui dire :

– Il faut qu'elle continue. Elle est exceptionnelle.

Clémence ramenait sa fille au logis en lui répétant les compliments qu'elle avait reçus pour elle. Plectrude les accueillait avec la grâce d'une diva.

— De toute façon, l'école maternelle n'est pas obligatoire, concluait Denis avec un fatalisme amusé d'homme soumis.

Hélas, le cours préparatoire, lui, était obligatoire.

En août, comme son mari s'apprêtait à y inscrire Plectrude, la maman protesta :

— Elle n'a que cinq ans !

— Elle aura six ans en octobre.

Cette fois, il tint bon. Et le 1er septembre, ce ne fut plus deux mais trois enfants qu'ils conduisirent à l'école.

La petite dernière n'y était d'ailleurs pas opposée. Elle était plutôt faraude à l'idée d'essayer son cartable. On assista donc à une rentrée étrange : c'était la mère qui pleurait en voyant s'éloigner l'enfant.

Plectrude déchanta vite. C'était très différent des leçons de ballet. Il fallut rester assise pendant des heures sans bouger. Il fallut écouter une femme dont les propos n'étaient pas intéressants.

Il y eut une récréation. Elle se précipita dans la cour pour faire des bonds, tant ses pauvres jambes n'en pouvaient plus d'immobilité.

Pendant ce temps, les autres enfants jouaient ensemble : la plupart se connaissaient déjà depuis l'école maternelle. Ils se racontaient des choses. Plectrude se demanda ce qu'ils pouvaient bien se dire.

Elle se rapprocha pour écouter. C'était un bruissement ininterrompu, produit par un grand nombre de voix, qu'elle ne parvenait pas à attribuer à leurs propriétaires : il y était question de la maîtresse, des vacances, d'une certaine Magali, d'élastiques, et donne-moi un Malabar, et Magali c'est ma copine, mais tais-toi t'es trop bête, maaaaiheuuuu, t'as pas des Carambar, pourquoi je ne suis pas dans la classe de Magali, arrête, on jouera plus avec toi, je le dirai à la maîtresse, ouh la rapporteuse, d'abord t'avais qu'à pas me pousser, Magali elle m'aime plus que toi, et puis tes chaussures elles sont moches, arrêteuh, les filles c'est bête, je suis content de ne pas être dans ta classe, et Magali...

Plectrude s'en fut, épouvantée.

Ensuite, il fallut encore écouter la maîtresse. Ce qu'elle disait n'était toujours pas intéressant ; au moins était-ce plus homogène que le bavardage des mômes. C'eût été supportable s'il n'y avait eu ce devoir d'immobilité. Heureusement, il y avait une fenêtre.

– Dis donc, toi !

Au cinquième « dis donc, toi ! », et comme la classe entière riait, Plectrude comprit qu'on s'adressait à elle et tourna vers l'assemblée des yeux stupéfaits.

– Tu en mets du temps à réagir ! dit la maîtresse.

Tous les enfants s'étaient retournés pour regarder celle qui avait été prise en faute. C'était une sensation atroce. La petite danseuse se demanda quel était son crime.

– C'est moi qu'il faut regarder, et pas la fenêtre ! conclut la femme.

Comme il n'y avait rien à répondre, l'enfant se tut.

– On dit : « Oui, madame » !

– Oui, madame.

– Comment t'appelles-tu ? demanda l'institutrice, l'air de penser : « Je t'ai à l'œil, toi ! »

– Plectrude.

– Pardon ?

– Plectrude, articula-t-elle d'une voix claire.

Les enfants étaient encore trop petits pour être conscients de l'énormité de ce prénom. Madame, elle, écarquilla les yeux, vérifia sur son registre et conclut :

– Eh bien, si tu cherches à faire ton intéressante, c'est réussi.

Comme si c'était elle qui avait choisi son propre prénom.

La petite pensa : « Elle en a de bonnes, celle-là ! C'est elle qui cherche à faire son intéressante ! La preuve, c'est qu'elle ne supporte pas de ne pas être regardée ! Elle veut se faire remarquer mais elle n'est pas intéressante ! »

Cependant, puisque l'institutrice était le chef, l'enfant obéit. Elle se mit à la regarder avec ses grands yeux fixes. Madame en fut déstabilisée mais n'osa pas protester, de peur de donner des ordres contradictoires.

Le pire fut atteint à l'heure du déjeuner. Les élèves furent conduits dans une vaste cantine où régnait une odeur caractéristique, mélange de vomi de môme et de désinfectant.

Ils durent s'asseoir à des tables de dix. Plectrude ne savait pas où aller et ferma les yeux afin de ne pas devoir choisir. Un flot la mena à une tablée d'inconnus.

Des dames apportèrent des plats au contenu et aux couleurs non identifiables. Paniquée, Plectrude ne put se décider à mettre ces corps étrangers dans son assiette. On la servit donc d'autorité et elle se retrouva devant une gamelle pleine de purée verdâtre et de petits carrés de viande brune.

Elle se demanda ce qui lui valait un sort aussi cruel. Jusqu'alors, pour elle, le déjeuner avait été une pure féerie où, à la lueur des chandelles, protégée du monde par des tentures de velours rouge, une maman belle et vêtue avec magnificence lui apportait des gâteaux et des crèmes qu'elle n'était même pas forcée de manger, au son de musiques célestes.

Et là, au milieu des cris d'enfants moches et sales, en une salle laide où ça sentait bizarre, on jetait dans son assiette de la purée verte et on lui signifiait qu'elle ne quitterait pas la cantine sans avoir tout avalé.

Scandalisée par l'injustice du destin, la petite se mit en devoir de vider la gamelle. C'était épouvantable. Elle avait un mal fou à déglutir. A mi-parcours, elle vomit dans l'assiette et comprit l'origine de l'odeur.

– Beuh, t'es dégueulasse ! lui dirent les enfants.

Une dame vint enlever la gamelle et soupira : « Ah ! là là ! »

Au moins, elle ne fut plus obligée de manger ce jour-là.

Après ce cauchemar, il fallut encore écouter celle qui, sans succès, cherchait à faire son intéressante. Elle notait sur le tableau noir des assemblages de traits qui n'étaient même pas beaux.

A quatre heures et demie, Plectrude fut enfin autorisée à quitter ce lieu aussi absurde qu'abject. A la sortie de l'école, elle aperçut sa maman et courut vers elle comme on court vers le salut.

Au premier regard, Clémence sut combien son enfant avait souffert. Elle la serra dans ses bras en murmurant des paroles de réconfort :

– Là, là, c'est fini, c'est fini.

– C'est vrai ? espéra la petite. Je n'y retournerai plus ?

– Si. C'est obligé. Mais tu t'habitueras.

Et Plectrude, atterrée, comprit qu'on n'était pas sur cette planète pour le plaisir.

Elle ne s'habitua pas. L'école était une géhenne et le resta.

Heureusement, il y avait les cours de ballet. Autant ce que l'institutrice enseignait était inutile et vilain, autant ce que le professeur de danse enseignait était indispensable et sublime.

Ce décalage commença à poser quelques problèmes. Après plusieurs mois, la plupart des enfants de la classe parvenaient à déchiffrer les lettres et à en tracer. Plectrude, elle, semblait avoir décidé que ces choses-là ne la concernaient pas : quand arrivait son tour et que la maîtresse lui montrait une lettre inscrite au tableau, elle prononçait un son au hasard, toujours à côté de la plaque, avec un manque d'intérêt un peu trop manifeste.

L'institutrice finit par exiger de voir les parents de cette cancre. Denis en fut gêné : Nicole et Béatrice étaient de bonnes élèves et ne l'avaient pas habitué à ce genre d'humiliation. Clémence, sans l'avouer, ressentit une obscure fierté : décidément, cette petite rebelle ne faisait rien comme tout le monde.

— Si ça continue comme ça, elle va redoubler son CP ! annonça la maîtresse menaçante.

La maman ouvrit des yeux admiratifs : elle n'avait jamais entendu parler d'un enfant qui redoublait son cours préparatoire. Cela lui parut une action d'éclat, une audace, une insolence aristocratique. Quel enfant oserait redoubler son CP ? Là où même les plus médiocres s'en tiraient sans trop d'embarras, sa fille affirmait déjà crânement sa différence, non, son exception !

Denis, lui, ne l'entendit pas de cette oreille :

— Nous allons réagir, madame ! Nous allons prendre la situation en main !

— Le redoublement est-il encore évitable ? demanda Clémence, pleine d'un espoir que les tiers interprétèrent à l'envers.

— Bien sûr. Du moment qu'elle parvient à lire les lettres avant la fin de l'année scolaire.

La maman cacha sa déception. C'était trop beau pour être vrai !

— Elle les lira, madame, dit Denis. C'est bizarre : cette petite a pourtant l'air très intelligente.

— C'est possible, monsieur. Le problème, c'est que ça ne l'intéresse pas.

« Ça ne l'intéresse pas ! releva Clémence. Elle est formidable ! Ça ne l'intéresse pas ! Quelle personnalité ! Là où les mômes avalent tout sans broncher, ma Plectrude fait déjà le tri entre ce qui est intéressant et ce qui ne l'est pas ! »

— Ça ne m'intéresse pas, Papa.

— Enfin, c'est intéressant, d'apprendre à lire ! protesta Denis.

— Pourquoi ?

— Pour lire des histoires.

— Tu parles. Dans le livre de lecture, la maîtresse nous lit parfois des histoires. C'est tellement embêtant que j'arrête d'écouter au bout de deux minutes.

Clémence applaudit mentalement.

— Tu veux redoubler ton CP ? C'est ça que tu veux ? s'emporta Denis.

— Je veux devenir danseuse.

— Même pour devenir danseuse, tu dois réussir ton CP.

L'épouse s'aperçut soudain que son mari avait raison. Elle réagit aussitôt. Dans sa chambre, elle alla chercher un gigantesque livre du siècle dernier.

Elle prit la petite sur ses genoux et feuilleta

avec elle, religieusement, le recueil de contes de fées. Elle eut soin de ne pas lui faire la lecture, de se contenter de lui montrer les très belles illustrations.

Ce fut un choc dans la vie de l'enfant : elle n'avait jamais été aussi émerveillée qu'en découvrant ces princesses trop magnifiques pour toucher terre, qui, enfermées dans leur tour, parlaient à des oiseaux bleus qui étaient des princes, ou se déguisaient en souillons pour réapparaître encore plus sublimes, quatre pages plus loin.

Elle sut à l'instant, avec une certitude à la portée des seules petites filles, qu'elle deviendrait un jour l'une de ces créatures qui rendent les crapauds nostalgiques, les sorcières abjectes et les princes abrutis.

– Ne t'inquiète pas, dit Clémence à Denis. Avant la fin de la semaine, elle lira.

Le pronostic était au-dessous de la vérité : deux jours plus tard, le cerveau de Plectrude avait tiré profit des lettres assommantes et vaines qu'il croyait ne pas avoir absorbées en classe et trouvé la cohérence entre les signes, les sons et le sens. Deux jours plus tard, elle lisait cent fois mieux que les meilleurs élèves du CP. Comme quoi il n'est qu'une clef pour accéder au savoir, et c'est le désir.

Le livre de contes lui était apparu tel le mode d'emploi pour devenir l'une des princesses des illustrations. Puisque la lecture lui était désormais nécessaire, son intelligence l'avait assimilée.

– Que ne lui as-tu montré ce bouquin plus tôt ? s'extasia Denis.

– Ce recueil est un trésor. Je ne voulais pas le gâcher en le lui montrant trop tôt. Il fallait qu'elle soit en âge d'apprécier une œuvre d'art.

Deux jours plus tard, donc, la maîtresse avait constaté le prodige : la petite cancre qui, seule de son espèce, ne parvenait à identifier aucune lettre, lisait à présent comme une première de classe de dix ans.

En deux jours, elle avait appris ce qu'une

professionnelle n'avait pas réussi à lui enseigner en cinq mois. L'institutrice crut que les parents avaient une méthode secrète et leur téléphona. Denis, fou de fierté, lui raconta la vérité :

— Nous n'avons rien fait du tout. Nous lui avons seulement montré un livre assez beau pour lui donner envie de lire. C'est ce qui lui manquait.

Dans son ingénuité, le père ne se rendit pas compte qu'il commettait une grosse gaffe.

La maîtresse, qui n'avait jamais beaucoup aimé Plectrude, se mit dès lors à la détester. Non seulement elle considéra ce miracle comme une humiliation personnelle, mais en plus elle éprouva envers la petite la haine qu'un esprit moyen ressent vis-à-vis d'un esprit supérieur : « Mademoiselle avait besoin que le livre soit beau ! Voyez-vous ça ! Il est assez beau pour les autres ! »

Dans sa perplexité rageuse, elle relut de bout en bout le livre de lecture incriminé. Y était narrée la vie quotidienne de Thierry, petit garçon souriant, et de sa grande sœur Micheline, qui lui préparait des tartines pour son goûter et l'empêchait de faire des bêtises, car elle était raisonnable.

— Enfin, c'est charmant ! s'exclama-t-elle au terme de sa lecture. C'est frais, c'est ravissant ! Qu'est-ce qu'il lui faut, à cette péronnelle ?

Il lui fallait de l'or, de la myrrhe et de l'encens, de la pourpre et des lys, du velours bleu nuit semé d'étoiles, des gravures de Gustave Doré, des fillettes aux beaux yeux graves et à la bouche sans sourire, des loups douloureusement séduisants, des forêts maléfiques – il lui fallait tout sauf le goûter du petit Thierry et de sa grande sœur Micheline.

L'institutrice ne perdit plus une occasion d'exprimer sa haine envers Plectrude. Comme celle-ci restait la dernière en calcul, la maîtresse l'appelait « le cas désespéré ». Un jour où elle ne parvenait pas à effectuer une addition élémentaire, Madame l'invita à retourner à sa place en lui disant :

— Toi, ça ne sert à rien que tu fasses des efforts. Tu n'y arriveras pas.

Les élèves de CP étaient encore à cet âge suiviste où l'adulte a toujours raison et où la contestation est impensable. Plectrude fut donc l'objet de tous les mépris.

Au cours de ballet, en vertu d'une logique identique, elle était la reine. La professeur s'extasiait sur ses aptitudes et, sans oser le dire (car ce n'eût pas été très pédagogique envers les autres enfants), la traitait comme la meilleure élève qu'elle ait eue de son existence. Par conséquent, les petites filles vénéraient Plectrude et jouaient des coudes pour danser auprès d'elle.

Ainsi, elle avait deux vies bien distinctes. Il y avait la vie de l'école, où elle était seule contre tous, et la vie du cours de ballet, où elle était la vedette.

Elle avait assez de lucidité pour se rendre compte que les enfants du cours de danse seraient peut-être les premières à la mépriser, si elles étaient au cours préparatoire avec elle. Pour cette raison, Plectrude se montrait distante envers celles qui sollicitaient son amitié

— et cette attitude exacerbait encore davantage la passion des petites ballerines.

A la fin de l'année, elle réussit son CP de justesse, au prix d'efforts soutenus en calcul. Pour la récompenser, ses parents lui offrirent une barre murale, afin qu'elle pût effectuer ses exercices devant le grand miroir. Elle passa les vacances à s'entraîner. Fin août, elle tenait son pied dans la main.

A la rentrée scolaire l'attendait une surprise : la composition de sa classe était la même que celle de l'année précédente, à une notoire exception près. Il y avait une nouvelle.

C'était une inconnue pour tous sauf pour elle, puisque c'était Roselyne du cours de ballet. Ebahie de bonheur d'être dans la classe de son idole, elle demanda l'autorisation de s'asseoir à côté de Plectrude. Jamais auparavant cette place n'avait été sollicitée : elle lui fut donc attribuée.

Plectrude représentait pour Roselyne l'idéal absolu. Elle passait des heures à contempler cette égérie inaccessible qui, par miracle, était devenue sa voisine à l'école.

Plectrude se demanda si cette vénération résisterait à la découverte de son impopularité scolaire. Un jour, comme l'institutrice remarquait sa faiblesse en calcul, les enfants se permirent des commentaires bêtes et méchants sur leur condisciple. Roselyne s'indigna de ce procédé et dit à celle qu'on raillait :

— Tu as vu comment ils te traitent ?

La cancre, habituée, haussa les épaules. Roselyne ne l'en admira que plus et conclut par :

— Je les déteste !

Plectrude sut alors qu'elle avait une amie.

Cela changea sa vie.

Comment expliquer le prestige considérable dont jouit l'amitié aux yeux des enfants ? Ceux-ci croient, à tort d'ailleurs, qu'il est du devoir de leurs parents, de leurs frères et sœurs, de les aimer. Ils ne conçoivent pas qu'on puisse leur reconnaître du mérite pour ce qui relève, selon eux, de leur mission. Il est typique de l'enfant de dire : « Je l'aime parce que c'est mon frère (mon père, ma sœur...). C'est obligé. »

L'ami, d'après l'enfant, est celui qui le choisit. L'ami est celui qui lui offre ce qui ne lui est pas dû. L'amitié est donc pour l'enfant le luxe suprême – et le luxe est ce dont les âmes bien nées ont le plus ardent besoin. L'amitié donne à l'enfant le sens du faste de l'existence.

De retour à l'appartement, Plectrude annonça avec solennité :

– J'ai une amie.

C'était la première fois qu'on l'entendait dire cela. Clémence en eut d'abord un pincement au cœur. Très vite, elle parvint à se raisonner : il n'y aurait jamais de concurrence entre l'intruse et elle. Les amis, ça passe. Une mère, ça ne passe pas.

– Invite-la à dîner, dit-elle à sa fille.

Plectrude ouvrit des yeux terrifiés :

– Pourquoi ?

– Comment, pourquoi ? Pour nous la présenter. Nous voulons connaître ton amie.

La petite découvrit à cette occasion, que

quand on voulait rencontrer quelqu'un, on l'invitait à dîner. Cela lui parut inquiétant et absurde : connaissait-on mieux les gens quand on les avait vus manger ? Si tel était le cas, elle n'osait imaginer l'opinion qu'on avait d'elle à l'école, où la cantine était pour elle un lieu de torture et de vomissements.

Plectrude se dit que, si elle voulait connaître quelqu'un, elle l'inviterait à jouer. N'était-ce pas dans le jeu que les gens se révélaient ?

Roselyne n'en fut pas moins invitée à dîner, puisque tel était l'usage pour les adultes. Les choses se passèrent très bien. Plectrude attendit avec impatience que les mondanités s'achevassent : elle savait qu'elle dormirait avec son amie, dans sa chambre, et cette idée lui paraissait formidable.

Ténèbres, enfin.

— Tu as peur du noir ? espéra-t-elle.

— Oui, dit Roselyne.

— Moi pas !

— Dans le noir, je vois des bêtes monstrueuses.

— Moi aussi. Mais j'aime ça.

— Tu aimes ça, les dragons ?

— Oui ! Et les chauves-souris aussi.

— Ça ne te fait pas peur ?

— Non. Parce que je suis leur reine.

— Comment le sais-tu ?

— Je l'ai décidé.

Roselyne trouva cette explication admirable.

— Je suis la reine de tout ce qu'on voit dans le noir : les méduses, les crocodiles, les serpents, les araignées, les requins, les dinosaures, les limaces, les pieuvres.

— Ça ne te dégoûte pas ?

— Non. Je les trouve beaux.

— Rien ne te dégoûte, alors ?

— Si ! Les figues sèches.

— C'est pas dégoûtant, les figues sèches !

— Tu en manges ?

— Oui.

— N'en mange plus, si tu m'aimes.

— Pourquoi ?

— Les vendeuses les mâchent et puis elles les remettent dans le paquet.

— Qu'est-ce que tu racontes ?

— Pourquoi crois-tu que c'est tout écrasé et moche ?

— C'est vrai, ce que tu dis ?

— Je te le jure. Les vendeuses les mâchent et puis les recrachent.

— Beuh !

— Tu vois ! Il n'y a rien de plus dégoûtant au monde que les figues sèches.

Elles se pâmèrent d'un dégoût commun qui les porta au septième ciel. Elles se détaillèrent longuement l'aspect répugnant de ce fruit desséché en poussant des cris de plaisir.

— Je te jure que je n'en mangerai plus jamais, dit solennellement Roselyne.

— Même sous la torture ?

— Même sous la torture !

— Et si on t'en enfonce dans la bouche, de force ?

— Je jure de vomir ! déclara l'enfant, avec la voix d'une jeune mariée.

Cette nuit éleva leur amitié au rang de culte à mystères.

En classe, le statut de Plectrude avait changé. Elle était passée de la condition de pestiférée à celle de meilleure amie adulée. Si au moins elle avait été adorée par une cloche de son espèce, on eût pu continuer à la déclarer indésirable. Mais Roselyne était quelqu'un de bien sous tous rapports aux yeux des élèves. Son seul défaut, qui consistait à être une nouvelle, était une tare très éphémère. Dès lors, on se demanda si on ne s'était pas trompé au sujet de Plectrude.

Evidemment, ces discussions n'eurent jamais lieu. C'est dans l'inconscient collectif de la classe que ces réflexions circulèrent. Leur impact n'en fut que plus grand.

Certes, Plectrude demeurait une cancre en calcul et en beaucoup d'autres branches. Mais les enfants découvrirent que la faiblesse en certaines matières, surtout quand elle atteignait des degrés extrêmes, avait quelque chose d'admirable et d'héroïque. Peu à peu, ils comprirent le charme de cette forme de subversion.

L'institutrice, elle, ne semblait pas le comprendre.

Les parents furent à nouveau convoqués.

– Avec votre permission, nous allons faire passer des tests à votre enfant.

Il n'y avait pas moyen de refuser. Denis en ressentit une humiliation profonde : on considérait sa fille comme une handicapée. Clémence exulta : Plectrude était hors norme. Quand bien même on détecterait que la petite était une débile mentale, elle prendrait cela comme un signe d'élection.

On soumit donc à l'enfant toutes sortes de suites logiques, d'énumérations absconses, de figures géométriques avec énigmes hors de propos, de formules pompeusement appelées algorithmes. Elle répondit mécaniquement, le plus vite possible, pour dissimuler une violente envie de rire.

Fut-ce le hasard ou le fruit de l'absence de

réflexion ? Elle obtint un résultat si excellent que c'en était effarant. Et ce fut ainsi qu'en l'espace d'une heure, Plectrude passa du statut de simplette à celui de génie.

— Je ne suis pas étonnée, commenta sa mère, vexée de l'émerveillement de son mari.

Ce changement de terminologie comportait des avantages, comme ne tarda pas à le remarquer la petite. Avant, quand elle ne s'en sortait pas avec un exercice, l'institutrice la regardait avec affliction et les plus odieux des élèves se moquaient d'elle. A présent, quand elle ne venait pas à bout d'une opération simple, la maîtresse la contemplait comme l'albatros de Baudelaire, que son intelligence de géante empêchait de calculer, et ses condisciples avaient honte d'en trouver sottement la solution.

Par ailleurs, comme elle était réellement intelligente, elle se demanda pourquoi elle ne parvenait pas à résoudre des calculs faciles, alors que, pendant les tests, elle avait répondu correctement à des exercices qui la dépassaient.

Elle se souvint qu'elle n'avait absolument pas réfléchi pendant ces examens et conclut que la clef était dans l'irréflexion absolue.

Dès lors, elle prit soin de ne plus réfléchir quand on la mettait devant une opération et de noter les premiers chiffres qui lui passaient par la tête. Ses résultats n'en devinrent pas meilleurs, mais ils n'en devinrent pas pires non plus. Elle décida par conséquent de conserver cette méthode, qui, pour être d'une inefficacité égale à la précédente, était défoulante à ravir. Et ce fut ainsi qu'elle devint la cancre le plus estimée de France.

Tout eût été parfait s'il n'y avait eu, à la fin de chaque année scolaire, ces formalités ennuyeuses destinées à sélectionner ceux qui auraient le bonheur de passer dans la classe supérieure.

Cette période était le cauchemar de Plectrude qui n'était que trop consciente du rôle du hasard dans ces péripéties. Heureusement, sa réputation de génie la précédait : quand le professeur voyait l'incongruité de ses résultats en mathématiques, il en concluait que l'enfant avait peut-être raison dans une autre dimension et passait l'éponge. Ou alors, il questionnait la petite sur son raisonnement, et ce qu'elle disait le laissait pantois d'incompréhension. Elle avait appris à mimer ce que les gens croyaient être le langage d'une surdouée. Par exemple, au terme d'un charabia échevelé, elle concluait par un limpide : « C'est évident. »

Ce n'était pas du tout évident pour les maîtres et maîtresses. Mais ils préféraient ne pas s'en vanter et donnaient à cette élève leur *nihil obstat*.

Génie ou pas génie, la fillette n'avait qu'une obsession : la danse.

Plus elle grandissait, plus les professeurs s'émerveillaient de ses dons. Elle avait la virtuosité et la grâce, la rigueur et la fantaisie, la joliesse et le sens tragique, la précision et l'élan.

Le mieux, c'est qu'on la sentait heureuse de danser – prodigieusement heureuse. On sentait sa jubilation à livrer son corps à la grande énergie de la danse. C'était comme si son âme n'avait attendu que cela depuis dix mille ans L'arabesque la libérait de quelque mystérieuse tension intérieure.

Qui plus est, on devinait qu'elle avait le sens du spectacle : la présence d'un public augmentait son talent, et plus les regards dont elle était l'objet avaient d'acuité, plus son mouvement était intense.

Il y avait aussi ce miracle de sveltesse qui ne la lâchait pas. Plectrude était et restait d'une minceur digne d'un bas-relief égyptien. Sa légèreté insultait aux lois de la pesanteur.

Enfin, sans jamais s'être consultés, les professeurs disaient d'elle la même chose :

— Elle a des yeux de danseuse.

Clémence avait parfois l'impression que trop de fées s'étaient penchées sur le berceau de l'enfant : elle craignait que cela ne finisse par attirer les foudres divines.

Heureusement, sa progéniture s'accommodait du prodige sans aucun problème. Plectrude n'avait pas empiété sur les domaines de ses deux aînées : Nicole était première en sciences et en éducation physique, Béatrice avait la bosse des mathématiques et le sens de l'histoire. Peut-être par diplomatie instinctive, la petite était nulle dans toutes ces matières – même en gymnastique, où la danse semblait ne lui être d'aucun secours.

Ainsi, Denis avait coutume d'attribuer à chacun de ses rejetons un tiers des accès à l'univers : « Nicole sera une scientifique et une athlète : pourquoi pas cosmonaute ? Béatrice sera une intellectuelle à la tête peuplée de nombres et de faits : elle fera des statistiques historiques. Et Plectrude est une artiste débordante de charisme : elle sera danseuse ou leader politique, ou les deux à la fois. »

Il concluait son pronostic par un éclat de rire qui était de fierté et non de doute. Les enfants l'écoutaient avec plaisir, car de telles paroles étaient flatteuses : mais la plus jeune ne pouvait se défendre d'une certaine perplexité, tant devant ces oppositions qui lui paraissaient ennemies du savoir que devant l'assurance paternelle.

Elle avait beau n'avoir que dix ans et ne pas être en avance pour son âge, elle avait quand même compris une grande chose : que les gens, sur cette terre, ne récoltaient pas ce qui leur semblait dû.

Par ailleurs, avoir dix ans est ce qui peut arriver de mieux à un être humain. A fortiori à une petite danseuse auréolée du prestige de son art.

Dix ans est le moment le plus solaire de l'enfance. Aucun signe d'adolescence n'est encore visible à l'horizon : rien que l'enfance bien mûre, riche d'une expérience déjà longue, sans ce sentiment de perte qui assaille dès les prémices de la puberté. A dix ans, on n'est pas forcément heureux, mais on est forcément vivant, plus vivant que quiconque.

Plectrude, à dix ans, était un noyau d'intense vie. Elle était au sommet de son règne. Elle régnait sur son école de danse, dont elle était l'étoile incontestée, toutes tranches d'âge

confondues. Elle régnait sur sa classe de septième, qui menaçait de devenir une cancrocra-
tie, tant l'élève la plus nulle en mathématiques,
sciences, histoire, géographie, gymnastique,
etc., était considérée comme un génie.

Elle régnait sur le cœur de sa mère qui avait
pour elle un engouement infini. Et elle régnait
sur Roselyne, qui l'aimait autant qu'elle l'admirait.

Plectrude n'avait pas le triomphe écrasant.
Son statut extraordinaire ne la transforma pas
en l'une de ces pimbêches de dix ans qui se
croient au-dessus des lois de l'amitié. Elle avait
pour Roselyne un dévouement et lui vouait un
culte égaux à ceux de son amie pour elle.

Une obscure prescience semblait l'avoir
avertie qu'elle pouvait perdre son trône. Cette
angoisse était d'autant plus vraisemblable
qu'elle se rappelait l'époque où elle était la risée
de sa classe.

Roselyne et Plectrude s'étaient déjà mariées
plusieurs fois, le plus souvent l'une à l'autre,

mais pas obligatoirement. Il pouvait aussi arriver qu'elles épousassent un garçon de leur classe qui, lors de fabuleuses cérémonies, était représenté par son propre ectoplasme, parfois sous forme d'un épouvantail à son effigie, parfois sous forme de Roselyne ou de Plectrude déguisée en homme – un chapeau claque suffisait à ce changement de sexe.

En vérité, l'identité du mari importait peu. Du moment que l'individu réel ou imaginaire ne présentait pas de vices rédhibitoires (gourmette, voix de fausset ou propension à commencer ses phrases par : « En fait... »), il pouvait convenir. Le but du jeu était de créer une danse nuptiale, genre de comédie-ballet digne de Lulli, avec des chants improvisés à partir des paroles le plus tragiques possible.

En effet, il était inévitable qu'après de trop courtes noces, l'époux se transformât en oiseau ou en crapaud, et que l'épouse se retrouvât enfermée dans une haute tour avec une consigne invivable.

– Pourquoi ça se termine toujours mal ? demanda un jour Roselyne.

– Parce que c'est beaucoup plus beau comme ça, assura Plectrude.

Cet hiver-là, la danseuse inventa un jeu sublime d'héroïsme : il s'agissait de se laisser ensevelir par la neige, sans bouger, sans opposer la moindre résistance.

– Faire un bonhomme de neige, c'est trop facile, avait-elle décrété. Il faut devenir un bonhomme de neige, en restant debout sous les flocons, ou un gisant de neige, en se couchant dans un jardin.

Roselyne la regarda avec admiration sceptique.

– Toi, tu feras le bonhomme, et moi le gisant, enchaîna Plectrude.

Son amie n'osa dire ses réticences. Et elles se retrouvèrent toutes les deux sous la neige, l'une allongée à même le sol et l'autre debout. Cette dernière cessa très vite de trouver ça drôle : elle avait froid aux pieds, envie de bouger, aucune envie de se transformer en monument vivant, et en plus elle s'ennuyait car, en dignes statues, les deux fillettes étaient tenues de se taire.

Le gisant, lui, exultait. Il avait gardé les yeux ouverts, comme les morts avant l'intervention d'un tiers. En se couchant par terre, il avait abandonné son corps : il s'était désolidarisé de la sensation glaciale et de la peur physique d'y laisser sa peau. Il n'était plus qu'un visage soumis aux forces du ciel.

Sa féminité d'enfant de dix ans n'était pas présente, non qu'elle fût encombrante : le gisant n'avait conservé que le minimum de lui-même afin d'opposer le moins de résistance possible au déferlement livide.

Ses yeux grands ouverts regardaient le spectacle le plus fascinant du monde : la mort blanche, éclatée, que l'univers lui envoyait en puzzle, pièces détachées d'un mystère immense.

Parfois, son regard scrutait son corps, qui fut enseveli avant son visage, parce que les vêtements isolaient la chaleur qui s'en dégageait. Puis ses yeux regagnaient les nuages, et peu à peu la tiédeur des joues diminuait, et bientôt le linceul put y déposer son premier voile, et le gisant s'empêcha de sourire pour ne pas en altérer l'élégance.

Un milliard de flocons plus tard, la mince silhouette du gisant était presque indiscernable, à peine un accident dans l'amalgame blanc du jardin.

La seule tricherie avait consisté à ciller parfois, pas toujours exprès d'ailleurs. Ainsi, ses yeux avaient conservé leur accès au ciel et pouvaient encore observer la lente chute mortelle.

L'air passait au travers de la couche glacée, évitant au gisant l'asphyxie. Il ressentait une impression formidable, surhumaine, celle d'une lutte contre il ne savait qui, contre un ange inidentifiable – la neige ou lui-même ? – mais aussi d'une sérénité remarquable, si profonde était son acceptation.

En revanche, sur le bonhomme, cela ne prenait pas. Indiscipliné et peu convaincu de la pertinence de cette expérimentation, il ne pouvait s'empêcher de remuer. Par ailleurs, la position debout favorisait moins l'ensevelissement — et encore moins la soumission.

Roselyne regardait le gisant en se demandant ce qu'elle devait faire. Elle connaissait le caractère jusqu'au-boutiste de son amie et savait qu'elle lui interdirait de se mêler de son salut.

Elle avait reçu la consigne de ne pas parler mais elle décida de l'enfreindre :

— Plectrude, tu m'entends ?

Il n'y eut pas de réponse.

Cela pouvait signifier que, furieuse de la désobéissance du bonhomme, elle décidait de le punir par le silence. Une telle attitude eût été dans son caractère.

Cela pouvait aussi signifier quelque chose de très différent.

Tempête sous le crâne de Roselyne.

La couche de neige était devenue si épaisse sur le visage du gisant que, même en cillant, il ne pouvait plus l'évacuer. Les orifices qui jusque-là étaient restés libres autour des yeux se refermèrent.

D'abord, la lumière du jour parvint encore à passer au travers du voile, et le gisant eut la sublime vision d'un dôme de cristaux à quelques millimètres de ses pupilles : c'était beau comme un trésor de gemmes.

Bientôt, le linceul devint opaque. Le candidat à la mort se retrouva dans le noir. La fascination des ténèbres était grande : il était incroyable de découvrir qu'en dessous de tant de blancheur régnait une telle obscurité.

Peu à peu, l'amalgame se densifia.

Le gisant s'aperçut que l'air ne passait plus. Il voulut se lever pour se libérer de ce bâillon, mais la couche glacée avait gelé, formant un igloo aux proportions exactes de son corps, et il comprit qu'il était prisonnier de ce qui serait son cercueil.

Le vivant eut alors une attitude de vivant : il cria. Les hurlements furent amortis par les centimètres de neige : il n'émergea du monticule qu'un gémissement à peine audible.

Roselyne finit par l'entendre et se jeta sur

son amie qu'elle arracha au tombeau de flocons, transformant ses mains en pelleteuse. Le visage bleu apparut, d'une beauté spectrale.

La survivante poussa un cri de délire :

— C'était magnifique !

— Pourquoi tu ne te levais pas ? Tu étais en train de mourir !

— Parce que j'étais enfermée. La neige avait gelé.

— Non, elle n'avait pas gelé. J'ai pu la retirer à la main !

— Ah bon ? C'est que le froid m'avait rendue trop faible pour bouger, alors.

Elle dit cela avec une telle désinvolture que Roselyne, perplexe, se demanda si ce n'était pas une simulation. Mais non, elle était vraiment bleue. On ne peut pas faire semblant de mourir, quand même.

Plectrude se mit debout et regarda le ciel avec reconnaissance.

— C'est formidable, ce qui m'est arrivé !

— Tu es folle. Je ne sais pas si tu te rends compte que, sans moi, tu ne serais plus vivante.

– Oui. Je te remercie, tu m'as sauvée. C'est encore plus beau comme ça.

– Qu'est-ce qu'il y a de beau là-dedans ?

– Tout !

La petite exaltée rentra chez elle et en fut quitte pour un gros rhume.

Son amie trouva qu'elle s'en était tirée à bon compte. Son admiration pour la danseuse ne l'empêchait pas de penser qu'elle déraillait : il fallait toujours qu'elle mît en scène son existence, qu'elle se projetât dans le grandiose, qu'elle organisât de sublimes dangers là où régnait le calme, qu'elle en réchappât avec des airs miraculés.

Roselyne ne put jamais se débarrasser du soupçon que Plectrude était restée volontairement enfermée sous son linceul de neige : elle connaissait les goûts de son amie et savait qu'elle eût trouvé l'histoire beaucoup moins admirable si elle en était sortie elle-même. Pour complaire à ses propres conceptions esthétiques, elle avait préféré attendre d'être sauvée. Et elle se demandait si elle n'eût pas été capable de se laisser mourir plutôt que d'enfreindre les lois héroïques de son personnage.

Certes, elle n'eut jamais la confirmation de ses supputations. Elle essayait parfois de se prouver le contraire : « Après tout, elle m'a appelée à l'aide. Si elle avait vraiment été folle, elle n'aurait pas crié au secours. »

Mais d'autres faits troublants avaient lieu, qui l'intriguaient. Quand elles attendaient le bus ensemble, Plectrude avait tendance à se tenir sur la rue et à y demeurer même quand il passait des voitures. Roselyne la ramenait alors, d'un geste autoritaire, sur le trottoir. A cet instant précis, la danseuse avait une expression bouleversée de plaisir.

Son amie ne savait pas ce qu'elle devait en penser. Cela l'énervait un peu.

Un jour, elle résolut de ne pas intervenir, pour voir. Elle vit.

Un camion fonçait droit sur Plectrude qui n'en restait pas moins sur la chaussée. Il était impossible qu'elle ne s'en fût pas aperçue. Et pourtant, elle ne bougeait pas.

Roselyne se rendit compte que son amie la

regardait droit dans les yeux. Cependant, elle se répétait ce leitmotiv intérieur : « Je la laisse se débrouiller, je la laisse se débrouiller. »

Le camion approchait dangereusement.

– Attention ! hurla Roselyne.

La danseuse demeura immobile, les yeux dans les yeux de son amie.

A la dernière seconde, Roselyne l'arracha à la rue en l'attrapant d'un bras furieux.

Plectrude en eut la bouche déformée de jouissance.

– Tu m'as sauvée, dit-elle en un soupir extatique.

– Tu es complètement folle, s'emporta l'autre. Le camion aurait très bien pu nous faucher toutes les deux. Tu aurais voulu que je meure à cause de toi ?

– Non, s'étonna l'enfant, l'air de ne pas avoir envisagé cette éventualité.

– Alors ne recommence plus jamais !

Elle se le tint pour dit.

En son for intérieur, Plectrude se repassa mille fois la scène de la neige.

Sa version en était très différente de celle de Roselyne.

En vérité, elle était à ce point danseuse qu'elle vivait les moindres scènes de sa vie comme des ballets. Les chorégraphies autorisaient que le sens du tragique se manifestât à tout bout de champ : ce qui, dans le quotidien, était grotesque, ne l'était pas à l'opéra et l'était encore moins en danse.

« Je me suis donnée à la neige dans le jardin, je me suis couchée sous elle et elle a élevé une cathédrale autour de moi, je l'ai vue construire lentement les murs, puis les voûtes, j'étais le gisant avec la cathédrale pour moi seul, ensuite les portes se sont refermées et la mort est venue me chercher, elle était d'abord blanche et douce, puis noire et violente, elle allait s'emparer de moi quand mon ange gardien est venu me sauver, à la dernière seconde. »

Tant qu'à être sauvée, il valait mieux l'être à la dernière seconde : c'était beaucoup plus beau comme ça. Un salut qui n'eût pas été ultime, c'eût été une faute de goût.

Roselyne ne savait pas qu'elle jouait le rôle de l'ange gardien.

Plectrude eut douze ans. C'était la première fois qu'un anniversaire lui donnait un vague pincement au cœur. Jusque-là, une année de plus, ça lui paraissait toujours bon à prendre : c'était un motif de fierté, un pas héroïque vers des lendemains forcément beaux. Douze ans, c'était comme une limite : le dernier anniversaire innocent.

Treize ans, elle refusait d'y penser. Ça sonnait horrible. Le monde des teenagers l'attirait aussi peu que possible. Treize ans, ce devait être plein de déchirures, de malaise, d'acné, de première règles, de soutiens-gorge et autres atrocités.

Douze ans, c'était le dernier anniversaire où elle pouvait se sentir à l'abri des calamités de l'adolescence. Elle caressa avec délectation son torse plat comme le parquet.

La danseuse alla se blottir dans les bras de

sa mère. Celui-ci la cajola, la dorlota, lui dit des petits mots d'amour, la frictionna – lui prodigua les mille tendresses exquises que les meilleures des mères donnent à leurs filles.

Plectrude adorait ça. Elle fermait les yeux de plaisir : aucun amour, pensait-elle, ne pourrait lui plaire autant que celui de sa mère. Etre dans les bras d'un garçon, ça ne la faisait pas rêver. Etre dans les bras de Clémence, c'était l'absolu.

Oui, mais sa mère l'aimerait-elle toujours autant quand elle serait une adolescente boutonneuse ? Cette idée la terrifia. Elle n'osa pas poser la question.

Dès lors, Plectrude cultiva son enfance. Elle était comme un propriétaire terrien qui, pendant des années, aurait disposé d'un domaine gigantesque et qui, suite à une catastrophe, n'en aurait plus possédé qu'un petit arpent. Faisant contre mauvaise fortune bon cœur, elle entretenait son lopin de terre avec des trésors de soin et d'amour, bichonnant les rares fleurs d'enfance qu'il lui était encore possible d'arroser.

Elle se coiffait de nattes ou de couettes, se vêtait exclusivement de salopettes, se promenait en serrant un ours en peluche sur son cœur, s'asseyait sur le sol pour nouer les lacets de ses Kickers.

Pour se livrer à ces comportements de môme, elle n'avait pas à se forcer : elle se laissait aller au versant favori de son être, consciente que, l'année suivante, elle ne le pourrait plus.

De tels règlements peuvent sembler bizarres. Ils ne le sont pas pour les enfants et les petits adolescents, qui observent avec minutie ceux des leurs qui sont soit en avance soit en retard, avec des admirations aussi paradoxales que leur mépris. Ceux qui exagèrent soit leurs avances soit leurs retards s'attirent l'opprobre, la sanction, le ridicule ou, plus rarement, une réputation héroïque.

Prenez une classe de cinquième, de quatrième, et demandez à n'importe quelle fille de cette classe lesquelles de ses consœurs portent déjà un soutien-gorge : vous serez étonné de la précision de la réponse.

Dans la classe de Plectrude – cinquième,

déjà – il y en eut bien quelques-unes pour se moquer de ses couettes, mais c'était précisément des filles qui étaient en avance du côté du soutien-gorge, ce qui leur valait plus de dérision que de louanges : on pourrait donc supposer que leurs railleries compensaient leur jalousie pour le torse plat de la danseuse.

L'attitude des garçons envers les pionnières du soutien-gorge était ambiguë : ils les reluquaient tout en tenant sur elles des propos très méprisants. C'est d'ailleurs une habitude que le sexe masculin conserve sa vie durant, que de calomnier haut et fort ce qui hante ses obsessions masturbatoires.

Les premières manifestations de la sexualité apparurent à l'horizon de la classe de cinquième, inspirant à Plectrude le besoin de se barder d'une innocence prononcée. Elle eût été incapable de mettre des mots sur sa peur : elle savait seulement que si certaines de ses condisciples se sentaient déjà prêtes pour ces « choses bizarres », elle ne l'était pas, elle. Elle s'appliquait inconsciemment à en avertir les autres, à grand renfort d'enfance.

Au mois de novembre, on annonça l'arrivée d'un nouveau.

Plectrude aimait les nouveaux. Roselyne fût-elle devenue sa meilleure amie si elle n'avait pas été une nouvelle, cinq ans auparavant ? La petite danseuse se trouvait toujours des atomes crochus avec ces inconnus plus ou moins effarés.

L'attitude consciente ou non de la plupart des mômes consistait à se montrer impitoyable envers le nouveau ou la nouvelle : la moindre de ses « différences » (il pelait une orange avec un couteau, ou alors s'exclamait « crotte ! » à la place du classique « merde ! ») suscitait des gloussements.

Plectrude, elle, s'émerveillait de ces comportements étranges : ils lui inspiraient l'enthousiasme de l'ethnologue face aux mœurs d'une peuplade exotique. « Cette manière de peler son orange avec un couteau, c'est beau, c'est étonnant ! » ou encore : « Crotte, c'est tellement inattendu ! » Elle allait au-devant des nouveaux avec l'accueillante générosité d'une Tahitienne recevant des marins européens et brandissant son sourire en guise de collier d'hibiscus.

Le nouveau était particulièrement poignant quand il poussait l'incongruité jusqu'à arriver en cours d'année scolaire au lieu de se joindre au troupeau de septembre.

C'était le cas de ce nouveau nouveau. La petite danseuse était déjà dans les meilleures dispositions envers lui quand il entra. Le visage de Plectrude se figea en un mélange d'horreur et d'admiration.

Il s'appelait Mathieu Saladin. On lui trouva une place au fond, près du chauffage.

Plectrude n'écouta pas un mot de ce que le professeur racontait. Ce qu'elle éprouvait était extraordinaire. Elle avait mal à la cage thoracique et elle adorait ça. Mille fois elle voulut se retourner pour regarder le garçon. En général, elle ne se privait pas de contempler les gens jusqu'à l'impolitesse. Là, elle ne pouvait pas.

Vint enfin la récréation. En des temps plus ordinaires, la petite danseuse fût venue au-devant du nouveau avec un sourire lumineux, pour le mettre à l'aise. Cette fois, elle restait désespérément immobile.

En revanche, les autres étaient fidèles à leurs habitudes hostiles :

— Dis donc, le nouveau, il a fait la guerre du Viêt-nam, ou quoi ?

— On va l'appeler le balafré.

Plectrude sentit la colère monter en elle. Elle dut se retenir pour ne pas hurler :

— Taisez-vous ! Cette cicatrice est splendide ! Je n'ai jamais vu un garçon aussi sublime !

La bouche de Mathieu Saladin était fendue en deux par une longue plaie perpendiculaire, bien recousue mais terriblement visible. C'était beaucoup trop grand pour évoquer la marque postopératoire d'un bec-de-lièvre.

Pour la danseuse, il n'y eut aucune hésitation : c'était une blessure de combat au sabre. Le patronyme du garçon lui évoquait les contes des *Mille et Une Nuits*, en quoi elle n'avait d'ailleurs pas tort, car c'était un nom de lointaine origine persane. Dès lors, il allait de soi que le garçon possédait un sabre recourbé. Il avait dû s'en servir pour taillader quelque infâme croisé venu revendiquer le tombeau du Christ. Avant de mordre la poussière, le chevalier chrétien, en un geste vengeur d'une mesquinerie révoltante (car, enfin, Mathieu Saladin s'était contenté de le couper en morceaux, ce qui était bien normal par les temps qui couraient), lui avait lancé son épée en travers de la bouche, inscrivant pour jamais ce combat sur son visage.

Le nouveau avait des traits réguliers, classiques, à la fois aimables et impassibles. La cicatrice n'en était que mieux mise en valeur. Plectrude, muette, s'émerveillait de ce qu'elle ressentait.

— Et alors, tu ne vas pas accueillir le nouveau, comme d'habitude ? dit Roselyne.

La danseuse pensa que son silence risquait d'attirer l'attention. Elle rassembla son courage, respira un grand coup et marcha vers le garçon avec un sourire crispé.

Il était justement avec un immonde gaillard du nom de Didier, un redoublant, qui essayait de s'accaparer Mathieu Saladin, histoire de se vanter d'avoir un balafré parmi ses relations.

– Bonjour, Mathieu, bafouilla-t-elle. Je m'appelle Plectrude.

– Bonjour, répondit-il, sobre et poli.

Normalement, elle ajoutait une formule tarte et gentille, du style : « Sois le bienvenu parmi nous » ou : « J'espère que tu t'amuseras bien avec nous. » Là, elle ne put rien dire. Elle tourna les talons et retourna à sa place.

– Drôle de prénom, mais très jolie fille, commenta Mathieu Saladin.

– Ouais, bof, murmura Didier en jouant les blasés. Si tu veux de la gonzesse, prends pas une gamine. Tiens, regarde Muriel : moi, je l'appelle Gros Seins.

– En effet, constata le nouveau.

– Tu veux que je te présente ?

Et avant même d'avoir sa réponse, il prit le garçon par l'épaule et le conduisit au-devant de la créature au torse avantageux. La danseuse n'entendit pas ce qu'ils se dirent. Elle eut en bouche un goût amer.

La nuit qui suivit cette première rencontre, Plectrude se tint ce discours :

« Il est pour moi. Il est à moi. Il ne le sait pas, mais il m'appartient. Je me le promets : Mathieu Saladin est pour moi. Peu importe que ce soit dans un mois ou dans vingt ans. Je me le jure. »

Elle se le répéta pendant des heures, comme une formule incantatoire, avec une assurance qu'elle ne retrouverait plus avant longtemps.

Dès le lendemain, en classe, elle dut se rendre à l'évidence : le nouveau n'avait pas un regard pour elle. Elle dardait sur lui ses yeux superbes sans qu'il les remarquât le moins du monde.

« S'il n'était pas blessé, il serait simplement beau. Avec cette cicatrice, il est magnifique », se répétait-elle.

Sans qu'elle le sût, cette obsession pour cette marque de combat était riche de signification, Plectrude se croyait la vraie fille de Clémence et de Denis et ne savait rien des circonstances de sa naissance véritable. Elle ignorait l'extraordinaire violence qui avait salué son arrivée parmi les vivants.

Pourtant, il devait y avoir une région, dans ses ténèbres intérieures, qui s'était imprégnée de ce climat de meurtre et de sang, car ce qu'elle éprouvait en contemplant la cicatrice du garçon était profond comme un mal ancestral.

Consolation : s'il ne s'intéressait pas à elle, il fallait reconnaître qu'il ne s'intéressait à personne d'autre. Mathieu Saladin était d'humeur égale, ses traits étaient peu mobiles, son visage n'exprimait rien en dehors d'une politesse neutre qui était destinée à tous. Il était de grande taille, très mince et très frêle. Ses yeux avaient la sagesse de ceux qui ont souffert.

Quand on lui posait une question, il prenait le temps de la réflexion et ce qu'il répondait était toujours intelligent. Plectrude n'avait jamais rencontré un garçon aussi peu stupide.

Il n'était ni particulièrement fort ni spectaculairement mauvais en aucune matière. Il atteignait dans chaque branche le niveau correct qui lui permettait de ne pas se faire remarquer.

La petite danseuse, dont les résultats étaient constants de nullité avec les années, l'admirait pour cela. Encore heureux qu'elle eût gagné la sympathie et une certaine estime auprès de ses pairs : sinon, elle eût eu encore plus de mal à supporter les réactions que suscitaient ses réponses.

— Pourquoi nous sortez-vous de telles pitreries ? demandaient certains professeurs, atterrés de ce qu'elle disait.

Elle eût voulu leur dire que ce n'était pas exprès. Mais elle avait le sentiment que cela aggraverait son cas. Tant qu'à provoquer les fous rires de la classe entière, autant plaider la préméditation.

Les professeurs croyaient qu'elle était fière des réactions du groupe et les suscitait. C'était le contraire. Quand ses bourdes déclenchaient l'hilarité générale, elle avait envie de se terrer.

Un exemple parmi des centaines : comme le thème du cours était la ville de Paris et ses monuments historiques, Plectrude fut interro-

gée sur le Louvre. La réponse attendue était le
Carrousel du Louvre ; la petite répondit :

– L'arc de triomphe de Cadet Rousselle.

La classe applaudit à cette nouvelle ânerie
avec l'enthousiasme d'un public saluant son
comique.

Plectrude était désemparée. Ses yeux cher-
chèrent le visage de Mathieu Saladin : elle vit
qu'il riait de bon cœur, avec attendrissement.
Elle soupira d'un mélange de soulagement et
de dépit : soulagement, car c'eût pu être pire ;
dépit, car c'était une expression très différente
de celle qu'elle avait espéré provoquer chez lui.

« Si seulement il pouvait me voir danser ! »
pensait-elle.

Hélas, comment lui révéler son don ? Elle
n'allait quand même pas venir au-devant de lui
et lui sortir de but en blanc qu'elle était l'étoile
de sa génération.

Comble de malchance, le nouveau ne fré-
quentait guère que Didier. Il ne fallait pas
compter sur ce mauvais sujet pour le lui
apprendre : Didier se fichait de Plectrude et du
ballet comme de l'an 40. Il ne parlait que de

revues cochonnes, de football, de cigarettes et de bière. Fort de son année de plus, il jouait à l'adulte, prétendait qu'il se rasait, ce qui était difficile à croire, et se vantait de ses succès auprès des filles de quatrième ou de troisième.

A se demander ce que Mathieu Saladin trouvait à la compagnie de ce débile. Au fond, il était clair qu'il ne lui trouvait rien : il côtoyait Didier parce que Didier voulait s'afficher avec lui. Il se souciait du redoublant comme d'une guigne. Il ne le gênait pas.

Un jour, au prix d'un courage fantastique, elle vint parler à son héros pendant la récréation. Elle s'entendit lui demander quel chanteur il aimait.

Il répondit aimablement qu'aucun chanteur ne le convainquait et que, pour cette raison, il avait constitué un groupe rock avec quelques amis :

— On se réunit dans le garage de mes parents pour créer la musique qu'on voudrait entendre.

Plectrude faillit s'évanouir d'admiration.

Elle était trop amoureuse pour avoir de la présence d'esprit et ne dit donc pas ce qu'elle eût voulu dire .

– J'aimerais bien vous entendre jouer, ton groupe et toi.

Elle demeura muette. Mathieu Saladin en conclut que cela ne l'intéressait pas ; il ne l'invita donc pas dans son garage. S'il l'avait fait, elle n'eût pas perdu sept ans de sa vie. Petites causes, grands effets.

– Et toi, tu aimes quoi, comme musique ? demanda le garçon.

Ce fut un désastre. Elle était encore à l'âge où l'on écoute la même musique que ses parents. Denis et Clémence adoraient la bonne chanson française, Barbara, Léo Ferré, Jacques Brel, Serge Reggiani, Charles Trenet : si elle avait donné l'un de ces noms, c'eût été une réponse excellente et hautement respectable.

Mais Plectrude eut honte : « A douze ans, tu n'es même pas fichue d'avoir tes propres goûts ! Tu ne vas pas lui répondre ça : il comprendrait que c'est la musique de tes parents. » Hélas, elle n'avait aucune idée de qui étaient les bons chanteurs de la fin des années soixante-dix. Elle ne connaissait qu'un seul nom et ce fut celui qu'elle cita :

— Dave.

La réaction de Mathieu Saladin ne fut pas vraiment méchante : il éclata de rire. « Pas de doute, cette fille est une rigolote ! » pensa-t-il.

Elle eût pu tirer parti de cette hilarité. Malheureusement, elle la vécut comme une humiliation. Elle tourna les talons et s'en alla. « Je ne lui adresserai plus jamais la parole », se dit-elle.

Commença pour elle une période de décadence. Ses résultats scolaires, de mauvais qu'ils avaient toujours été, passèrent à exécrables. La réputation de génie qui jusque-là avait semé le trouble dans l'âme des professeurs ne suffisait plus.

Plectrude y mettait du sien : elle semblait avoir opté pour le suicide scolaire. Non sans griserie, elle se fracassait contre les bornes de la nullité et les faisait voler en éclats.

Ce n'était pas exprès qu'elle répondait des énormités aux questions des professeurs : son seul choix était de ne plus se contrôler. Désormais, elle se laisserait aller, elle dirait ce que sa pente intérieure de cancre lui dicterait, ni plus ni moins. Le but n'était pas d'attirer l'attention (même si, pour être sincère, cela ne lui déplaisait pas) mais d'être rejetée, renvoyée, expulsée comme le corps étranger qu'elle était.

Le reste de la classe l'entendait proférer des monstruosités géographiques (« le Nil prend sa source dans la mer Méditerranée et ne se jette nulle part »), géométriques (« l'angle droit bout à quatre-vingt-dix degrés »), orthographiques (« le participe passé s'accorde avec les femmes sauf quand il y a un homme dans le groupe »), historiques (« Louis XIV devint protestant quand il épousa Edith de Nantes ») et biologiques (« le chat a les yeux nubiles et les griffes nyctalopes ») avec admiration.

Admiration du reste partagée par la fillette elle-même. En effet, ce n'était pas sans un étonnement extatique qu'elle s'entendait dire de telles bourdes : elle n'en revenait pas de contenir tant de perles surréalistes et prenait conscience de l'infini qui était en elle.

Quant aux autres élèves, ils étaient persuadés que l'attitude de Plectrude était pure provocation. Chaque fois que le professeur l'interrogeait, ils retenaient leur souffle, puis ils s'émerveillaient de l'aplomb naturel avec lequel elle sortait ses trouvailles. Ils croyaient que son but était de se moquer de l'institution scolaire et applaudissaient à son courage.

Sa réputation franchit les limites de la classe. A la récréation, tout l'établissement venait demander aux élèves de cinquième « la dernière de Plectrude ». On se racontait ses hauts faits comme une chanson de geste.

La conclusion était toujours identique :

— Elle y va fort !

— Tu y vas un peu fort, non ? s'emporta son père en voyant son carnet de notes.

— Je ne veux plus aller à l'école, Papa. Ce n'est pas pour moi.

— Ça ne se passera pas comme ça !

– Je veux devenir petit rat de l'Opéra de Paris.

Cela ne tomba pas dans l'oreille d'une sourde.

– Elle a raison ! dit Clémence.

– Tu la défends, en plus ?

– Bien sûr ! C'est un génie de la danse, notre Plectrude ! A son âge, il faut qu'elle s'y donne corps et âme ! Pourquoi continuerait-elle à perdre son temps avec des participes passés ?

Le jour même, Clémence téléphona à l'école des petits rats.

L'habituelle école de danse de la fillette se montra enthousiaste :

– Nous espérions que vous prendriez une telle décision ! Elle est faite pour ça !

On lui écrivit des lettres de recommandation où l'on parlait d'elle comme de la future Pavlova.

Elle fut convoquée par l'Opéra afin de passer un examen. Clémence hurla en recevant la lettre de convocation, qui ne signifiait pourtant rien.

Le jour fixé, Plectrude et sa mère prirent le RER. Le cœur de Clémence battait encore plus fort que celui de la petite quand elles arrivèrent à l'école des rats.

Deux semaines plus tard, Plectrude reçut sa lettre d'admission. Ce fut le plus beau jour de la vie de sa mère.

En septembre, elle commencerait l'école de l'Opéra, où elle serait pensionnaire. La fillette vivait un rêve. Un grand destin s'ouvrait devant elle.

On était en avril. Denis insista pour qu'elle terminât et réussît son année scolaire :

— Comment ça, tu pourras dire que tu t'es arrêtée en quatrième.

La petite trouva dérisoire cette entourloupe. Cependant, par affection pour son père, elle donna un coup de collier et obtint de justesse les résultats suffisants. Elle avait désormais la faveur de tous.

Le collège entier savait pourquoi elle partait et s'en enorgueillissait. Même les professeurs dont Plectrude avait été le cauchemar déclaraient qu'ils avaient toujours senti le « génie » de cette enfant.

Les pions vantaient sa grâce, les dames de la cantine louangeaient son manque d'appétit, le professeur d'éducation physique (branche dans laquelle la danseuse brillait par sa faiblesse) évoquait sa souplesse et la finesse de ses muscles ; le comble fut atteint quand ceux des élèves qui n'avaient jamais cessé de la haïr depuis le cours préparatoire se flattèrent d'être ses amis.

Hélas, le seul être de la classe que la petite eût voulu impressionner manifesta une admiration polie. Si elle avait mieux connu Mathieu Saladin, elle eût su pourquoi son visage était si impassible.

En vérité, il pensait : « Et merde ! Moi qui pensais avoir cinq ans devant moi pour arriver à mes fins ! Et elle qui va devenir une étoile ! Je ne la reverrai plus jamais, c'est certain. Si au moins elle était une amie, j'aurais un prétexte pour la rencontrer à l'avenir. Mais je n'ai jamais vraiment lié amitié avec elle et je ne vais pas me conduire comme ces ploucs qui font semblant de l'adorer depuis qu'ils savent ce qui l'attend. »

Le dernier jour de classe, Mathieu Saladin lui dit au revoir avec froideur.

« Encore heureux que je quitte le collège, soupira la danseuse. Je vais cesser de le voir et je penserai peut-être moins à lui. Ça lui est parfaitement égal, que je m'en aille ! »

Cet été-là, ils ne partirent pas en vacances : l'école des rats coûtait cher. A l'appartement, le téléphone sonnait sans cesse : c'était un voisin, un oncle, un camarade, un collègue, qui voulait venir voir le phénomène.

— Et elle est belle, en plus ! s'exclamaient-ils à sa vue.

Plectrude avait hâte d'être pensionnaire afin d'échapper à ce défilé permanent de badauds.

Pour se désennuyer, elle ruminait son chagrin d'amour. Elle montait au sommet de son arbre dont elle enlaçait le tronc en fermant les yeux. Elle se racontait des histoires et le cerisier devenait Mathieu Saladin.

Elle les rouvrait et prenait conscience de la sottise de son attitude. Elle enrageait : « Qu'il est bête d'avoir douze ans et demi et de plaire à tout le monde sauf à Mathieu Saladin ! »

La nuit, dans son lit, elle se racontait des histoires beaucoup plus intenses : Mathieu Saladin et elle étaient enfermés dans un tonneau que l'on jetait dans les chutes du Niagara. Le tonneau explosait sur des rochers et c'était tour à tour elle ou lui qui était blessé ou inanimé et qu'il fallait sauver.

Les deux versions avaient du bon. Quand c'était elle qu'il fallait sauver, elle adorait qu'il plonge pour la rechercher au fond des remous, qu'il l'enlace pour la ramener à la vie puis que, sur la berge, il lui fasse la respiration artificielle ; quand c'était lui qui était blessé, elle le sortait de l'eau et se racontait ses plaies dont elle léchait le sang, se réjouissant des nouvelles cicatrices qui allaient le rendre encore plus beau.

Elle finissait par ressentir des frissons de désir qui la rendaient folle.

Elle attendait la rentrée comme une libération. Ce fut une incarcération.

Elle savait qu'à l'école des rats régnerait une discipline de fer. Pourtant, ce qu'elle y découvrit surpassa de loin ses pressentiments les plus délirants.

Plectrude avait toujours été la plus mince de tous les groupements humains dans lesquels elle s'était aventurée. Ici, elle faisait partie des « normales ». Celles qu'on qualifiait de minces eussent été appelées squelettiques en dehors du pensionnat. Quant à celles qui, dans le monde extérieur, eussent été trouvées de proportions ordinaires, elles étaient en ces murs traitées de « grosses vaches ».

Le premier jour fut digne d'une boucherie. Une espèce de maigre et vieille charcutière vint passer en revue les élèves comme si elles avaient été des morceaux de viande. Elle les sépara en trois catégories à qui elle tint ces discours :

— Les minces, c'est bien, continuez comme ça. Les normales, ça va, mais je vous ai à l'œil. Les grosses vaches, soit vous maigrissez, soit vous partez : il n'y a pas de place ici pour les truies.

Ces aimables hurlements furent salués par l'hilarité des « minces » : on eût dit des cadavres qui rigolaient. « Elles sont monstrueuses », pensa Plectrude.

Une « grosse vache », qui était une jolie fillette d'un gabarit parfaitement normal, éclata en sanglots. La vieille vint l'engueuler en ces termes :

– Pas de sensibleries ici ! Si tu veux continuer à t'empiffrer de sucres d'orge dans les jupes de ta maman, personne ne te retient !

Ensuite, on mesura et pesa les jeunes morceaux de viande. Plectrude, qui aurait treize ans un mois plus tard, mesurait un mètre cinquante-cinq et pesait quarante kilos, ce qui était peu, surtout compte tenu du fait qu'elle était tout en muscles, comme une danseuse qui se respecte ; on ne lui en signifia pas moins que c'était un « maximum à ne pas dépasser ».

A toutes ces fillettes, ce premier jour à l'école des rats donna l'impression d'une éviction brutale de l'enfance : la veille, leurs corps étaient encore des plantes aimées que l'on arrosait et chérissait et dont la croissance était espérée comme un merveilleux phénomène naturel, garant des beaux lendemains, leurs familles étaient des jardins de terre grasse où la vie était lente et douillette. Et là, du jour au lendemain, on les arrachait à ce terreau humide et elles se retrouvaient dans un monde sec, où un œil âpre de spécialiste extrême-oriental décrétait que telle tige devait être allongée, que telle racine devait être affinée, et qu'elles le seraient, de gré ou de force, car, depuis le temps, on avait des techniques pour cela.

Ici, pas de tendresse dans les yeux des adultes : rien qu'un scalpel guettant les dernières pulpes de l'enfance. Les petites venaient d'effectuer un voyage instantané dans les siècles et dans l'espace : elles étaient passées en quelques secondes de la fin du IIe millénaire en France à la Chine médiévale.

C'était peu dire qu'en ces murs régnait une discipline de fer. L'entraînement commençait tôt le matin et se terminait tard le soir, avec d'insignifiantes interruptions pour un repas qui ne méritait pas ce nom et pour une plage d'études pendant laquelle les élèves savouraient si profondément le repos du corps qu'elles en oubliaient l'effort intellectuel requis.

A ce régime-là, toutes les filles maigrirent, y compris celles qui étaient déjà trop maigres. Ces dernières, loin de s'en inquiéter comme l'eussent fait des personnes de bon sens, s'en réjouirent. On n'était jamais trop squelettique.

Contrairement à ce que le premier jour avait laissé supposer, le poids n'était pourtant pas la principale préoccupation. Les corps étaient tellement exténués par les heures interminables d'exercices que l'obsession était simplement de s'asseoir. Les moments où l'on n'employait pas ses muscles étaient vécus comme des miracles.

Dès le lever, Plectrude attendait le coucher. L'instant où l'on confiait au lit sa carcasse douloureuse de fatigue pour l'y abandonner pendant la nuit était si voluptueux qu'on ne parvenait pas à penser à autre chose. C'était la seule détente des fillettes ; les repas, à l'opposé, étaient des moments d'angoisse. Les professeurs avaient tant diabolisé la nourriture qu'elle en paraissait alléchante, si médiocre fût-elle. Les enfants l'appréhendaient avec terreur, dégoûtées du désir qu'elle suscitait. Une bouchée avalée était une bouchée de trop.

Très vite, Plectrude se posa des questions. Elle était venue dans cet établissement pour y devenir une danseuse, pas pour y perdre le goût de vivre au point de ne pas avoir d'idéal plus élevé que le sommeil. Ici, elle travaillait la danse du matin au soir, sans avoir le sentiment de danser : elle était comme un écrivain forcé de ne pas écrire et d'étudier la grammaire sans discontinuer. Certes, la grammaire est essentielle, mais seulement en vue de l'écriture : privée de son but, elle est un code stérile. Plectrude ne s'était jamais sentie aussi peu danseuse que depuis son arrivée à l'école des rats. Dans le cours de ballet qu'elle avait fréquenté les années précédentes, il y avait place pour de petites chorégraphies. Ici, on faisait des exercices, point final. La barre finissait par évoquer les galères.

Cette perplexité semblait partagée par beaucoup d'élèves. Aucune n'en parlait et, cependant, on sentait le découragement se répandre parmi les enfants.

Il y eut des abandons. Ils semblaient avoir été espérés par les autorités. Ces défections en entraînaient d'autres. Ce dégraissage spontané enchantait les maîtres et meurtrissait Plectrude, pour qui chaque départ équivalait à un décès.

Ce qui devait arriver arriva : elle fut tentée de partir. Ce qui l'en empêcha fut la sourde impression que sa mère le lui reprocherait et que même ses excellentes explications ne serviraient à rien.

Sans doute les chefs de l'école attendaient-ils l'abandon d'une liste déterminée de personnes car, du jour au lendemain, leur attitude changea. Les élèves furent convoquées dans une salle plus grande que d'habitude, où on leur tint d'abord ce langage :

— Vous avez dû observer, ces derniers temps, de nombreux départs. Nous n'irons pas jusqu'à dire que nous les avons délibérément provo-

qués, nous n'aurons cependant pas l'hypocrisie
de les regretter.

Il y eut un silence, sans doute dans le seul
but de mettre les enfants mal à l'aise.

– Celles qui sont parties ont prouvé qu'elles
n'avaient pas vraiment envie de danser ; plus
exactement, elles ont montré qu'elles n'avaient
pas la patience nécessaire à une danseuse véritable. Savez-vous ce que certaines de ces péron-
nelles ont déclaré, en annonçant leur défec-
tion ? Qu'elles étaient venues pour danser et
qu'ici, on ne dansait pas. Qu'est-ce qu'elles
s'imaginaient,   celles-là ?   Qu'après-demain,
elles nous interpréteraient *Le Lac des cygnes* ?

Plectrude se rappela une expression de sa
mère : « battre le chien devant le loup ». Oui,
c'était bien cela : les professeurs étaient en train
de battre les chiens devant les loups.

– Danser, cela se mérite. Danser, danser sur
une scène devant un public, est le plus grand
bonheur du monde. A dire vrai, même sans
public, même sans scène, danser est l'ivresse
absolue. Une joie si profonde justifie les sacri-
fices les plus cruels. L'éducation que nous vous

donnons ici tend à présenter la danse pour ce qu'elle est : non pas le moyen, mais la récompense. Il serait immoral de laisser danser des élèves qui ne l'auraient pas mérité. Huit heures à la barre par jour et un régime de famine, cela ne paraîtra dur qu'à celles qui n'ont pas assez envie de danser. Alors, que celles qui veulent encore partir partent !

Plus aucune ne partit. Le message avait été bien reçu. Comme quoi l'on peut accepter les pires disciplines, pourvu qu'elles vous soient expliquées.

La récompense arriva : on dansa.

Certes, ce fut deux fois rien. Mais le simple fait de quitter la barre pour s'élancer, sous les regards des autres, au centre de la salle, d'y virevolter quelques instants et de sentir combien son corps possédait l'art de ce pas était affolant. Si dix secondes pouvaient procurer tant de plaisir, on osait à peine rêver de ce qu'on éprouverait en dansant deux heures.

Pour la première fois, Plectrude plaignait

Roselyne qui n'avait pas été reçue à l'école des rats. Elle ne serait jamais qu'une jeune fille ordinaire pour qui la danse serait un délassement. A présent, Plectrude bénissait la dureté de ses professeurs, qui lui avaient appris que cet art était une religion.

Ce qui, jusque-là, l'avait scandalisée, lui semblait maintenant normal. Qu'on les affamât, les abrutît à la barre de rabâchages techniques des heures d'affilée, qu'on les injuriât, qu'on traitât de grosses vaches des gamines sans aucune rondeur, tout cela désormais lui paraissait acceptable.

Il y avait même des choses bien pires qui, au début, lui donnaient envie de crier à l'atteinte aux droits de l'homme et qui, à présent, ne la révoltaient plus. Celles qui présentaient plus tôt que d'autres des signes de puberté se voyaient obligées d'avaler des pilules interdites qui bloquaient certaines mutations de l'adolescence. Au terme d'une petite enquête, Plectrude s'aperçut que personne n'avait ses règles à l'école des rats, pas même dans les classes supérieures.

Elle en avait discuté en cachette avec une grande qui lui avait dit :

– Pour la plupart des élèves, les pilules ne sont même pas nécessaires : la sous-alimentation suffit à bloquer le cycle menstruel et les modifications physiques qu'entraîne l'apparition des règles. Pourtant, il y a quelques dures à cuire qui parviennent quand même à devenir pubères malgré les privations. Celles-ci doivent prendre la fameuse pilule qui arrête les menstruations. Le tampon, c'est l'objet introuvable de l'école.

– N'y a-t-il pas des filles qui ont leurs règles en cachette ?

– Tu es folle ! Elles savent que c'est contre leur intérêt. C'est elles-mêmes qui demandent la pilule.

Cette conversation, en son temps, avait scandalisé Plectrude. A présent, elle admettait les pires manipulations, elle trouvait magnifiques les lois spartiates de l'établissement.

Son esprit était subjugué, à la lettre : sous le joug des professeurs, leur donnant raison en tout.

Heureusement, à l'intérieur de sa tête, la voix de l'enfance encore proche, plus savamment contestataire que celle de l'adolescence, la sauvait, qui lui susurrait d'hygiéniques énormités : « Sais-tu pourquoi ce lieu s'appelle l'école des rats ? On dit que c'est le nom des élèves, mais c'est celui des professeurs. Oui, ce sont des rats, des pingres, avec de grandes dents pour ronger la viande sur le corps des ballerines. Nous avons du mérite à avoir la passion de la danse alors qu'ils l'ont si peu : eux, ce qui les intéresse, en bons rats qu'ils sont, c'est de nous ratisser, de nous bouffer. Rats, ça veut dire avares, et si ça n'était que d'argent ! Avares de beauté, de plaisir, de vie et même de danse ! Tu parles qu'ils aiment la danse ! Ils sont ses pires ennemis ! Ils sont choisis pour leur haine de la danse, exprès, parce que s'ils l'aimaient, ce serait trop facile pour nous. Aimer ce qu'aime son professeur, ce serait trop naturel. Ici, on exige de nous ce qui est surhumain : se sacrifier pour un art haï de nos maîtres, trahi cent fois par jour par la petitesse de leur esprit. La danse, c'est l'élan, la grâce, la générosité, le don absolu – le contraire de la mentalité d'un rat. »

Le dictionnaire Robert lui fournit l'alimentation qu'elle n'avait plus. Plectrude lut avec gourmandise et délectation : « rat d'égout, être fait comme un rat, face de rat, radin, rapiat ». Oui, vraiment, l'école portait bien son nom.

Il y avait pourtant une salubrité réelle à choisir des professeurs abjects. L'institution pensait, non sans raison, qu'il eût été immoral d'encourager les ballerines. La danse, art total s'il en fut, requérait l'investissement entier de l'être. Il était donc obligatoire d'éprouver la motivation des enfants en sapant jusqu'aux bases leur idéal. Celles qui ne résisteraient pas ne pourraient jamais avoir l'envergure mentale d'une étoile. De tels procédés, pour monstrueux qu'ils fussent, relevaient du comble de l'éthique.

Seulement, les professeurs ne le savaient pas. Ils n'étaient pas au courant de la mission suprême de leur sadisme et l'exerçaient par pure volonté de nuire.

C'est ainsi qu'en secret, Plectrude apprit aussi à danser contre eux.

En trois mois, elle perdit cinq kilos. Elle s'en réjouit. D'autant qu'elle avait remarqué un phénomène extraordinaire : en passant au-dessous de la barre symbolique des quarante kilos, elle n'avait pas seulement perdu du poids, elle avait aussi perdu du sentiment.

Mathieu Saladin : ce nom qui auparavant la mettait en transe la laissait désormais de glace. Pourtant, elle n'avait pas revu ce garçon, ni eu de ses nouvelles : il n'avait donc pu la décevoir. Elle n'avait pas non plus rencontré d'autres garçons qui eussent pu lui faire oublier celui qu'elle aimait.

Ce n'était pas davantage l'écoulement du temps qui l'avait refroidie. Trois mois, c'était court. Et puis, elle s'était trop observée pour ne pas remarquer l'enchaînement des causes et des effets : chaque kilo en moins emportait dans sa fonte une part de son amour. Elle ne le regrettait pas, au contraire : pour pouvoir le regretter, il eût fallu qu'elle éprouvât encore du sentiment. Elle se réjouissait d'être débarrassée de ce double fardeau : les cinq kilos et cette encombrante passion.

Plectrude se promit de retenir cette grande loi : l'amour, le regret, le désir, l'engouement – toutes ces sottises étaient des maladies sécrétées par les corps de plus de quarante kilos.

Si par malheur un jour elle pesait à nouveau ce poids d'obèse et si, en conséquence, le sentiment recommençait à torturer son cœur, elle connaîtrait le remède à cette pathologie ridicule : ne plus manger, se laisser descendre en dessous de la barre des quarante kilos.

Quand on pesait trente-cinq kilos, la vie était différente : l'obsession consistait à vaincre les épreuves physiques du jour, à distribuer son énergie de manière à en avoir assez pour les huit heures d'exercices, à affronter avec courage les tentations du repas, à cacher fièrement l'épuisement de ses forces – à danser, enfin, quand on l'aurait mérité.

La danse était la seule transcendance. Elle justifiait pleinement cette existence aride. Jouer avec sa santé n'avait aucune importance pourvu que l'on pût connaître cette sensation incroyable qui était celle de l'envol.

Il y a un malentendu autour de la danse classique. Pour beaucoup, elle n'est qu'un univers ridicule de tutus et de chaussons roses, de maniérismes à pointes et de mièvreries aériennes. Le pire, c'est que c'est vrai : elle est cela.

Mais elle n'est pas que cela. Débarrassez le ballet de ses afféteries gnangnan, de son tulle, de son académisme et de ses chignons romantiques : vous constaterez qu'il restera quelque chose et que cette chose est énorme. La preuve en est que les meilleurs danseurs modernes se recrutent à l'école classique.

Car le Graal du ballet, c'est l'envol. Aucun professeur ne le formule comme ça, de peur d'avoir l'air d'un fou furieux. Mais qui a appris la technique de la sissone, de l'entrechat, du grand jeté en avant, ne peut plus en douter : ce qu'on cherche à lui enseigner, c'est l'art de s'envoler.

Si les exercices à la barre sont si ennuyeux,

c'est parce que celle-ci est un perchoir. Quand on rêve de s'envoler, on enrage d'être contraint à s'amarrer à un morceau de bois, des heures durant, alors que l'on sent dans ses membres l'appel de l'air libre.

En vérité, la barre correspond à l'entraînement que les oisillons reçoivent au nid : on leur apprend à déployer leurs ailes avant de s'en servir. Pour les oisillons, quelques heures suffisent. Mais si un humain a le projet invraisemblable de changer d'espèce et d'apprendre à voler, il est normal qu'il doive y consacrer plusieurs années d'exercices exténuants.

Il en sera récompensé au-delà de ses espérances quand viendra le moment où il aura le droit de quitter le perchoir – la barre – et de se jeter dans l'espace. Le spectateur sceptique ne voit peut-être pas ce qui se passe dans le corps de la danseuse classique à cet instant précis : c'est une folie véritable. Et que cette démence respecte un code et une discipline de fer n'enlève rien au côté insensé de l'affaire : le ballet classique est l'ensemble des techniques visant à présenter comme possible et raisonnable l'idée de l'envol humain. Dès lors, comment s'étonner des atours grotesques voire grand-guignolesques dans lesquels cette danse s'exerce ? S'attend-on vraiment à ce qu'un projet aussi dingue soit celui de gens sains d'esprit ?

Cette longue incise s'adresse à ceux chez qui le ballet ne suscite que le rire. Ils ont raison de rire, mais qu'ils ne se contentent pas de rire : la danse classique cache aussi un idéal terrifiant.

Et les ravages que ce dernier peut exercer dans un jeune esprit équivalent à ceux d'une drogue dure.

A Noël, il fallut passer de courtes vacances dans sa famille.

Aucune élève de l'école des rats ne s'en réjouissait. Au contraire, cette perspective les emplissait d'appréhension. Des vacances : à quoi cela pouvait-il bien servir ? Cela se justifiait du temps où le but de la vie était le plaisir. Mais cette époque, qui était celle de l'enfance, était révolue : à présent, le seul sens de l'existence était la danse.

Et la vie de famille, composée essentiellement de repas et d'avachissement, était en contradiction avec l'obsession nouvelle.

Plectrude se dit que c'était ça, aussi, quitter l'enfance : ne plus se réjouir à l'approche de Noël. C'était la première fois que cela lui arrivait. Elle avait eu raison, l'an passé, de tant craindre l'âge de treize ans. Elle avait vraiment changé.

Tous le constatèrent. Sa maigreur les frappa : sa mère fut la seule à s'en émerveiller. Denis, Nicole, Béatrice et Roselyne, qu'on avait invitée, désapprouvèrent :

— Tu as un visage en lame de couteau.

— Elle est danseuse, protesta Clémence. Il ne fallait pas vous attendre à ce qu'elle nous revienne avec des joues rondes. Tu es très belle, ma chérie.

Au-delà de sa maigreur, une modification plus profonde les laissa d'autant plus perplexes qu'ils ne lui trouvèrent pas de nom. Peut-être n'osèrent-ils simplement pas la formuler tant

elle était sinistre : Plectrude avait perdu beaucoup de sa fraîcheur. Elle qui avait toujours été
une fillette rieuse manquait à présent de cet
entrain qu'on lui avait connu.

« C'est sans doute le choc des retrouvailles »,
pensa Denis.

Mais cette impression s'accentua au fil des
jours. C'était comme si la danseuse était
absente : sa bienveillance apparente cachait mal
son indifférence.

Quant aux repas, ils semblaient la torturer.
On avait l'habitude qu'elle mange très peu ;
maintenant, elle n'avalait carrément plus rien,
et on la sentait tendue aussi longtemps qu'on
n'avait pas quitté la table.

Si ses proches avaient pu voir ce qui se passait dans la tête de Plectrude, ils se seraient
inquiétés encore davantage.

D'abord, le jour de son arrivée, ils lui avaient
tous semblé obèses. Même Roselyne, une adolescente mince, lui parut énorme. Elle se
demandait comment ils supportaient leur
embonpoint.

Elle se demandait surtout comment ils toléraient cette vie vaine qui était la leur, cette mollesse étale et sans but. Elle bénissait son existence dure et ses privations : elle au moins, elle allait vers quelque chose. Ce n'était pas qu'elle avait le culte de la souffrance, mais elle avait besoin de sens : en cela, déjà, elle était adolescente.

En aparté, Roselyne lui raconta les mille histoires de leur classe. Elle pouffait et s'excitait :

— Et tu sais quoi ? Eh bien Vanessa, elle sort avec Fred, oui, le type de troisième !

Très vite, elle fut déçue de l'absence de succès qu'elle récoltait :

— Tu as été dans leur classe pendant plus longtemps que moi et tu t'en fous, de ce qui leur arrive ?

— Ne le prends pas mal. Si tu savais comme tout cela est loin de moi, maintenant.

— Même Mathieu Saladin ? demanda Roselyne, fine mouche du passé mais pas du présent.

— Bien sûr, dit Plectrude avec lassitude.

– Ça n'a pas toujours été comme ça.

– Ça l'est.

– Il y a des garçons à ton école ?

– Non. Ils prennent leurs cours séparément. On ne les voit jamais.

– Rien que des filles, alors ? Quelle galère !

– Tu sais, on n'a pas le temps de penser à ces choses-là.

Plectrude n'eut pas le courage de se lancer dans ses explications sur la barrière qui séparait les plus de quarante kilos des moins de quarante kilos, mais elle en sentait plus que jamais la réalité. Qu'est-ce qu'elle s'en fichait, de ces ridicules flirts scolaires ! Cette pauvre Roselyne lui faisait d'autant plus pitié qu'elle portait désormais un soutien-gorge.

– Tu veux que je te le montre ?

– Quoi ?

– Mon soutif. Tu n'arrêtes pas de le zieuter pendant que je te parle.

Roselyne souleva son tee-shirt. Plectrude hurla d'horreur.

En son for intérieur, la petite, qui avait appris à danser contre ses professeurs, apprit aussi à vivre contre sa famille. Elle ne lui disait rien mais elle observait les siens avec consternation : « Comme ils sont affalés ! Comme ils sont soumis aux lois de la pesanteur ! La vie, ce doit être plus et mieux que ça. »

Elle trouvait que leur existence, à l'inverse de la sienne, n'avait aucune tenue. Et elle avait honte pour eux. Parfois, elle se demandait si elle n'était pas une orpheline qu'ils avaient adoptée.

— Je t'assure qu'elle m'inquiète. Elle est très maigre, dit Denis.

— Oui, et alors ? C'est une danseuse, répondit Clémence.

— Les danseuses ne sont pas toujours aussi maigres qu'elle.

— Elle a treize ans. A cet âge, c'est normal.

Rassuré par cet argument, Denis put trouver le sommeil. La capacité d'auto-aveuglement des parents est immense : partant d'un constat exact – la fréquence de la maigreur chez les adolescents –, ils gommaient les circonstances. Leur fille était très fine par nature, certes : sa maigreur actuelle n'en était pas naturelle pour autant.

Les fêtes passèrent. Plectrude retourna à l'école, pour son plus grand soulagement.

– J'ai parfois l'impression d'avoir perdu une enfant, dit Denis.

– Tu es égoïste, protesta Clémence. Elle est heureuse.

Elle se trompait doublement. D'abord, la fillette n'était pas heureuse. Ensuite, l'égoïsme de son mari n'était rien comparé au sien : elle eût tellement voulu être ballerine et, grâce à Plectrude, elle assouvissait cette ambition par procuration. Peu lui importait de sacrifier la santé de son enfant à cet idéal. Si on le lui avait dit, elle eût ouvert de grands yeux et se fût exclamée :

– Je ne veux que le bonheur de ma fille !

Et c'eût été de sa part franchise absolue. Les parents ne savent pas ce que leur sincérité cache.

Ce que Plectrude vivait à l'école des rats ne s'appelait pas le bonheur : il faut à ce dernier un minimum de sentiment de sécurité. La fillette n'en avait pas l'ombre, en quoi elle avait raison : à son stade, elle ne jouait plus avec sa santé, puisqu'elle jouait sa santé. Elle le savait.

Ce que Plectrude vivait à l'école des rats s'appelait l'ivresse : cette extase se nourrissait d'une dose énorme d'oubli. Oubli des privations, de la souffrance physique, du danger, de la peur. Moyennant ces amnésies volontaires, elle pouvait se jeter dans la danse et y connaître la folle illusion, la transe de l'envol.

Elle était en train de devenir l'une des meilleures élèves. Certes, elle n'était pas la plus maigre, mais elle était sans conteste la plus gracieuse : elle possédait cette merveilleuse aisance du mouvement qui est la plus suprême injustice de la nature, car la grâce est donnée ou refusée à la naissance sans qu'aucun effort ultérieur ne puisse pallier son manque.

Et puis, ce qui ne gâtait rien, c'est qu'elle

était la plus jolie. Même à trente-cinq kilos, elle ne ressemblait pas à ces cadavres dont les professeurs louaient la maigreur : elle avait ses yeux de danseuse qui illuminaient son visage de leur beauté fantastique. Et les maîtres savaient, sans pour autant en parler à leurs élèves, que la joliesse compte énormément dans le choix des danseuses étoiles ; à cet égard, Plectrude était de loin la mieux lotie.

C'était sa santé qui la tracassait en secret. Elle n'en parlait à personne mais, la nuit, elle avait si mal aux jambes qu'elle devait s'empêcher de crier. Sans avoir aucune notion de médecine, elle en soupçonnait la raison : elle avait supprimé jusqu'à la moindre trace de produits laitiers dans son alimentation. En effet, elle avait remarqué qu'il lui suffisait de quelques cuillerées de yaourt maigre pour se sentir « gonflée » (encore eût-il fallu voir ce qu'elle appelait « gonflée »).

Or, le yaourt maigre était le seul laitage admis dans l'établissement. S'en passer revenait à éliminer tout apport en calcium, lequel était censé cimenter l'adolescence. Si fous que fussent les adultes de l'école, aucun ne recommandait de se priver de yaourt, et même les élèves les plus décharnées en mangeaient. Plectrude bannit cet aliment.

Cette carence entraîna très vite d'atroces douleurs dans les jambes, pour peu que la petite restât immobile quelques heures, ce qui était le cas la nuit. Pour éliminer cette souffrance, il fallait se lever et bouger. Mais le moment où les jambes se remettaient en mouvement était un supplice digne d'une séance de torture : Plectrude devait mordre un chiffon pour ne pas hurler. Elle avait à chaque fois l'impression que les os de ses mollets et de ses cuisses allaient se rompre.

Elle comprit que la décalcification était la cause de ce tourment. Pourtant, elle ne put se décider à reprendre de ce maudit yaourt. Sans le savoir, elle était victime de la machine intérieure de l'anorexie, qui considère chaque privation comme irréversible, sauf à ressentir une culpabilité insoutenable.

Elle perdit encore deux kilos, ce qui la confirma dans l'idée que le yaourt maigre était

« lourd ». Lors des vacances de Pâques, son père lui dit qu'elle était devenue un squelette et que c'était horrible, mais sa mère rabroua aussitôt Denis et s'extasia sur la beauté de sa fille. Clémence était le seul membre de sa famille que Plectrude voyait encore avec plaisir : « Elle au moins, elle me comprend. » Ses sœurs et même Roselyne la regardaient comme une étrangère Elle ne faisait plus partie de leur groupe : ils ne se sentaient rien de commun avec cet assemblage d'ossements.

Depuis qu'elle était descendue plus bas que trente-cinq kilos, la danseuse éprouvait encore moins de sentiments. Elle ne souffrit donc pas de cette exclusion.

Plectrude admirait sa vie : elle se sentait comme l'héroïne unique d'une lutte contre la pesanteur. Elle l'affrontait par le jeûne et par la danse.

Le Graal était l'envol et, de tous les chevaliers, Plectrude était la plus proche de l'attein-

dre. Que lui importaient les douleurs noctur-
nes en regard de l'immensité de sa quête ?

Les mois, les années s'écoulèrent. La danseuse s'intégra à son école comme une carmé-
lite à son ordre. En dehors de l'établissement,
point de salut.

Elle était l'étoile montante. On parlait d'elle
en haut lieu : elle le savait.

Elle atteignit l'âge de quinze ans. Elle mesurait toujours un mètre cinquante-cinq et
n'avait donc pas même grandi d'un demi-cen-
timètre depuis son entrée à l'école des rats. Son
poids : trente-deux kilos.

Il lui semblait parfois qu'elle n'avait jamais
eu de vie avant. Elle espérait que son existence
ne changerait jamais. L'admiration d'autrui,
réelle ou fantasmée, lui suffisait comme rap-
port affectif.

Elle savait aussi que sa mère l'aimait follement. Mine de rien, la conscience de cet amour
lui servait de colonne vertébrale. Un jour, elle
parla de ses problèmes de jambes à Clémence ;
celle-ci se contenta de lui dire :

– Que tu es courageuse !

Plectrude savoura le compliment. Pourtant, en son for intérieur, elle eut l'impression que sa mère eût dû lui dire quelque chose de très différent. Elle ne savait pas quoi.

—

Ce qui devait arriver arriva. Un matin de novembre, comme Plectrude venait de se lever en mordant son chiffon pour ne pas hurler de douleur, elle s'effondra : elle entendit un craquement dans sa cuisse.

Elle ne pouvait plus bouger. Elle appela à l'aide. On l'hospitalisa.

Un docteur qui ne l'avait pas encore vue examina ses radios.

– Quel âge a cette femme ?

– Quinze ans.

– Quoi ? ! Elle a l'ossature d'une ménopausée de soixante ans !

On l'interrogea. Elle dévoila le pot aux roses : elle ne prenait plus aucun produit laitier depuis deux années – à l'âge où le corps en a des besoins démentiels.

– Vous êtes anorexique ?

– Non, voyons ! s'insurgea-t-elle de bonne foi.

– Vous trouvez que c'est normal de peser trente kilos à votre âge ?

– Trente-deux kilos ! protesta-t-elle.

– Vous croyez que ça change quelque chose ?

Elle recourut aux arguments de Clémence :

– Je suis ballerine. Il vaut mieux ne pas avoir de rondeurs dans mon métier.

– Je ne savais pas qu'on recrutait les danseuses dans les camps de concentration.

– Vous êtes fou ! Vous insultez mon école !

– A votre avis, que faut-il penser d'un établissement où on laisse une adolescente s'autodétruire ? Je vais appeler la police, dit le médecin qui n'avait pas froid aux yeux.

Plectrude eut l'instinct de protéger son ordre :

– Non ! C'est ma faute ! Je me suis privée en cachette ! Personne ne savait.

– Personne ne voulait savoir. Le résultat, c'est que vous vous êtes cassé le tibia rien qu'en tombant par terre. Si vous étiez normale, un mois de plâtre suffirait. Dans votre état, je ne sais combien de mois vous allez devoir le garder, ce plâtre. Sans parler de la rééducation qui suivra.

— Mais alors, je ne vais pas pouvoir danser pendant longtemps ?

— Mademoiselle, vous ne pourrez plus jamais danser.

Le cœur de Plectrude cessa de battre. Elle sombra dans une sorte de coma.

Elle en sortit quelques jours plus tard. Passé le moment exquis où l'on ne se souvient de rien, elle se rappela sa condamnation. Une gentille infirmière lui confirma la sanction :

— Votre ossature est trop gravement fragilisée, surtout dans les jambes. Même quand votre tibia sera rétabli, vous ne pourrez pas recommencer la danse. Le moindre saut, le moindre choc pourrait vous briser. Il faudra des années de suralimentation en produits laitiers pour vous recalcifier.

Annoncer à Plectrude qu'elle ne pourrait plus danser revenait à annoncer à Napoléon qu'il n'aurait jamais plus d'armée : c'était la priver non pas de sa vocation mais de son destin.

Elle ne pouvait pas y croire. Elle interrogea tous les médecins possibles et imaginables : il n'y en eut pas un pour lui laisser une lueur d'espoir. Il faut les en féliciter : il eût suffi que l'un d'entre eux lui accordât un centième de chance de guérison et elle s'y fût accrochée au point d'y laisser la vie.

Après quelques jours, Plectrude s'étonna que Clémence ne fût pas à son chevet. Elle demanda à téléphoner. Son père lui dit qu'à l'annonce de la terrible nouvelle, sa mère était tombée gravement malade :

– Elle a de la fièvre, elle délire. Elle se prend pour toi. Elle dit : « Je n'ai que quinze ans, mon rêve ne peut pas être déjà fini, je serai danseuse, je ne peux pas être autre chose que danseuse ! »

L'idée de la souffrance de Clémence acheva Plectrude. Dans son lit d'hôpital, elle regardait le goutte-à-goutte qui la nourrissait : elle avait vraiment la conviction qu'il lui injectait du malheur en guise d'aliment.

Aussi longtemps que le moindre mouvement lui fut interdit, Plectrude resta à l'hôpital. Son père venait parfois lui rendre visite. Elle demandait pourquoi Clémence ne l'accompagnait pas.

— Ta mère est encore trop malade, répondait-il.

Cela dura des mois. Personne d'autre ne vint la voir, ni de l'école des rats, ni de sa famille, ni de son ancien collège : comme quoi Plectrude n'appartenait plus à aucun monde.

Elle passait ses journées à ne faire strictement rien. Elle ne voulait rien lire, ni livres ni journaux. Elle refusait la télévision. On diagnostiqua une dépression profonde.

Elle ne pouvait rien avaler. Encore heureux qu'il y eût le goutte-à-goutte. Ce dernier lui inspirait pourtant du dégoût : il était ce qui la rattachait à la vie, malgré elle.

Quand ce fut le printemps, on la ramena chez ses parents. Son cœur battait à l'idée de revoir sa mère : ce souhait lui fut refusé. La petite s'insurgea :

— Ce n'est pas possible ! Elle est morte ou quoi ?

— Non, elle est vivante. Mais elle ne veut pas que tu la voies dans cet état.

C'était plus que Plectrude n'en pouvait supporter. Elle attendit que ses sœurs fussent au lycée et que son père fût sorti pour quitter son lit : elle pouvait à présent se déplacer à l'aide de béquilles.

Elle tituba jusqu'à la chambre parentale, où Clémence était en train de dormir. En la voyant, la petite la crut morte : elle avait le teint gris et lui parut encore plus maigre qu'elle. Elle s'effondra à côté d'elle en pleurant :

— Maman ! Maman !

La dormeuse s'éveilla et lui dit :

— Tu n'as pas le droit d'être ici.

— J'avais trop besoin de te voir. Et puis maintenant c'est fait, et c'est mieux comme ça : je préfère savoir comment tu es. Du moment que tu es vivante, le reste m'est égal. Tu vas recommencer à manger, tu vas aller mieux : nous allons guérir toutes les deux, maman.

Elle remarqua que sa mère restait froide et ne l'étreignait pas.

— Serre-moi dans tes bras, j'en ai tellement besoin !

Clémence demeurait inerte.

— Pauvre maman, tu es trop faible même pour ça.

Elle se redressa et la regarda. Comme elle avait changé ! Il n'y avait plus aucune chaleur dans les yeux de sa mère. Quelque chose était mort en elle : Plectrude ne voulut pas le comprendre.

Elle se dit : « Maman se prend pour moi. Elle a cessé de manger parce que j'ai cessé de manger. Si je mange, elle mangera. Si je guéris, elle guérira. »

La petite se traîna jusqu'à la cuisine et prit une tablette de chocolat. Ensuite, elle revint dans la chambre de Clémence et s'assit sur le lit, près d'elle.

— Regarde, maman, je mange.

Le chocolat traumatisa sa bouche qui avait

perdu l'habitude des aliments, a fortiori d'une friandise aussi riche. Plectrude s'efforça de ne pas montrer son malaise.

– C'est du chocolat au lait, maman, c'est plein de calcium. C'est bon pour moi.

C'était donc ça, manger ? Ses entrailles tressaillaient, son estomac se révoltait, Plectrude se sentit sur le point de tourner de l'œil, mais elle ne s'évanouit pas : elle vomit – sur ses genoux.

Humiliée, désolée, elle resta immobile à contempler son œuvre.

Ce fut alors que sa mère dit, d'une voix sèche :

– Tu me dégoûtes.

La petite regarda l'œil glacial de la femme qui venait de lui lancer une telle condamnation. Elle ne voulut pas croire ce qu'elle avait entendu et vu. Elle s'enfuit aussi vite que ses béquilles le lui permettaient.

Plectrude tomba sur son lit et pleura autant que l'on peut pleurer. Elle s'endormit.

Quand elle s'éveilla, elle sentit un phénomène invraisemblable : elle avait faim.

Elle demanda à Béatrice, qui entre-temps était rentrée, de lui apporter un plateau.

– Victoire ! applaudit sa sœur qui ne tarda pas à lui ramener du pain, du fromage, de la compote, du jambon et du chocolat.

La petite ne prit pas ce dernier qui lui rappelait trop le récent vomissement ; en compensation, elle dévora le reste.

Béatrice exultait.

L'appétit était revenu. Ce n'était pas de la boulimie mais de saines fringales. Elle mangeait trois copieux repas par jour, avec une attirance particulière pour le fromage, comme si son corps la renseignait sur ses besoins les plus urgents. Son père et ses sœurs étaient ravis.

A ce régime, Plectrude reprit rapidement du poids. Elle retrouva ses quarante kilos et son beau visage. Tout allait pour le mieux. Elle parvenait même à ne pas éprouver de culpabilité, ce qui pour une ancienne anorexique est extraordinaire.

Comme elle l'avait prévu, sa guérison guérit

sa mère. Celle-ci quitta enfin sa chambre et revit sa fille, qu'elle n'avait plus aperçue depuis le jour où elle avait vomi. Elle la regarda avec consternation et s'écria :

— Tu as grossi !

— Oui, maman, balbutia la petite.

— Quelle idée ! Tu étais si jolie avant !

— Tu ne me trouves pas jolie, comme ça ?

— Non. Tu es grosse.

— Enfin, maman ! Je pèse quarante kilos.

— C'est bien ce que je disais : tu as grossi de huit kilos.

— J'en avais besoin !

— C'est ce que tu te dis pour avoir bonne conscience. Tu avais besoin de calcium, pas de poids. Si tu t'imagines que tu as l'air d'une danseuse, maintenant !

— Mais maman, je ne peux plus danser. Je ne suis plus une danseuse. Sais-tu combien j'en souffre ? Ne retourne pas le fer dans la plaie !

— Si tu en souffrais, tu n'aurais pas tant d'appétit.

Le pire était la voix dure avec laquelle cette femme lui assena son verdict.

– Pourquoi me parles-tu comme ça ? Ne suis-je plus ta fille ?

– Tu n'as jamais été ma fille.

Clémence lui raconta tout : Lucette, Fabien, l'assassinat de Fabien par Lucette, sa naissance en prison, le suicide de Lucette.

– Qu'est-ce que tu me racontes ? gémit Plectrude.

– Demande à ton père – enfin, à ton oncle –, si tu ne me crois pas.

La première incrédulité passée, la petite parvint à dire :

– Pourquoi me dis-tu ça aujourd'hui ?

– Il fallait bien te l'avouer un jour, non ?

– Bien sûr. Mais pourquoi de cette façon si cruelle ? Jusqu'ici, tu as été pour moi la meilleure des mères. Là, tu me parles comme si je n'avais jamais été ta fille.

– Parce que tu m'as trahie. Tu sais combien je rêvais que tu sois danseuse.

– J'ai eu un accident ! Ce n'est pas ma faute.

— Si, c'est ta faute ! Si tu ne t'étais pas stupidement décalcifiée !

— Je t'avais parlé de mes douleurs aux jambes !

— C'est faux !

— Si, je t'en avais parlé ! Tu m'avais même félicitée pour mon courage.

— Tu mens !

— Je ne mens pas ! Tu trouves que c'est normal, une mère qui félicite sa fille d'avoir mal aux jambes ? C'était un appel au secours et tu ne l'as même pas entendu.

— C'est ça, dis que c'est ma faute.

La mauvaise foi de Clémence laissa Plectrude sans voix.

Tout s'effondrait : elle n'avait plus de destin, elle n'avait plus de parents, elle n'avait plus rien.

Denis était gentil mais faible. Clémence lui ordonna de cesser de féliciter Plectrude pour son appétit retrouvé :

— Ne l'encourage pas à grossir, voyons !

— Elle n'est pas grosse, bégaya-t-il. Un peu ronde, peut-être.

Le « un peu ronde » signifia à la petite qu'elle avait perdu un allié.

Dire à une fille de quinze ans qu'elle est grosse, voire « un peu ronde », quand elle pèse quarante kilos, revient à lui interdire de grandir.

Une fillette, face à un tel désastre, n'a que deux possibilités : la rechute dans l'anorexie ou la boulimie. Par miracle, Plectrude ne sombra ni dans l'une ni dans l'autre. Elle conserva son appétit. Elle avait des fringales que n'importe quel médecin eût trouvées salutaires et que Clémence déclarait « monstrueuses ».

En vérité, c'était une santé suprême qui intimait à Plectrude d'avoir faim : elle avait des années d'adolescence à rattraper. Grâce à sa frénésie de fromage, elle grandit de trois centimètres. Un mètre cinquante-huit, c'était quand même mieux qu'un mètre cinquante-cinq, comme taille adulte.

A seize ans, elle eut ses règles. Elle l'annonça à Clémence comme une merveilleuse nouvelle. Celle-ci haussa les épaules avec mépris.

— Ça ne te fait pas plaisir, que je sois enfin normale ?

— Combien pèses-tu ?

— Quarante-sept kilos.

— C'est bien ce que je pensais : tu es obèse.

— Quarante-sept kilos pour un mètre cinquante-huit, tu trouves ça obèse ?

— Regarde la vérité en face : tu es énorme.

Plectrude, qui avait retrouvé le plein usage de ses jambes, alla se jeter sur son lit. Elle ne pleura pas : elle ressentit une crise de haine qui dura des heures. Elle tapait du poing sur son oreiller et, à l'intérieur de son crâne, une voix hurlait : « Elle veut me tuer ! Ma mère veut ma mort ! »

Jamais elle n'avait cessé de considérer Clémence comme sa mère : peu lui importait qu'elle fût sortie de son ventre ou non. Elle était sa mère parce qu'elle était celle qui lui avait vraiment donné la vie – et c'était la même qui, à présent, voulait la lui retirer.

A sa place, nombre d'adolescentes se seraient suicidées. L'instinct de survie devait être sacrément ancré en Plectrude car elle finit par se relever en disant à haute et calme voix :

— Je ne te laisserai pas me tuer, maman.

Elle se reprit en main, autant que cela était possible à une fille de seize ans qui avait tout perdu. Puisque sa mère était devenue folle, elle serait adulte à sa place.

Elle s'inscrivit à un cours de théâtre. Elle y fit grande impression. Son prénom y contribua. S'appeler Plectrude, c'était à double tranchant : soit on était laide et ce prénom soulignait votre laideur, soit on était belle et l'étrange sonorité de Plectrude démultipliait votre beauté.

Ce qui fut son cas. On était déjà frappé quand on voyait entrer cette jeune fille aux yeux superbes et à la démarche de danseuse. Quand on apprenait son prénom, on la regardait davantage et on admirait ses cheveux sublimes, son expression tragique, sa bouche parfaite, son teint idéal.

Son professeur lui dit qu'elle avait « un physique » (elle trouva cette expression étrange : tout le monde n'avait-il pas un physique ?) et lui conseilla de se présenter à des castings.

Ce fut ainsi qu'on la sélectionna pour jouer le rôle de Géraldine Chaplin adolescente dans un téléfilm ; en la voyant, l'actrice s'exclama : « Je n'étais pas si belle à son âge ! » On ne pouvait pourtant nier une certaine parenté entre ces deux visages d'une minceur extrême.

Ce genre de prestations rapportait à la jeune fille un peu d'argent, pas assez, hélas, pour lui permettre de fuir sa mère, ce qui était devenu son but. Le soir, elle rentrait à l'appartement le plus tard possible, afin de ne pas croiser Clémence. Elle ne pouvait cependant toujours l'éviter et se voyait alors accueillie d'un :

– Tiens ! Voilà Bouboule !

Dans le meilleur des cas. Dans le pire, cela devenait :

– Bonsoir, Dondon !

On pourrait mal comprendre comment des propos aussi surréalistes la blessaient à ce

149

point ; ce serait ignorer l'air dégoûté avec lequel ces commentaires lui étaient assénés.

Un jour, Plectrude osa répliquer que Béatrice, sept kilos de plus qu'elle, ne recevait jamais de remarques aussi désobligeantes. A quoi sa mère répondit :

– Ça n'a rien à voir, tu sais bien !

Elle n'eut pas l'audace de dire que non, elle ne savait pas bien. Tout ce qu'elle comprit, c'est que sa sœur avait le droit d'être normale et pas elle.

Un soir, comme Plectrude n'avait pu trouver de prétexte pour ne pas dîner avec les siens, et comme Clémence prenait un air scandalisé chaque fois qu'elle avalait une bouchée, elle finit par protester :

– Maman, cesse de me regarder comme ça ! Tu n'as jamais vu quelqu'un manger ?

– C'est pour ton bien, ma chérie. Je m'inquiète de ta boulimie !

– Boulimie !

Plectrude regarda fixement son père, puis ses sœurs, avant de dire :

— Vous êtes trop lâches pour me défendre !
Le père balbutia :

— Ça ne me dérange pas que tu aies bon
appétit.

— Lâche ! lança la jeune fille. Je mange moins
que toi.

Nicole haussa les épaules.

— J'en ai rien à foutre, de vos conneries.

— Je n'en attendais pas moins de toi, grinça
l'adolescente.

Béatrice respira un grand coup puis elle dit :

— Bon, maman, j'aimerais que tu laisses ma
sœur tranquille, d'accord ?

— Merci, dit la jeune fille.

Ce fut alors que Clémence sourit et clama :

— Ce n'est pas ta sœur, Béatrice !

— Qu'est-ce que tu racontes ?

— Crois-tu que le moment soit bien choisi ?
murmura Denis.

La mère se leva et alla chercher une photo
qu'elle jeta sur la table.

— C'est Lucette, ma sœur, qui est la vraie
mère de Plectrude.

Pendant qu'elle racontait l'histoire à Nicole

et Béatrice, la petite avait saisi la photo et regardait avidement le joli visage de la morte.

Les sœurs étaient abasourdies.

– Je lui ressemble, dit l'adolescente.

Elle pensa que sa mère s'était suicidée à dix-neuf ans et que ce serait son destin à elle aussi : « J'ai seize ans. Encore trois ans à vivre, et un enfant à mettre au monde. »

Dès lors, Plectrude eut, pour les nombreux garçons qui tournaient autour d'elle, des regards qui n'étaient pas de son âge. Elle ne pouvait les dévisager sans penser : « Voudrais-je un bébé de celui-ci ? »

Le plus souvent, la réponse intime était non, tant il paraissait inimaginable d'avoir un enfant avec tel ou tel godelureau.

Au cours de théâtre, le professeur décida que Plectrude et un de ses camarades joueraient une scène de *La Cantatrice chauve*. Ce texte intrigua si profondément la jeune fille qu'elle se procura les œuvres complètes d'Ionesco. Ce

fut une révélation : elle connut enfin cette fièvre qui pousse à lire des nuits entières.

Elle avait souvent essayé de lire, mais les livres
lui tombaient des mains. Sans doute chaque être
a-t-il, dans l'univers de l'écrit, une œuvre qui le
transformera en lecteur, à supposer que le destin
favorise leur rencontre. Ce que Platon dit de la
moitié amoureuse, cet autre qui circule quelque
part et qu'il convient de trouver, sauf à demeurer incomplet jusqu'au jour du trépas, est encore
plus vrai pour les livres.

« Ionesco est l'auteur qui m'était destiné »,
pensa l'adolescente. Elle en conçut un bonheur
considérable, l'ivresse que seule peut procurer
la découverte d'un livre aimé.

Il peut arriver qu'un premier coup de foudre
littéraire déchaîne le goût de la lecture chez
l'intéressé ; ce ne fut pas le cas de la jeune fille,
qui n'ouvrit d'autres livres que pour se persua-
der de leur ennui. Elle décida qu'elle ne lirait
pas d'autres auteurs et s'enorgueillit du prestige
d'une telle fidélité.

Un soir, comme elle regardait la télévision, Plectrude apprit l'existence de Catherine Ringer. En l'entendant chanter, elle ressentit un mélange d'engouement et d'amertume : engouement, parce qu'elle la trouvait formidable ; amertume, parce qu'elle eût voulu faire très précisément ce métier, alors qu'elle n'en avait ni la capacité, ni les moyens, ni la moindre notion.

Si elle avait été le genre de fille qui a une nouvelle ambition par semaine, ce n'eût pas été très grave. Ce n'était hélas pas son cas. A dix-sept ans, Plectrude avait peu d'enthousiasme. Ses cours de théâtre ne la passionnaient pas. Elle eût vendu son âme pour reprendre la danse, mais les médecins, s'ils avaient constaté un net progrès dans sa recalcification, étaient unanimes pour lui interdire son ancienne vocation.

Si la découverte de Catherine Ringer fut un tel choc pour l'adolescente, c'est parce qu'elle lui donnait, pour la première fois, un rêve étranger à la danse.

Elle se consola en pensant qu'elle allait mourir dans deux ans et qu'entre-temps elle devrait mettre un enfant au monde : « Je n'ai pas le temps d'être chanteuse. »

Au cours de théâtre, Plectrude eut à jouer un passage de *La Leçon* d'Ionesco. Pour un comédien, obtenir l'un des rôles principaux dans une pièce de son auteur préféré, c'est à la fois Byzance et Cythère, Rome et le Vatican.

Il serait faux de dire qu'elle devint la jeune élève de la pièce. Elle avait toujours été ce rôle, cette fille si enthousiaste face aux apprentissages élus qu'elle en venait à les pervertir et à les démolir – encouragée et devancée en cela, bien entendu, par le professeur, grand masticateur de savoir et d'étudiants.

Elle fut l'élève avec tant de sens du sacré que cela contamina la partie adverse : celui qui reçut le rôle du professeur fut automatiquement choisi par Plectrude.

Lors d'une répétition, comme il lui disait une réplique d'une vérité prodigieuse (« La philologie mène au crime »), elle lui répondit qu'il serait le père de son enfant. Il crut à un procédé langagier digne de *La Cantatrice chauve* et acquiesça. La nuit même, elle le prit au mot.

Un mois plus tard, Plectrude sut qu'elle était enceinte. Avis à ceux, s'ils existent, qui ne verraient encore en Ionesco qu'un auteur comique.

PLECTRUDE avait l'âge de sa propre mère quand elle accoucha : dix-neuf ans. Le bébé fut appelé Simon. Il était beau et bien portant.

L'adolescente ressentit une fabuleuse bouffée d'amour en le découvrant. Elle ne se doutait pas qu'elle aurait à ce point la fibre maternelle et le déplora : « Ça ne va pas être facile de se suicider. »

Elle était pourtant déterminée à aller jusqu'au bout : « J'ai déjà mis de l'eau dans le vin de mon destin en renonçant à tuer le père de Simon. Mais moi, je n'y couperai pas. »

Elle berçait le petit en lui murmurant :

— Je t'aime, Simon, je t'aime. Je mourrai parce que je dois mourir. Si j'avais le choix, je resterais auprès de toi. Je dois mourir : c'est un ordre, je le sens.

Une semaine plus tard, elle se dit : « C'est maintenant ou jamais. Si je continue à vivre, je vais trop m'attacher à Simon. Plus j'attendrai, plus ce sera difficile. »

Elle n'écrivit aucune lettre, pour cette noble raison qu'elle n'aimait pas écrire. De toute manière, son acte lui paraissait si lisible qu'elle ne voyait pas la nécessité de l'expliquer.

Comme elle ne se sentait aucun courage, elle décida de revêtir ses plus beaux vêtements : elle avait déjà remarqué que l'élégance donnait du cœur au ventre.

Deux ans plus tôt, elle avait trouvé aux puces une robe d'archiduchesse fantasmatique en velours bleu nuit, avec des dentelles couleur de vieil or, si somptueuse qu'elle était importable.

« Si je ne la mets pas aujourd'hui, je ne la mettrai jamais », se dit-elle, avant d'éclater de rire en prenant conscience de la profonde vérité de cette pensée.

La grossesse l'avait un peu amaigrie et elle flottait dans la robe : elle s'en accommoda. Elle lâcha sa chevelure magnifique qui lui tombait jusqu'aux fesses. Quand elle se fut composé un maquillage de fée tragique, elle se plut et décréta qu'elle pouvait se suicider sans rougir.

Plectrude embrassa Simon. Au moment de sortir de chez elle, elle se demanda comment elle allait procéder : se jetterait-elle sous un train, sous une voiture, ou dans la Seine ? Elle ne s'était même pas posé la question : « Je verrai bien », conclut-elle. « Si on se soucie de ce genre de détails, on ne fait plus rien. »

Elle marcha jusqu'à la gare. Elle n'eut pas le courage de se précipiter sous les roues du RER. « Tant qu'à mourir, autant mourir à Paris, et de moins vilaine façon », se dit-elle, non sans un certain sens des convenances. Elle monta donc dans le train, où, de mémoire de banlieusards, on n'avait jamais vu une passagère d'aussi superbe allure, d'autant qu'elle souriait d'une oreille à l'autre : la perspective du suicide la mettait d'excellente humeur.

Elle descendit dans le centre de la ville et

marcha le long de la Seine, à la recherche du pont qui favoriserait le mieux son entreprise. Comme elle hésitait entre le pont Alexandre-III, le pont des Arts et le Pont-Neuf, elle marcha longtemps, effectuant d'incessants allers-retours pour reconsidérer leurs mérites respectifs.

Finalement, le pont Alexandre-III fut recalé pour magnificence exagérée et le pont des Arts éliminé pour excès d'intimité. Le Pont-Neuf fut élu qui la séduisit tant par son ancienneté que par ses plates-formes en demi-lune, idéales pour les réflexions de dernière minute.

Hommes et femmes se retournaient sur le passage de cette beauté qui ne s'en rendait pas compte, tant son projet l'absorbait. Elle ne s'était plus sentie aussi euphorique depuis l'enfance.

Elle s'assit sur le bord du pont, pieds dans le vide. Beaucoup de gens adoptaient cette position qui n'attirait plus l'attention de personne. Elle regarda autour d'elle. Un ciel gris pesait sur Notre-Dame, l'eau de la Seine frisait au vent. Soudain l'âge du monde frappa Plec-

trude : comme ses dix-neuf années seraient vite
englouties dans les siècles de Paris !

Elle eut un vertige et son exaltation tomba :
toute cette grandeur de ce qui dure, toute cette
éternité dont elle ne ferait pas partie ! Elle avait
apporté à la terre un enfant qui ne se souvien-
drait pas d'elle. Sinon, rien. La seule personne
qu'elle avait aimée d'amour était sa mère : en
se tuant, elle obéissait à celle qui ne l'aimait
plus. « C'est faux : il y a aussi Simon. Je l'aime.
Mais vu combien l'amour d'une mère est nocif,
il vaut mieux que je le lui épargne. »

Sous ses jambes, le grand vide du fleuve
l'appelait.

« Pourquoi ai-je attendu ce moment pour
sentir ce qui me manque ? Ma vie a faim et soif,
il ne m'est rien arrivé de ce qui peut nourrir et
abreuver l'existence, j'ai le cœur desséché, la tête
dénutrie, à la place de l'âme j'ai une carence,
est-ce dans cet état qu'il faut mourir ? »

Le néant vrombissait sous elle. La question
l'écrasait, elle fut tentée d'y échapper en laissant
ses pieds devenir plus lourds que son cerveau.

A cet instant précis, une voix hurla, de loin :

161

– Plectrude !

« M'appelle-t-on de chez les morts ou de chez les vivants ? » se demanda-t-elle.

Elle se pencha vers l'eau, comme si elle allait y voir quelqu'un.

Le cri redoubla d'intensité :

– Plectrude !

C'était une voix d'homme.

Elle se retourna en direction du hurlement.

Ce jour-là, Mathieu Saladin avait éprouvé le besoin incompréhensible de quitter son XVIIe arrondissement natal pour se promener le long de la Seine.

Il profitait de cette journée douce et grise quand il avait vu venir en sens inverse, sur le trottoir, une apparition : une jeune fille d'une splendeur sidérante, vêtue comme pour un bal costumé.

Il s'était arrêté pour la regarder passer. Elle ne l'avait pas vu. Elle ne voyait personne, avec ses grands yeux hallucinés. Ce fut alors qu'il l'avait reconnue. Il avait souri de joie : « Je l'ai retrouvée ! On dirait qu'elle est toujours aussi folle. Cette fois-ci, je ne la lâche plus. »

Il s'était livré à ce plaisir qui consiste à suivre en secret une personne qu'on connaît, à observer ses comportements, à interpréter ses gestes.

Quand elle avait enjambé le Pont-Neuf, il n'avait pas eu peur : il l'avait vue avec un visage joyeux, elle n'avait pas l'air désespéré. Il s'était accoudé au bord de la Seine et penché pour regarder son ancienne camarade de classe.

Peu à peu, il avait trouvé que Plectrude avait une attitude des plus louches. Son exaltation même lui avait paru suspecte ; quand il avait eu la nette impression qu'elle allait se jeter dans le fleuve, il avait hurlé son prénom et couru vers elle.

Elle le reconnut aussitôt.

Ils eurent le prélude amoureux le plus court de l'Histoire.

— Tu as quelqu'un ? demanda Mathieu sans perdre une seconde.

— Célibataire, avec un bébé, répondit-elle aussi sec.

— Parfait. Tu me veux ?

— Oui.

Il empoigna les hanches de Plectrude et les retourna à cent quatre-vingts degrés, pour qu'elle n'eût plus les pieds dans le vide. Ils se roulèrent un patin afin de sceller ce qui avait été dit.

— Tu n'étais pas en train de te suicider, par hasard ?

— Non, répondit-elle par pudeur.

Il lui roula un nouveau patin. Elle pensa : « Il y a une minute, j'étais sur le point de me jeter dans le vide, et maintenant je suis dans les bras de l'homme de ma vie, que je n'avais plus vu depuis sept ans, que je croyais ne plus jamais revoir. Je décide de remettre ma mort à une date ultérieure. »

Plectrude découvrit une chose surprenante : on pouvait être heureux à l'âge adulte.

– Je vais te montrer où j'habite, dit-il en l'emmenant.

– Que tu es rapide !

– J'ai perdu sept ans. Ça m'a suffi.

Si Mathieu Saladin avait pu se douter du nombre d'engueulades que cet aveu allait lui valoir, il l'eût bouclée. Combien de fois Plectrude ne lui cria-t-elle pas :

– Et dire que tu m'as laissée attendre sept ans ! Et dire que tu m'a laissée souffrir !

A quoi Mathieu protestait :

– Toi aussi, tu m'as laissé ! Pourquoi ne m'avais-tu pas dit que tu m'aimais, à douze ans ?

– C'est le rôle du garçon ! coupait Plectrude, péremptoire.

Un jour, comme Plectrude entamait le couplet du déjà célèbre « et dire que tu m'as laissée attendre sept ans ! », Mathieu y coupa court par une révélation :

– Tu n'es pas la seule à avoir été à l'hôpital. De douze à dix-huit ans, j'ai été hospitalisé six fois.

— Monsieur s'est trouvé une nouvelle excuse ? Et pour quels bobos te soignait-on ?

— Pour être plus complet, sache que, de un à dix-huit ans, j'ai été hospitalisé dix-huit fois.

Elle fronça les sourcils.

— C'est une longue histoire, commença-t-il.

A l'âge d'un an, Mathieu Saladin était mort.

Le bébé Mathieu Saladin marchait à quatre pattes dans le salon de ses parents, explorant l'univers passionnant des pieds de fauteuil et des dessous de table. Dans une prise de courant, il y avait une rallonge qui ne donnait sur rien. Le bébé s'intéressa à cette ficelle qui s'achevait sur un demi-bulbe des plus saisissants : il le mit dans sa bouche et saliva. Il reçut une décharge qui le tua.

Le père de Mathieu ne put accepter cette sentence électrique. Il conduisit le bébé chez le meilleur médecin de la planète dans l'heure qui suivit. Personne ne sut ce qui se passa, mais il rendit la vie au petit corps.

Encore fallait-il lui rendre une bouche :

Mathieu Saladin n'avait plus rien qui correspondît à cette appellation : ni lèvres, ni palais. Le médecin l'envoya chez le meilleur chirurgien de l'univers qui préleva ici un peu de cartilage, là un peu de peau, et qui, au terme d'un minutieux patchwork, reconstitua, sinon une bouche, au moins sa structure.

— C'est tout ce que je peux faire cette année, conclut-il. Revenez l'an prochain.

Chaque année, il réopérait Mathieu Saladin et rajoutait quelque chose. Puis, il terminait par les deux phrases devenues rituelles. Ce fut le sujet de plaisanteries de l'enfance et de l'adolescence du miraculé :

— Et si tu es bien sage, l'an prochain, on te fera une luette (une arrière-bouche, une membrane vélaire, une courbure palatale, une gingivo-plastie, etc.).

Plectrude l'écouta, au sommet de l'extase.

— C'est pour ça que tu as cette sublime cicatrice à la moustache !

— Sublime ?

— Il n'y a rien de plus beau !

Ils étaient vraiment destinés l'un à l'autre,

ces deux êtres qui chacun, de manière si différente, au cours de la première année de leur
existence, avait côtoyé la mort de beaucoup
trop près.

Les fées, décidément trop nombreuses, qui
avaient accablé la jeune fille d'épreuves à la
mesure des grâces dont elles l'avaient parée, lui
envoyèrent alors la pire des plaies d'Egypte :
une plaie de Belgique.

Quelques années avaient passé. Vivre le parfait amour avec Mathieu Saladin, musicien de
son état, avait donné à Plectrude le courage de
devenir chanteuse, sous un pseudonyme qui
était un nom de dictionnaire et qui convenait
ainsi à la dimension encyclopédique des souf-
frances qu'elle avait connues : Robert.

Il est régulier que les plus grands malheurs
prennent d'abord le visage de l'amitié : Plectrude rencontra Amélie Nothomb et vit en elle
l'amie, la sœur dont elle avait tant besoin.

Plectrude lui raconta sa vie. Amélie écouta
avec effarement ce destin d'Atride. Elle lui

demanda si tant de tentatives de meurtre sur sa personne ne lui avaient pas donné le désir de tuer, en vertu de cette loi qui fait des victimes les meilleurs des bourreaux.

— Votre père a été assassiné par votre mère quand elle était enceinte de vous, au huitième mois de sa grossesse. On a la certitude que vous étiez éveillée, puisque vous aviez le hoquet. Donc, vous êtes témoin !

— Mais je n'ai rien vu !

— Vous avez forcément perçu quelque chose. Vous êtes un témoin d'un genre très spécial : un témoin *in utero*. Il paraît que, dans le ventre de leur mère, les bébés entendent la musique et savent si leurs parents font l'amour. Votre mère a vidé le chargeur sur votre père, dans un état de violence extrême : vous avez dû le ressentir, d'une manière ou d'une autre.

— Où voulez-vous en venir ?

— Vous êtes imprégnée de ce meurtre. Ne parlons même pas des tentatives d'assassinat métaphoriques que vous avez subies et que vous vous êtes imposées par la suite. Comment pourriez-vous ne pas devenir meurtrière ?

169

Plectrude, qui n'y avait jamais songé, ne put dès lors qu'y penser. Et comme il y a une forme de justice, elle assouvit son désir d'assassinat sur celle qui le lui avait suggéré. Elle prit le fusil qui ne la quittait pas et qui lui était utile quand elle allait voir ses producteurs et tira sur la tempe d'Amélie.

« C'est tout ce que j'ai trouvé pour l'empêcher d'élucubrer », expliqua-t-elle à son mari, compréhensif.

Plectrude et Mathieu, qui avaient en commun d'avoir souvent traversé le fleuve des Enfers, regardèrent le macchabée avec une larme au coin des yeux. Cela renforça encore la connivence de ce couple très émouvant.

Dès lors, leur vie devint, à une syllabe près, une pièce d'Ionesco : « Amélie ou comment s'en débarrasser ». C'était un cadavre bien encombrant.

L'assassinat a ceci de comparable avec l'acte sexuel qu'il est souvent suivi de la même question : que faire du corps ? Dans le cas de l'acte sexuel, on peut se contenter de partir. Le meurtre ne permet pas cette facilité. C'est aussi pour cette raison qu'il constitue un lien beaucoup plus fort entre les êtres.

A l'heure qu'il est, Plectrude et Mathieu n'ont toujours pas trouvé la solution.

*La composition de cet ouvrage
a été réalisée par I.G.S. Charente Photogravure,
à l'Isle-d'Espagnac,
l'impression et le brochage ont été effectués
sur presse Cameron dans les ateliers
de **Bussière Camedan Imprimeries**
à Saint-Amand-Montrond (Cher),
pour le compte des Éditions Albin Michel.*

A Rose for
Virtue

A Rose for
Virtue

NORAH
LOFTS

Cover Photography: Amanda Thomas
Styling: Susie Wilkinson
Thanks to St Agnes' church, Bristol and Siubhan Macdonald

First published in 1971
This edition published in 2009
By arrangement with the Author's Estate and Tree of Life Publishing

The History Press
The Mill, Brimscombe Port
Stroud, Gloucestershire, GL5 2QG
www.thehistorypress.co.uk

British Library Cataloguing in Publication Data.
A catalogue record for this book is available from the British Library.

ISBN 978 0 7524 4871 8

Typesetting and origination by The History Press
Printed in Great Britain

Mother said, ending her story, 'And so I asked him to join us here this evening.'

She arranged herself a little more comfortably on the sofa.

Eugène said, with a gasp and a stare, 'You asked General Bonaparte! Here! Wh—what did he say?'

'He accepted. I cannot say graciously,' Mother said with one of her smiles, very sweet but just tinged with mockery. 'A trifle brusque. In fact what he said was, "I'll come. What time?" And I told him, nine o'clock.'

'He'll walk in as the clock strikes,' Eugène said; and not critically, not implying any slur upon the mannerliness of a man who could ignore the convention of being half an hour late for any purely social gathering.

'I cannot see why,' Mother said. 'I told him nine o'clock.'

'He's a soldier. He'll be punctual,' Eugène said.

Eugène was born to hero-worship as some people are born to write verse or compose music; one, at least, of his school masters was always wonderful, three, at least, of his school-fellows witty, clever, good-natured beyond belief. He was frequently disillusioned but never cured. The natural outlet for boyish enthusiasm and emulation was closed to him; even when our father was alive we had seen little of him: he and Mother had not been happily married. Yet, retrospectively, Eugène had spared a little sentiment and adulation for Father and as a result had found a new idol.

Someone had conceived the notion that the rather shaky calm in France would be bolstered up if no private citizen were allowed to possess any weapon. A law ordering the confiscation of all arms had been passed and Eugène seemed to be in danger of losing what he now regarded as almost a holy relic – Father's sword. Saying nothing to anybody Eugène had gone off and somehow managed to talk or wheedle his way into the presence of General Bonaparte, and plead to be allowed to keep this sword. The General had said, 'Keep it. Use it for France.' Eugène came home in triumph; possessed of a new hero, but disconsolate because he had been too much overcome to express his gratitude properly. Mother said, 'You can write a nice little letter.' For Mother the two words were almost inseparable, what was nice was usually little, what was little usually nice. Eugène tried, tore up several attempts, asked my help, was still not satisfied and finally told Mother that he wished she would go and thank General Bonaparte in person.

Mother is … well agreeable is too weak a word and to say that she is anxious to please is denigrating. If someone of whom she is fond told her to go and jump in the Seine she would not do it; nor would she, on the other hand, say 'Nonsense.' She would circle about, asking why this peculiar order had been given; asking who would benefit by such action; and in the end the person who said it would be left with the impression that she had been willing, at least, so to jump. It is a talent. I wish I had inherited it. When Eugène said that he wished she would go, she agreed that it would be a civil gesture, but she was too busy. That again was typical of her; she is capable of doing nothing, and doing it beautifully, all day long. Inside Eugène, however, alongside the hero-worshipper lie half a dozen other characters, all of them strong, and one is a nagger. He can go on and on. Over this matter he wore Mother down, talked her out of one excuse after another and in the end she went; and had had, she said, a very interesting little talk and had issued her invitation.

I know that it is the rule when recalling some momentous occasion in life to claim having had some feeling of premonition. On this day, though, I felt a certain interest in the man who had shot into prominence so quickly – and 'shot' is an apt word; and though I was willing, though not anxious to see Eugène's latest hero, my overriding thought was a drearily practical one. Another mouth to supply with food and drink. I was almost thirteen; aged a little by recent events. I knew that strictly speaking Mother could not afford to have parties at all. For two years we had lived from hand to mouth and the debts were mounting up daily. We were in the same position as thousands of other people in post-Revolutionary France. My father had died on the guillotine in 1794; Mother had been imprisoned and if Robespierre's Reign of Terror had lasted only two days longer, she would have been beheaded too. We were without property or resources in France and although Mother's own family in Martinique did their best to spare us a little they were themselves in difficulties. The Revolutionary spirit had reached even the West Indies and there had been slave revolts which had greatly reduced the productivity of the sugar plantations. And what small allowances were sent from Martinique did not always reach us, for the new Government was very corrupt; there were itching palms and sticky fingers at all levels.

Mother seemed to be incapable of living within her means. She had never known extreme wealth but she had generally been able to have whatever she wanted and even now, in near penury, she lived in elegant style, buying clothes lavishly, always in the latest fashion, keeping servants, giving parties, filling the house full of flowers. Occasionally she would think, for one dismayed moment, about her debts and then the happy, carefree spirit which was one of her charms would get the upper hand and she would say that things were so bad that they could only improve. I had a suspicion then, a suspicion later confirmed, that she had no idea how much she owed; she had no head for figures. I have no natural gift for them, but I can understand them if I try; there is the difference between us.

The difference stems, I suppose, from our upbringing. Mother spent the first sixteen years of her life as the pampered daughter of a sugar planter, waited on hand and foot by slaves, moving in the best circles of the island's society. She then came to France and was married to my father, the Viscount de Beauharnais; and even when the marriage failed my father's parents seemed to take her side and saw that she was provided for. My Martinique grandparents were equally generous and as soon as Eugène was old enough to be placed in boarding school, Mother and I went to visit them, and stayed for three years.

My early girlhood had been very different. Happy enough – Mother saw to that; she wanted everybody to be happy – but unsettled. A father I saw seldom, frequent changes of residence and one experience which few girls of my class have ever had.

We were back in France when the Revolution broke out and my father, though an aristocrat, adopted its ideals with enthusiasm. (That he should die because he had a title was one of the many ironies of the time.) He insisted, and being our father he had the power to insist, that Eugène and I should be taken away from the schools where we then were and apprenticed to useful trades. Eugène was sent to a cabinetmaker's and I to a dressmaker's. We did not serve our full articled time, but we did see something of a humbler way of life and learned something of the value of money. We had then the less-uncommon experience of having our father guillotined, our mother taken away in the night and threatened with the same fate. The threat of the worst kind of insecurity that a child can know – loss of both parents – was very close to us then. Neither of us was ever able to share fully again Mother's carefree attitude.

On this particular evening, for instance, Eugène worried and nagged and I worried with him. Mother must be dressed and ready, down in the salon by nine o'clock. The General would arrive, he repeated, as the clock struck. I did not nag – there was no need – but I did worry; for Mother is one of those people who cannot hurry. Every movement she makes is slow and languid and perhaps for that reason, graceful. I could just see Eugène and me, ready and alone, receiving a man of great importance whom Eugène had met once, briefly, and I had not met at all. He might take offence. We all knew that General Bonaparte was a parvenu, and a Corsican at that; such people take offence where none is intended.

Eugène nagged and I worried and Mother drifted about, inspecting the food on the buffet table, complaining mildly about the wine.

'I suppose I can no longer expect to be served with the best, owing what I do,' she said. 'But this was a gift from Barras and I hoped for better things.' Then, as usual, she turned from grievance to laughter. 'Well, if anyone, drinking this, pulls a sour face, I shall refer him to Barras.'

'Mother, please, will you go upstairs and get ready,' Eugène said.

'I must just see …' Mother said. She went and stood stock still in front of a great bowl of hot-house flowers, which, helped by me, she had spent an hour arranging that afternoon. Arranging flowers was the one task she undertook willingly, and she did it with great skill. I thought the flowers looked perfect, but she had to twitch one here and there, pull a piece of trailing fern forward, study the effect with her head slightly on one side, think better of it and push it back.

Poor Eugène took out his handkerchief and dabbed his forehead.

However, she went away at last. Eugène made a sign to me and I obeyed at once and offered my help.

'No, thank you, darling. Marion can manage. Too many people simply leads to confusion.'

I said to Eugène when we were alone, 'I think she will be ready. Everything is so much simpler now.'

That was quite true. Fashions had changed completely; the elaborate styles, the panniers, the tightly laced-in waists of the old days had gone; everything must be simple and based on the styles of ancient Rome. Gone were the days when it took four hours to torture a woman's hair into the semblance of a ship in full sail, or a windmill, or a nest with fledgling birds in it. We all wore our hair short, curled if necessary. Simply running a comb through was enough. Mother could easily make herself ready in the half-hour she had allowed herself. If she gave her mind to it.

Half reassured on this point, Eugène found something else to worry about.

'Did you hear what she said about the wine?'

'Yes. It is not very good, but it was a present.'

'From Paul Barras.' Eugène spoke the name with disgust and scowled. 'I shan't drink any. I'd advise you not to.'

'His name is Barras, not Borgia,' I said, trying to make a joke. Eugène's nerves were already frayed enough. But I knew what he meant and I wished not to talk about it.

At this time – the January of 1796 – I was a boarder at Madame Campan's very select school for young ladies, where I had a good many friends and an enemy or two, as is usual. And even the most select young ladies are given to gossip. At thirteen I knew what are called the facts of life; I also knew what was being said about my mother. It was not pleasant; talk inspired by jealousy never is. Paul Barras, who was at that moment the most power-ful man in France, was a known libertine and he had certainly befriended Mother and taken her into the centre of the gay, rather raffish society of the day. An attractive widow, looking younger than her thirty-three years, living apparently well though with no visible means and moving in that circle, was an easy target for slander. But there was no proof then – nor has there been later – that she was his mistress. Mother was not a woman who needed to take a man into her bed in order to retain his goodwill. Those who said that in order to obtain favours one must bestow them did not know Mother well. She had that indefinable thing called charm. When she was in the Cannes, that most dreadful prison of all, the very anteroom to the Place de la Guillotine, a young man lost his heart to her. He also was under the shadow of death, but he bribed the guards to take her some of the better food which he was allowed because he was a general – about to be beheaded because he was not consistently successful; and he sent her letters; one, in quite extravagant terms, saying that if they must die, he hoped that they would go to death in the same tumbrel; to die in such company would be an honour. She certainly had not been *his* mistress. She shared a dismal room with, I think, eighteen other women.

Nevertheless, I did not want to discuss the gossip with Eugène. We were both home for a day or two's leave from our respective schools and he was so excited at the prospect of General Bonaparte coming to our house. Nothing must spoil this evening. So as we waited, growing more and more nervous I said, 'Tell me about him.' I did not mean tell me about how he had driven the English out of Toulon, or saved the Government in Paris with well-placed guns and the willingness to fire on the mob. Eugène knew what I meant.

'Nothing much to look at,' Eugène said as he had said before, of the won-derful school master who was so short-sighted that he fell over his own feet, and of the sullen school-friend who, brought home for the day, ate almost frenziedly and hardly spoke a word. 'But,' Eugène said, 'there is something ... It's hopeless to try to put it into words. You'll see for yourself. Wonderful ... And just two minutes left.'

Mother came in as the clock struck.

She looked very lovely in her white muslin gown, the high waist defined by a dark green ribbon, a similar piece tied around her head, wound through the dark red curls. My day-at-home dress and coiffure were very similar except that my ribbons were blue.

The clock crawled. Ten minutes past. Fifteen minutes.

'You see, my dear boy; there was no need to hurry me.'

'He isn't coming,' Eugène said.

'Don't look so downcast,' Mother said. 'There'll be another evening.'

'Yes. When I'm back at school.'

'Then we must see what can be arranged,' Mother said; ready to promise anything so long as *this* evening should be happy. She put her hand on his arm and gave him her most cajoling smile. 'Don't spoil a holiday evening by being sulky.'

The other guests arrived between half past nine and ten and as usual I was called upon to play the harp, which I was glad to do for I had not yet acquired the art of conversing easily with people so much older than I, some of them important and some of them clever. And with me there was, at all social gatherings, another problem. Madame Campan had been one of Queen Marie Antoinette's ladies-in-waiting and within her school taught and insisted upon the old courtly manners, the phrases and the curtsies that had been done away with at the Revolution, when everybody must dress and behave like a peasant. But times were changing again; it was no longer dangerous to behave well, but it might be unacceptable. The uncertainty was reflected by Madame Campan herself; in school, in the most prominent place, there was a portrait of the unfortunate Queen; on its back in clear black script and properly framed were some phrases from the Constitution drawn up by the Revolutionary Government. Whenever anyone of known political views visited the school – which was often since it was now partly nationalised – the picture was reversed and Marie Antoinette's face was turned to the wall.

On this evening I played softly, the music a background for conversation. I was aware of Eugène approaching and standing near by and when I came to the end of a tune he touched my arm.

'Imagine,' he said. 'Barras brought a message. General Bonaparte was detained and sent an apology. But Barras is giving a dinner party tomorrow evening and has invited us all. And *he* will be there, for certain.'

Eugène's current hero was always simply *he*.

To tease Eugène I said, 'I should hope so if he is giving the party.'

'Stupid! You know what I mean.'

'I know,' I said, 'and I'm glad for you.'

I was a little puzzled at my inclusion. Eugène, fifteen and well-grown, might well be asked – escort for his widowed mother, an extra man – but I, though allowed to be present at Mother's parties, had never received such an invitation before.

'Are you sure I am asked?'

'Oh yes. Barras made a special point of it.'

I thought – Oh well, I suppose I am growing up: thirteen in April this year. Mother was married at sixteen. Neither the prospect of growing up, nor of attending my first formal dinner party elated me very much. But when Eugène said, 'Isn't it wonderful?' I agreed that it was. I had inherited some of Mother's desire to please, though in me it was limited to those of whom I was fond.

2

The Luxembourg Palace had seen some bad times; it had been a prison in the days of the Terror and now a good deal of it was hired out as apartments, but the part which Barras, as head of the Directoire Government, occupied was very fine indeed. Barras had been born an aristocrat, had, like my father, turned Revolutionary, but fared better. He knew, as many of the new men did not, how rooms should be furnished, tables set and servants trained.

This was my real introduction to the great world and I felt rather shy, though I did my best to conceal it, shyness being something of which Madame Campan disapproved. I looked around to see if there were anyone else of my own age; there was not and that increased my feeling of being out of place. I could see one young man, standing alone and looking rather out of place, though if he felt shy he also concealed it well under a look of arrogance and disdain. He was thin as a bone, his uniform was shabby. I wondered whether he could be an emigré, one of those who had fled when the Revolution broke out. They were beginning to come back now and many of them were poor. Perhaps this young man was one, glad to be asked to Barras's table where he could be sure of getting a good meal. He did look hungry.

Barras, having greeted us all very genially, paying Mother and me the compliment of saying that we looked like sisters, went across to the young man I had noticed and brought him over to us.

'May I present General Bonaparte. Citizeness Beauharnais, her daughter Hortense and her son Eugène whose acquaintance you have already made.'

Eugène was dark rose-red to the tips of his ears. Mother said, very sweetly, 'I also have had the honour of making your acquaintance, General Bonaparte.'

'I remember,' he said. I am sorry about last evening. I was unavoidably detained.'

Mother's policy of refusing to be hurried served her. Many women would have said quickly that it did not matter. She took her time and thought of something more flattering.

'We were all very much disappointed. Eugène particularly; but as I told him there is always another day.'

By the way he looked at her one would have imagined that she had uttered some words of the most profound and enlightening philosophy.

He said, 'I must remember that. Another day; always another.' I had a curious feeling that he meant it differently.

Mother put her hand on Eugène's shoulder. 'Eugène was so certain that if you came it would be as the clock struck nine that he positively harried me.'

'He was right,' the General said. 'Had I been able to come I should have been on time.'

Mother said, 'I sometimes think that chopping up time, snip, snip, snip,' she mimicked with two fingers the action of scissors, 'is a mistake. But that may be because I grew up on an island where time mattered so little.'

'And I spent my youth on one where ten minutes made the difference between the quick and the dead.' Abruptly he switched his attention to me. 'So this is Hortense.'

I had been observing that his boots were badly polished and that his hair was peculiar. It was very dark and plentiful but it had a dry, lifeless look; it was badly cut, too, loose floppy strands of it falling down over his forehead. But when he turned his gaze to me I regretted all my rather unfavourable and denigrating observations because I felt that he knew, could see straight through my head, read my thoughts.

But he spoke kindly. 'You go to school, Hortense?'

'Yes, General. To Madame Campan's at St Germain-en-Laye.'

'You like it there?'

'Oh yes, very much.'

'Then I take it that you are a good scholar.'

'Not very good. I do my best.'

'And what more can anyone do?'

Then the tall double doors were flung open and dinner was announced.

To my immense relief I was seated next to Mother, on her left hand; on my left was General Bonaparte and on his left was Madame Tallien, one of Mother's friends and admittedly the prettiest and wittiest woman in the world. And perhaps the luckiest. Perhaps one of the bravest. During the Terror she had aided emigrés to escape; she had been accused and condemned and everybody said that it was in order to save her, then his mistress, from the guillotine, that Tallien had moved to overthrow Robespierre and so end the Terror and thus save Mother and hundreds of other innocent people.

I need not have worried – as I had done – about the necessity of making dinner-table conversation. As soon as we were seated the General leaned across me in an unmannerly way and said, 'Where were you when time meant so little?'

She told him about Martinique; the warmth, the fruit, the flowers, the easy-going ways. He then told her about Corsica, rocky, arid, unfertile. Mother could eat and talk at the same time; he took no interest in his food at all. He would take a mouthful and then lean across to me again, making it difficult for me to reach my plate. It was a delicious dinner, too. I hoped that Barras, on Mother's right, and Madame Tallien on the General's left, would presently claim a little attention, but they seemed to be equally engrossed with their other neighbours.

'But you are eating nothing, General,' Mother said at last.

'Food doesn't mean much to me. There is a necessary minimum of course. Beyond that I don't bother.'

'But it is one of life's pleasures. By your standard I am very greedy I am afraid.'

'Yet you look as though you lived on sea-foam and rose petals,' he said. Then, as though saying it had embarrassed him he bent over his plate and took a few mouthfuls of *coq au vin* disposing of the food as though it were something he had to put away in the least possible time. I thought it was a very pretty compliment and apt; and surprising, coming from him.

I took advantage of having free access to my own plate but was soon cut off again. Having eaten his necessary minimum he leaned forward and said, 'I may sound ignorant. Is your gown muslin?'

Mother looked a little startled. 'Yes.'

'Indian?'

She laughed. 'I hope so. The price I paid!'

'No good Frenchwoman should wear it!' He sounded quite violent. 'Friend Barras here should pass a law against it.' Mother took it – and so did I – that he was objecting to the transparency of the material. There were prudes who did.

Mother said gently, soothingly, 'But one wears other garments under the muslin.'

'It comes from India and India belongs to the English. Every time you buy it you enrich some fat English merchant. French women should stick to good French stuff – silk, satin, velvet. Next time you are tempted by muslin, Citizeness, think of the weavers, starving in Lyons.'

'Such materials are still associated with … with the old times and therefore out of favour.'

'It's high time such nonsense was forgotten!' He said that brusquely, and then with a complete change of voice and manner went on, '*You* should wear white satin, embroidered with roses, with here and there a diamond, the dewdrop in the heart.'

That touch of poetry again. And strange that he should twice have mentioned roses, for which Mother had a passion.

'It sounds delightful,' Mother said. 'But with my affairs in their present condition, alas unattainable.'

To that he made no answer; he just looked at her, and I could tell from that look that if he had white satin and diamonds in his gift they would be hers instantly.

I pushed my chair back and gave up all attempt to eat. I occupied myself by composing a poem in the romantic style, all about a lady whom to see was to love. I had a small gift for versification. I could toss off rhymed couplets, often irreverent, sometimes amusing, about any event at school, a mistress, the food. It was almost too easy. Salted cod-fish, cheap, nourishing, too frequently served and unpopular, did not make me groan; it made me say:

> *When in his wisdom god*
> *Created fish called cod*
> *He little thought how often we*
> *Would mourn that creativity.*

My real verses nobody, not even Eugène knew about.

The dinner over I found Eugène who seemed to think that I had been supremely favoured, seated next to *him* at dinner, and wanted to know what had been said. I told him it was mostly about Martinique and Corsica and the iniquity of wearing muslin.

'Was anything said about me?'

'Now let me think,' I said, playing for time, trying to think up some acceptable lie – not too bad a lie. Here again all the old ideas had been thrown out, everybody was an atheist now and I was a long time and a long way from Martinique where an old negress had told me that for every lie your lips spoke your feet must take a step on Hell's red-hot pavement. (I had actually told one just then and the thought of my feet on red-hot cobbles had sent me wailing to Mother who dismissed that idea completely but said that it was better to tell the truth. And then there was Madame Campan who talked a great deal about honour; honour included telling the truth, even to your own disadvantage.)

However, to please Eugène I was prepared to tell a lie, if I could think of one not likely to be contradicted. I was spared that step on Hell's pavement, for at that moment General Bonaparte joined us and said to Eugène, 'Well, and how soon do you propose to use that sword for France?'

It was the kind of half-jocular question that people put to the young. Eugène took it seriously, stood up very straight and said, 'At the first possible moment, sir.' Clipped and sudden as though he had had an order.

He looked at General Bonaparte with that bright, eager, willing look that reminded me of Mother's pug dog. And at the back of my mind I added that look, and a dog, to my poem about the lady whom everyone loved.

The front of my mind observed that General Bonaparte had not accepted Eugène's answer in quite the spirit in which it was offered. He said, rather sombrely, 'And that may be sooner than you think.'

And then Mother was there, just behind me, saying over my shoulder, 'Oh, I hope not. Eugène is only fifteen. Still at school.'

Eugène loved Mother, but he looked at her with positive hatred.

General Bonaparte said, 'He would be safe with me. I would never let a promising young soldier within reach of an enemy until he had been trained to be dangerous. I hate waste.' He turned that measuring look on Eugène and said, 'Two years or less ... But I must remember that you,' he was now looking at Mother, 'dislike the idea of time being cut up, snip, snip.' He imitated exactly her imitation of the scissors.

We all laughed. The back of my mind went to work on the phrase *safe with me*. He certainly had, when he chose, a way with words. Safe with me held, in three words, such assurance, such promise. It struck home to me perhaps because I had never known what it was to feel safe with anyone; loved by, cared for, but never safe with, simply because the people who loved me and cared for me had not themselves been safe. And to this reflection I added a question – How could even General Bonaparte speak with such complete assurance? In a lost battle, in a retreat, how could Eugène or any other young soldier be safe with him?

On our way home to the Rue Chantereine Mother seemed unusually quiet. I thought that perhaps the mention of Eugène being a soldier soon had depressed her. Or perhaps so much rather intense talk during the dinner had tired her; she tired easily and she was easily bored and the talk had differed from the light give-and-take of ordinary social chat. Or again she may not have liked Eugène's new hero much and, unable to praise him fulsomely enough, thought silence the best policy.

Marion had been told not to sit up; her wages were probably in arrears in which case too much demand must not be made upon her; so I went in to act as lady's maid and to enjoy a little bedtime chat. Even as I helped Mother out of her dress its material did not provoke any comment about muslin. I remembered the starving weavers in Lyons and having hung Mother's dress away, I fingered my own and said, 'General Bonaparte almost spoiled my dinner, leaning between me and my plate; and he has spoiled my pleasure in this dress forever. What did you think of him?'

She was smoothing out and winding around her fingers the ribbon that had been around her curls.

'A funny little man,' she said, in an absent-minded way. Then she added, 'I don't know why but he made me *nervous*.'

3

The information that Madame Campan wished to see me in her private sitting room did not cause me a pang. She was going to congratulate me for having at last won the most coveted trophy – The Rose For Virtue. I wore it pinned to my dress, and unless I did something almost unthinkably disgraceful it would be mine for a month.

It was not easily come by, for it was awarded by vote as well as by marks for work and behaviour and general demeanour: to win it one must be popular with one's school-fellows as well as approved of by one's teachers – sometimes irreconcilable aims. It was a very old silk rose, a relic of Madame Campan's better days; it had seen the Court of Marie Antoinette. It was now faded and frayed and its petals were held together with a piece of wire.

Madame Campan made no remark about the rose; but she smiled and invited me to sit down on a stool near the chair in which she sat. It was a cold spring evening and she had a small fire. With an invalid husband to support and child to bring up and three motherless nieces to educate, she could not afford much in the way of comfort, even for herself.

She said, 'Hortense, I have a piece of excellent news to impart to you. I have received a letter from your mother.'

That in itself was news; Mother disliked letter-writing and would defer it from day to day, always intending to write – tomorrow. I looked at Madame Campan with interest, wondering what could be the excellent news that had made Mother set pen to paper.

'Your mother asked me to tell you that General Bonaparte has made her a proposal of marriage which she has accepted. They are to be married very shortly.'

Sheer surprise made me speechless. For one thing I had never imagined Mother re-marrying, which was absurd of me. But she had been married once, and very unhappily … And there was the suddenness of it. And above all that she should choose to marry him, the funny little man who made her feel nervous.

And sitting there, unable to say anything, I was aware of Madame Campan's eye upon me, assessing the value of training. How did a properly-brought-up young lady receive news that astonished her out of her wits?

Control, I thought, I must show self-control, but it was useless; I had no more control of this situation than a man, stepping suddenly on to a patch of slippery ice in the roadway, has control of his legs. I tried. I knew that the correct thing to do was to say – *Madame, thank you for telling me. I hope they will be happy.* I knew what was required of me, I had the words ready. I actually opened my mouth … And that was too much. There I was, crying, crying ….

Madame Campan did not speak nor move; she knew, I suppose, that nobody can cry like that for long. Presently, like someone almost drowned, I had to come up for air, breathing through my mouth, using my handkerchief.

I said, 'I am sorry, Madame. I allowed myself to be overcome by surprise. And by the thought that our mother would not love us so much.'

'Naturally you were surprised. The other thought is ridiculous. The feeling a woman entertains for her children and that she entertains for her husband are entirely different. Your mother has made a very wise decision. You are young, Hortense, but not, I think, too young to understand that these are very troubled times and life for a woman with no husband and no property can be most difficult.'

I nodded, thinking of the debts. Would they now be paid? By that young man who looked so poor?

'It will be an excellent thing for all of you. And for Eugène, of course, a chance in a million.'

I nodded again. 'Does Eugène know?'

'Not yet. I sent a message asking him to come.' She looked at the clock. 'He should be here in half an hour.'

Eugène's school was within walking distance. 'Eugène will be delighted,' I said.

'So I supposed. And that is why I told you first. So that you might be composed when he arrived.' She had evidently expected that I should fail in this test for composure. But she was kind. She put her arm around me and gave me a brief little hug. 'Now run upstairs and bathe your eyes, then come back here.'

When I came down Eugène was there – he must have run all the way; and Madame Campan had broken the news to him. Delight is too mild a term. He was elated almost out of his mind. He embraced me, lifting me off my feet and twirling me round.

'Isn't it wonderful? Isn't it the most marvellous thing that ever happened? The most wonderful man in the world to be our *father*, Hortense. Unbelievable!'

I was so *grateful* to Madame Campan for her wisdom and forethought. I thought how dreadful it would have been if she had waited and told us together and I had cried. It would have ruined Eugène's pleasure. As it was the bad moment was over; so far over that I could now ask myself – Why bad? Why had I wept?

Madame Campan had produced from her ill-furnished store a bottle of wine. We drank. 'To their happiness.' (Happiness with a funny little man who made her feel nervous.)

'And to his success in his new command,' Eugène said, raising his glass again.

'Wherever that may be,' Madame Campan replied. She sipped and gave Eugène a quizzical look. 'I suppose,' she said, 'that in your place where everybody is a politician, General Bonaparte's destiny is already decided.'

Looking very knowing and sophisticated and young, young beyond belief, Eugène said, 'Well, the odds are fifty to one that he will be given command in Italy.'

Madame Campan laughed.

'Even at such odds, if one plunged … But to bet when one *knows* is not quite …'

'You *know*, Madame Campan?' Eugène asked eagerly.

'Let us say that I have very good reason to *think*, Eugène. Thirty thousand French soldiers, ragged, bare-footed, starving and mutinous, stranded. The competition to take command there will not be very strong. And whom else could they send?'

'Who indeed? And he as good as promised to find a place for me.' I could see his thoughts running forward. 'We shall see him at the wedding?'

'I think not. No mention was made of it, Eugène. And your mother did not give a date; she merely said it would be soon.' Eugène looked dashed. 'You will miss little. Weddings are not what they were. A mere civil ceremony.'

'Well, I shall write to General Bonaparte.' I knew what that letter would be; half congratulation, half supplication.

'Hortense must write, too,' Madame Campan said. 'When a new member joins a family that is already established it is more than ever essential to make him feel welcome.'

If in future days anyone who had been in contact with Madame Campan ever behaved less than impeccably it was not for lack of admonition.

That evening before undressing I went to remove the rose from my breast. It was gone and all I was left with was the pin and a bit of twisted wire. Madame Campan's brief embrace or Eugène's boisterous one had proved too much for the poor frail flower.

4

Two days after the wedding my step-father left for Italy, and in an incredibly short space of time hard-riding couriers began to bring in news of battles fought and won. In the fifteen days between 10th April and 25th April that wretched ragged army had won four battles and driven the Austrians out of that part of northern Italy known as Piedmont. Morning after morning before we left the breakfast table for the classroom Madame Campan would read out the latest news and all eyes would turn on me, the step-daughter of this wonder-working man. I always coloured and attempted that difficult thing, to look dutifully pleased without looking complacent or smug.

On the morning when Madame Campan asked me to remain behind when the others dispersed my immediate thought was that I had not looked sufficiently pleased or had been guilty of wearing a look which she would call a smirk. However, what she had to tell me was that I was to go home that morning.

'There is nothing to be alarmed about, Hortense. Your mother writes that she is slightly unwell and would like your company.'

I was alarmed. For all her look of fragility I had never known Mother to suffer even a common cold. However, when I reached home, although she was in bed and looking rather paler than usual, she seemed well enough. About what ailed her she was evasive.

'The worst is over now. I shall be up and about in a day or two. It is a trifling indisposition, best ignored. But I thought it would cheer me to see you, darling. And presently – there is no hurry – I need your help with something.' As she said that she looked at the table beside the bed. There was the usual vase of flowers, lilies-of-the-valley, the month being May, a five-branched candle-stand of silver, new to me, and, also new to me a kind of casket, gold or at least silver gilt, supported by four little cherubs, one to each corner and with its curved lid encrusted with what I took at first glance to be pearls. I thought – Impossible! It would be worth a fortune.

Mother said as though following my thought, 'He sent you a present too. On my dressing table. No. To the left, just by the scent bottle.'

'What, this? For *me*?'

'So it said. He can write quite plainly when he wants to.'

Unbelieving I picked up and examined the trinket. It was a watch. There was the brooch, shaped like a rather full flattened rose, set with dark, richly red stones and suspended from it by three slender chains. The dial surrounded by pearls and backed with more of the dark red stones. It was the most beautiful ornament I had ever seen.

'This is for me? Are you sure?'

'It was packed separately. And he wrote, "The watch is for Hortense." I could read that. It was not the usual scribble. Yes, darling, it is yours and very pretty, don't you think?'

'Absolutely beautiful. I shall never dare wear it – at school I mean. Everybody would be so envious.'

'I rather think that envy is something we must learn to live with. If this goes on … But it need not worry us now. Enjoy your pretty present.'

I wound it and pinned it on. The brooch, smaller and darker in colour but not un-rose-like lay on my chest, exactly where The Rose For Virtue had lain so briefly. I kept looking down at it, lifting and tuning the watch, checking the time every ten minutes while Mother and I ate the meal which Marion brought in on two trays.

I thought Mother ate less heartily than usual. I mentioned it and she said, 'Lying in bed is not very conducive to appetite.'

I said, 'It is a beautiful day. Could Marion and I help you down and into the garden?'

She looked as she did when anyone tried to hurry her. 'No. Not today. Perhaps tomorrow, or the next day. We'll see.'

Presently I said, 'What did you want me to help you with?'

'All those letters. He writes every day, sometimes twice a day. Here and there I can make out a sentence but for the most part … And then when I did write, as best I could, he said my letter was cold. Here they are.' She reached out for the casket, opened it and tipped out on to the rose-coloured bed-cover a lot of letters and a magnifying glass. She had at least tried! But not very hard or very successfully or she would never have handed such letters to *me*. There was not a coarse fibre in her nature; indeed her wish that everything should be 'nice' verged upon prudery.

The letters were the reverse of nice; they were the violent, passionate outpourings of a love so complete as to be shocking. They were all villainously written, though the degrees of illegibility varied and there were sentences which, even with the use of the magnifying glass, I could not decipher. After the first few minutes I realised that there was a kind of pattern; when he wrote of ordinary things, yesterday's success, tomorrow's plans, the writing was no more than difficult; when he wrote of his love, it deteriorated. I could see exactly where and why Mother had abandoned the attempt to read.

I had read more than was decent, more than was good for me, when the thought struck me that these were meant for her eyes alone.

'Mother, I can't. They're so …'

'I know, darling. But do try. I am sure there are things I should answer. There is one that begins, "I am writing this with the paper propped against my saddle," I could read that perfectly well, and not another word.'

I said, 'They are love-letters.'

'He is … very much attached to me and inclined to express himself extravagantly,' she said, reducing this raw agony of longing into something within her comprehension, something nice and little. 'Don't bother with those parts. Read me the pieces about my going to Italy to join him. I know he is anxious for me to do so. Does he mention any actual arrangements?'

I looked down again and read, 'Take wings and fly. Come, come, but travel carefully …' I also read, 'A kiss upon your heart, another a little lower, another lower still, far lower …'

It was not just my face, my whole body was one burning blush.

I shot her a furtive look as though I had been caught out in some indescribably shameful act. She had taken one of the lilies-of-the-valley from the vase and was passing it slowly before her nose.

Presently I said, 'He is most eager for you to go to Italy … He says it is quite safe now … He says he wants you to share his triumph …'

'One of them says something about the roads being bad. I could read that. I cannot possibly go yet. I could not bear the jolting. I tried to explain that.'

Picking about to find some reference to the state of the roads, I came upon some deliriously happy sentences which informed me what she had explained, and also why she was now in bed and looking rather pale. I could hardly refer to her pregnancy since, so far as she knew, I was still in a state of ignorance about such things.

Tipping the letters out as she had done, she had disordered them and I thought – Of course, he urged her to join him *before* he knew; now that he knows he will understand why she cannot travel. For some reason that thought comforted me.

Mother said, 'I must write to him. Perhaps tomorrow.'

I recognised the Martinique word. It was a fact that quite a long time before Mother and I went there on our visit my grandparents' house had burned down. It had been, they said, very beautiful and there was a picture of it, brought by Mother when she came to France and still in her possession, which confirmed this statement. After the fire the family had moved into a building, formerly a sugar store and there they lived. Not in discomfort and not in squalor, but in a makeshift way because they were always going to have the house re-built – tomorrow or if not tomorrow the day after. My grandfather died, my grandmother would die, in the storehouse.

'If you wrote and thanked him for that pretty watch,' Mother said, 'I am sure that he would be pleased, and the letter could go with mine. Look through the rest of those, darling, and see if I there is anything else that you can make out and should be answered.'

The fact that I was only doing what I had been told did not alleviate my sense of shame, almost of guilt. As I read I thought how right I had been on that evening at the Luxembourg to detect the poet in him. I sensed that such letters were unusual, even for a man very deeply in love, so I felt it unlikely that I should ever be addressed in such terms, but if by any chance I should ever inspire such love how willingly I would respond, how hard I would try to write answers that were not completely unworthy. The strange thought occurred to me that if any woman but Mother had behaved so casually over letters written straight from the heart I should have disliked her and thought her hateful and heartless. But Mother was Mother.

One thing that I could decipher was that my step-father intended shortly to send his eldest brother Joseph to Paris. 'I hope that he will win your friendship, He deserves it. Nature has given him a heart that makes him always gentle and kind.'

In due time Joseph Bonaparte arrived and although there was a certain resemblance I could not help thinking of our art classes at school. We had a very gifted teacher and sometimes he brought a picture of his own for us to copy. Joseph Bonaparte seemed a rather poor copy of his brother. He was in fact only a year older, but his fleshiness and pompous manner made him seem the senior by many years. This was particularly noticeable when he said with that kind of heavy humour which so often disguises a rebuke, 'Napoleon was very naughty! He defied the good Corsican custom of asking the head of the family for permission to marry. It distressed our mother very much.'

Mother gave him a sweet smile and said, 'There was so little time. So many good old customs are casualties in time of war.'

She was by this time up and about again and I had gathered from Marion, indirectly, that there would be no baby. The furtively handed-about schoolgirl talk had not included the word miscarriage, but I was learning fast. I have sometimes wondered whether the truth is that we are all born, not with the knowledge, but with the ability to acquire and accept it. Like language. Could it be that a French child, born in another country, never having heard French spoken, might, suddenly confronted with it, show an aptitude? Something like that with me, the language, the attitudes, the penalties of love I seemed to know before I knew. 'Such a loss,' Marion said and I knew what had been lost and had thought – Now Mother can take the rough road to Italy.

I was also as well-informed, or at least half-informed enough, to real-ise that it was a pity that on this, Joseph Bonaparte's first visit, Hippolyte Charles should arrive.

He had for some time been a friend of Mother's, nice to look at, good company, kind, amusing. My informant about sex had missed out miscar-riage and also hermaphrodite, but my knowledge of the latter had preceded my knowledge of the former. I was quite accustomed to Hippolyte. Later in life I knew others, and of all the many variations of people, they adhere most closely to a given pattern.

They live on a borderline; they dress and for the most part act like men. Often exceptionally brave. Mother's Hippolyte had been in one of the early battles in Italy, wounded, mentioned in dispatches and sent home to conva-lesce. He had, as they all have, a waspish wit. Mother would say, 'Oh, such an unkind thing to say,' and he would say, 'But would you not have *adored* to say it yourself, if you had thought of it first.' His speech and behaviour were mannered, the one given to over-emphasis, the other to gestures. To him and to all his kind endearments come so easily as to be worthless.

He came in on this evening carrying a bunch of white roses, which, with a flourish, he presented.

'My dear, the very *first*. I thought it would be such a *change* for you to be Our Lady of Roses for one evening. Our Lady of *Victories* does sound rather *stern*.'

People were beginning to call Mother that. Soldiers particularly had seen a link between Bonaparte's marriage and his sudden successes. Most of them were simple men, reared in the religion which the Revolution had abolished. For them a pretty prostitute, enthroned in Notre Dame as the Goddess of Reason, was a poor substitute for Our Lady, Mother of God. Superstition moved in to fill the empty space.

'But how kind,' Mother said. As usual she took her time, smiling and bur-ying her face in the flowers. Then she made the introduction, calling Joseph her brother-in-law, come directly from Italy.

'With news of great battles,' Hippolyte said in his gay, light, voice. 'And loot from sacked cities.'

'There has been fighting,' Joseph said, and I at least could hear the added – And you were not there.

'Nothing to equal Lodi,' Hippolyte said 'The General loaded cannon with his own hands.' As though by accident he flung back his swaggering Hussar cloak with its red fox fur border, exposing his bandaged arm. The sleeves of his jacket and shirt had been cut away. He accompanied this gesture with a small catlike smile, more eloquent than words.

The conversation went on with that slight edginess that results from dislike at first sight. Joseph explained that one of his missions was to take Mother back to Italy with him.

'But, sir, that would be to sack Paris. What has poor Paris done to be so ravaged?'

'I am afraid it will be a little time before I feel well enough to travel,' Mother said.

'But you *look* better. Last time I saw you, you were in bed and very *wan*.'

Perhaps the custom of receiving people in one's bedroom was unknown in Corsica: Joseph Bonaparte looked shocked. He said stiffly, 'We can allow a day or two. I have other errands. A letter to the Minister of War. Another to Director Barras. And then of course there is Eugène.'

'What about him?' Mother asked, for her sharply.

'My brother has found a niche for him on his staff.'

'But Eugène is so young. Only fifteen.'

'Far too young,' Joseph agreed in a voice that informed me that the appointment met with his disapproval. 'But my brother is exceptionally conscious of family responsibilities.'

Hippolyte said, 'My dear, you need have *no* fear for Eugène. Junior members of the staff are kept *well* behind the lines, with the maps, the re-mounts – and the civilians.' Joseph Bonaparte was a civilian!

Mother, in her own way, was also aware of family responsibilities, and as soon as her own position was less precarious, had undertaken to pay for two of my cousins, Emilie and Stephanie de Beauharnais, at Madame Campan's. They were not sisters and in looks and character were quite unlike one another. They were installed but still feeling new when I returned to school in June; so they clung to me rather, but I did not allow them to interfere with my real friendship with one of Madame Campan's nieces, Adèle Aguie. Fortunately her two sisters liked my cousins and the six of us formed a little close-knit group until rebuked by Madame Campan who said that one of the objects of education was to acquire the art of sociability. I took this remark to heart and my efforts to be more affable to all, allied to the knowledge that I must not seem to be proud because my step-father and my mother were being treated like royalty in Italy, gained me so much popularity that in one way at least, my later schooldays were an ill preparation for real life. I became unduly sensitive to the slightest criticism, convinced that anyone whom I liked must surely like me, deluded into the belief that I had inherited at least some part of Mother's charm.

5

Mother had left for Italy in June and knowing how much she hated writing and how fully occupied she would be I did not expect much in the way of letters. There were two brief ones; she had arrived safely and been given a wonderful reception; she was well, so was Bonaparte; they hoped I was and both sent their love. The second was much the same; she had seen Eugène who was in his element and indescribably happy; the scenery was magnificent; the weather warm; she was becoming accustomed to being treated like a queen and living in palaces, but looked forward to coming back to Paris and seeing me and settling down into our dear cosy little house.

When her third letter came it was so much thicker that I thought it must contain an enclosure from Eugène. But it was in fact a long letter and for once she had written as she spoke, the pen a tool, not an impediment.

'Darling, I am so very sorry, I have terrible news for you. If you were here I could hold you in my arms and break it gently. To write it seems so cruel.' In the blink between one line and another I thought Eugène? Bonaparte? 'Fortunè is dead. We went to stay at a castle and there was a horrid mastiff which took him up and shook him as though he were a rat and broke his neck.'

First the fright, then the relief. I was tremulous. I thought – Only Fortunè – and then wondered whether it was heartless to think that.

Fortunè had been given to Mother when he was a puppy. He was supposed to be a King Charles spaniel, but he had grown up into a kind of pug with a nasty disposition. He was Mother's dog, jealous of and inclined to snap at anyone who went near her. He had learned to tolerate Eugène and me and a few other people but he did it with bad grace. However, he had once done us sterling service. In those dreadful days when Mother was imprisoned, Eugène and I, with Fortunè on a leash, had spent hours outside the place, hoping that we might see her from a window, or that she might see us. One day Eugène said, 'I believe that if we loosed him he'd get in. We could tie a note under his collar. Let's try.' So we wrote that we were well – untrue, for grief and fear was wearing us down – and that Citizeness Lanoy, the dressmaker to whom I had been apprenticed and in whose house we were living, was being kind to us – true. The prison doorway, well-guarded, often opened and closed and as it opened to admit somebody on a legitimate errand, Eugène slipped the leash and said, 'Go find.' Fortunè went cringing in, poor stray dog, hoping for a crust. Presently, speeded by a kick from the ruffian who kept the door, he limped out. The note was still under his collar and we feared the worst. But when we looked we realised that Fortunè had found Mother. She had written on the back of the note that she was well and we must not worry or give up hope.

Many dogs would have shrunk from facing that janitor again, but Fortunè was brave; and it was not always the same man.. Some were kind and once he came out with a great meaty bone which Citizeness Lanoy took away from him – he had lost his appetite, too – and washed and put in her soup pot. Afterwards, with Mother home and safe, we asked how she had ever persuaded Fortunè to leave her and come out to us and she said, 'I told him "Go home!" I've always held that he understood every word I said.'

So now he was dead. I paid him a little tribute of grief and read on.

Darling, I have now met the whole family and they do not like me though I have done my best. His mother is formidable, much annoyed that he should have married without her permission and to somebody who is not a Corsican. At our first meeting she looked me over and did not smile; she then made a remark, in Italian. Very rude, some old peasant saying about telling a woman's age, like a fowl's, by the neck. I was not pretending to be young – with Eugène there, looking very smart and at least twenty, how could I? And there are so many of them, three sisters, four brothers, all under the old woman's thumb, all against me and not sufficiently respectful to him. But for him where would they be, who would ever have heard of them? Still Bonaparte is so much attached to them and they are my family now so I must try to be friends though it is hard with his mother saying I am too old to have children. Darling, there is talk of sending the youngest one, Caroline, to Madame Campan's. If this should happen, please be friendly to her for my sake; even if we old ones cannot be you young ones must.'

I could not help wondering who had taken the trouble to translate to Mother two hurtful remarks made in Italian.

When Eugène wrote it was with more rancour.

They are so rude and Mother tries so hard. The other evening I saw Pauline B. stick her tongue out behind Mother's back and when she saw me looking she stuck it out at me. I'd have done something even ruder but remembered that I was in uniform. How the General came to have such a horrid family is a mystery to everybody. It is a pity about poor old Fortunè, but he was getting very crotchety. The General didn't think he should sleep on the bed and when he tried to move him Fortunè bit him. If they do send Caroline B. to your school just look out.

Caroline arrived at Madame Campan's. She was fair and rather pretty and seemed much older than she was, which was almost a year younger than I. Madame Campan virtually handed her over to me. 'You can explain the rules, Hortense, and perhaps help her with her lessons. Her education has been much interrupted.' Interrupted? It had never begun; she was dreadfully ignorant and not a bit ashamed. She was very angry at being sent to school at all; she had fallen in love with one of her brother's officers, Joachim Murat. 'It is so unfair,' she said to me once. 'Napoleon caught Pauline kissing Leclerk behind a screen and said the only thing for it was for them to marry. So then Joachim and I kissed in the open and let ourselves be caught, and I was sent to school!'

She sulked, she resented rules, disliked us all and yet had a wish to be popular and to win prizes. She drew better than she did anything and on one occasion, minding what Mother had said, I helped her with a drawing and she did win a prize. Then, in order to make me feel small, she said, 'It was not such a very good picture. It was the name. Everybody is anxious to curry favour with the Bonapartes now.'

I said, 'If you think Monsieur Isabey would be influenced ... And in any case, in competitions drawings are only numbered. The names that match the numbers are known only to Madame Campan.'

'And you think she wouldn't ... Really, Hortense Beauharnais, you are as soft and simple as your mother.'

Everything, Mother's example, Madame Campan's training, fell away and I was again the wretched forced-to-be-tough creature of my apprentice days. My hand shot out and slapped her, hard, across the face. A voice, not mine, shouted, 'You keep your tongue off my mother!' She would have hit me back, but I was ready for it and ducked so that her hand hit the empty air and my head was in a position to butt, a trick I had learned, being small, during those difficult days. The butt sent her backwards and a chair fell over with a crash which brought people running. By the time they arrived Caroline had me by the hair and was shaking me as the mastiff had shaken Fortunè and I was kicking her shins.

'Nothing of the kind has ever occurred here,' Madame Campan said. 'Hortense, you are the older, you may speak first and give, if it is possible, some explanation of this most unseemly conduct.'

I said, 'Madame, we were only rehearsing.'

'Rehearsing? What? A scene between two fishwives?'

'Market women,' I said, 'in a scene I planned for the play at the end of the year. Caroline and I both allowed ourselves to be carried away, to play our parts too thoroughly. Everyone thought we were really quarrelling.'

Madame Campan said, 'Hmmmm,' a long-drawn-out and non-committal sound. I waited for the accusation of telling lies, possibly even a sentence of expulsion. Her standards were very high and her waiting list long. 'Have you anything to add to that, Caroline?'

'No … madame. It was like Hortense said.' I could see us both being expelled. What for? Fighting like gutter children, telling lies. And why did you fight? Because of something she said about Mother. Appalling!

'I should be interested to see the script of this play, Hortense.'

'It is not quite ready, Madame Campan. It is not a fair copy, yet.'

'How soon will you have a fair copy?'

I said, desperately, 'Perhaps by the end of next week, madame.'

'I shall look forward to receiving it then on Saturday evening. And a copy is always useful, is it not? Caroline could copy each page as you complete it. It will be useful practice in handwriting. And in order that you may have time to devote to it you will both be excused from art and music lessons and from walks. And, yes, I think from supper. A tray will be brought to you at the scene of your labours which for the sake of privacy will be the garden room.'

This was a kind of extension to the classroom which had been the drawing room, and because it was made largely of glass and had no means by which it could be heated, was never used except in summer. In effect Caroline and I had been sentenced to ten days' imprisonment in what, in late October, was a very cold cell. To one another's distasteful company for hours on end. And, as we were to learn, prison food, at least at supper time.

'That was quick and cunning,' Caroline said. 'I shouldn't have thought you had it in you.'

'I didn't want to be expelled in disgrace. Over something *you* started.'

She ignored the reproach and said, 'Nor did I. When Napoleon comes back it would do me no good to be in disgrace. When I talk to him again about Joachim, I mean.'

'I'm being punished for your behaviour,' I said, 'and my punishment is far worse than yours. I have to write a play in ten days.'

'With a quarrel in it.'

'Yes,' I said, drearily realising the extent to which I had committed myself. I had written or largely contributed to school plays, and that was why that shoddy explanation had shot into my head at that crucial moment, but nothing I had ever had to deal with was even remotely concerned with quarrelling market women. School plays were always pretty, romantic, unrealistic. If something like a death *had* to happen, it was always off-stage.

'I know,' Caroline said. 'A Vendetta. Do you know what a Vendetta is? Well, it is a quarrel, it can begin between two people, over the simplest thing and goes on and on with whole families … Take us. You hurt me more than I hurt you, I hadn't time to tear a handful of hair out. In Corsica that would mean that my brother would have to fight your brother and so on until there wasn't a Bonaparte or a Beauharnais left. We could write a play that began with a squabble between two market women and ended with everybody dead.'

'Including Madame Campan. Of shock when she read it! In case you don't know, school plays always have happy endings and if we have to spend ten days in misery we might as well produce something that can be used.' I was still furious with her. 'You may have noticed that *I* was told to write the play; *you* were told to copy it. So be quiet and allow me to think.'

She said, quite meekly, 'I was only trying to help.' I saw that the whole disgraceful, distasteful episode had given me an ascendancy which neither my seniority nor attempts to be kind had established. I took full advantage of it.

While Caroline and I laboured away with our chill-stiffened fingers and I made sudden changes, crossing things out, putting things in *after* she had made a copy, my step-father had led his troops almost to Vienna; the Austrians asked for an armistice and he dictated his peace terms.

Mother sent me a string of pearls and a letter saying that she intended to visit Venice. 'I have heard so much about it and such an opportunity may not come again. I need a little respite from public life which I find very wearing, so much standing and smiling …' Of what public life involved I then knew nothing except little things, gathered from books and pictures, and from Madame Campan's reminiscences. Public life, it seems, had been too much for Marie Antoinette, born to it, and she had taken refuge in pretending to be a milkmaid, in a dairy where every utensil was of silver or fine china. I could well understand how Mother, always at her best in intimate settings, would be tired and bored by vast impersonal receptions. Eager as I was to see her I could not begrudge her a brief respite.

My step-father's journey back to Paris was one long triumphal procession; never, since the ancient days of Rome, had a returning soldier been given such a reception. As he neared Paris I thought of his entering the little house in the street now renamed Rue de la Victoire, with nobody there to receive him. I asked Madame Campan if she thought I should go home. She did not answer immediately and when she did she spoke with less than her usual certainty.

'I am inclined to think that you would do well to wait – at least until you are sent for. General Bonaparte acted somewhat independently over this peace treaty; the Directors may feel affronted. And the way in which he is being welcomed will breed envy, which in politics can be dangerous. Caroline must go of course as soon as her family arrives, but I think you should wait.'

I had an uncomfortable and quite inexplicable feeling that this caution was not entirely due to political thought; for the first time I saw that Mother's failure to come home with him might be sinister.

For me the situation was resolved by my grandfather Beauharnais. He was a kindly, ineffectual old man who had survived the failure of his career in the Navy, the failure of his marriage and who had, for as long as I could remember, been living in fairly penurious retirement in a modest house in Versailles. Emilie and Stephanie and I had lately spent our holidays there and when, one morning, early, I was sent for and found him in Madame Campan's parlour, I imagined that he had come to take us all out for the day.

'Do as you think best, of course,' Madame Campan was saying as I entered. There were flecks of colour high up on the cheekbones of her sallow face and I guessed that they had been arguing. My grandfather was better dressed than usual in the shabby, elegant clothes of a bygone day. As he kissed me I could smell the lavender and rosemary that had preserved them from moth.

'The Marquis, your grandfather, has come to take you to Paris, Hortense,' Madame Campan said crisply. 'Dress in your best, but warmly.'

In the broken-down hired carriage my grandfather explained that General Bonaparte had arrived in Paris overnight, that the news had reached him by accident and that he thought that he and I should, if possible, be the first to give him a family welcome.

'I don't know what all this talk is about,' he said, gently querulous. 'Your dear mother isn't the most sensible of women, but there's no harm in her, there never was. But for us – you and me to hold aloof at this minute would give entirely the wrong impression. He has restored French morale and liberated Italy, he's a great man, but he's human and will appreciate the family touch.'

In the re-named street our small, but rather elegant, house had been transformed into a kind of Army headquarters; it was full of men, soldiers standing or sitting about – their job done, civilians, government officials I guessed, moving more quickly, waiting less patiently. But as soon as my grandfather had given our names we were admitted. We climbed the familiar stairs and were ushered into the room where, rather less than a year ago, Mother had drifted about re-arranging the flowers, decrying the wine and Eugène had sweated with impatience.

From behind a makeshift table, a board set up on trestles, scattered with maps and papers and, incongruous among them, a dish with half a roast chicken on it, my step-father stood up, came forward and embraced me.

He had changed a little. The sun in Italy had browned his skin and bleached his hair. He still looked thin and hungry, despite all those official banquets which Mother and Eugène had written about, meals lasting a full four hours.

My grandfather made a fulsome little speech. I said, 'I have been so very proud, ever since Mondivi.'

He said, 'I am sorry, Hortense, that your mother and brother are not here. You know where she is? And I sent Eugène with the deputation to the Pope to explain the terms of the treaty and how it would affect the Papal States.'

'A great honour, for one so young,' my grandfather said.

'He's a very steady boy. And growing up rapidly. You've changed in the year since I last saw you, Hortense. Much prettier.' I blushed.

He talked on, saying that if the weather held Mother should be back in a few days; his own family would arrive tomorrow or next day, then Caroline and I must have a holiday and join in the festivities. Somebody opened the door and said, 'Excuse me, General,' and we were dismissed, but very kindly.

Outside my grandfather said, 'That went well and refutes all this gossip about a disagreement.'

'Between the General and Mother?'

'Yes. All nonsense. Had there been anything in it we should not have been received as we were.'

He seemed pleased to have proved something to himself and I meditated the word *prettier*. It hinted at improvement, but upon what? Vanity was not much encouraged by Madame Campan; one must be neat and clean, dressed correctly but inconspicuously; these rules observed, appearance was of no great importance compared with deportment, self-control, diligence. But like every other girl I longed to be thought pretty, to be pretty.

Oddly enough it was a remark made by Madame Bonaparte and repeated to me, disparagingly, by Caroline, that gave me more confidence than could be gleaned from a looking-glass in which reflection varies, or from things said by girls – I wish my hair curled like yours, and so on. 'My mother says that you are exactly like your mother.'

'Oh. In what way?'

'Every way. Looks, frivolous behaviour, smooth tongue.'

'I take that as the highest possible compliment. When next I see your mother I shall thank her.'

Hardy as she was, Caroline blenched. 'For God's love, Hortense, no! She'd box my ears if she knew I had repeated ...'

'Then why did you?'

'Because I am so miserable. So angry with everybody. Napoleon treats you as though you were grown up and me like a child. There's not all that difference in our ages. You are allowed to dance with anybody; if Joachim partners me once there are black looks all round. It just is not fair. If you went to Napoleon today and said you wanted to marry … well, say General Dubroc, he'd pat you on the head and give you his blessing, whereas when I say I want to marry Joachim they laugh. And Napoleon tells me to copy your behaviour.'

'I shouldn't dream of marrying anybody yet. And you are far too young …'

'By silly French standards! Mother was not much older than I am now when she married.'

I thought to myself – She was never any age, she was never young, she will never be old. Completely inhuman, cut out of Corsican rock. In the gay gatherings which Caroline and I, and presently Emilie and Stephanie were allowed to attend that winter, Madame Bonaparte in plain black, wearing no jewels, unsmiling, immensely dignified, was a remarkable figure. Her dark eyes, deep-set under hooded lids, missed nothing and although she spoke only a few words of French with a heavy Italian accent and refused to learn more, I think she understood it. One does not listen, closely attentive for hours, to talk one does not understand. My step-father, her second son, now had money enough, his pay as general, his share of the loot that came in creaking carts up from Italy to France, fabulous presents given to him by the liberated cities; his mother, well provided for and established in a large house, still made bean and onion soup and the traditional pasta with her own hands. People laughed about her and called her a peasant, but she was as classless as she was ageless. I should have admired her had she not been so hostile to Mother who really did her best to placate, even giving her precedence in doorways.

Well, if that grim old woman thought that I was like Mother, I was well content. Privately I doubted whether I was frivolous in quite the way she condemned, meaning, I think, extravagant. Mother's latest extravagance was to refurnish our house with a military motif; the beds were all curtained to look like tents; there were stools in the form of drums and an ancient cannon up-ended to hold a bowl of flowers.

Possibly one of the things which angered Caroline was that my mother positively thrust new dresses and shoes upon me while hers took the opposite attitude. When Caroline wailed, 'I don't know what to wear; all my dresses are so old,' Madame Bonaparte replied, 'Had you but one dress you would know what to wear!'

Despite the joy of being reunited with Mother, the plenitude of pretty dresses and being treated as a grown-up and allowed to attend receptions and balls, I was not completely happy during those festive weeks. Below the surface gaiety there were undercurrents, both inside and outside the family. All the Bonapartes except Pauline – now married and in Italy – and Jerome – away at sea – were now in Paris and saying worse things about Mother than that she was extravagant. They said that she had met Hippolyte Charles in Venice and that the slowness of her Alpine crossing was due less to the weather than to her reluctance to part with her lover. Stories like this were eagerly seized upon by the cynical society of the day and not least by those busy currying favour. No one said anything directly to me, but I heard things.

I once heard Talleyrand say, in his beautiful, clear voice, 'Husbands should *pay* fellows like Hippolyte Charles. They keep the *real* ones away.' I took that to indicate that he shared my opinion of Hippolyte's harmlessness, and he should know; he was a man of the world if ever there was one. But it showed what had been the subject of the conversation; so did the little nudges and whispers which recognised my proximity. Talleyrand was not an admirable character; he had been a bishop, but had left the Church and married. He was notorious for his infidelities. During the Revolution he had been an emigré, presumably Royalist; but he had come back to France, made an alliance with Barras and was now Foreign Minister. He was a wit and one of his quips affected my life a little.

It was at one of those dinner parties for which I still felt too young and the conversation had been political. The Directory Government was now in such bad repute that anyone who took office under it said he had no choice, he had been forced to accept it. There was some talk about this, and Talleyrand, seated almost directly opposite to me, said, 'Ah yes. I have in my office a long list of people who have registered themselves as anxious to be forced.'

I laughed, partly because the remark had humour in it and partly, I admit, to show that I was there, and not deaf or dumb. Other people laughed too, a little belatedly, Monsietir Talleyrand's comments were so often barbed that there was just that second of wondering – Was that meant for me? So, laughing just that little too soon I attracted his attention. His serious attention, a taking stock. Then across the flowers he spoke to me.

'Mademoiselle, will you accept a word of advice from an old man?'

I knew he meant himself. It is a pose which many men, a little older than they enjoy being, adopt with young girls, inviting contradiction. So I said the right thing. 'But of course. Where is this old man?' I looked about as though expecting to see some hoary-headed ancient.

'In a pretty woman,' he said, quite seriously, 'a sense of humour is a two-edged knife with no handle. Dear child, rid yourself of it.'

Now his neighbours at table and mine were looking at me; 'dear child' said like that was offensive. I felt as I had felt just before I smacked Caroline's face. I said in a mock-sweet way, 'Thank you, monsieur. I will remember. Advice on any subject, from an expert, is valuable.'

Everybody knew what a womaniser he was and the laughter was hearty, spiked with malice. I loathed myself.

Mother said, 'But, darling, I can't see that you said anything wrong. That kind of talk … I'm no good at it, too slow. I never think of the right thing to say until it is at least half an hour too late. Why are you so upset?'

'Because it is not how I wish to *be*. But when I am provoked … something comes over me. I hate it.'

'Darling, that is silly. You did nothing wrong. That kind of remark is well-regarded. I only wish I had the wit and the knack.'

We were in her bedroom. I had waited until Marion had gone and then come in to unburden myself, seek a word of comfort. So far it had not been said and never would, I thought, as the door opened and my step-father came in. 'It was his bedroom, too. I was the intruder. I would have got up to go, but Mother had her arm round me and tightening her clasp held me down.

He said, 'And now what is the matter?' speaking as though about a thousand things had recently gone wrong and this was the last straw.

I said, 'Nothing,' and I would have gone then, taking my trivial misery with me. But Mother said, 'Poor Hortense, she is a little upset.'

He said, 'Who? What?' The words dropped like flints. I thought of all he had to concern with and to bother about. I began to cry.

'It's such a horrible world,' I said.

Mother began, 'No, darling, don't say that. There's so much …'

'Of course it's a horrible world.' It's abominable. Not worth shedding a tear over.' He spoke gruffly, but his eyes met mine with a look of such translucent understanding that I thought – *He knows. He feels as I do.* Why that thought should so jolt me as to set my heart racing I did not know. I had never been deprived of sympathy and understanding … It was the look that was new and disturbing. I tried to shift my gaze and could not.

'It's the only world we have. We have to make the best of it and get on top of the blockheads.'

'Dear me,' Mother said in her easy, soothing way, 'you sound a little upset, too.'

'I am.' He kicked one of the drum-shaped stools out of the way and began to walk up and down. 'They won't be *told*. Invade England! Invade my ... I can *make* soldiers. Ships I know nothing about – and all those who did got their heads lopped off. So England has a navy, we have a mess of men and ships. We'd be massacred.' He turned, stopped, said, 'I wonder ...' I saw the skin whiten around his mouth. He dashed for the door and was gone.

'He can't really work with Barras and the rest,' Mother said. 'In fact the only way for him to be happy would be to have one Director, and he that one.'

'I'm sorry I made such a fuss about so little. I'm not really old enough. Mother, I think I would like to go back to school. Would you mind?'

'I should miss you, darling. But it would ease things with Caroline and Emilie and Stephanie. They need another year and resent going back. And of course if you went back they wouldn't have a leg to stand on.' She then said one of those incongruously shrewd things. 'All the same, Hortense, you must not look upon school as a refuge.'

We now had two love-sick girls at school, Caroline and my cousin Emilie. Caroline had failed to convince either her brother or her mother that she was old enough to marry and that Joachim Murat was the only man in the world for her. Her fury and frustration were exacerbated by the sight of Emilie being visited, being wooed by Louis Bonaparte.

'When he comes to see her, what do they *do*? she demanded, savagely scornful. 'Sit in the parlour and compare their symptoms?'

Unkind but with a kernel of truth. I thought them ideally suited. Louis Bonaparte, fourth of the five brothers, had been with my step-father during the Italian campaign and had contracted some obscure form of rheumatism. He had also had a fall from a horse and injured his knee. He could now neither dance nor ride and Emilie hated dancing and was afraid of horses. She was sickly in a vague way, prone to headaches and stomach upsets and spent a day every month in bed. She had had an unhappy life; her father died, her mother re-married, badly, and had several other children to whom, until Mother rescued her, Emilie had acted as unpaid nursemaid and servant. Mother, who believed in food, attributed Emilie's frailty and low spirits to lack of it. 'The only time the poor child ever had a proper meal was in your grandfather's house and that far too seldom.' Both Emilie and Louis were quite nice-looking, in a way, and there again they matched. She was very fair, almost faded, but with pretty features; he was dark and pale and sombre, much more like a poet than a soldier. Of all her children he was the one upon which Madame Bonaparte had stamped her image least clearly.

'Of course in Napoleon's eyes Louis can do no wrong. He's the pet lamb. Napoleon brought him up – and nobody finds fault with his own handi-work. And all this nonsense about Louis saving his life at Arcola. Joachim told me the truth. Napoleon fell into a ditch and grabbed Louis and Louis fell on top of him. Louis struggled out and Napoleon grabbed him. And that made Louis a hero. Imagine,' Caroline said inconsequently, 'their wedding. Louis holding his elbow on his knee, Emilie holding her head. It'd make you laugh if you didn't want to spit. And I don't even know where Joachim is.'

Military movements were being mysteriously conducted. The invasion of England had not been attempted, nor openly abandoned. Eugène's last letter to me had been sent from Marseilles and said nothing about future plans. On my recent visits home I had noticed a change in the kind of people around Mother's table, fewer soldiers and politicians, more men of a scholarly type.

'And wherever he is,' Caroline went on, 'he's seducing some stupid bitch. But he knows and I know that he belongs to me, really. We'd have run off and been married but that would have ruined his career. My dear brother can carry a grudge. So here I must wait and watch that silly milk-and-water Miss ...'

The year 1797 sped away; the New Year came and the sense of waiting, of something impending, increased. I thought I was about to be informed when Mother and my step-father came to Madame Campan's one morn-ing, taking us all by surprise and proposing to take Emilie and me out for a picnic lunch. It was early in the year for eating out of doors and the day though sunny was not warm. As Emilie and I donned our outdoor clothes I rather wondered why Caroline and Stephanie had not been included, but when we reached the carriage I saw that my parents had a man with them, and five was as many as the carriage would hold comfortably.

We drove into the forest and ate a delectable lunch and drank a good deal of wine. The man was a general, his name Antoine Lavalette. He was stout, growing bald and seemed to be doing his best to be amiable, even gay, while burdened by a secret worry. Only a well-bred man could have managed so well. My step-father was in such boisterous high spirits that he might have been the one having an unexpected day's holiday and eating delicious food. The meal over, he took Mother and me by the arm and said, 'Now, a good brisk walk!' and almost pulled us away. General Lavalette, worry now in the ascendant, offered his arm to Emilie who took it shyly. I felt sorry for her; Louis Bonaparte was the only man with whom she had ever been at ease.

But there was nothing I could do; in a deceptively slight frame my step-father had muscles of iron, Mother and I were literally in tow.

I wonder that Mother stood it so long, she hated moving fast and walking for the sake of walking. Presently she said, 'Oh Bonaparte, surely this will do. I rather think I have twisted my ankle.'

'Take a little rest,' he said, glancing back along the path. I looked, too; there was no sign of the others. Emilie, like Mother, was no walker.

We ambled back and there was General Lavalette, all worry banished, beaming and Emilie looking quite stunned. She was ordinarily so pale that one would have thought she could look no paler, but she did, and her very light blue eyes looked quite dark.

'Mademoiselle Beauharnais has done me the great honour of accepting my hand,' General Lavalette said. He wore the very look with which Fortunè would emerge from the prison doorway – I did it!

My step-father slapped him on the back and congratulated him. Mother hugged and kissed Emilie, shook Lavalette's hand. I kissed Emilie – whose face was icy and stiff.

Back at school she broke down and cried.

'Why did you agree?' I asked.

'I had no choice. You see he began by telling me that Louis is to marry somebody else. And it is true he hasn't come so often lately.' She cried even harder. 'It was all arranged, by that brother of his.'

Everything pointed that way. It seemed strange that Mother should have played a part in such a plot.

'Whom is Louis to marry?'

'I don't know. Somebody with a dowry and a fine family.'

'Well, even so I don't see why you said yes. Look, Emilie, write and say you didn't mean it, or have changed your mind.' I handed her a dry clean handkerchief. 'It may not even be true about Louis. Caroline would surely know and would have mentioned it.' And in what terms! Any mention of any marriage made her storm.

'It's true. General Lavalette said General Bonaparte told him so. And then he said that he had always admired me and General Bonaparte approved and so did your mother. You could see they did. What could I say?'

'You could have said no. You still can.'

'Don't keep saying that. It's too late. We're to be married next week.'

'Next week!' Now I sounded shocked.

'If you go on crying like that you'll make your head ache,' I said, after I had thought over the suddenness of it all. 'Look, Emilie, I'll write … or go into Paris tomorrow and explain to them that you made a mistake. I'm sure Mother wouldn't wish … Nor would he. He's not unkind.'

Emilie then said something which made me see that I was wasting sympathy, at least in part.

'Oh, no! You mustn't do that. I might not get a husband at all.'

Just then Madame Campan – obviously forewarned – came in and chose to assume that Emilie was crying from joy and because it was the maidenly thing to do. More embraces and congratulations; and an explanation of the haste; soldiers had so little time between campaigns. And how nice it would be for Emilie to have an establishment of her own and how fortunate she was to have a man of family, not an upstart as so many were these days. One would have thought that Emilie had won a prize in a lottery.

And perhaps Madame Campan's attitude was the right one. Under my eyes Emilie changed. She had never been of much importance in her own right, never played a major part in any scene. Now she was the centre of attention; whisked out of school to be a war-time bride, envied, a romantic figure. She slipped into her new role so easily that one could only assume that she would make an excellent wife.

Emilie was married, a week later, quietly, in my grandfather Beauharnais's house at Versailles. Caroline and I were present.

'That was neatly managed,' Caroline said as we rode home. 'But if Nablione thinks he'll dispose of me so easily he will learn.' She often called my stepfather by his rather nasal-sounding Italian name when she was angry.

'You think it was … contrived?'

'I'm as sure as if I'd done it myself. He's saving Louis up for something, a *good* marriage. Me too, the clown! But Louis he can deal with; I bet he promised him an Egyptian princess and a palace on the Nile and a couple of pyramids. Me he couldn't bribe with the Papal crown.'

'Why an Egyptian?'

'Holy Mother of God,' she said, putting her hand to her mouth. 'I shouldn't have *said*… You *would* notice … Well, look, I've had a letter at last.' She touched her bodice and the paper crackled. 'From Joachim. A special messenger brought it. They're going to India. But Egypt first. And if the English knew they'd get their fleet into the Mediterranean. That's why everything has been so secret. And it is a secret. You're not supposed to know. Yet. In a few days I suppose everybody will know.'

'I shan't say anything,' I said.

'What was the name of that Egyptian girl who went about rolled up in a carpet?'

'I don't know. I never heard of her.'

'Oh yes you do. She had herself rolled in a carpet and then she put some pearls in vinegar and they melted and she was the most beautiful woman in the world. You know …'

'Oh. Cleopatra?'

'That's it. Well, Egypt may be full of them. The one thing I do know is that Joachim might go to bed with a dozen, snakes and all, but he wouldn't marry one.'

I thought – How very nice to be so *sure*.

'What makes me so furious is the waiting. This thing may take a year.'

7

Fifty thousand men embarked from Toulon and Mother stood on a balcony over the harbour and waved to each contingent as it passed. Our Lady of Victory. It was not only of soldiers that she took leave; on his staff my step-father was taking writers and artists, geologists, archaeologists and the engineers who were to study the possibility of cutting through the isthmus and making a canal between the Mediterranean and the Gulf of Suez. Egypt, part of the Turkish Empire, had been for centuries a land of mystery. Now, as Madame Campan said with enthusiasm, it was to be properly explored. 'We may learn the secret of the Sphinx.'

Perhaps the Sphinx had no secret to be revealed, but it was one of the experts on that expedition who found in a place called Rosetta a monument which, because it bore the same inscription in three languages, broke, as it were, the secret code of history and opened many hitherto keyless doors into the past.

It was a time of anxiety and it lasted more than the year which Caroline had foreseen. I worried about Eugène and about my step-father, and in a less personal way about all those fifty thousand men who were in danger not only from the enemy but from unaccustomed heat and strange diseases. In one letter Eugène mentioned flies as a source of torment. But at first the news was good; our troops won two battles and Egypt lay quiet. Before the battle fought near the famous Pyramids my step-father said, 'Soldiers, forty centuries of history look down on you.' I thought that a very poetic thing to say, so did Madame Campan – only she called it inspiring – but Caroline, still angry with her brother, said contemptuously, 'He might know that, he was always reading about such things. But what would it mean to soldiers? Most of them can't count above ten.'

None the less there was a curiously romantic streak in her too. She seemed immune from worry about Joachim Murat though casualties in the cavalry were always heaviest – 'Death rides pillion to all,' was the expression. She would say, 'Oh, Joachim knows how to take care of himself,' or 'Joachim was born lucky.' But once she said with real feeling, 'I should know. Whatever hit him would hit me. So as long as I am all right I know he is.'

Then the bad news came, bringing in the long period of no news. The English fleet moved into the Mediterranean and in the Battle of the Nile completely destroyed ours. After that they controlled the sea and the French in Egypt could receive neither reinforcements nor supplies, and the French in France were dependent upon rumours.

Mother had gone from Toulon to Plombières, a watering-place in the Vosges mountains. Its waters were good for many complaints and to drink from one spring was regarded as a sure cure for sterility in women. Not that Mother could be called sterile; she had Eugène and me, within a few weeks of her marriage to Bonaparte she had suffered a miscarriage, but since then, nothing.

History is said not to repeat itself; one wonders. For once again it had been arranged that as soon as Mother had taken the magical waters and Egypt was safe, she should join my step-father in that country. But before she had completed her 'cure', the balcony on which she sat sewing collapsed, and she fell twenty-five feet on to a hard stone pavement. She broke no bones, but was badly shaken and terribly bruised. By the time she was able to travel English patrol boats controlled all sea routes and there was nothing for her to do but to come back to Paris and give her full attention to Malmaison.

I, for one, should never have bought it and hundreds of other people, looking for a country property not too far from Paris, must have felt the same, for nobody had lived in the château for many years, and when we first saw it, it had that desolate, haunted look of a place once occupied, now deserted. Its very name was ill-omened and was derived, it was said, from its having once been a refuge for lepers.

Mother went from room to room on that first visit, looking for evidence of the roof's failure to keep out the rain, sniffing for decay. 'Nobody could call it derelict,' she said at last. 'It was beautiful once, and could be again. And think of the garden.'

The grounds were spacious and though parts were overgrown and neglected other parts were well cultivated, let out on very short tenancies to people who wanted to grow stuff for the Paris market.

'Bonaparte said he wanted a place to come back to. And I have always wanted a real garden of my own.'

Shortage of money no longer worried her. Joseph Bonaparte had obtained some official post and had been left with orders to supply Mother with what she needed. She threw herself happily into the business of making Malmaison beautiful. In this she was helped by Hippolyte Charles, now out of the Army and engaged in some kind of business which left him free to spend unlimited time on the choosing of fabrics and colours and the placing of pictures and other beautiful things, statues, fountain-heads and urns which had been brought from Italy and stored because there was no room for them in the Paris house, or in the tiny garden. Adèle and I went there often and from one visit to the next saw vast changes.

Mother seemed to take the war and the lack of news calmly. 'If anything had happened to Bonaparte the English would have been the first to let us know. And that is true of Eugène, too.'

The English papers were busy smearing both Mother and my step-father; she was supposed to be committing adultery with Hippolyte Charles, he with the wife of one of his generals who had followed her husband to the war. To back up such libels the English claimed to have intercepted some correspondence destined for France, including a letter to Mother from Eugène who would never, knowing the risk of such a letter falling into the wrong hands, have written it. Eugène, so cautious, so discreet, was supposed to have written rebuking Mother for not having joined our step-father while it was possible to do so, and for her present behaviour which had provoked retaliation. Whoever invented or forged that letter did not know my brother, I thought, for it ended with a completely uncharacteristic note of self-pity. The whole situation, Eugène was said to have written, put him in a most difficult position, torn between his loyalty to his general and his loyalty to Mother and on the point of being forced to resign his staff appointment.

Not Eugène's style at all. But some people believed it. There were sinister little signs. Fewer people wished to see how the beautification of Malmaison was progressing, or, when Mother was back in the Rue de la Victoire, came to her parties. And Joseph Bonaparte ceased to hand out money, so the debts mounted again.

One October night I was roused by somebody shaking me by the shoulder. I thought – Another bad dream! I dreamed often, and very vividly and always in extremes, either everything was so beautiful and wonderful and happy as to be indescribable, or so terrible and frightening – like Adèle kissing me good night and turning into a wolf.

This was a bad one. I had never seen Madame Campan in her night-cap, her features distorted by the light of a candle, wavering. *This will pass*, I said to myself, *I shall wake*.

She said, 'Try not to wake everybody. Get up. Dress warmly. General Bonaparte is safely home. In France. Your mother is going to meet him and wishes you to go with her. I will leave the candle.'

Half asleep, half awake, I pulled on my clothes, stumbled downstairs. Outside the door, darker in the dark, really only distinguishable by its lamps, was the carriage. I clambered in.

'All possible speed,' Mother called and the headlong drive began. She hugged me. She felt flimsily clad.

'I was dining with Barras when the news came,' she explained. 'But his brothers had been told first. They are ahead. We must overtake them. I must get there first.'

I had my warm winter cloak and we shared it, huddling together as the carriage hurtled south. It was a nightmare journey. We changed horses, we changed drivers, made our little necessary visits, hastily drank water and got back into the carriage taking with us whatever was handiest to eat as we went along. Mother, who hated fast driving, kept urging greater speed; but as the hours and the miles rolled away and we had not overtaken the other carriage, she put a hopeful interpretation on the fact. 'They stopped to sleep at some inn and are now behind us,' she said. 'I shall have him to myself and everything will be well.'

We had slept as we could, short spells of unconsciousness due to exhaustion, from which, roused by a jolt or a tilt at a too-sharply turned corner, one woke and felt worse.

We clattered into Lyons quite early on a wet, blustery morning. There were triumphal arches in the streets; the laurels had lasted well, the flowers had withered, the tiny ribbons blowing limply. In open spaces what had been bonfires were heaps of dead ash.

'He had been and gone,' Mother said. 'By the other road. And they met him ...'

She had two ways of crying; she could cry beautifully, the tears welling up and making her eyes look enormous and then spilling without damage, no reddened eyelids or nose, no snuffles. She could cry like an ordinary woman and she did so now as the carriage turned and sped towards Paris. I held her as the sobs shook her, I said, 'Mother, don't!' I said, 'It does no good.' From sheer weariness and misery I cried with her. I did not ask what she feared. From the first my step-father's family had wanted him to divorce her and her carelessness over Hippolyte Charles had played into their hands. Too few people thought as Talleyrand did about the harmlessness of the Hippolytes of this world and somebody at Malmaison itself, probably someone who was disgruntled at not being paid, had started a story that she and Hippolyte had walked about the garden, hand in hand. I knew that the caressing gesture came so easily to her; she would have taken anybody by the hand and said – 'Oh look, the first rose.' But that kind of thing was outside most people's understanding. So was my down-to-earth thought that if she had been conducting a clandestine love-affair she would have been more careful, would have had me home and Adèle to stay with me, so that pursuing her own interests we should have been the ideal chaperones, present, but not ubiquitous.

It was night when we reached Paris and our house seemed deserted, though blazing with lights everywhere. As we tumbled out of the carriage I had a sensible thought. I said, 'Tidy yourself. Change your dress.' There are clothes designed to stand up to the exigencies of travel, but Mother wore one of her frail, lacy evening dresses, soiled, muddy about the hem. We had not taken so much as a comb with us, we had once or twice splashed our faces with water from a pump or horse-trough in an inn yard, drying them on my petticoat. How I looked I do not know, but Mother in her draggled finery looked – dissolute.

She ignored me and hurried into the house. I followed and saw her go upstairs, tripping over the muddied flounce, already torn when she had left the carriage at some point. I thought – Fatal!

Somebody said, 'Hortense!' and there was Eugène. I should hardly have known him, he had grown so much, was burned dark brown and had a moustache. We hugged each other.

'Where have you *been*?'

'To Lyons. To meet him. There and back without a stop – except to change horses.'

'How witless! He thought Mother had …' He broke off.

Nobody would have believed that Mother's delicate hands could beat so heavily on a closed door. That the door should be locked told me something; people do not lock doors against nothing. He had seen us arrive.

'Bonaparte. Let me in! Please, I beg of you. Let me in! You must let me in!'

'If only she'd been here,' Eugène said. Coming back to an empty house … After all he has been through.'

I tried to think of something undreary to say. 'Eugène, I am so glad to see you. Getting no news. I couldn't help worrying.'

'We were both wounded at Acre,' Eugène said, not without pride. Mother had ceased to hammer the door and was moaning and crying. 'This isn't much of a homecoming.' We stood, linked in misery. Then Marion appeared at the head of the stairs, her brown face grey. She beckoned us, and as we neared her said, 'Chillun, you gotta do it. Gotta get that door open.' We went along to the door where Mother seemed to have collapsed, Marion raised her and said, 'Wailing and beating your hands to rags don't help none. You try,' she looked at Eugène.

Eugène put on a firm face and took a deep breath. He rapped smartly on the door and called, 'General,' in a firm, unemotional voice.

No answer.

'Sir, you must admit me. Or give me some reason. This is the home we share.'

Another breath-holding silence.

Eugène said, 'Hortense is here, half dead. She went to Lyons to meet you. Is this how you welcome her?'

The silence lasted long enough to make us feel that we had failed; then the lock clicked and the door began to open. Mother slipped past us and ran into the room. The door closed again.

Marion said, 'You always did have a good head on you. They'll be all right now.' She vanished.

'I somehow feel,' Eugène said solemnly, 'that I shall never marry. Too much of a strain.'

'On other people,' I said.

He laughed then and said he was hungry. So was I. We went into the deserted kitchen and found food which we ate in our fingers and he told me all the news. 'And we didn't turn back from Acre because it withstood us, or because of being wounded. It was because the Sultan of Turkey was pouring fresh men into Egypt. We gave them the soundest thrashing and might have been on our way to the East again except for the papers.' His face changed.

'What papers?'

'Some I'm positive the English *intended* he should have. A mixed lot, some French, some English. Reports about the Government here being on the verge of collapse. And … and other things.'

I knew what he meant. But in the silent house there had been no sound of that door opening and closing, of anyone ejected or stalking away in anger.

'If *that* is settled,' Eugène said, following my glance ceilingwards, 'he can deal with the Government. I think we may see changes.'

8

We saw changes. Within a month the Directory had been swept away, the whole constitution of government changed. France was henceforth to be ruled by three Consuls; of whom my step-father was first. His brother Lucien, a skilled politician and a good orator, took credit for the rearrangement of things, and so did Joachim Murat who at a crucial moment had arrived at a heated debate at the head of a detachment of soldiers, but the truth was that the people of France were yearning for firm, settled government and looked to the one man they thought capable of supplying it.

Despite the fact that Murat had helped with the *coup d'état*, my step-father was still opposed to his marriage with Caroline. He clung as long as he could to the argument that Caroline was too young, but she, Adèle and I were out of school and embarked upon the world and of the three of us, Caroline was in many ways the most mature, the most sought-after. She had two proposals from men to whom Bonaparte seemed to have no objection. 'I spit upon them,' she said, and one had the feeling that she was not speaking entirely metaphorically.

Mother said, sweetly reasonable, 'But if she is old enough to marry at all, why not Joachim? I am not arguing …' – since that reunion after his return from Egypt, she had lost confidence in a way that perhaps I was the only one to notice.

'He's a good cavalry officer – not the best, but good. He is also the son of an inn-keeper. Not a fit match for my sister.'

Mother, seeming not to realise that she was, after all, arguing, said, 'Lucien's wife is an inn-keeper's daughter.'

She was, but a very nice, sensible woman.

'That was before … Murat is very big and very handsome. And he very much wants to be my brother-in-law. Years ago Caroline took a childish fancy to him and in her pig-headed way sticks to it.'

'I think she is in love,' Mother said.

'She knows as much about love as you do about mathematics! What do you say, Hortense?'

Taken by surprise I could think of only one safe thing to say.

'I am no judge. I have never been in love.'

'Pray God you never may be.' He gave me a look which put me on the defensive. I said, 'If ever I were, I daresay I should behave much as Caroline is doing.'

'I should trust you to have more sense.'

However, he gave in, and Caroline, ecstatically triumphant, was married to Joachim in January 1800. My step-father did not attend the wedding which was held at Joseph Bonaparte's magnificent country house, Mortefontaine: he gave as his excuse that he was too busy and busy he certainly was, but everyone knew that he could have spared a day had he wanted to. Perhaps the ceremony was gayer, certainly the talk was freer for his absence, for despite the family's almost deliberate use of the Italianate form of his name, and references to him as 'Little Brother', he could awe them if he chose, and he had a streak – unexpected in a soldier – of puritanism. He disliked coarse talk or remarks containing the double entendre which were regarded as so witty and would show his disapproval by a blank, glowering stare, an abrupt remark, or even by walking away. Some people, in my place, would have found this inconsistent with the outpourings in those letters, but I understood.

As First Consul he was given an official residence in Paris; for a few weeks it was the Luxembourg Palace, then we moved to The Tuileries, a move which dismayed Mother. Both were palaces, but the Luxembourg, much of it let out as apartments, and more closely associated with the Directory than with Royalty, had been in size, in atmosphere and in status, reduced to near-ordinariness. The Tuileries was very different. Here Louis XVI and Marie Antoinette had lived out their last *hopeful* days; here they had been mobbed by the roughest elements of Paris; from here – it was still possible to see the doorway, the gateway – they had made their abortive effort to escape. For Mother, born romantic, ardent Royalist at heart, it was a very short step from 'Marie Antoinette walked here' to 'Marie Antoinette walks here'. She swore the place was haunted and everything contributed to a creepy feeling, if not positive belief. The space alone. Space for a thronged Court, for ladies-in-waiting, officials, flunkeys, sentries. We moved in, still a private family. Usurpers? And although the mob had smashed and looted there was enough left to *link*. Mother, for instance, once looked into a mirror and swore that she saw not herself, but Marie Antoinette. Marion hearing her scream, ran up to see why, and fainted. My step-father said, 'Morbid imagination!' but he ordered the removal of that mirror and several other relics of the past.

In the late spring war was resumed in Italy where the Austrians had taken advantage of Bonaparte's absence in Egypt to regain what they had lost. They were defeated at Marengo and again at Hohenlinden into Bavaria, then they sued for peace and again my step-father dictated the terms, this time not merely as a successful, rather headstrong general, but as First Consul of France. Again, in Italy, he was treated like a king and when he returned to

France there was behind the rapturous welcome given to the hero a hint of something more, as though there was a growing recognition of the fact that he was unique and irreplaceable, more than a soldier, more than a statesman. Portraits of him, some of them villainously reproduced, were to be seen in the humblest homes, sometimes in the place on the wall formerly occupied by a holy picture, in very conservative families side by side with one. The mystique had begun and so had the ridiculously premature talk of his need for an heir. He saw how ridiculous it was; 'One cannot bequeath a consul-ship. Who worries whether a mayor or a harbour-master has a son or not?'

Like any normal man he would have liked to be a father; his letter to Mother when she told him that she was pregnant, his behaviour to Eugène and me; his interest in the young generally – he wanted every French child to have some education – proved that; but he was clear-sighted enough to distinguish between a personal disappointment and the kind of dynastic dis-aster which the Family were trying to make of his childlessness. He was even capable of making a joke about it. 'A wise child knows and picks his father. Maybe mine is waiting until he sees more than my sword and Malmaison to inherit.'

In such talk I thought I saw a double purpose. A desire to reassure Mother who had been twice more to Plombières. And a discontent with what he had achieved, a sort of challenge to the gods, to Fate, to the people of France – Give me something for a boy to inherit, I will then bother myself …

An enemy, not a friend or relative, made the move which changed every-thing and a single female garment played such a part that it seemed idiotic.

It was December and eight of us were going to the Opera; Mother, Bonaparte, Eugène, Caroline, Adèle, General de Broc, General Rapp and me. Since we had taken up residence in The Tuileries, Adèle had lived with us and I had a great hope that Eugène, occupying what he firmly called bachelor's quarters in one wing, might, if exposed to Adèle's unusual combi-nation of sweet temper and quiet wit, prettiness and sound sense, change his mind about marriage. Caroline was with us because Joachim was tone-deaf and could not bear opera, and she was so far pregnant that this outing might well be her last.

There were two carriages waiting. Bonaparte, Mother, Eugène and Caroline should have ridden in the first, the rest of us in the second. Mother came out wearing one of the new Kashmir shawls which were all the rage. It was as though the India merchants, failing to sell their muslin, had invented a wrap, so light, so warm, patterned in such beautiful and versatile colours that no woman – however French and loyal – could resist it.

Mother's was new and very beautiful, but Bonaparte looked at it with disgust.

'You cannot appear in public wearing that! Change it!'

Then, as was his way when annoyed, he underlined the offence by pretending to be in a great bustle.

'We shall be late. We're late as it is. I shan't wait. Get in, get in.' Caroline, of necessity, was rather slow, so he seized Adèle, pushed Eugène, called to de Broc and whirled off. Mother said to me, 'Fetch my blue silk one, darling.' It took me about two minutes.

We had reached the Rue Saint-Nicais when the end of the world seemed to come. There was a deafening explosion, the carriage lifted and rocked, the glass in its windows shattered. Mother screamed and fell forward. For a horrified moment I thought she was mortally wounded, dead. The carriage had come down on its wheels, however, and as soon as the plunging horses were under control we could take stock. I was holding Mother and there was blood on the blue of her shawl.

'She is hurt,' I said.

'The blood is from your own hand,' General Rapp said. I looked down and saw the wound which I had not felt, a piece of flying glass had made a long, but not deep, diagonal cut across the back of my hand. He lifted Mother back into her seat and handed me his handkerchief. 'I think it is only a swoon,' he said, and Mother stirred, and came round.

'Bonaparte?'

'He missed it by a minute,' Caroline said. 'It was meant for him.'

'Are you all right, Caroline?' I asked. Such a shock might well have precipitated the birth. But she, like her mother, was made of Corsican rock.

'Quite all right. Pull yourself together, Josephine. Nobody's hurt.' Except for my trivial wound we were uninjured, but a number of people in the street had been hurt, some fatally.

The street ahead was blocked and we were obliged to turn and make a detour. I turned Mother's shawl so that the blood spatters did not show, I wound the handkerchief tightly round my hand and hid it under the folds of a gauzy scarf I wore. Mother was still trembling when we arrived at the Opera and her face was so pale that the rouge looked as though it had been thrown at her.

'You're late,' my step-father said irritably as we entered the box. 'Why are you so late? What's the matter? Why do you look like that?'

'We were nearly blown up,' Caroline said.

'Anybody hurt? Rapp?'

'No. He went back to see what happened exactly,' I said.

'Then we must appear calm. We don't want a panic.'

The piece was Haydn's *Creation* and it was not given the attention it merited. Even the assumed calm in our box was disturbed when General Rapp came softly in and reported twenty-four people dead or injured by the explosion, many others suffering cuts from broken window glass.

'How ghastly to make so many poor people perish in order to get rid of one man,' Bonaparte said. It was a comment straight from the heart and I always remembered it when people said that to him human lives were of no importance.

Somebody brought the news and spread it through the audience; there was sibilant talk, heads turning, eyes staring. At the end, as we stood up to leave there was a tumult, cheering and clapping as though another great victory had just been announced.

'Most people are not anxious to be rid of me,' my step-father said, not complacently but with a kind of brooding thoughtfulness.

At the head of a long line of waiting carriages stood the one in which he had come in a rage, thus missing by a minute, or two at most, the explosion intended to end his life, and another to take the place of the broken-windowed one. Mother, Eugène and Caroline, as in the original placing, entered the first carriage, but he did not take his place in it. Nor in the second. A thin cold sleet was beginning to fall. Through the almost pearly curtain that it made against the lights at the front of the Opera and the lights of the waiting carriages, he turned and walked away in the direction of the Rue Saint-Nicais.

Answering a question that had not been asked, a reproach that had not been levelled, General de Broc said, 'We and your brother, mademoiselle, are under orders.'

Their orders had been to go to The Tuileries and keep the ladies company. Even Eugène interpreted this order with military precision. Mother, before donning the shawl which had saved eight people from death or severe injury, had left orders that the fires in the two private rooms should be banked and food for an informal supper – the kind she loved best – prepared and left in the dining room.

Time gave a kind of jolt, taking me back to that other evening, four years ago, in the little house in the Rue Chantereine – waiting for Bonaparte, Eugène impatient, Mother placid, myself a little nervous. There was the similarity, no sooner recognised than denied, for all was different now. We were different.

The food was ignored, except by Caroline. Conversation was disjointed. 'He insisted upon going alone.' 'He wanted to see for himself,' the men said.

Mother, still shaken, lay on a sofa, accepted a glass of wine and spilled it. 'What could there be to *see*?' she wailed. 'The assassins may be still lying in wait.'

'Not in the Rue Saint-Nicais. The last place he would be expected to be,' Eugène said.

General Rapp said, 'The assassins are miles away by now.'

Time lagged.

When at last he came in – knowing as much about the affair as anyone could know at that moment, what had caused the explosion, how many dead, how many injured – under his air of gravity I could see a secret excitement. His eyes were particularly bright and luminous and although he spoke again with regret about the casualties I had a feeling that he was not altogether displeased by the evening's events. I went to bed very puzzled.

It was never ascertained who had placed and fired the keg of gunpowder which had missed him so narrowly. Some people accused the extreme Republicans who saw in the Consulate a threat of dictatorship; others accused the extreme Royalists. To judge by the extreme dismay and apprehension which the attempt provoked there were few extremists of either kind left; France and Bonaparte were becoming more and more closely identified. What would become of France if anything happened to the First Consul? To that nobody gave the rational answer – Two would be left, a third could be elected. The focus was on Bonaparte. As he said himself, 'Nobody tries to blow up nonentities.'

Caroline had her baby, a beautiful boy who was to be called Achille. 'There's only one thing wrong with him, his surname,' my step-father said.

Mother made another visit to Plombières.

And with the signing of the Treaty of Amiens which brought peace with England, thousands of English people came to Paris, hoping to catch at least a glimpse of the man who so lately had been 'The Monster', 'The Corsican Ogre'. And of his wife, that immoral woman. They found a gay, but so far as The Tuileries was concerned, intensely respectable society. Even dress must be modest; my step-father disapproved of the fashionable *décolletage* and once rebuked two ladies who had not regarded the unwritten rules by loudly ordering the fire to be piled higher.

'And higher,' he said, in that flinty, carrying voice that all Bonapartes could use when they chose. 'I am so much afraid that these ladies will catch cold.'

Among the English who were allowed not only to see, but to be received by and spoken to by the First Consul of France, was the statesman named Fox who went back and reported, with typical condescension, that my step-father seemed to be a young man slightly overcome by his meteoric rise. That was one of the most obtuse judgments ever made.

9

One morning, towards the end of that hot gay summer, Adèle and I coaxed Roustam, an ex-slave whom my step-father had brought from Egypt and treated half as servant, half as pet, to allow us to paint his portrait. We had wanted to try for a long time; the shade of his skin, dark copper with undertones of blue as well as his turban and robe, offered a challenge; but Roustam had resisted us – he had an inborn contempt for women and a superstitious prejudice against being painted and it had taken a direct order from his 'Effendi', as he called Bonaparte, to get him to stand, looking like a thunder cloud surrounded by a rainbow.

We were busy, a little elated by our triumph, when the door opened and one of my step-father's secretaries appeared. There were three of them and I liked Monsieur Bourrienne least. He had once been rather too familiar in his behaviour to me; some time ago now, when I had been inexperienced, ill-equipped to deal with unwanted advances, a little unsure – Does this mean what I think it means? – a little afraid of hurting feelings. I had rebuffed him, clumsily, a little, I thought afterwards, too seriously.

He now said, 'Mademoiselle, I have a message from the First Consul.'

'Deliver it. I am listening.'

'It is of a private nature.'

I was just beginning to get that peculiar metallic blending of brown and blue. I said, 'Oh bother!' The paint ready mixed, the elusive subject there. 'You go on,' I said to Adèle. 'Get the face, the rest can be put in afterwards.'

I got up and went into the tiny anteroom or lobby, no more than the end of a passage, enclosed, off which the apartments which Adèle and I occupied led. It contained one table, marble-topped, one chair, a candle-stand and a statue of some unknown ancient lacking a nose.

'Well,' I said. 'What is it?'

'I have been commissioned to communicate to you the ardent wish of the First Consul – and of your mother.'

I thought – A joke! They want me to arrange some entertainment. Write some topical verse, take Mother's place at some boring function and have taken this over-emphatic, pompous approach for fun.

'Tell me,' I said. 'I am prepared for the worst.'

'It is their wish that you should marry Monsieur Louis Bonaparte.'

I began to laugh – a joke if ever there was one – then I stopped, brought up short by the look on Bourrienne's face.

'Why you? I … I saw him … I saw the First Consul … last evening. I breakfasted with my mother …'

'Neither wished to speak.'

'This is true? Not a joke?' Bourrienne's grave face slipped sideways and blended with that of the noseless Roman, the candle-stand swayed, the solid table tilted. Then I was in the chair, guided, supported by gentle hands.

'It is a shock to you, mademoiselle. To me also. I should not have chosen to be the one to say it. I did as I was ordered to do.'

The chair, though not designed for sitting in, was solid, had arms. Once I was in it, elbows on the arms of it, hands against my face, the room steadied and I could think.

I said, 'Surprised, Monsieur Bourrienne. Both by the suggestion, and the manner of its presentation.' I intended to resist this fantastic idea, but with the least possible drama and the least offence to anyone. Bourrienne was a gossip. I did not want him going around saying that the very mention of the match had shocked me so much that I fainted, or was speechless.

'I am of the opinion that the First Consul and madame suspected that the suggestion would be unwelcome and shrank from witnessing your dismay.'

'Why dismay? As I see it, it is an honourable proposal.'

Bourrienne gave a slight shrug.

'Then I take it, mademoiselle, that I may say that you received it favourably.'

'Good gracious, no! How could I make such a momentous decision without thought? Even had I seen some indication …' That was part of the shock; Louis Bonaparte had never evinced the slightest interest in me, never so far as I could remember even gone out of his way to fetch me an ice or a glass of wine. It would be worse than marrying a complete stranger with whom some kind of contact might be established upon closer acquaintance.

'I must think it over,' I said, as lightly as I could.

'They are prepared for that and proposed that you should allow yourself a week.'

That was a shock, too. I forced myself to be calm.

'It may take rather longer; but you may say that I am considering. Thank you, Monsieur Bourrienne.'

That should have dismissed him and he did turn to go. Then he swung about and said, 'I offended you once. I take the risk again. Don't do it. You wouldn't be happy with that spineless, self-centred …' He gave a kind of choke. 'You of all people …' he said.

I got up and on legs that felt flaccid and too long, returned to the sitting room, sank into another chair and said to Adèle, 'Send Roustam away …'

He went, as much affronted at being so summarily dismissed as he had been by the order to allow himself to be painted.

'What is it? You look ill.'

I told her as briefly as possible and she said, 'Oh no!' Then her Aunt Campan side, common sense with a flavour of cynicism, came uppermost and she said, 'Darling, I am afraid that you will find this very difficult to get out of. You cannot even plead a former attachment – that would count with Aunt Josephine.'

'I never felt one. There are several men I have liked … to – dance with … talk to … ride with, but not one I wished to marry. Louis Bonaparte I don't even like.'

'No, I know.' She looked and sounded gloomy. 'It's nothing I can help with. I can't even advise.' The need to say or do something was there however and presently she said, with no great certainty, 'There's nothing actually against him, though. And people do say that arranged marriages often turn out best.'

'You speak as though it were inevitable. I'm not going to do it, Adèle. I'd sooner …' What? The days were gone when the alternative to a distasteful marriage was a convent. Caroline Bonaparte, refusing one of her unwanted suitors, had said in rage that she would sooner join the prostitutes under the arcades of the infamous Palaise Royale. People had been known to say, 'I'd sooner die than do this, or that.' I was not yet so desperate; the first shock was receding and Adèle had helped in a negative way to restore my spirit. '… remain unmarried for the rest of my life,' I said. 'I was given a week to make up my mind, but I won't deceive them. I shall go and tell Mother now.'

Adèle reached out and took me by the wrist.

'Darling, don't say anything that might … bounce back. Resist by all means. To the utmost, but don't get into a position where … Oh, you know what I mean.'

Poor Mother. She employed to the utmost all her little devices for evading what was not acceptable. She reminded me that I was eighteen. She said that Louis was young and attractive. She said that if Bonaparte allowed any other Frenchman to marry me it would cause jealousy and accusations of favouritism; and that if I married a foreigner it would entail my living out of France. Therefore …

I waited until she had run down. There are a number of pretty things, not exactly toys, animated by clockwork, wound up, capable of giving a predicted performance and at times Mother's behaviour was not unlike theirs. The last remark of this prepared defence was that Louis was in love with me.

I said, 'Mother, that is not true and you must know it. He may have been in love with Emilie, but he was very easily put off and since then he has been in love with himself and his rheumatism.'

She said, helplessly, 'Hortense, that is unkind.'

'Maybe. But there are times when one must face the truth, however unkind, and this is one of them.'

Her look, her very voice changed. She said, 'Very well; we will face it. *Unless you marry Louis, Bonaparte will divorce me.*'

For the second time that morning everything slithered, Mother on the rose brocade couch, the flowers, the high window beyond which a single chestnut tree had begun to change colour, they all melted and whirled, but I was sitting down and did not need to be supported and guided. Things righted themselves and I could speak.

'Why?'

'Because he must have an heir. And it must be a Bonaparte. I am thirty-eight. Plombières has done nothing for me. The hope of a child of our own ... But they are proposing to make Bonaparte First Consul for life, with the right to name his heir. It must be a Bonaparte.'

'Joseph,' I said, 'Lucien. Louis himself. Even Jerome.'

Mother said, 'I never thought you were stupid. Name one of them – and not a *boy* between them to decide – the others would swoop like vultures. Louis is free to marry; Louis he looks upon as though he were his son. Louis married to you ... Darling, you are my daughter, and there are the soldiers who look upon me ... *His* brother, *his* almost son and *my* daughter ... the child, at least the son, of such a marriage would be acceptable to all.'

I sat and thought. I could see the logic, and also the absurdity.

'Even so. Suppose I agree – which I do not – to marry Louis – next week, and had a baby in the shortest possible time – a boy, what kind of heir would that be?'

'As much an heir as if I ... As if my last visit to Plombières had been ... effective.' She was absurdly embarrassed, talking in this fashion to me, who, for all she knew, or should have assumed, did not know how babies were made, or how long they took to gestate. 'It would be what is needed now, some assurance for the future. It would settle things. And there would be time for the baby to grow up. Bonaparte is only thirty-two.'

'I'm sorry, Mother. I simply cannot face the prospect of spending my life with Louis Bonaparte.'

'Then you do not care what happens to me.'

I thought – if she were drowning, or trapped in a burning house, I should at least attempt to save her: I would nurse her through a contagious illness.

Why should this be so different? The answer was simple; the other situations were imaginary and demanded only a limited courage, this was fact and involved a life-sentence. But she looked so stricken that I weakened.

'I will think about it.'

She began to cry. 'Bless you, my darling. I knew I could rely upon you.'

'No. That you must not do. I only said I would think.'

'Do bear in mind ...' She dabbed her eyes and steadied her voice. 'Love is so strange. I came to France to marry your father, a man I had never seen so how could I love him? But I did. I loved him so much that when he was unkind to me it broke my heart. Then, quite suddenly, I ceased to love him. Or take Bonaparte, I did not love him. I married him partly because he was so insistent and I was in such a muddle, and had you and Eugène to consider: but I came to love him and now ...' More tears rose. 'I think you would come to love Louis – if you gave him a chance to endear himself to you.'

In love, out of love, in love again. I thought of Emilie, now completely devoted to her Antoine. I thought of Caroline, steadfast as a rock. To me the word as applied to an emotion between a man and a woman was almost abstract, concerned with books and plays and operas and songs and other people's experience. Despite my ignorance I had an inner certainty that between me and Louis it could never exist. In saying that I would think about my decision I had merely copied Mother's evasiveness, or fallen victim to the Martinique habit of deferring until tomorrow.

Nothing was said for a week.

At almost every game he ever played my step-father would cheat if he could, less for the joy of winning than for the delight he took in pointing out afterwards how he had outwitted everybody. In chess it is not easy to cheat, but it is easy to lose by missing opportunities.

He and I were playing in a small room to one side of the larger one where other, noisier games were going on; and I let him win because now the week was up and the time had come for me to speak. I wanted to put him in a good humour to start with. Instead I made him irritable and he said, 'What is the matter with you? You're playing like a novice.'

A good opening.

'I have something on my mind,' I said. 'The week's grace is expended and I have to tell you that I cannot marry Louis.'

He said, 'Oh, so that's it. Now we know where we are.' He pushed the table so that the pieces fell over and some rolled to the floor. 'Why not?'

'I have no feeling for him – except that I have no wish to marry him.'

'Because of his health? You see yourself saddled with an invalid? Believe me, Louis's ills are largely imaginary. He has great potential – not so far realised. Ill health is his alibi. Married to – yes, I think it safe to say – the most eligible young woman in the world, and given responsibility, he will be a different man. Hortense, I know men. I know Louis. I brought him up. I know you, too. Your happiness and well-being closely concern me. Nothing – certainly no political consideration – would have made me suggest this had I thought you ill-suited. I rebuffed that English duke and that German prince on your behalf; neither of them knew what a book was. Louis does and with you that should count in his favour.'

It should have, but did not. Louis had written, and published, a novel, *Marie or the Pains of Love*, which I had found sentimental to the point of sickliness, and more than a little tasteless since it was a thinly disguised account of his abortive affaire with my cousin Emilie whom he had abandoned without protest.

It was all of a piece with something difficult to put a name to. It had evidenced itself in a small way, over the plays we organised at Malmaison. Louis, offered a minor part, refused outright; offered a major role he would say he would perform if he felt well enough. When it came to the point he always did, but he missed, or was late for, most rehearsals and when he did come invariably demanded some complete alteration to suit himself, his damaged knee, his ailing arm.

I said, 'I am sure everything was taken into consideration. But the fact remains, I cannot, I will not marry Louis.'

He said, 'You *must*. Listen …' I listened. He said nothing new.

It was all just as Mother had explained a week ago; his need, France's need for a boy, a Bonaparte. I listened as one does to a tale twice told. I thought, as I had done all this week … Joseph had daughters but was not yet too old to beget a son; Lucien had daughters, and as his good, sensible wife, the daughter of an inn-keeper, was dead, he could marry again; Jerome was still very young and Louis, being free, might make some other woman a good husband.

Why me?

'Louis's son would be a Bonaparte whoever he married,' I said when my step-father ended his argument.

'But I want *his* son to be *your* son. This child will be my heir. Surely you can see … I esteem you very highly, Hortense. *Your* child, with *my* name. Failing a son of my own what better could I ask?'

The words were ordinary enough, but his voice and his look had a compelling urgency, not precisely frightening, but upsetting, embarrassing. I remembered Adèle saying that I might find this difficult to get out of. It was being difficult in a way that I had not foreseen. My heart was hammering and when I spoke I sounded breathless.

'I value your esteem. Within reason I would do anything to please you. But I cannot marry Louis.'

To have an excuse for looking away I began to right the fallen chessmen. He reached out and took me by the wrist.

He said, 'Has nothing I have said …' Then a terrible thing happened. His face turned ashen, his eyes seemed to bulge, his whole body went rigid. The fit or whatever it was communicated itself to me through his fingers, now so hard-clenched on my wrist that I bore the bruises for a fortnight. It was a vibration that seemed to shake the marrow of the bones.

I thought – He is dying; I have killed him! The cataleptic grip on my wrist prevented me from moving. I tried to call and could not. I could only sit there and share something much worse than pain.

It lasted perhaps a minute in countable time. Then his hand relaxed and fell away. He wiped his face, streaming with sweat. Mine was wet, too.

'Now you know … Nobody knows.'

'What is it?'

'Nothing. A very mild form of epilepsy. I very rarely … and not without warning. You're not to say a word, mind you.'

'Oh no; Would you like some water? Some wine?' I wanted to get away, from him, from the little room, from the memory of this inexplicable thing that we had shared, and which I could never speak about.

'No. And there is no need to look so frightened, child. Alexander the Greek had it, so did Julius Caesar – it is the commanders' curse. Now, we were talking about you and Louis. Are you going to refuse me the only thing I ever asked of you?'

'I must. I'm sorry.'

'Now that you know how much it means to me? To your Mother. To France.'

I suppose that virtually I began to yield then. Something inside me had given way and there was no support from without. The one person who might have understood – and helped me – my brother Eugène – was in Italy. Adèle understood but was helpless, resigned to the inevitable from the start. Mother began to come into my bedroom in the middle of the night – 'Darling, I simply cannot sleep, I am so worried.' Once she said, weeping, that Lucien Bonaparte, who had been to Spain on some diplomatic mission, was back with a lyrical wordy description and a portrait of a young Spanish infanta who would only too readily marry the First Consul of France once he was divorced.

That night I said, 'Mother, would it matter so much? We could go and live in peace at Malmaison.' She had so often expressed a preference for private life.

She said, 'You are like your father, utterly heartless.'

Then one day Madame Campan, for whom I had always felt a great affection and admiration, made a call and steered the talk on to the subject of marriage. I hated to think that she had been primed. She did not mention Louis by name and everything she said applied as equally to Adèle who was there, as to me. She had seen many marriages, she said, and the happiest were those arranged by parents, on a solid basis of suitability, compatibility, as in the taking of a business partner. Romantic attachments simply led to disillusion in her experience. Since Adèle, at least so far as I knew, had never had a romantic attachment, and I certainly had not, the remark seemed irrelevant. What she said next was not; it was a generalisation, but spoken with authority.

'The main purpose of marriage is the begetting of children. In one's children one lives again.'

Adèle and I were both eighteen. Nobody had yet made her a serious offer; those made to me had been rebuffed; we were both approaching the end of our eligible time and the remark seemed unkind, setting such a value upon something that neither of us might ever have. Before she left she managed to bring the conversation – or rather her monologue – round to the subject of duty, saying that she very much hoped that no girl of hers would ever shirk from her duty, once it had been pointed out to her.

And then, to complete my sense of being like a besieged city, beset on every side and with dwindling resources, Louis Bonaparte began to pay me marked attention. In public and in family gatherings he was never far from my side, he paid me stiff little compliments, discovered that he too had a liking for musk and that his knee was now well enough to enable him to dance. For my part I discovered that Mother's theory about a thing *being* so if firmly enough assumed to *be* so was not without basis. Everyone assumed that Louis was paying court to me, everybody, Louis included, assumed that his attentions were welcome. My own inertia contributed to give this impression and although inside me a remnant of common sense screamed its protest and urged me to escape while I could, almost before I knew it, it was too late. Mother was saying that she knew I should not fail her; my stepfather said that nothing in his life had ever made him so happy.

Louis asked me to marry him during a ball at Malmaison, early in December. He sounded very loving, and also rather humble and diffident. By this time I had argued myself into believing – not that I was in love with him, but that for me the kind of love one read about would remain abstract, purely a thing of the mind. Had I been capable of it, I thought, I should have felt it by now, well on into my nineteenth year. In default it seemed reasonable to accept a man who appeared to be in love with me, who had definitely improved upon closer acquaintance, and whom everybody wished me to marry …

Everywhere, except in my mind, joy exploded. The very same papers which only three years ago had attacked the morals of both Bonaparte and Mother, turned on full floods of flattery and sentiment over another Bonaparte marrying another Beauharnais. Congratulations and good wishes and presents began to pour in. The presents in their number and value were proof positive that my step-father was no longer regarded as a successful soldier who had reached high state office. In all but name he was monarch, his brother and his step-daughter, by association, royal. Mother ordered me a wedding dress of great splendour; my step-father gave me a magnificent parure of diamonds with earrings to match, miniature chandeliers.

10

Louis and I were married on 3rd January, 1802, so our engagement was brief and during it Louis had played the lover to perfection; on any day when we did not meet he sent me flowers and letters, often including little poems, trite – but one should not be over-critical. When, about four days before the wedding, Louis seemed to change a little I thought – He is nervous, too! Or his rheumatism, always worse in winter, is troubling him.

On the day of the wedding – we were to have a civil ceremony early in the evening and then, because my step-father had recently made a Concordat with the Pope which restored France to the Catholic Church without giving priests any political power or returning the property which, before the Revolution, the Church had owned, we were to have a religious ceremony as well, I looked at the resplendent wedding dress, hastily but beautifully made, of white satin, embroidered all over by little skilled women, blinking and yawning and something – a kind of repulsion – came over me. I thought – It may be necessary to kill the calf, to put a wreath around its neck … No! So I wore to my wedding a plain white silk dress and the string of pearls which Mother had sent me from Italy.

At the civil ceremony Bonaparte's fellow Consuls acted as witnesses; then we drove to The Tuileries where an altar had been set up, and were married by Cardinal Capara. Caroline and Joachim Murat shared the nuptial blessing which had been unavailable to them when they were married.

Brought up in a godless age, almost literally the product of the Age of Reason, I had not expected the one ceremony to mean more than the other, yet it did. I stood there and understood the meaning of marriage and I beat off the feeling of being fraudulent by making up my mind that Louis should never know that I did not love him and had married him because I was weak and the pressure upon me strong. Hundreds of people, I reminded myself, married every day for reasons totally disassociated from emotion, and they seemed to manage. I would do better, I thought; I would behave as though for me Louis was the one man in the world, the one I had chosen. I would be loyal, faithful, amiable and never by word or deed betray the fact that in me something was lacking.

What was lacking I knew from seeing Caroline and Joachim. Their quarrels were notorious, they were both high-tempered and violent, they had been known to throw plates at one another in a rage. But they were in love … I thrust that thought aside; some people can walk tight-ropes, I thought, turn somersaults, foresee the future: and some people fall in love. Never having been so was, in the circumstances, an advantage.

Nothing so far as I, in my ignorance, could judge, went wrong between us when we bedded. Louis was experienced and I possibly no more awkward than the average virgin bride. It did once occur to me to think that he wished I were Emilie and that perhaps this accounted for a certain lack of enthusiasm, as well as for his glum mood the last few days. The idea that to him I was second best caused me no pain at all.

His spirits were no higher in the morning and he grumbled because we were to dine at The Tuileries. 'I've a good mind to send an excuse,' he said. I asked if he were feeling unwell; he said he was all right, so then I ventured to say, 'They are leaving for Lyons in the morning. Perhaps we should say goodbye.'

At Lyons Bonaparte was to meet some Italian statesmen to discuss the setting up of a Republic in Italy, and now Louis said, sardonically, 'Unless they keep their wits about them they'll be offering him the crown.'

No more was said on the subject and when the time came we dressed and drove from the Rue de la Victoire – my step-father had given us the house there as part of his wedding present – to The Tuileries, where Mother embraced me and whispered, 'All right?' – a question which I answered with a smile and a nod. My step-father pinched my cheek and said I looked as though marriage agreed with me. At that I blushed and he said to Louis, 'You are fortunate to have married a sweet girl who can blush.'

Louis received this remark in silence and there was a second or two of rather awkward silence before Mother hurried in with one of her smoothing-over remarks. 'Alas, my blushing days were over before we met, Bonaparte.' He then touched her cheek and said, 'You do very well with the rouge, my dear.' We then went in to dinner, just the four of us.

Presently Louis said, 'Madame Bonaparte, would you give me a complete list of all your Beauharnais relatives? I think they should be informed of our marriage.'

Bonaparte said, 'But everyone has been informed. Not merely the Beauharnais family. I instructed the various ambassadors. Yours was no private marriage, my boy. It was an affair of state.' The words may have been a little pompous, but his manner was genial. Louis laid down his knife and fork and said angrily, 'You should have told me. You may be head of this state, you are not yet head of the family.'

'I know that. With our mother and Joseph still alive – and long may they live.'

Mother said, 'I have been thinking. We shall be away for some time. Would you like to spend your honeymoon at Malmaison?'

The question was addressed to me, but before I could most joyfully accept, Louis said, 'Thank you; no. The country in mid-winter does not appeal to me.'

'But the house is so warm. I took care of that. I should think it is the warmest house in Europe.'

'The whole place is like a hot-house,' my step-father said.

'And some very curious things grow in hot-houses,' Louis said, making the inoffensive remark sound as though it meant something obscure.

'Oh yes; indeed they do,' Mother said brightly. 'You would be astonished at the gifts I receive, seeds or cuttings from the ends of the earth. Once one is known to have a hobby … Even English sea-captains send me things. And it is a curious thing – every plant I deal with myself seems to flourish.'

'So I have observed,' Louis said, again with that undertone.

The evening jarred on. Apart from Louis's first protest absolutely nothing was said which, reported word for word or written down word for word, could convey any idea of the unpleasantness of the atmosphere. The time came to leave – Mother and Bonaparte were to make an early start in the morning. Louis said, 'I wish you a safe journey, Nablione. Rumour has it that you will come back not as President of the Cisalpine Republic but as King of Italy.'

Up to that moment my step-father had shown either an uncharacteristic deafness to barbed remarks or that astounding patience which he exercised towards all his family, but when Louis said that he gave the barking little laugh which I knew was often a sign of his displeasure.

'I don't take crowns,' he said. 'I shall give them. Be a good boy, Louis, and you shall have one. One day.'

On the way home Louis said, as though arguing, though I had not said a word: 'Oh yes, I know he did everything for me. The moment he had his miserable sub-lieutenant's pay, he sent for me, kept me. He mended my boots, patched my clothes, cooked wretched little meals in a pan over a smoky fire. But he treated me like a dog. I was his first *subject*. Once he caught me reading Rousseau when I should have been studying and he treated me like a delinquent private soldier; bread and water, sleep on boards for forty-eight hours. And that was years ago. Now he is insufferable, he has even given France back to God!'

I had kept myself quiet during the evening, a little unsure, answering when spoken to, proffering trivial, innocuous remarks. Now something seemed to be required of me, some words sympathetic to Louis, derogatory of Bonaparte, and they just would not be spoken. So I evaded the issue by asking where this happened, and how old he was at the time, and which of Rousseau's books he had been reading.

Back home I went into my bedroom where my maid was waiting to help me undress. Waists – and therefore corsets – were back in fashion again, and I was half-unlaced when Louis came through the door that led to his dressing room. Aware that my undressing had reached its least attractive stage I snatched up a shawl and flung it round me.

Louis said to the girl, 'You may go. I can give madame any further help she needs.' He sounded amiable again; the girl simpered a little. As soon as she had gone he said, very angrily, 'Don't you know better than to act the prude in front of your husband? What will that girl think? You know how they talk. They'll be saying you don't love me. That you were forced to marry me.'

The attack seemed so unwarranted, and was so sudden, coming on top of a spoiled evening – the last I should spend with Mother for some time – that I began to cry.

'Were you?'

'What?'

'Forced to marry me?'

'Who could have forced me? I'm not a slave.'

I had the horrible idea that my step-father might have let slip some reference to my reluctance. I reached for my handkerchief and the silk shawl slipped. There I stood, wearing a half-laced corset, and very little else.

'Did you wish to marry me?'

I had always been considered quick-witted and apt with words. Now I was confused, fumbling.

'As soon as I was sure that you wished to marry me. A girl,' I said, 'can't go about with her heart on her sleeve.'

He considered that and then said, 'No. Of course. There. I'm sorry I made you cry.' I had the lunatic notion that he was not sorry at all, glad rather. But he helped me to finish undressing and said, 'I came in to say that we'll go to Malmaison if you wish.'

'You decide, Louis. Truly I don't mind at all.'

'We'll go,' he said. 'We'll make a foursome of it. You bring Adèle and I'll bring Jean Coustan.'

That suggestion pleased me. I had not been quite sure what difference my marriage would make to the old friendship between Adèle and me; three is an awkward number.

'That would be perfect,' I said.

It could have been. Captain Coustan was young, supremely amiable, rather stupid. Some snow fell, enough to transform the garden and the country-side into a fairyland place but not enough to prevent us taking long walks or driving, which suited Louis better. One evening Madame Campan invited us all to St Germain. She had provided a supper which I am sure she could ill afford and afterwards the girls staged an entertainment, all centred around me, things I had done, or written, even my verse about the cod; even my winning – and so quickly losing – the Rose for Virtue. A rather small girl came on to the stage wearing a rose of pink paper so huge that she was almost invisible. She chanted:

> *I am Hortense Beauharnais,*
> *I wore the rose for one whole day.*
> *Where it went to no one knows.*
> *Welcome Hortense! Goodbye rose!*

She then pulled or released whatever held the petals in place so that they scattered. There was laughter, in which I joined. Everyone knew that I had been the last to win and wear that rose which had never actually been replaced; after that catastrophe the rose had become purely symbolic, some words – 'The Rose for Virtue has been awarded to so-and-so, whose name is entered in the list.'

Louis stood up abruptly and said, 'We must go.'

In the carriage he said, 'I shall never go there again.'

I was becoming accustomed to his changes of mood, so sudden that in another man, one would have thought – drunk, sober; but Louis, careful of his delicate stomach, hardly drank at all.

'You mustn't be too hard on them, Louis,' Captain Coustan said. 'Poor little dears, they did their best.'

'The usual excuse for poor performance and bad taste,' Louis said and did not speak again all the way home.

Next evening we stayed at home. Louis sat by the fire, reading; Adèle and I were working at some embroidery; Jean Coustan was at the table, trying out some puzzles, metal links and loops which, with cunning and sleight of hand, could be made to take certain patterns. The one he worked at should have ended as one ring with others on it, like a chatelaine's keys, but in his hands it went wrong and ended as a series of links, like a dog collar. In order not to disturb Louis who seemed to be engrossed in his book, Jean reached out, touched Adèle on the arm, motioned to her to draw my attention, held up the chain with a grimace, put it round his neck and mimed 'Bow-wow!' We both laughed and Adèle, less careful of Louis than I was said, 'It did that to me when I first tried it. I'll show …'

Louis closed his book with a bang and said, 'I am going to bed.' He went, leaving us feeling a little silly, more than a little guilty.

Jean Coustan said, 'I suppose if you're reading … I never tried it myself. For pleasure, I mean…' Adèle gave me a long look.

Across the bed in which we might or might not indulge in what people call connubial relationships, Louis said, 'What do you take me for?'

'I don't know what you mean by that, Louis. The noise? We were very sorry to have disturbed you.'

'Only women of light morals make mock of their husbands.'

Absolutely astounded I said, 'But we were not mocking *you*. We weren't even laughing *at* Captain Coustan. He laughed at himself and we shared his amusement.'

'You saw the symbol and laughed.'

'What symbol?'

'The collar. You may as well know that if you insist upon humiliating me I shall leave you.'

Half of me cried – Do that, the sooner the better; you spoil everything! The other half thought about the gossip and the scandal, about Mother and Bonaparte coming back to find a marriage ended almost before it had begun.

I said, 'Honestly, Louis, I do not know what you are talking about. I seem to offend you without wishing to, without even knowing why. What have I done? How have I humiliated you?'

'That remains to be seen.'

'And what does that mean? Louis, please tell me. What have I done; or said …'

'We shall see,' he said cryptically. He went off and slept in his dressing room.

I said, 'Adèle, I am beginning to think that he is not quite right in the head. He looks so wild and is – incoherent. Can you see anything symbolic about that collar?'

'Yes. Marriage. He has been rather spoiled, you know. Never having to care or even think about anybody but himself. He probably finds the responsibility difficult to face up to. Settling down, it takes a little time.'

She spoke with a deliberate soothing manner which in fact did anything but soothe.

'Is that sufficient reason for trying to pick quarrels with me? For saying things that don't make sense. And if he finds marriage such a responsibility, how will he act when he hears that he is to be a father?'

It was a rough-handed way of imparting such news. Adèle turned pale, her eyes widened and darkened.

'Not yet, surely. Less than a month …'

'Ten days overdue.' She looked confused.

'I believe,' she said, 'that just being married … can disturb!'

'I thought that – for a day or two, but now …'

Adèle said, 'Darling, what am I thinking of? I should have said – How lovely! And congratulated you and wished you well. I do, I do. You took me by surprise. And think how delighted your parents will be!'

'That was the aim of the whole thing,' I said.

By March, when I decided to tell Louis and Mother and my step-father, I was feeling better about everything. The baby would be mine, something to love, both a justification and a compensation for a marriage made joyless by Louis's unpredictable moods. There would be short spells when I thought that we had at least achieved friendliness, and then over some trivial things, or even over nothing at all, he would turn surly and either maintain a sulky silence or say hurtful things.

In March I was at least enlightened, with a shock which almost lost me the baby.

I said, 'Louis, if all goes well I shall have a baby in October.' It had been one of our friendly days and I thought I had chosen my opportunity well.

'What time in October?'

'I cannot tell exactly. Fairly early in the month, I think.'

That wild look came over him.

'If that child is born *one day* too soon, I shall disown it and leave you forever.'

My heart stopped, and my breathing; my mind stayed active just long enough to think – This is death! After that, nothing.

It was so momentary that Louis did not notice and when I – no, not I, but a Hortense irrevocably changed – could see and feel, he stood just as he had, glaring at me.

I said, 'And who is supposed to have forestalled you?'

'Nablione.'

'And you don't know a virgin when you bed with one?'

'It can be feigned.'

'Go away,' I said. 'I am about to be sick.'

So far I had done well, a faint queasiness on waking, but now I was sick as nobody ever was on dry land. Between spasms I thought – I did not deny it; I did not defend myself; I behaved like a guilty woman. The thought nause-ated me again. Then I thought – No child can survive in a body so racked and wrenched; I shall be left with nothing, and it is all Louis's fault. For a little while the full enormity of what he had said escaped me. I was simply

68

angry with him for having believed it and repeated it to me and thus made me ill. Then as I realised the implications I understood everything, even Adèle's look of dismay. I bore in mind that the subject of an ugly rumour is always the last to hear it. So now everyone in France knew. Presently I was able to be sorry for Louis even while still blaming him for over-credulity.

I had told him on Friday because I intended to break the news to Mother at the routine Sunday supper gathering of the Family, a thing no Bonaparte within reach of Paris would miss, acrimonious as such meetings often were. I knew that Mother found them trying and I had imagined myself whispering the news to her so that she could gloat over it in secret and then at a likely moment impart it to my step-father. Now I felt that I could not face the Clan. I had every excuse for lethargy; I would write Mother a note and ask Adèle to place it in Louis's dressing room.

She took it and said, 'Hortense, we have been friends for eight years and it is as a friend that I speak. You must not stay skulking here.' I had announced my intention of keeping to my bed, or at least my room.

'You must get up and out-face them and everybody else. If you take to your bed now, or shun company, you countenance the lie. They'll say you are so far gone as not to be fit to be seen.

It is the most horrible situation and you are the last person it should have happened to – but there is no justice in this world. And yet … well, in a way there is. You better than most can do this, carry it off, if you make up your mind to. Come on, up you get. I will help you dress.'

The face in the glass was different; as though I had lived ten years since Friday, or been at death's door. What had been considered pretty and girl-ish, the gloss, the curves that hide indecision and an unwelcome marriage had left virtually untouched, because I still retained a little hope that duty brought its own reward, were gone now. After the first recoil I took heart. Prettiness, ebbing away, had left a kind of beauty. I thought, inconsequently, that one day I should look, not like my own mother – a rose gently fading – but like *theirs*, that rocky old Corsican.

'You must look *splendid*,' Adèle said. 'This is to be a great moment.' So she prepared me to look splendid. Fastening the diamond parure, the wedding gift that I had not worn at my wedding, Adèle said, 'He is back …' I halted in the fixing of an earring and heard Louis moving about in the next room. Not man enough to stay away from the brother he thought had cuckolded him and the wife who had lost her virginity before marriage. Not man enough to face me even to ask how I was.

I opened the door between the two rooms, this time catching him at a disadvantage. He had evidently been in the process of changing his shirt when he saw my note and now stood, half-naked, with the paper in his hand. With his hair ruffled, his torso bare, he looked oddly vulnerable. I said, more gently than I intended to speak, 'I feel better and intend to go, after all.'

'Very well. Excuse me, I am late as it is.'

I sat down on the end of the bed; I said, 'Louis, I swear your suspicion is absolutely unfounded. I swear this child is yours. I intend to tell Bonaparte this evening how vilely we have both been traduced, ask him to add his denial to mine and see that the person who started the rumour goes to gaol.'

'It was Lucien who warned me. Too late. Four days before the wedding. And if you mention it to Napoleon I shall divorce you at once. With the maximum of publicity. The people who believe that our sister Pauline was his mistress won't boggle over you.'

That left me completely speechless. We drove in silence to The Tuileries, where, as I had planned, I told Mother who immediately told Bonaparte. He informed everybody by embracing me and making a great fuss. Then he said, 'Mind it's a boy, Hortense. If it is a girl I shall disown her.'

Louis said, waspishness wrapped in jocularity, 'But, Nablione, even you would find that a trifle difficult. Unless you pass a new law making it legal for a man to disown what belongs to another man.'

My step-father laughed, neither too soon, nor too heartily.

He said, 'You have me there, Louis. I should have said that if it's a girl we'll ear-mark a good husband for her and hope for better luck next time.'

Madame Bonaparte said in her faulty, nasal French, 'A boy it will be, Nablione. One can always tell. Did I tell you, Caroline? A boy I said, a boy it was.'

'*How* can you tell?' my step-father asked.

'That Hortense should be here tonight. The little boys are so good, so not troublesome, almost to the end. Then they are hard to bear and hard to rear. It is in balance.' She moved her work-worn, but elegant hands in an eloquent gesture. 'I should know,' she said.

11

One hears of things so tragic or so cruel that one thinks – I could never have lived through that! Certainly if someone had told me, on the eve of my wedding, how it would turn out I should have said – I cannot bear it, and run away. But it had happened, and I bore it, and by June I was not only bearing the situation, I was indifferent to it. The placidity of advancing pregnancy wrapped me round and I became impervious to Louis's moods. They were not invariably bad. Sometimes for as long as three days on end anyone could have kept us under the closest observation and seen and heard nothing to hint that we were not a most mundane married couple awaiting a baby; then he would get upset about something and turn sour.

In May he decided to go to a watering-place, Barèges in the Pyrenees and take a cure. He was insistent that I should go with him. Then I did stir from my lethargy and protested that jolting over roads well known to be bad, would not be suitable to my condition.

'Are you afraid of being out of reach of Dr Baudeloque?' Dr Baudeloque had been chosen as my obstetrician; he was supposed to be the best in France – that was in the world. He had already told me that the baby would be born in the first half of October. Louis knew that so the question was deliberately insulting. I ignored it. Afterwards it did occur to me to wonder whether Louis had believed Lucien to the point of expecting the baby to be born before October and wished it to be born somewhere at a distance and with some excuse for being premature. Fortunately both Mother and my step-father protested so much, the one vociferously, the other with authority, that Louis went alone, and I moved back to The Tuileries and to Malmaison where old servants often forgot that I was Madame Louis and called me Mademoiselle Hortense. This gave me an obscure pleasure; and then I would think – how perverse, to be eagerly looking forward to one's baby and yet wishing oneself unmarried.

When Louis returned – depressed because the cure had done him no good – we did not go back to what had been Mother's little house. My step-father had bought us another, larger one, in the same street; 'more of a family house', as he expressed it.

There were other changes, too. The decision to make Bonaparte First Consul for life, with the privilege of naming his heir, had been taken and the date for the public announcement fixed – 15th August, his thirty-third birthday. He was also given the palace of St Cloud as a summer residence, Malmaison being considered no longer large enough or grand enough.

'So this,' Mother said, speaking of the birthday party she was planning, 'will be the last time Malmaison will be used as anything but a private residence and I am very glad. It will seem more like home.'

I was a little dubious about attending this party. Bulk had come upon me suddenly, and though Mother's own dress maker, Leroy, had designed me some deceptive dresses, my condition was obvious.

'From things that Bonaparte has said about other women I gather that he does not care to see pregnant women. Aesthetically, he is right,' I said.

'He does not feel that way about you, darling. In fact he said the other evening that whereas most women look horrible you grew lovelier. Like a flower, he said. You must come. It is his birthday; and there is so much to celebrate.'

So I went and after supper, when the dancing began, I found myself sharing a sofa with the Second Consul, Monsieur Cambaceres, a notorious glutton. Beside him, even now, I was sylphlike. He had actually had a piece carved out of his private dining table to accommodate his bulk. The sofa stood by the windows, all wide open on this warm night and the scent of stocks and other flowers most sweet after dark, drifted in. The music made conversation a little difficult and quite unnecessary; after a few civilities Cambaceres was content to sit and digest and I was content to sit and watch the dancing, noting the subtle little differences in steps and styles that had developed since I last danced.

Then Bonaparte, who did not dance, came and stood by the sofa. Cambaceres wallowed to his feet. Bonaparte did not sit down. He stood and said, 'Not dancing, Hortense?'

I laughed. 'It would take Atlas to partner me now.'

'And here he is.' He jerked his head and a most enormous young man approached and bowed. Six foot four at least and not, like many tall men, lanky and ill-put together.

'You've been shirking your duty, Mac,' Bonaparte said. 'My daughter wishes to dance. Take her twice round the floor, carefully. Come on, Hortense. Exercise is good.' He held out his hands, lifted me from the sofa and gave me into the giant's arms.

I had never felt so conspicuous in my life. I was sorry for the young man, too; not properly introduced, given such an extraordinary order. He behaved as though he had been told to carry a very frail basket of eggs — some already cracked — through a crowded market place full of people intent upon smashing them all. I could not even make up for my slowness and heaviness by sprightly conversation, his head was far above me. We went round the perimeter of the room twice, as bidden, and back to the sofa where my step-father waited.

Next morning the *Journal de Paris*, in a fulsome account of the celebratory party, included the remark that Madame Louis Bonaparte, despite being seven months pregnant, had taken part in the dancing.

'Give Nablione his due, he is a strategist,' Louis said. 'The English papers have been saying that the child was already born.'

'One can hardly blame them,' I said. 'When those who know the truth can be so suspicious.'

My baby was born on 10th October. A boy, as Madame Bonaparte had predicted, and as she had said of boys, 'hard to bear'.

Everybody, even Adèle – though I suspected her of trying to build for the future – praised Louis's behaviour. I was aware of him, every now and again as I struggled, biting my hand, or the sheet in an attempt not to scream; he looked white-faced and distressed. Dr Baudeloque muttered that devoted husbands were a nuisance at such times; the midwife said she had never seen a husband suffer so much.

At last it was over and Mother, who had been with me throughout, said, 'Darling, it's a boy. A lovely little boy,' and shed a few beautiful tears.

When Louis came in the midwife said proudly, 'A boy, monsieur. Here is our Dauphin.'

'Never use that word,' Louis snapped and turned and went out.

Afterwards Mother tried to explain away this odd behaviour. 'I think Louis felt the word ill-omened. That poor little boy …' The last Dauphin of France had died in the Temple prison seven years earlier; some said of a long standing illness, some said of ill-treatment. Very ardent Royalists believed that he had been smuggled out and replaced by a deaf-mute boy already dying.

I thought, as all mothers do, that my baby was the most beautiful ever born. I lay in bed surrounded by loving care – except from Louis who disappeared for two days – with flowers, presents, letters of congratulation and good wishes. After two days I was allowed visitors and the first was my step-father, beside himself with joy. He must hold the baby and did so, with an awkward kind of tenderness that was touching, looked at the soft unformed features and declared that here was a true Bonaparte and said that he must be named Napoleon Charles. Charles was the name of the man who had fathered the Family.

That was the beginning of the wrangling, doomed to go on, changing ground but not essence.

First the name. Louis contested, rightly, that a firstborn son should bear his father's name; the baby should be called Louis Charles. When it came to the registering Louis actually wrote 'Louis...' and Bonaparte snatched the pen, crossed out that word and wrote 'Napoleon Charles'.

I lay back in post-delivery euphoria and thought of the child as Baby and now and then savoured the irony. Louis once so anxious to repudiate ...

Mother had found me an excellent wet-nurse, a solid healthy peasant woman who had borne twins, breast fed them both and then, a month before my baby was born had had another child. She had, I swear, milk for four. When her own Marie and my Napoleon Charles had fed so full that the milk dribbled out of their mouths she would squeeze her breasts and the milk would still run.

The time was not long past when for a woman above the line of absolute poverty to breast-feed her own child would have been unthinkable, but times had changed, it was now the fashionable thing to do. Fashionable or not, I would have done it had I been able. It would have extended for a little while that communion which birth severed. But my chest had produced nothing but a stupid little hacking cough.

I was grateful to Mother for having found me such a good human milch cow, so when she said that she had found the perfect governess I made only the faintest protest. 'A little early,' I said.

'Oh, not a teacher,' Mother said, 'a controller of the nursery. To oversee everything. Madame de Boubers has had such a sad life and she is so proud. To take charity irks her. She would do anything. In fact at this minute she is doing some menial job. I forget what, there are so many of them.'

There were so many of them. Royalists who had fled from the Revolution drifted back and found things changed; the houses they had lived in either burnt or dropping through decay into ruin, their acres alienated. That Mother was extravagant nobody could deny, but how much she gave away to such people, nobody, not even I could ever reckon. Ever since my stepfather came back from Egypt, Mother had been beset by petitioners wanting some little post or place, or a loan to start a business.

I agreed to see Madame de Boubers. No more than that. She had an air of quiet competence, unusual in many of Mother's protégées and her manner was neither supercilious nor sycophantic. She was looking for a post, she said, but would only undertake the one I offered if allowed a reasonably free hand. 'I have my own ideas about bringing up children. Regular hours, plenty of fresh air, good plain food. I believe in kindness, but not in indulgence.'

'And no interference?' I asked, smiling.

'Well, if the parents say one thing and the governess another the result is confusion.'

I engaged her.

The question of the name having been settled – somewhat high-handedly – the matter of the formal adoption came up. Here Louis refused to yield and I agreed with him in so far as I wished to have control of my own child.

'But, my dear girl, it would be the merest formality,' my step-father said. 'Should I dream of taking your child from you, or usurping your authority? It's just that I want the thing tied up. You must speak to Louis and make him see sense. When war breaks out again, as it inevitably must, I want to leave a tidy situation behind me.'

Louis gave me no chance to speak on the subject; before I had said half a sentence he said, 'Tell him, if he wants a son, to get one of his own.'

Spoken in private that was excusable; but Louis said it again, more vehemently, in circumstances which made it unforgivable.

We are all at The Tuileries. Poor Madame de Boubers' freedom from interference had not lasted long. When the First Consul said, 'Bring the baby,' rules about regularity went overboard. In the palace a room adjourning the private dining room had been fitted as a night nursery, with a crib, far more elaborate than the one at home, a comfortable chair for the governess, a table at which she could take her meals and – a typical Bonaparte touch – a lamp with a shade, opaque on the side towards the crib, transparent on the other. Full fed and sound asleep, Napoleon Charles would be transported, laid in the crib and left until my step-father said, 'Bring the baby.' He liked him asleep, but preferred him awake and would gently pummel him until he roused.

'At this stage perhaps it does not matter so much. He soon goes to sleep again. Later on it will mean trouble,' Madame de Boubers said. But even she, I noticed, did not put up the resistance that she would have done had Louis or I proposed to show off the baby at our table, after bedtime.

That there was an element of showing off in Bonaparte's attitude towards Napoleon Charles even I could not deny. Mixed up with a genuine affection there were other elements; possessiveness and a desire to tease by the provoking of that emotion so prevalent in the Family as to need no provocation, jealousy.

On this particular evening the family gathering was smaller than usual; just Madame Bonaparte, Caroline and Joachim Murat, Louis, myself.

When bidden I fetched the baby, telling Madame de Boubers we would go home as soon as possible. My step-father took him, woke him, said, 'There, you see, he knows me already. Isn't he beautiful? And intelligent? And what a proper little Bonaparte!'

There he deceived himself. At the age of three months Napoleon Charles was beginning to look far more like Eugène than anyone. His hair was fair, his eyes a greyish blue and his whole head and face more squarish than that of any Bonaparte.

Caroline said, 'My Achille at that age was bigger.'

'But not so forward,' Bonaparte said. He cleared a space on the table, laid the baby on it and rolled him gently to and fro. 'Now, Louis, what about it. My adopted son and the next … First Consul of France, eh?' There was the slightest possible hesitation before the title.

Louis said, elaborately casual, 'Nablione, you should learn to listen. I said no and I meant it. If you'd listened to advice years ago you'd now have a boy of your own.'

The inference was obvious and Mother sat there.

Madame Bonaparte intervened. She snapped her fingers and broke into a tirade in Italian, turning her dark shining eyes from one son to another. The rapid, angry words dropped like stones. Mother, wearing her stricken look, glanced at me and then away again. Murat reached out a long arm and moved a branched candlestick away from where the baby, momentarily abandoned, rolled.

My step-father, if not yet the most powerful then certainly the most talked-about man in the world, listened to the old woman's speech with the same look of naughty-boy-caught-out, as did Louis. She ended with a sharp rap of her knuckles on the table and sat back.

Louis said, 'Very well then.'

Caroline, with a courtesy one hardly expected of her, looked at Mother, Joachim and me, sitting together, and said, 'She said they were not to quarrel.' It had taken a great many words to say that much.

'I shall go to Italy,' Louis said.

'The sun will be good for you,' my step-father said.

'Taking my wife and child.'

'Not long since you taunted me about making laws to suit myself,' my step-father said. 'I could pass one forbidding the export of any French child and have you stopped at the frontier.'

No more was said about adoption, or Italy. Louis decided to try the waters at Montpellier and did not even suggest taking us. Just as he left, in fact the carriage was waiting, he said, 'You must promise me something. Never to spend a night at St Cloud.'

If he meant what I thought, why St Cloud especially and not Malmaison? I did not ask, lest that should be included in the embargo. So I promised and found it difficult to keep my word. My step-father insisted that Napoleon

Charles should accompany me in order to be exhibited, no longer to the family only, but to ambassadors, high officials and foreign visitors. Mother could never understand why I must drive back to Paris, sometimes late at night, sometimes in bad weather and Madame de Boubers grumbled. My excuses sounded fatuous, an appointment early next morning with dressmaker, hairdresser, music master. Mother would say why did I not arrange things better, or why not send a message, but I kept my word until a day in March.

It was a beautiful day, warm and sunny. My step-father, having neglected his lunch in order to play with the baby, said to Mother and me, 'Get your things on. I'll have a holiday this afternoon and take you for a drive.'

We went down to find that he had meant this literally; he was in the driving seat of the low open carriage, a new one called the English carriage because it was a style of vehicle made popular by the influx of visitors from across the Channel. It was drawn by two perfectly matched black horses.

We had a pleasant drive. Bonaparte was in high spirits, pretending to be a coachman, calling us 'Madame', asking Mother if she would give him a good reference and how about a rise in pay. All silly perhaps, but harmless, and an example of how he could throw off the cares of state and revert to youth.

Within sight of the palace again he suddenly lashed the horses into a wild gallop and Mother called, 'Not so fast or you will get no reference at all …' He took no notice and we approached the gateway at a speed far too fast. The right-hand side of the carriage struck the stone pillar; there was a check and a jolt that threw him from his seat and Mother and me together as the carriage, its wheels splintered, sagged.

Nimbler than she was I climbed out and reached him first and saw that he would have been flung farther but for the fact that he still held the reins. In that cataleptic grip that I remembered. Instinctively I bent over him, hiding him. I called to her, 'Fetch somebody. He isn't hurt.' The horses were plunging about and I tried with my right hand to add my weight to his on the reins and with my left to save his head from bumping on the ground.

His clutch on the rein relaxed just as two men from the stable-yard came running, followed by Mother, deathly pale and holding her side.

Bonaparte said, 'I'm all right. See to the horses. Josephine, there's no …' Blood began to pour from his nose. Mother wailed, 'He has hurt himself.'

He found his handkerchief and from behind it said, 'Help me up. Best thing that could happen. Save the doctor a job.'

He was on his feet when Roustam arrived.

'Effendi. Can carry.'

'When I'm dead, damn your hide! Take my arm.'

Blood, I know, makes much of itself, but by the time we were indoors his handkerchief, mine, Mother's, were all soaked and so was the front of his coat.

'Don't try the stairs,' Mother said. 'Sit down. Lie down. Rest.'

'If ever I needed a bath ...' my step-father said. 'I'm sorry. I know women can't bear ... But it's nothing ...' From behind the handkerchiefs, wadded together with blood, he gave me a reminding, a warning, an appealing look.

He liked very hot baths, long-lasting. He once said that in a hot bath one could think without worrying.

When he had gone to his bath Mother said, 'I thought he was dead. Everything went *grey*. Do you think I should send for Dr Corvisart?'

'What could he do – except bleed him and that surely is unnecessary.'

Mother looked at me uncertainly and then laughed.

'My dearest, dearest girl, nobody will ever know what a comfort you are to me ...' We clung together, both laughing a little hysterically, women who had been frightened, had exercised self-control and now gave way. 'And to think,' she said, 'that if I had had my wilful way, you would never have been born. Darling, doesn't that sound a dreadful thing to say? But it is true. Your father had behaved so abominably and we were living apart and then your grandfather Beauharnais urged me. Try once more, he said. And I did and had you, my darling.'

I tried to imagine the unimaginable – my own non-existence. The great world, millions of people, but no Hortense de Beauharnais, no *me*. I was I because of that brief reconciliation ... Everything that had happened to me, about me, all I had ever done or said or felt ...'

A dizzying thought, all concerned with measureless space and infinite time and chance, things against which we rear our pitiable defences, being so busy, thinking ourselves so important.

My step-father came in, looking not so much pale as greenish. Mother made him lie on her sofa and because he was feeling apologetic he did so, but awkwardly as though lying on a sofa were an art, one he had not acquired.

'I'm sorry to have given you both such a fright. I took the turn too fast. But no harm done, eh?' We assured him, no harm. A ready assumption of blame can be guard against accusation.

Mother said that she must go and change; I said I must go home. They both said no. I must stay; they needed my company after the upset of the afternoon.

I also had been upset, though forcing myself to stay calm, resourceful. Otherwise I should never have said what I did when my step-father, only half jocularly, remarked, 'It is too quiet for her here. We are getting old. Hortense finds the night life of Paris attractive.'

'That is unfair. You neither of you understand. I gave Louis my word not to spend a night here.'

Mother said, 'Why on earth not?' in genuine astonishment.

Bonaparte said, 'That was cautious of him. But nobody's going to attempt to blow up St Cloud. We are more than adequately guarded. You and the child are safer here than in your own house.'

He spoke most naturally, but I could see that he understood.

'So Hortense will stay,' he went on. 'You go and make yourself pretty, my dear. Hortense will arrange my pillows. Gentlemen on sofas always have their pillows arranged.'

As soon as we were alone he said, 'Now first. She didn't see, did she?'

'No. I stood between you.'

'I thought I should get home. That is why I drove like that. Now second. I'm sorry, more sorry than I can say about that vile slander. Sorrier still that Louis should be such a fool. He should know that I've been accused of everything short of cannibalism. Try to ignore it. Never let the world see a wound.'

'I try not. I no longer blame it entirely for things being so wrong between Louis and me. If it hadn't been that it would have been something else. We're utterly ill-suited. In fact,' I said, putting a wish into words for the first time, 'now that the aim of the marriage has been accomplished I wish we could live apart.'

'Oh, no, no! You must never say that. You haven't given it a fair trial. Fourteen months. That would be a scandal. You must put that thought clean away. I know Louis can be difficult but he's sound at heart. You must hold on, Hortense, hold on …'

Two servants came in to set up a table by the side of the sofa. Mother on her way to her room had given the order. So the conversation lapsed there and was not resumed.

I spent that night at St Cloud. Next day, there was a formal reception at The Tuileries. They were routine now, and except for Mother, as stiff and mannered as any at a Royal Court. Ladies stood in a semi-circle, gentlemen in another behind them. The First Consul, looking severe, moved around, a few civil words to each, seldom a smile. Mother followed him, exercising to the full her gift of charm, of never forgetting a face or a name, of making the most complete stranger feel that she had been waiting, all her life, for this meeting. Both Mother and my step-father liked me to trail behind them. The First Consul had acknowledged the existence of each person, Mother had made them feel like human beings, my function, I often thought, was to prevent them dropping dead of boredom while the round was completed.

The only variation, so far, had been when Bonaparte had carried Napoleon Charles on his round; then he did seem human.

On this occasion, remembered because it was memorable, Mother and I, Madame de Boubers holding the baby, clad in his best, waited in the anteroom and Bonaparte, ordinarily a stickler for time, was at least ten minutes late. He wore his withdrawn, preoccupied look, but he went to Madame de Boubers and took the baby from her, went almost to the door of the salon, from behind which came the sound of voices, carefully muted and then turned back, walked up and down, holding Napoleon Charles in such an unusually careless way that I was alert, fearful that he would drop him. When he did, however, it was into Madame de Boubers's arms. Then he said, 'Are you ready?' to Mother and me – ready and waiting for what seemed a long time.

He was slightly more brusque than usual, but Mother took her time, so that, following her I was at some little distance from my step-father when he paused in front of Lord Whitworth, the British Ambassador. To say that Lord Whitworth was a typical Englishman would be to subscribe to a theory that experience renders untenable, but he was tall and fair, solid but not fat, imperturbable, always beautifully dressed and well mannered. The Englishman as the Englishman would wish to see himself.

Bonaparte halted and addressed him as though he were King of England, Prime Minister, Parliament. In a flow of vituperative he accused the English of double-dealing, perfidy, of looking upon the Treaty of Amiens like a cracked plate to be thrown away … 'It never was more to you than a chance to catch your breath. You never wanted peace, you wanted war. Well, you can have it.'

He turned and, ignoring the rest of the people waiting to be acknowledged, strode out. It was a horrible moment. Lord Whitworth came forward, breaking the line, bowed over Mother's hand, and then over mine. 'If you will excuse me, madame,' then he, too, went away. And there was confusion.

'I know, I know,' Bonaparte said. 'I was hasty. But I had been talking to Talleyrand and then there was that great carthorse of an Englishman … And I let myself go. But now they will learn. This time I shall not fight with one hand tied behind me, begging another gun, another pair of boots for a barefoot soldier. I can now order boots and guns and mobilisation and I shall hit them where it hurts most. The English are a nation of shopkeepers. I will close their shop.'

12

War was not actually declared until two months later and in the meantime Louis came home, no better in health and out of humour not only with me but with all the world. Whom he had left to spy upon me I never discovered, but my single night at St Cloud had been reported and almost his first words to me were, 'You gave me a solemn promise and broke it at the first opportunity.'

I explained about the accident, but he would not be appeased. 'You are not to be trusted. I should be justified in separating from you entirely.'

'For spending a night under my mother's roof?'

'For deceiving me and flaunting my wishes.'

I was the more angered because since my talk with my step-father I had argued myself round to a determination to try again, let the past be the past and to bury old grievances. The truth was that there was a great difference between Louis absent – and a rather pitiable figure with his ailments and his search for cures – and Louis in the flesh with that sombre accusative eye and carping tongue.

His next squabble was with his brother, and that for a most unusual reason. With talk of war in the air Bonaparte had been looking to his army and among the promotions was that of Louis to the rank of Brigadier-General. 'And that means leaving my own regiment. He knew that and only did it to annoy me.'

The outcome of that was that Louis kept his newly-gazetted rank but was to be allowed to stay with his own regiment, then stationed at Compiegne, a pleasant little garrison town. We were to take up residence there and Mother gave us a farewell ball.

Louis no longer danced, had not in fact danced since just before our wedding, but even if he joined card games in adjoining rooms he would leave them occasionally and look in, gathering material for next day's catechism. Why had I danced three times in one evening with so-and-so? What had another man said to make me laugh so much?

On this evening, towards the end, I danced with an Italian whose name, if I ever knew it, I have forgotten. The best partner I ever had. And as sometimes happened when one couple were giving a particularly good performance, others drew away. When the music stopped on this occasion somebody clapped – an unheard of thing to do, and I turned to give whoever it was a glance of disdainful rebuke. Drawing attention to me, I thought; I shall hear about *this* on the way home or first thing tomorrow morning.

The trouble with words is that they have been so much used as to lose meaning. 'My heart stood still', 'my heart turned over', 'my breath stopped'. Yet there is truth in the very triteness. I looked at the offender, and he looked at me … I must have tottered or gasped or given some other sign of discomposure for my partner asked, rather anxiously, if he had made me dance too vigorously. I managed to say, no indeed, seldom had I enjoyed a dance so much.

I was twenty years old, a married woman, a mother and what had happened, in one exchange of glances, was what every green girl dreams of; love at first sight, eye speaking to eye across a crowded room.

He was a stranger. I did not even know his name. I might never see him again. But I had looked and loved, and was changed.

Louis said, 'I hope the applause pleased you.'

Next day – my last in Paris for a while – several people called to say goodbye and my footman was kept busy. Presently he said, 'Madame de Souza and Captain de Flahaut.'

Madame de Souza I knew well and liked; she was the wife of the Portuguese Ambassador, but born a Frenchwoman and she had a quality that I can only describe as resolute cheerfulness. Her smile was warm and kind, her laughter ready and hearty, her conversation easy and spontaneous, like birdsong.

Captain de Flahaut, following her in, was the young man who had clapped.

'I've brought this naughty boy of mine to apologise for his behaviour last night. You must forgive him. He has no manners but that is not my fault. He has been in the army since he was fifteen.'

He said, 'My mother wrongs me. I have manners – all bad. But I should be sorry to think that I had annoyed you – irrevocably, madame.'

In Martinique the dark-skinned people talked of zombies, people who had died and been raised, by magic, to something like life again. I felt like one.

He had a beautiful voice, deep and so flexible that it could tilt 'irrevocably' into a question, 'You do forgive me?' There were other people in the room and I suppose I took leave of them. My heart thudded, so loud to me that I thought someone must notice, my face felt hot, my knees and hands shaky. I tried to avoid looking at him and could not.

The zombie tried to take refuge in its motherhood; rang the bell, asked for her baby to be brought in. Sat down, baby in lap, married woman, mother, staid, 'Keep away from me! Too late!'

An unwise move, for he came and knelt beside me, taking one of Napoleon Charles's hands and saying how like a starfish, and the nearness, the crisp brown hair, the way it grew on forehead and neck … The zombie knew hungers that Hortense never dreamed of. Hortense had thought about love at first sight, the glance of recognition, but she had been both innocent and ignorant, physical involvement for her meaning an exchange of kisses, walking hand-in-hand. The zombie knew more and wanted more. And was afraid. Glad that it was leaving for Compiegne next day.

There was the old, old compulsion, to talk about the beloved. To use the name, as pious people say 'God'.

I said to Adèle who was helping me gather my last, most personal things together, 'I did not know, did you, that Madame de Souza had been married before. Had been Madame de Flahaut?'

'Oh yes. Years ago. People have either forgotten or choose to pretend to. There was a scandal. Everybody said that she was Talleyrand's mistress and the child was his. I think this could be given to the poor, don't you?' She held up a petticoat with a draggle-tail flounce. I said, 'What have the poor done to deserve such affliction?' She laughed. The zombie said, 'But how do you know? You could hardly have been born.'

'I must have overheard gossip, either when she came back from exile, or remarried, or something. She was an émigré, you know. My aunt Campan rather admired her for being self-supporting. She wrote a book and made … hats, I think.'

'Her son called with her this morning. He does not resemble Talleyrand in the least.' The zombie wanted Adèle to pursue this subject but Adèle said, 'It was probably mere rumour. That old man has such a bad reputation even now. Years ago he had only to ask a woman the time of day and talk would start.'

Life at Compiegne was very gay. Though, officially France was at war with England again, actual fighting had not started: England was seeking allies on the Continent and the First Consul was content for the moment to see that recruiting and training went on at full speed, and in pursuing his plans to ruin England's trade. But war was near enough to put a special sparkle into life in a garrison town and, owing to Louis's rank, I was first lady there, much sought after. I threw myself almost frenziedly into every activity, holding the zombie at bay. I became popular and this Louis resented. He had friends of his own but was not generally liked, partly because he was so careful of his dignity, but more because of his vacillation; an order issued one day would be rescinded on the next. In both these respects he was the exact opposite of Bonaparte who was so very sure of his superiority that he did not feel it imperilled by his sharing an ordinary soldier's meal. 'Let's see what they're giving you boys for dinner,' he would say, and woe betide the commissariat and the cooks if the food were not up to standard. 'An army marches on its belly,' he said. And before he gave an order he had thought about it, reasoned it through, visualised it in operation.

The Christmas festivities of 1803 ended early in January 1804 with a rather wild party, based on what had once been known as The Twelfth Night revels. It was the kind of thing in which Louis, with his intense self-consciousness, could not participate at all and he went home early. I stayed on and drank so many toasts that for the first time in my life I became a little inebriated. I had a good head for drink, Mother said I had inherited it from her father who ordinarily drank a bottle of rum a day with no apparent effect. On this evening it failed me. The place in which we had feasted and danced and romped was either a drill hall or a riding school and the bare walls had been hung with evergreens and bunting. There was some old superstition about all signs of Christmas being removed by midnight on the Twelfth Day. So, on the tick, with military precision, a squad of recruits, all in uniforms slightly too big for them, ran in to dismantle the decorations. At the same time, through another door, two men wheeled in a barrel on a handcart. The captain with whom I had danced the last whirling gallop looked at the boys and said, 'They're mainly from Calvados and they're going to have a treat. Their local cider-brandy.'

I looked at them and thought of Eugène, in his first too-big uniform.

Captain Leclos said, 'God knows where they'll be this time next year.' I looked at him and realised that he was young, too, not quite so young, but young. 'I suppose … dare I suggest it? … you wouldn't stay and drink a tiny glass with them? It would be so deeply appreciated. They're all horribly homesick.'

'I should love to,' I said. Several other women, reluctant to end the evening, stayed too; and the boys had the hall stripped in a few minutes, working away with a deadly intensity as though striking camp or looting an enemy town.

We drank to the First Consul, to Mother, to the New Year, to the army, to Captain Leclos who had provided this treat, to Louis, 'Damnation to the English'; I wondered how many of them, given a map, could have found England, France, Calvados, for that matter. We drank to absent friends and 'To the little boy, ma'am.'

I made my own contribution, because they were so young and touching and the Calvados was very potent.

Raising my glass for what I knew must positively be the last time, I said, 'To that Marshal's baton hidden in your knapsack.' It was a phrase my step-father had used in a speech comparing the old method of promotion by rank and influence to the new one of ability. It was received with roars of approval. For a moment every awkward, homesick boy was a Marshal.

Then I went home, and found Louis sitting up waiting for me. Where had I been? Did the dancing not end at midnight? With whom had I been? I tried to explain, but my head was spinning and my tongue tripped me.

'And now you are drunk,' he said.

So I was, too drunk to hold a promise that I had made to myself months ago – never again to give him the satisfaction of seeing me cry. I sat in a chair and wept, not just for myself, for everything, everybody in an abominable world. I even wept for English boys in uniforms too big for them, not knowing where France was. And for all of whom it could be said – God knows where they will be next year at this time.

Louis was astonishingly kind.

He helped me undress; he helped me into bed. He joined me there. Hortense was drunk; the zombie, ravening for what it could not have, snatched at what was offered. In March when we were suddenly recalled to Paris, I knew that I was pregnant again.

At Compiegne we had heard nothing and it was a shock to us to find Paris looking like a city besieged, guards at the gates, demanding credentials, barricades at street corners, soldiers everywhere.

At The Tuileries we learned what had happened. There had been a plot, foiled just in time, to assassinate Bonaparte, this time not by blowing up his carriage but by stabbing him in his bed. Several of his army officers – all with Royalist connections – were involved, and so were some of the palace staff, bribed to be deaf and blind at a certain hour. Roustam, whom nobody could bribe, was to have been drugged.

Fouché, who had been Chief of Police but was so no longer because my step-father disapproved of him, had maintained his secret contacts and exposed the plot, just in time. Arrests had been made and trials were pending.

Mother was so nervous that the slightest sound made her jump. Bonaparte was behaving much as he had done after the former attempt; there was the same calm front and behind it the kind of secret satisfaction, as though his enemies, moving against him, had done him good rather than harm. At the same time he had gathered his family about him and had made Joachim Murat military governor of Paris.

But for Mother the guillotine would have been busy again. All those brought to trial were condemned and for days their mothers, sisters, wives, daughters, came begging her to intervene. Each one exonerated her own man – led away by others, too old, too young to exercise judgment, once a good soldier, potentially a good soldier.

Mother, so little politically minded that she was capable of denouncing the plotters as treacherous beasts, and at the same time weeping in sympathy with the treacherous beasts' women folk, actually saved dozens of lives with one laconic, shrewd remark.

'Once they're dead they'll be martyrs,' she said.

My step-father gave her a sharp, sudden look.

'Who's been quoting Tertullian to you?' Mother looked completely blank. 'He said it, about Christians – The blood of martyrs is the seed of the Church.' He gave a meditative grunt and after a second or two said, 'Well, we don't need martyrs. Cadoudal was the ringleader, I can't spare him, or the two generals, or the pair that came from England to start the rot. The others can live to see the result of their handiwork.'

¢ 13 ¢

With our return to Paris it was impossible for me to avoid Charles de Flahaut, who was now on Joachim Murat's staff. I tried to do so because just as Louis distrusted me, I distrusted the zombie. I had only to see him, or hear his voice, or even the mention of his name, to be thrown into a state of mind and of body of which I was ashamed. I was so afraid of having to dance with him that I stopped dancing altogether and sat about, months before it was necessary, with the middle-aged and the old and the lame.

Sometimes, at a safe distance, with a crowd of people between us, I would look and look, asking myself why? He had the average good looks of a healthy young man, nothing outstanding except a kind of … jauntiness is the wrong word, a compactness, a self-assurance … they also are wrong. I was far from being the only one susceptible to whatever it was; dozens of women were crazy about him. Caroline was one. As the wife of his commanding officer she had the right to the rather exaggerated, stylised attentions usual in the circumstances, but I could see, by the way she leaned when she took his arm, by the way she smiled, by the very manner in which she called him or pulled him by the hand into or out of a group that he meant more than the others. And there was a Polish girl who came on a visit. She was as beautiful as a fawn and immensely rich; she had inherited estates said to be the size of Brittany, and at any given moment the jewels she was wearing would have constituted a sizeable fortune. She actually asked him to marry her and even Caroline said what a chance, and what a fool he was to refuse. But he did, and that lovely young creature, having cried herself silly, went home – she said to free all her serfs and go into a convent.

During this time his attentions to me were never conspicuous, but they were constant in a curious, covert way. Let the seat beside me be vacant for a moment and there he would be, with some ordinary remark that anyone could overhear and think nothing of, but with the look. I told myself fiercely that the look meant nothing – something to do with the way his eyes were set. Something that meant nothing, while seeming to mean all. His eyes were the colour of sherry, with little green flecks that seemed to dance and shift. His mouth was wide and rather thin, the upper lip sharply cut, the reverse of voluptuous, rather hard, capable of being cruel – so Hortense would think, trying to be cool, analytical, defensive, while the zombie thought of kisses … 'Long as my exile, sweet as my revenge,' as the English Shakespeare wrote.

87

Of course, during this little space, this month of April, when we were making merry because the plot had been foiled, and when other plans were afoot, I had an ordinary life to lead. One morning I went to The Tuileries and found Mother shedding some real, damaging tears.

'Didn't I tell you,' she said, 'that this place boded me no good? Darling, I was about to send for you. I needed someone to talk to.'

'What about? What has happened? What is the matter?'

'He told me, last night. In bed. I'm not supposed to say anything. For a day or two. But I am so distraught ...'

'You can tell me,' I said.

'Now they want everything changed. They want him to be Emperor. Emperor of the French, with a throne and a crown. And he means to accept.'

That he should accept such an offer did not surprise me; that it should have been made, or discussed, or proposed, did. From the time when some Revolutionary had declared that to be royal was to be a monster and Louis XVI had paid for his accident of birth on the guillotine everything that had been done in France had been done under the cloak, admittedly a bit widespread, of Republicanism, with the titles and the names of institutions all harking back to ancient Rome. But – I remembered with a little jerk – the Roman Republic had ended as the Roman Empire ...

I said, 'Darling, why should that distress you so much? You will make a most beautiful Empress.'

'I think not,' she said, shaking her head. 'My enemies will see in this an opportunity to be rid of me. Up to now everything has been makeshift, improvised; and for that a named heir was enough, if not entirely satisfactory. This will be very different. They'll talk about a dynasty. They'll persuade him that only an emperor's son can succeed to an emperor's throne. They'll persuade him to divorce me and marry some fat German princess, sixteen years old.' She spoke the last words with an astonishing viciousness and then relapsed into tears.

I said, 'Has he ... Did he say, or even hint at such a thing?'

'No.' She dabbed at her eyes with a little lace-edged handkerchief, already completely sodden. 'No. He just told me what had been suggested ... But I feel it in my bones.'

The fact that I felt sorry for her did not prevent me feeling a pang of self-pity, too. In order to ward off this divorce, and to provide an acceptable heir, I had married Louis and ruined my life. All for nothing. Non-Non had never been formally adopted; the divorce still threatened. That was a bitter thought. When I had told her that it was silly to cry and ruin her looks over something that had not happened and might never happen, I added,

'Mother, if it came to the worst, would it not be possible to make a new, happy life, at Malmaison, free of all this?' I moved my hand to indicate the Palace of the Tuileries and all that it stood for.

'You cannot understand,' she said. 'My poor child, you have never been in love.'

True enough, I suppose. I had never loved Louis and what I felt for Charles de Flahaut was too largely based upon physical attraction and the activity of imagination to justify the name. I sensed that if the zombie were once given its head the resultant affaire would be as brief as it was disastrous. I hastily diverted my attention and said, 'I think you should behave as though you were absolutely certain of being crowned; as though you had never entertained one moment's doubt.'

Whether because of that advice or because of her natural ability to adapt herself to changing circumstances, from that time until May when the Senate waited upon Bonaparte and asked him to accept the throne, and addressed him as Emperor and Mother as Empress, she always wore in public, at least, an air of calm confidence. Only when alone with me did she betray fear and uncertainty, saying that she would not feel safe until after the Coronation which was to take place in December; saying that a lot could happen in seven months, that Joseph and Lucien Bonaparte were plotting together.

Certainly, at this time Joseph and Lucien were in our house more than was usual; closeted with Louis in the library and talking urgently, sometimes loudly. But their talk was not concerned with Mother directly; it was of the succession and of Non-Non. As Mother had foreseen, the establishment of the Empire had brought to the forefront the question of who should inherit. Both Joseph and Lucien had been very eager to be named as heir to the First Consulship, they were now doubly anxious not to see Non-Non properly adopted. Louis could not or would not see that when they said, 'Why should *he* have *your* son?', it was their own corn they were grinding.

Then one evening Lucien came alone, looking almost as wild as Louis at his wildest. We were dining alone and the sombre meal was about half-way through.

'I've done it!' Lucien said. 'Broken with him forever. And with Joseph. He sold himself.'

Louis half rose and said, 'We'll go to the library.'

'Everybody will know tomorrow,' Lucien said. He dragged up a chair and sat down. He had never been a welcome guest in my house and he knew it. I could never look at him or hear his name without remembering that he had dropped that poisonous insinuation which had ruined all hope of even a moderately happy marriage. Now, however, common courtesy forced me to ask had he dined. He said he was not hungry, but he accepted some wine, which he drank as though it were a dose of nauseous medicine.

Louis asked, in a curiously cool and detached way, 'What happened?'

'He tried to bargain with me. He offered me everything if I would divorce Alexandrine. There's some damned widowed Queen in Florence just waiting for a young husband, chosen by Nablione! Me! I refused absolutely and he flew into a temper. So did I. Arrogant God-Almighty. I shouted at him that he'd killed the Republic. "Like this," I said. Louis, I flung my watch on the floor and stamped on it.'

Most grown men having given way to a fit of rage that had led them to destroy their own possession would have been regretful, or shame-faced, or perhaps amused; but the Bonapartes were different. Lucien looked at Louis as though he expected to be applauded.

Louis said in that same way, 'So what now?'

'Italy. Tomorrow. You'll come?'

'Not tomorrow.'

'Soon then. While you are still your own man. Linger and he'll have you, body and soul. And your boy. Mother knew! She got away before the bargaining started. I shall go to her and live with the woman I chose, not one who was chosen for me. And my children will be mine.'

'So far my child is mine. And will remain so.'

'Don't be idiotic. You're next. Stay here and you'll be bought. Like Joseph.'

'What of Joseph?' Louis asked, rather as though Joseph had had a simple cold and he was enquiring how he did.

Lucien said, 'Laugh. Joseph is now a full colonel with an army record, false as Hell. Student of Artillery, staff officer, major and adjutant general. Slightly, but honourably wounded at Toulon. He is to have 350,000 francs a year for *expenses*!

'Uniforms,' Louis said, and laughed. Lucien joined him and then broke off abruptly and snapped, 'You see? Now, how soon can you get away?'

Louis fiddled with a fork, looking down as though its balance between his fingers was a matter of the utmost importance.

When he looked up he said, 'I see your point, Lucien. You had no choice. For myself I think I shall wait and see what I am worth.'

Lucien then did an incredible thing. He spat. Clear across the dining table, the white linen, the flowers, the glass and silver. Then having made this guttersnipe gesture he pushed back his chair, said two or three words in Italian and made for the door. Louis called, 'Tell Mother to keep a bed for me. I may be next.'

He laughed as Lucien slammed the door. Then, with one of his switches of mood, he rounded on me and said nastily, 'Most unedifying! A thing no Beauharnais would do.'

I said nothing.

'He's regretting it already poor fellow. And he thought that if I agreed to go with him, Nablione would recant ...'

Soon after this we all became royal. Joseph and Louis became Princes of France, Julie and I became Princess Joseph and Princess Louis. There were other titles too, both culled from the past; both carrying handsome emoluments. Joseph was made Grand Elector of the Empire, Louis was Constable of France.

The most immediate effect of our new status upon our lives – apart from the fact that among ladies-in-waiting, equerries and secretaries we lost all privacy – was a change of residence. We left our house in the Rue de la Victoire for a much larger and more magnificent one in the Rue Taitbout and acquired a country residence, Saint-Leu, a richly wooded estate, so old it included two châteaux standing side by side, one a medieval, fortified place, long-abandoned and ruinous, the other about a hundred years old. Ruins had become fashionable, people were erecting brand new ruins in their gardens to give the romantic, antique touch. We were not forced to such a device.

Louis was at Saint-Leu, estimating what superficial work the château needed, and I was supervising the packing for the move between the two Paris houses when what I shall always think of as *the* letter came. I was glad of that, for Louis's curiously inconsistent, watchful, jealous suspicion applied not only to my behaviour but to my correspondence. He never actually demanded to see a letter or asked from whom a letter came, but he kept a furtive observation. He would say he had lost a paper, could it possibly have got among mine? With nothing to hide I would say, 'I think it unlikely, but look for yourself,' and he would sit down at my writing table and search and peruse. Once something even more humiliating happened. I came home unexpectedly smitten with a terrible headache, and found his valet ferreting about in my bedroom, in the drawers of my chest. I said, 'Pierre, what are you doing here?' Taken by surprise, pallid, sweating, the man said, 'I do not rightly know. My master ordered me to look.'

'What for?'

'I do not know, madam. At least ... anything that was where it should not be. I didn't want to. I was only doing what I was told to do.' To my dismay he began to cry. I had never seen a man full-grown cry like a child before. And my head felt as though it were being split with an axe, blow on blow.

'And have you found anything where it should not be?'

'No,' he sobbed.

I said, 'Wait!' and went into my sitting room, found my latest dressmaker's bill, took it into the bedroom, opened a drawer and placed it under my handkerchiefs.

'There you are, Pierre. Something out of place. Find it, take it. And go.'

So, with this everlasting feeling – What are you up to? What is this about? I don't trust you an inch – hovering in the background, I was glad to receive this particular letter when I was alone.

It was addressed in the style that still seemed unfamiliar to me. Her Imperial Highness Princess Louis. It was signed, Adelaide de Souza. Madame de Souza wrote that she regretted that her absence from Paris, being on holiday in Portugal, prevented her from conveying her congratulations in person; but she did congratulate me and thought my elevation most apt. 'From the first I have always thought your nature and demeanour most royal.' Well-meant, I thought, a little fulsome. One must get used to flattery. A trifle familiar?

> *It is now a month since I have seen you, even at a distance, and I fear that in future you will be even less accessible. I do beg you not to forget me but to remember that to serve you, in however humble a way, is the dearest wish of my heart. I beg to assure you that there will always be one French soldier who while he draws breath will fight not only for France but for you – that is my son who shares to the full the respect and admiration that I have always felt for you. Madame, the high places in this world tend to be lonely; should you find this true the merest sign that my company would be welcome to you will bring to your side one who thinks of you as Hortense.*

I thought it a rather peculiar letter for one woman to have written to another, though I could not have said exactly why. Just that little bit off key, like an ill-tuned harp. Yet it had a sincerity about it and one of the first things I did when I was settled into the Rue Taitbout was to write and ask Madame de Souza to come and drink tea with me, in the English fashion, at four o'clock one afternoon. My step-father tolerated the drinking of tea so long as the leaves came from China not India. It was very expensive, and partly because of this, and because the fashion was relatively new, a certain mystique had grown up around the tea ceremony. Mere acquaintances, even enemies might make formal calls in the morning or attend dinner and supper parties but only friends, as a rule, took tea together.

Normally one of our new footmen would have brought in the heavy silver tray, set with fragile, shallow cup beautifully painted with flowers or birds, and normally one of my six ladies-in-waiting would have poured the tea. Of my six Mother had recommended five, mostly selected, as Madame de Boubers had been, from returned emigrées in reduced circumstances. The sixth was my dear Adèle, and since I had chosen one of her duty days it was easy for me to say that I should like to see Madame de Souza alone and make the tea-drinking as informal and intimate as possible. Adèle understood how much my new way of life conflicted with my liking for privacy.

We exchanged some casual remarks and then I said, 'Madame de Souza, I greatly appreciated your letter.'

Light eyes often react to surprise with a widening of the pupils. Madame de Souza's eyes were almost black, very bright and lively. In them surprise showed by a certain fixity of stare and a lifting of the upper lids.

'Your Imperial Highness is administering a rebuke? I should have written, I know. But we were in Portugal, visiting my husband's family. The posts from there are slow and I imagined that I should be back in Paris, able to offer my congratulations in person by the time a letter arrived. But it was remiss of me, and I apologise.'

'But I received a letter from you – at least it was signed with your name.'

'Then someone has taken my name in vain. I cannot think who it could be. Have you the letter still? May I see it?'

I took it from the drawer of my writing table. I had saved it because on second perusal I had decided that the worst thing Louis, if he ever read it, could say was that it was unduly familiar.

Madame de Souza glanced at it but did not read it. Then she gave a little rueful laugh.

'He really is incorrigible,' she said. 'Forgive him if you can. Blame me. There were circumstances connected with his upbringing which led me to indulge him so far as I could, and even five years in the army have failed to teach him sense.'

'Your son?'

'Who else?' She gave me a knowing, birdlike look. 'If you will forgive some plain speaking … You may remember the occasion when he annoyed you. He fell in love with you then – not knowing who you were. I enlightened him, of course, and pointed out his folly. Loyal wife, devoted mother, never the slightest whisper of scandal. Not, if you will excuse my saying so, *quite* a suitable object for a boy's romantic dreams to centre upon. But …' she spread her plump little hands in a gesture of defeat. 'Even your own most admirable behaviour – I often wondered whether you had *guessed* – failed to deter him.' She looked down at the letter and read it in a second. 'At least,' she said, looking up, 'unlike most such letters, this was written from the heart. That must be its excuse. That and his youth. He is only nineteen.'

I thought of that look, so experienced, of the taut, compact figure, the confident bearing of the lines that would presently be grooves running from cheekbone to jaw.

'I should have thought older,' I said, as much to myself as to her.

'War makes men of boys quickly. Outwardly at least. At heart …' she spread her hands again, 'he is a romantic boy. The Polish marriage would have been greatly to his advantage. But then,' she shrugged a shoulder, 'who am I to blame him? The tendency to let the heart rule the head he inherits from me. When I was young I was *incredibly* foolish. I paid for my folly, again and again. Now, of course, I enjoy a compensating cynicism.'

'Enjoy, Madame de Souza?'

'Oh, indeed. To have no illusions, to be impervious. It is so comfortable. You will reach this state one day – I hope by an easier road than mine.'

Perhaps I liked her because she was *his* mother, but there was more to it; I liked her for herself, for something that was simple and straightforward without being naïve. I liked her for the total lack of suggestiveness in her attitude and because she seemed to dismiss the whole thing as a boyish folly that made no demands upon me. I did not know another woman with whom this would have been possible. I had been obliged to give nothing away; she had in fact made it very easy for me to pretend that she and I were somewhat alike, two grown women watching the antics of a puppy.

But when she had gone I re-read the letter, kissed it, pressed it to my heart. I thought – The English duke, the German prince wanted to marry Bonaparte's step-daughter; Louis had married me under pressure and had come to hate me. But somebody loved me … Had fallen in love with me not knowing who I was.

14

Always, whenever Bonaparte was in Paris, Sunday evening was for the Family. Once a week, encapsuled in a French palace, The Tuileries or St Cloud, a decent, solid, middle-class Corsican family sat down together, ate the various pasta dishes, drank the rough Italian wines, laughed at old jokes, talked freely and quarrelled.

There were fewer now; old Madame Bonaparte with her unassailable dignity, her disapproval, had gone to Italy, Lucien had joined her there. Pauline, the pretty one, back from the West Indies where General Leclerk had died of yellow fever, had quickly married again and become Princess Borghese. She was in Italy, too. But on this evening that I remember so well we were still a considerable gathering. My step-father, Emperor of the French, Mother, Joseph and Julie, Elisa and her husband, Caroline and hers, Louis and me, now obviously pregnant again.

For Mother and me these had never been particularly happy occasions, but this evening was vile. Mother smiled and smiled and used Christian names just that little too much, with a kind of insistence, while my step-father threw titles about mockingly: 'The Empress feels …' 'How does Princess Joseph think…?' 'Princess Louis looks particularly blooming this evening.' 'Prince Joseph's uniform, you must all agree, is very handsome, if unorthodox.' Caroline made the briefest possible answers if directly addressed, 'Yes, Your Majesty', 'No, Your Majesty', but not echoing his teasing manner. Elisa did not speak at all. Murat looked uneasy and Baciocchi, born Italian, gave his attention to the simple food. Caroline ate nothing but drank glass after glass of water. Presently the Emperor noticed and said, 'What is the matter, Caroline? Lost your appetite?'

She said in her roughest voice, 'Yes. So would you if you had been treated as we have.'

Murat put his big brown hand on her arm and said, 'Caro! Not tonight. It is not the right time.'

'Then tell me what would be! Tell me that. Here we are. One family, around one table. Prince and Princess Joseph. Prince and Princess Louis. General and Madame Murat. Colonel and Madame Baciocchi.' She leaned forward, 'You must forgive me, Elisa, for naming you last, but with all this precedence being observed…' She then leaned back and looked straight at the Emperor. 'It is intolerable. If you did not think *me*, your sister, worthy of rank, what of Joachim, the best cavalry officer you ever had, or ever will? In what battles did these *Princes* ever lead a charge? And apart from that, Elisa and I are your sisters, your flesh and blood, Nablione. What sort of Emperor is it that has commoners for relatives?'

My step-father said, 'You have an argument there. Elisa, you feel the same way?'

Elisa opened her rather ugly mouth and said, 'Absolutely,' and shut it again with a snap, like somebody closing a purse.

Bonaparte laughed, not merrily, and said, 'Well, well. Really, anybody hearing you would think that I had cheated you both out of your inheritance left you by your father, the late king! This must be righted, never let it be said …' He broke off and I saw that pale shadow creep below his nose, around his mouth. He pushed back his chair, stood up and went away.

Where did he go when this thing threatened? I thought of the loneliness – not unlike mine.

Mother – cover up, smooth over, make all nice, acted as though she had that moment arrived, turned to Joseph and said, 'I understand that you leave for Boulogne tomorrow.'

'Yes,' he said with a defiant glance about the table, at Murat, Louis, Baciocchi, all with army rank older than his. 'My experience on the field may be limited but on the commissariat side I am a veteran.'

Murat said, 'So long as you arrange that we do not have to eat our horses, Joseph. Eating horseflesh always makes me feel like a cannibal.'

I said, 'I will just look in on Non-Non.'

In fact I did not turn aside to the room devoted to Non-Non's use, but hurried straight along through the communicating apartments. The first, like the dining room in which supper had been served, was brilliantly lighted; in the next candles were in process of being lighted; the third, a vast room, often used for receptions, had no light except what came through the tall windows. Day was ending and the sky was purplish with thunder; the room was thick with shadows.

Among the things which my step-father had brought back from the Near East were screens, heavy things made of some black wood, intricately carved and inlaid with mother-of-pearl. One of these stood on the far side of the room I was now crossing and as I neared it I became conscious of an unaccountable nervousness and thought of Mother and her claim to have seen ghosts in this place. Nonsense, I knew, but fright moved coldly down from the nape of my neck to between my shoulders. The fragments of mother-of-pearl caught what light there was and gleamed like small, evil eyes. But I walked on until one of the sections of the screen moved. Then I stood stock-still, waiting; what for I did not know. Nor, when the Emperor emerged from his hiding-place, was I instantly reassured; for one fraction of a second he looked like a disembodied face, floating; his dark greenish grey clothes merged with the shadows, his face was so pale that it seemed luminous.

I think I startled him as much as he did me.

'Why, Hortense!' he said. 'What are you doing here?'

'I saw. I came to see if you were all right.'

'Of course I am all right. That was sudden, though. And bad. And all Caroline's fault.' He smoothed his hair and then knuckled his cheeks. 'You're my sweet Hortense. Quite my favourite woman — after your mother, of course. You say you saw. Did anyone else?'

'No. I think one sees what one is prepared to see.'

'True. What excuse did you give for leaving the table?'

'I said I was going to look in on Non-Non.'

'We will look in on Non-Non,' the Emperor said and into that simple, ordinary sentence he managed to inject a sinister sound.

Madame de Boubers rose as we entered and curtsied and said, 'You wish him to be roused, sire,' with a blending of obligingness and disapproval that only she could manage. She moved towards the bed where Non-Non lay asleep — he had outgrown his various cribs. The Emperor elbowed her aside and lifted the child with none of the gentle preliminaries. Non-Non opened his eyes and his mouth and let out a roar of displeasure. Then he recognised Uncle Bona and smiled and made a grab for his hair.

The relationship between them was a strange one. After the first six months my step-father had ceased to handle the child gently and begun to toss and poke and pummel him in a way that was almost rough. Non-Non adored it, perhaps because it was a change from the soft, almost reverent handling to which he was accustomed. 'They're the toughest things on earth,' my step-father had once told Madame de Boubers, 'how else could they survive? They can fall from fourth floor windows and not damage themselves.' He also held the theory that anything a healthy child could swallow it could digest, and so far that had seemed to be true despite Madame de Bouber's forebodings.

Now, carrying Non-Non high, the Emperor moved towards the dining room. Madame de Boubers said, with agitation, 'Your Highness! He should be chambered. He has been asleep a long time. There may well be … an accident.'

But it was too late to do anything about that. My step-father carried the child to the family table and said, 'Clear a space,' and when space was cleared he attempted to lower Non-Non who still held on to his hair.

'See what strength he has already. And what sense. That's my boy! That's right, Baby, grab what you can and then hold on. Do you realise, Baby, that one day you will be Emperor of Europe …'

I recognised that remark for what it was – a getting-back at Caroline. Typically Bonapartish, mischievous, malicious. Non-Non, surrounded by people whom he recognised, in a familiar situation, expectant of sips of wine, pieces of fruit or cheese, released his hold on the Emperor's hair and looked about him, smiling.

It always seemed a little surprising to me that Louis and I should have produced such a child, so big, so lusty. I was perhaps an inch or two above average height but rather thin and small-boned; Louis was frail, pale. Non-Non, at this time still something short of two years old, was extraordinarily solid, big and heavy. I sometimes wondered whether his wet-nurse, that sturdy peasant woman, had left her mark upon him.

Non-Non's expectations on this evening were more than fulfilled. These family meals always ended with ice-cream, an Italian invention, and when Non-Non had had several spoonfuls and still said, 'More. Uncle Bona, more,' I felt obliged to intervene. I said, 'Sire, if you give him any more he will have colic and Madame de Boubers will scold me.'

'There,' the Emperor said, 'did you hear that? The Princess Louis called me "Sire". She is the only one with any manners.'

Caroline said, 'Sire, I apologise. Sire, I thought this was a family party, Sire.'

'So it was. Until you spoiled it. I tell you all,' his glance shot over Non-Non's innocent head and included them all, 'I will not be scolded or imposed upon. I must remind you, and sharply, that I am Emperor of France.'

Louis, who had been very silent, said, 'Emperor of the French Republic, was it not? A curiously ambivalent title.'

The Emperor said, 'My dear Louis – forgive me, Your Imperial Highness – if you feel obliged to mention that stinking carcass, the Republic, do it elsewhere, not at my table.'

Caroline said, 'So I spoiled your party, Nablione? Well, for the last time. Never, never again will I go anywhere where Julie and Hortense are Imperial Highnesses and I am Madame Murat. Even Pauline – and no thanks to you – is a Princess.'

The Emperor laughed. 'So that is where the shoe pinches! Well, we must see what can be done ... Ha, that's my boy! Show what you think of all this trumpery ...'

The little accident had come about, a spreading, yellowish stain on the white cloth between the fruit dishes, the flowers and the candlesticks. Non-Non beamed around with an air, unmistakable, of achievement.

Yet, in the end, family feeling was triumphant and the Emperor bestowed upon Elisa and Caroline and their husbands the titles they coveted. He had, however, still three 'commoner' relatives. Lucien, Jerome – the baby of the family who had married an American girl without consulting anyone – and old Madame Bonaparte, who had withdrawn from the glory of the new regime, and who had befriended Lucien in his disgrace. When eventually a title was bestowed on the mother, about a year later, it was unique and had nothing royal about it; she was to be known as Madame Mère. Probably she chose it herself, valuing maternity above all.

The autumn of 1804 was devoted to preparations for the Coronation which everyone was determined should be the most splendid and spectacular ever seen in France. The ceremony was to be performed by Pope Pius VII with whom the Emperor was now on good terms, having restored the Church in France, though with curtailed powers and less property than it had enjoyed before the Revolution.

There was a suggestion that the Coronation should take place in Rheims, the traditional crowning place of Kings of France, but my step-father decided that this would be too closely to associate himself with bygone, discredited things. Paris, he said, was his city and he would be crowned in Notre Dame.

I was awaiting another event, the birth of my child, due in the first week of October. With the idea of Non-Non's adoption shelved but not abandoned, I hoped for a girl who would belong to me wholly, at least until she was of marriageable age. I also hoped for an easy delivery, a hope encouraged by everyone who said that each childbirth was less painful than the one before. In my case neither hope was fulfilled. I had a hard, long labour and bore a second son, rather small and puny. My recovery was slow, largely because I developed a villainous cough which rattled my bones and seemed literally to shake the flesh from them. I tried dozens of remedies but nothing cured it. There was a palliative, a mixture heavily laced with laudanum which would stun the cough and daze me for an hour or two, but as soon as its effect wore off I coughed more and more violently as though to make up for the surcease.

There was a little unpleasantness about the new baby's name. Louis was determined that this son, whose paternity he had only once questioned and that indirectly, should bear his name. But when it came to the registration, which, our being royal now, must be done in the Emperor's presence, when Louis wrote 'Louis', the Emperor reached out, snatched the pen, crossed out the word and wrote 'Napoleon' and said, 'Now you can add Louis if you wish.' Louis was deeply offended.

The new baby had a wet-nurse, as carefully chosen as the other, but he throve much less well. The nurse was changed; changed again. It made no difference. Even his crying was different from that of Non-Non whose cries had always seemed to be demands for attention, certain of instant satisfaction. Napoleon Louis cried on a mournful, wailing note, protesting against something but without much hope. Madame de Boubers said, 'It seems strange, the routine is exactly the same. But we must not worry. Ailing babies often do well in the end.' We had been a little concerned about how Non-Non, so lively, boisterous and precocious, so accustomed to being the centre of attention, would take to a brother whom he might regard as a rival. We need not have worried; everything within Non-Non's scope was his; he had inherited to a full degree the Bonaparte trait of possessiveness; he accepted the baby as a new toy; took on the role of elder brother and guardian and always spoke of *my* baby, *my* little brother.

I was still in bed when Mother, on one of her daily visits, having kissed me and asked how I was, sat down and said happily, 'Darling, it seems that I worried unduly. Last evening Bonaparte told me to order my gown and robe for the Coronation. And he must have given it much thought. Down to the smallest detail.'

Mildly dazed by the dose I had taken so that my cough should not distress her, I asked, 'Is the dress the one he once described? Satin embroidered with roses with diamond dew drops in their hearts?'

She said, 'Fancy you remembering that! It seems so long ago. Well, not unlike ...' She launched out into a description of what she was to wear. Clothes had always been her passion and she spoke animatedly of the gown, to be embroidered not with roses but with bees – the symbol of the Empire, as lilies had been of the Bourbon monarchy, and of the mantle of velvet, lined with satin and bordered with fur. I listened, peacefully half-drugged, so glad for her sake that the period of uncertainty was over. Then suddenly she stopped, that stricken look came over her face and she said, 'Darling, I have just thought of something. Quite dreadful!'

'The weight of it?' I asked lightly.

She said, with rebuke in her voice, 'Nothing so frivolous, Hortense! I said *terrible*. Oh dear, and I was feeling so very happy. I must be blind not to have seen it before.'

'Seen what?'

'That the Pope cannot crown me. In his eyes a civil marriage is no marriage at all. How could he anoint and crown a woman who has lived in sin for eight years?'

'That applies equally to the Emperor. The Pope is not likely to come all the way to Paris and then refuse ...'

'With a man it is different. In the eyes of the Church I am merely a mistress and mistresses are not crowned.'

'But surely the Pope knew the circumstances when he agreed to officiate.'

'That is the point. He did not agree. He was forced. Bonaparte was obliged to threaten him to get him to come. He threatened to ban the Church in France again unless Pius came. And that shows how deep religion goes with him! So the old man will come and take revenge by refusing to crown me! And don't forget, there are three Bonapartes in Italy at this minute, all working against me; all good Catholics, all with access to the Pope. How delighted they will be. And here was I babbling like a fool about what I was to wear.'

She did not weep, but I could see by her pallor and her look of despair that she believed what she was saying. She looked very old at that moment, old and defeated. I tried to tell myself that she was the victim of her own suspicion and that what she feared was most unlikely to happen. Surely a Pope was unlikely to connive … And yet I could not be sure. Pauline, the most jealous and spiteful of them all, was in Italy, and such a public humiliation was just the kind of thing she might plan.

'Then you must strike first,' I said, forcing my mind to clarity. 'Say nothing. When Pius arrives, request a private audience. Tell him that you have *always* worried about not being properly married. Say you feel unfit to be crowned. Cry just a little. Ask him to suggest a little private pre-Coronation marriage ceremony. He could hardly refuse that to a penitent woman, anxious to atone.'

She thought that over and then said dubiously, 'It might work. I certainly cannot think of anything better. I can but try.' Colour returned to her face, her eyes always dark in distress, regained their blue and within a few minutes she was back on the subject of clothes; this time what I should wear. But just before she left she was serious again. She said, 'Darling, you are so clever, and so pretty. You've given Louis two beautiful boys. It does seem such a shame that you are not happier. You know there are times … Waking in the middle of the night when I think the whole thing was a most tragic mistake. Perhaps I should never … But I was in such a muddle. And I balance what it brought to me, and to you, against what it did for Eugène, and then sometimes I think that in fact what we do and what comes of it is not a matter of choice at all … That we do what we must, often to the hurt of ourselves and those we love.'

'Old man Calvin and his predestination?'

'No. Oh *no*. That was all about souls and such a cruel creed. I was thinking more about, well, physical things, what we do in this world. It is a little difficult to explain. But, darling, if your plan works and I am married, and crowned, I will tell you something I never told anybody.'

The year crept downhill, with worsening weather. My cough stayed with me, but it could be controlled by that one particular medicine which seemed to drop a veil, three layers of gauze, between me and whatever was going on. Dr Courvisart, the Emperor's own physician who had recommended it in the first place, worried about it, saying that he had advised it as a temporary relief, not as something to be taken regularly, in large quantities. Louis said that I was suffering from whooping cough; he could remember Jerome having this complaint and being cured by eating a fried mouse. What animals are edible and which inedible is a matter subject to no rational rules and I had not the quite prevalent feminine aversion to mice, but the idea of eating one, fried, repulsed me for no reason that I could give. So I was not cured; I continued to gulp down the laudanum compound when necessary and Dr Courvisart spoke gloomily about the link between laudanum and opium and the danger of becoming addicted and I tried to comfort him, saying that once the Coronation was over I would eschew the drug, retire to Saint-Leu and cough, if I must, all day and all night.

Pius arrived in November and his reception by the ordinary people was proof positive that in restoring the Church my step-father had once again gauged the ordinary man's mind and given the ordinary man what he needed. Foul as the weather was, thousands of people stood lining the roads, the men bare-headed, the women often on their knees as he passed. Pius VII was old and very frail, thin and bowed, but he bore the stamp of supreme authority. That my step-father resented. This was evident from the way he gloated over and repeated remarks made by old soldiers, anti-clerical in sentiment. Things like, 'This Coronation is only a puppet show. We crowned him at Lodi', and 'We made our little corporal into an Emperor without any help from Monsieur Pope'. A few really virulent anti-clerical veterans threatened to boycott the ceremony altogether, and though the Emperor said sternly that when he ordered a parade it must *be* a parade, he was secretly delighted by anything that smacked of anti-Papal sentiment. It was against such a background that Mother set about to carry out the plan I had suggested.

She did it successfully. After the requested private audience, she called upon me in order to report. She was all in black, her face with its still beautiful complexion, clear as a cameo against the cloud of black gauze, arranged so that it hid her hair and the age-betraying throat. Her ability to play any part she assigned herself had served her so well that even now, having gained her point, she was still all penitent and intensely self-reproachful at ever having doubted the Pope's integrity. Pius had indeed shown himself to be a very powerful ally and said that unless the Emperor took immediate steps to regularise the position, he doubted whether he could bring himself to crown *him*.

Three days before the Coronation an altar was set up in the Emperor's study at The Tuileries, and Madame Bonaparte's brother, Cardinal Fesch, performed the marriage ceremony. Two staff officers had acted as witnesses. Nobody else was present.

Divorce, which to a greater or lesser degree had threatened this marriage from the start, backed away; a proper church marriage could not be broken, as a civil one could be, at will. For the first time since those days when Bonaparte had been so infatuated, Mother felt truly secure. Happiness illuminated and rejuvenated her. It also enabled her to bear with equanimity the latest evidence of Bonaparte malice.

Old records of earlier Coronations had been studied and among the facts unearthed was that to bear the Queen's train was the highest honour, reserved for the most nobly born. Therefore Elisa, Pauline – now back from Italy – Caroline, Julie and I were to carry Mother's. Ignorant of, or ignoring tradition, the Bonaparte sisters rebelled; train carrying was for pages, it was humiliating, they would not do it, they would sooner stay away from the ceremony, they would rather die than be so degraded.

With that phenomenal patience that he almost invariably displayed towards his family the Emperor argued and coaxed, quoting precedence, naming great ladies who had been proud to be trainbearers to Queens. 'Yes,' Pauline retorted, 'Queens of royal birth. Show me proof that Princesses ever carried the train of a Creole upstart.'

That angered him and he said they could stay away and he might have held to that decision had Madame Bonaparte been going to be present. She was not, and to have none of his female relatives present except me, his stepdaughter, would give rise to talk. So he compromised; we were not to bear the train, we were to *support* it.

Of that superlatively grand and glittering ceremony I had but the haziest impression; I was so afraid that at some crucial moment my cough would shake me that I took a treble dose of the brew and went through the day in a kind of waking dream; I did not walk, I floated. I felt absurdly happy, profoundly calm. Two moments made an impact on my muffled consciousness. One was when Mother had to move forward and mount a few steps. We had had a rehearsal of the train-supporting, and now Julie and I assumed our part of the burden. The Bonaparte sisters pretended to, but instead of supporting, they pulled. 'Mother tottered and seemed about to fall backwards, Julie and I stumbled. Then the weight eased as they took their share and we all moved forward.

The other moment was when the Emperor's impatience seemed to get the better of him. It was a long ceremony and Pius was slow, setting a pace which all the attendant clergy must follow. Even the organ seemed to lag. When it came to the ultimate stage, to which all else had been moving and the Pope was about to place the crown on his head, Bonaparte took it, snatched it almost, and crowned himself. He then lifted the lighter, more delicate crown and put it on Mother's head. She had the presence of mind to sink down on her knees. That moment is immortalised in David's painting of the scene, though there is one discrepancy. The Emperor ordered that his mother should be painted in. Whether by accident or design, or because truth will sometimes insist upon asserting itself, that old, handsome, hawk-like face is there forever, staring upon the scene with an expression of derision and mockery, not far removed from contempt.

15

I had adhered to my intention to go to Saint-Leu and cough myself out, but there were all the celebrations and then there was Christmas. And Eugène, who had come to Paris for the Coronation, was still there, waiting to return, early in the year, with the Emperor who was to be crowned King of Italy, naming Eugène as his Viceroy. So I stayed on and dosed myself when occasion demanded.

Louis and I seemed to have reached, in three years, that state which most unhappy but unbroken marriages, and some happy ones, reach after a period much longer; nothing to hope for, nothing to fear. When we were alone together, which now happened seldom since the new status had completely altered our lives, we hardly spoke. I had learned not to offer comments which would immediately be contradicted or be twisted into something that I did not intend; he was very gloomy and more than usually withdrawn. His acidulous comments upon Eugène's appointment I took in silence, making a little allowance for the sourness, Louis would so have loved to be *sent* to Italy, into the sunshine and a basically feudal way of life and the company of Lucien whom he missed.

Charles de Flahaut I saw a few times, not often because Murat, perhaps a bit jealous and wary of Caroline, kept choosing him to go on military missions, and after all he was a soldier, and France was at war though sometimes this seemed difficult to accept. The Army for the Invasion of England was still mustering at Boulogne, the flat-bottomed boats being built in increasing numbers, the stores under Prince Joseph, that veteran commissariat man, mounting. But so far no shot had been fired. The Emperor, who had once declared the invasion of England to be impossible, was waiting for perfect sea conditions and the rehabilitation of the French navy. England was waiting for a continental ally.

I was waiting to go to Saint-Leu, with Madame de Boubers and the children, with Adèle and perhaps, for appearance's sake, one other of my ladies, Madame de Viry, sharp-tongued, witty, irreverent. But before I could get away and break through the routine of cough, dose, cough, dose, an idiotic thing happened.

Ostensibly the French press was free, but newspaper proprietors and journalists had learned that it was wise to adhere to the old proverb – Tell the true, but not the unpleasant, tell the pleasant but not the untrue. With an unpleasant truth or an untrue pleasantry, they could always get away by pretending to quote from foreign papers – as had happened during the Egyptian campaign.

It was not the English press, but the German which suddenly began to focus upon me and to be quoted. The Paris-based representative of a Berlin paper began to send reports that dismissed Mother, the Emperor, everybody else worth mentioning in a couple of lines and then took to describing in detail what I wore, how I looked, what I did, to whom I spoke. If for any reason I was not present at some function, I was still dragged in, 'All that this glittering occasion lacked was the presence of Princess Louis ...' That sort of thing. To be honest, I was not displeased; I was not extremely thin and to be called sylphlike and ethereal was comforting. It was also agreeable to learn that at some function to which I had gone half-drugged my behaviour had been distinguished by its gracious animation and my conversation by its wit.

The thing became a joke, with frequent references to my 'unknown admirer'. Even Madame de Viry, who had many friends and interests outside the Court circle, failed to identify whoever it was who reported to a German paper and had access not only to public but to many private functions. My own amusement became slightly tinged with uneasiness when one article, praising me as a lady who did not allow social pleasures to interfere with the duties of motherhood, described exactly the way I romped with Non-Non and what I wore while playing – garments I never wore on any other occasion. It gave me a feeling of being spied upon by a relentless if kindly eye and it seemed reasonable to suspect that the spy must be in my own household. Watchfulness and questioning, however, revealed nothing.

The laudatory remarks and articles ceased as abruptly as they had begun and the reports of what the Berlin papers were saying resumed their usual function of saying what no French paper dared say directly. Then the truth came out. My unknown admirer was a young man of respectable family and some private means who had been sent by the German paper to report upon the Coronation and the following festivities. At one point he had been warned that he had not been sent to Paris and paid in order to eulogise Princess Louis and that unless his articles became more inclusive he would lose his job. He had continued to write about me and had lost his job, gone out of his mind and been fetched home by his distressed parents. That was a sad story enough, but there was more to it. Other people besides me and Adèle and Madame de Viry had realised that someone, in contact with Germany, had enjoyed unusual freedom of access and the word 'spy' was being used in its serious sense. Police investigation had revealed that under a number of names and in several capacities the young man had wormed his way into almost everything except the Sunday family suppers. In one group of hired musicians he played the violin, in another the piano; he had acted as a temporary waiter, usher, scene-shifter. All harmless, except to himself, and all because, so his parents said in a public statement, because of his infatuation for me!

Louis's jealousy, which seemed to have died of inanition, sprang up, very lively and very vicious. It was absolutely absurd, he said, for me to say that I had never wittingly seen the young man, or spoken to him. No man in his senses would become so infatuated without some encouragement.

'But this poor fellow was not in his senses,' I pointed out, breaking my rule of silence. 'He has probably been a little mad for a long time.'

'Mad or sane,' Louis said, shifting ground a little, 'how could he know what games you play with Non-Non; or about that shabby old cloak. Answer me. How can you account for that?'

'I cannot.'

'Because you will not admit the truth. He was here. In this house. Admit it! Admit it!'

His face was so livid, his eyes so bulging, their whites streaked with red that for a moment I thought he was going to attack me, but he contented himself with verbal abuse. I was a liar, I was sly, I was unfaithful; I must be kept under constant surveillance in order to prevent worse scandals, and under surveillance I should be kept. He ended by giving orders that we move out immediately to Saint-Leu.

I was still a little curious as to how that unfortunate young man could have known what I wore when I played with Non-Non; none of his roles seemed to explain that. I wore the old blue cloak because we often played with a ball and Non-Non's aim was not yet very steady, nor was my catching good, the damp or muddy ball often hit my clothing. The garden of our Rue Taitbout house was entirely surrounded by walls, at least twelve feet high and against the one at the end there were several tall trees, which with those on the adjoining properties made a screen that should have ensured complete privacy. However, while the hasty packing was being done I went into the garden and stood on the stretch of lawn where Non-Non and I usually played and looked around and saw that from one house, not next door, nor directly across the street that ran parallel, there was a view from a single window at this time of the year when the trees were leafless. I called Adèle, pointed out the house and the window to her and asked her to go and make enquiries. She came back and said that the house contained ten apartments, one of which had been until lately occupied by the mysterious young man about whom such a fuss was being made. 'Such a very quiet, well-behaved young man, too,' the concierge had said.

When I offered this explanation to Louis he ridiculed it. The window was set at such an angle that it would be impossible for anyone standing at it to see into our garden, he said.

I said, 'But if a man stood at that window now, we could see him and naturally he could see us.'

Louis then said that he was tired of flimsy excuses and wished to hear no more on the subject.

Out at Saint-Leu his behaviour became more and more irrational, or at least only rational when viewed from the eye of his obsession. The weather was fine and pleasant for the time of year but we were allowed to take no drives except when Louis was able and willing to accompany us. Would-be visitors were repulsed, Her Imperial Highness was not well enough to receive anyone. In order to spare fuel we must all spend every evening together in one room, under Louis's gloomy eye. Music was forbidden, it made his head ache. Could we not play cards more quietly? He would sit with a book in his hand, but the reading was a pretence; most of the time he sat staring gloomily ahead. One day he went to Paris, saying he would spend the night there and the sense of freedom and gaiety that his absence caused was a measure of the repression we all felt in his presence. That evening we drank more wine than usual, and laughed at almost nothing, we had music and those who could do so sang. I could not because of my cough.

In the dark of that night I woke with a jolt and with that creepy feeling that I was not alone. I cried sharply, 'Who is there?'

Louis's voice asked, 'Whom did you expect? Who else could it be?'

He made a light and looked searchingly around the room. Such a wakening had given me a shock, I coughed and trembled. The implication of his action outraged me.

I said, coughing, 'You have neglected to look under the bed.'

'You've been lucky, so far,' he said cryptically. 'But you'll trip one day.'

I did not mention this midnight visitation even to Adèle; she knew a lot, having been with me from the first, but she was so much attached to me that to dwell upon a situation which she was impotent to relieve, seemed cruel. What my new ladies thought of Louis's general behaviour, what explanations they found or invented, I could not know.

Two or three days later, in pale sunshine, Adèle, Madame de Viry and I took Non-Non to walk and play in the garden which, like the one in Paris, was walled, the walls not so high. We played with the ball until Non-Non made one of his wild throws and sent the ball over into the heavily timbered ground outside. Furious with himself, he let out a roar. I said, 'Never mind. You have lots of balls.'

'I want that one. That is my best ball. I want it. I want it.'

Madame de Viry, who thought he was a spoiled child, gave him a cold look. Dear Adèle said, 'Perhaps we could find it. There is a little gate, at least a door, just along there,' she nodded towards the left. 'All right, Non-Non.'

She took his hand and said, 'We'll stay here and call, so that Mamma and Madame de Viry know where to look and they'll try to find it for you. If not I'll get you a new one, all red. You like red, don't you?'

'I want my ball.'

Madame de Viry and I hurried away, and there, as Adèle said, was a door which I had never noticed, perhaps because I had always been either playing with Non-Non or making plans for the garden. It was a door of solid oak-planks, roughly hewn and studded with nails, old enough to be contemporary with the original ruined château. It fastened on the inside with two heavy bolts, rusted and difficult to shift. But we moved them at last and walked back, calling and being answered. When we were level with Adèle and Non-Non, Adèle said, 'You're right now,' and Non-Non said, 'Find it.' Madame de Viry stopped and said, 'I hope you will forgive me. This is something I have felt I should say … Madame de Boubers is a most excellent governess … Please do not think that I am criticising her. But she is concerned only with the physical well-being. If that child's destiny is what we all hope and expect it to be, wilfulness may make things very hard for him. Self-control must be learned early, if it is to be learned at all.'

From over the wall the child of destiny called. 'Find it. I want my ball.'

There were fallen leaves, there was withered bracken. Madame de Viry abandoned her lecture, we searched, we poked, we stamped. We converged upon what had obviously once been a kind of path leading obliquely to that gate in the wall. It was overgrown, but relatively open and I said, 'It could have ricocheted off a tree trunk and rolled a little way.'

An angrier and more urgent voice than Non-Non's yelled, 'Stop! Come back. Stop! Back in!' There was Louis, looking quite demented. He made a little detour and got ahead of us along the path, then, waving his arms and shouting like a peasant driving animals, hustled us back through the door, slammed and bolted it and with his back to it said breathlessly, 'Now! Where were you going? Whom were you meeting?'

It was the most open display of mania he had yet made and I was morti-fied and frightened.

'Madame de Viry and I were looking for a ball that Non-Non threw over.'

'That's a likely tale! We'll have the truth now. Come on, I want the truth!'

'That *is* the truth,' Madame de Viry said quite truculently. 'Do you ques-tion my word?' She was very small, and facing Louis, in her russet cloak, she was rather like those miniature fowls, called Bantams from their place of origin in the Far East. 'Am I to understand that you suspect *me* of some clandestine assignation?' I thought her deliberate misreading of the situation most tactful. 'Allow me to say that did I not know better, I should suspect Your Imperial Highness of being inebriated.'

'You … You,' Louis began, stammering with rage. How that sentence would have ended, what he would have done or said we could not know, for Non-Non came trotting up.

'Did you find …?' Seeing us empty-handed he reddened and roared, 'I want it, I want it. It is my favourite …'

'Forget it,' Louis said. 'I'll give you a ride.' Neglecting for once to spare his weak arm he hoisted the child on to his shoulders and set off across the garden at a shambling jog-trot. Adèle joined Madame de Viry and me and we walked back to the house in an embarrassed silence, as though we had jointly witnessed some shaming thing.

Three men spent the afternoon walling up the garden gateway with bricks taken from the ruined château.

'It is very *sad*,' Madame de Viry said when she had finished her brutal, but understanding little discourse upon what she called the Italian Disease. 'I know it only too well, I had a very dear cousin … Very dear. I hoped to marry him. With him also it resulted in hallucinations. He was so positive that he had been cheated out of some property that he went to law and ruined himself. So I speak from experience. What one must remember is that it is an infirmity, to be pitied and excused. One must also remember that one does not accept everything a man says or does simply because he has toothache …'

I sat there, listening, quite stunned by the idea that Louis's jealousy and suspicion had nothing to do with what Lucien had said, or anything I, or anyone else had done. It was, if Madame de Viry were to be believed, the result of a disease which he had contracted by sleeping with a diseased girl in Italy; something of which, in my sheltered, my innocent, my ignorant life I had never even heard and now found very difficult to believe in.

I said, 'Is there no cure?'

She hesitated. 'I think it is too late. Taken in time … No, Your Highness, the brain is the last to be affected. The subject of the hallucinations may shift. There may be intermissions. My aim in speaking so frankly … on such a very distasteful subject, was to console you. Ever since I joined Your Highness's household I have had my suspicions, but I … However, what happened this morning could hardly be overlooked. We could hardly pretend that it had not happened … If I were to continue to attend you, I felt that I must speak out, or resign.'

I said, 'I am very grateful to you. I had no …' I broke off to cough, a shattering paroxysm, so bad that towards the end of it I knew what it felt like to die. I could not breathe in against the cough, could not draw in the air necessary for coughing. There was a roaring in my ears, sparks in front of my eyes. I thought – I am dying, help me, help! Then it was over and it seemed to have cured itself. I did not cough in the night, nor next day, nor the next, or the next.

When we went to our Paris house there was fresh evidence of Louis's hallucination. There my bedroom opened on one side to my private sitting room beyond which was a small anteroom out of which was a door to the nursery; on the other side, from close to my bed, there was another door which gave upon my dressing room which in turn had a door to a kind of landing off which were the doors of the rooms occupied by my ladies-in-waiting and a stairway leading up to the maids' quarters. The further door of my dressing room had been boarded over and hung with the same silk as the other walls; and that meant that any of my ladies, any maid could reach me only by going down twenty stairs, crossing the main entry, mounting twenty-eight slightly more shallow stairs, crossing the anteroom and the sitting room. Also, just below my bedroom window was a little sentry box, manned day and night. It was in order to make these re-arrangements that Louis had come into Paris on the day that ended in the night when he gave me such a scare.

Adèle said, 'How shameful!' and wept. My other four ladies grumbled, saying how inconvenient. Madame de Viry said, 'This is the sick mind which must be resisted. If Your Highness will give me permission to speak …' What she said and how she said it I do not know, I was not there, but her speaking was effective. The boarded-over doorway was unblocked. The sentry box remained, causing nobody any inconvenience. After that Louis's disease had a quiescent period, or perhaps the outbursts had purged his jealousy. There were no more scenes, and surrounded by people as we now were, flung back into a gay social life, there were fewer silent, solitary meals. My cough was better, Louis-Napoleon's health improved. The late spring and summer of that year 1805 was, domestically, a relatively happy time.

Outwardly it was a strange year with many comings and goings, troop movements, rumours and speculations as to where the fighting would be, and when it would break out. The Emperor was often absent from Paris, but he gave orders that this should make no difference; Mother, Pauline, Caroline and I were to set the fashion for gay, though decorous entertainments. Elisa was absent too. She had been created Duchess of a small Italian principality, Piombino, and was taking her new position very seriously indeed. Caroline disguised her jealousy by mockery. 'Elisa will have an army of sixty men, twenty of them officers, and she will hold a parade every day. Twice on Sundays.' In fact Elisa showed a good deal of my step-father's energy and administrative ability, concentrating upon making roads, setting up schools and improving the economic state of her tiny realm.

I had now resumed dancing. One of the privileges of being a Royal Princess was that I could choose my partners, and not be chosen. When Charles was in Paris it was sometimes a little awkward, and always very painful for me to ignore him as I felt I must. Once when I had done so, just before supper, he came and stood behind me during the meal and said, in a plaintive, muted voice, 'You are very unkind to me. Why?' I should have pretended not to hear. Instead I turned, met that look at close quarters and changed colour; whether I reddened or paled I did not know, but the whole of my face underwent a slight crepitation which must have shown, and my heart jumped up to above my collar bone and hammered there. The stare between us seemed to last for a very long time. Later that evening I saw Madame de Souza looking at me rather speculatively.

When at last I did dance with him it was by direct order. It was at Malmaison, in high summer, at one of Mother's private parties. The Emperor, who did not dance, but liked to favour certain ladies by inviting them to sit out a dance with him, led me off into the conservatory, saying that he had not seen enough of me lately. He seemed rather preoccupied and presently said, apropos of nothing, 'Everything now depends upon the fleet. Don't you find it remarkable to reflect that England, where there was no Revolution, stands or falls by the abilities of the son of a poor country parson? Our Villeneuve is a good man – the best I could find, but not a genius …' He brooded, then said, 'But if he had luck he could be across the Channel in no time. The flotilla is ready. Simply a question of moving back the men. This new Coalition is no problem …' He was, I realised, talking to himself; nothing was required of me except silence and an attentive attitude. I was actually thinking about the English, who in their papers, at least, had been so self-righteous, attacking his morals, and Mother's and mine, now depending for their lives on a man who for years had been the acknowledged lover of another man's wife, had a child by her. '…for your pretty little head,' the Emperor continued. 'But I always found you so easy to talk to, my dear. Now, you must not waste any more time on me. You must come and dance with some of these beautiful young men who may have little time left for dancing. Even the shortest, most victorious campaign brings some casualties. Give them something to remember as they march. Ha, here is de Flahaut, a most nimble performer. He will not tread on your toes …'

He pushed me towards Charles who was standing just inside the ball-room. He pushed me literally – since the dance just beginning was a waltz – into his arms.

When the waltz was first introduced it was severely criticised as being indecent, involving as it did far more contact between bodies than the older dances,
gavottes and minuets. Some older people refused to dance it at all, strict parents
forbade their daughters to waltz. Despite or perhaps because of this conservative disapproval the waltz had caught on as no dance had ever done and the
denouncements of it as a sensual, slightly indecent thing had endued it with a
sexual significance. All but a few people tried to waltz with ones they liked.

Dropping Hortense by the door of the conservatory, the zombie put its
right hand in Charles's left, its left hand, lightly, on his right upper arm. It
accepted his right hand around its waist, noted the strength, the warmth.
Part of it, but not all, that I want, the zombie said.

I felt myself go soft, yielding, weak. I seemed to have no bones, borne on
a wave, wafted on a breeze. Dumb.

He was dumb too, but as I weakened his hold strengthened. The stipu-
lated four inches which even waltz-acceptors decreed should separate two
waltzing bodies, lessened. From the meeting of our hands, from the spot
where my fingers touched the hard muscle of his arm something seemed
to spark and crackle, a pins-and-needles sensation. Words were not needed;
they would indeed have interfered, broken the spell.

The dreamy, romantic tune began to slow down, a prelude to its end, but
someone – perhaps someone like me who wished this dance to last forever
– must have given a signal and it went on.

Charles spoke then. He said, 'Something to remember for ever.'

I wanted to say – For me also, but I dared not make that admission.

'You will remember, too,' he said in a tone of quiet triumph. 'Say that you
will. When I am far away.'

I thought of the Emperor's words about those with little time left for
dancing. To my utter dismay I felt my eyes fill with tears. I was about to cry,
on a crowded ball-room floor. I bent my head, blinked, swallowed hard. I
said, 'It would be better to forget. It can come to no good.'

'Why not, when we were meant for each other.'

'It is too late.'

'Never say that. I shall come back.' I thought how all men went into battle
with that certainty. Hortense had a shuddering premonition that here was
one who would not come back. The zombie began a raging tirade about
time wasted, joy missed, comparing me unfavourably with those like Pauline
who when they loved showed it, braving scandal. Why, the zombie demanded,
should you set yourself up to be holy? With Louis so jealous of nothing, why
did you not give him reason to be and snatch what you could? Just think, the
zombie said, if an almost conventional dance-hold can do this to you …

'May I write to you?'

I said 'Oh no!' in such a tone of horror that I felt it demanded some explanation. 'I have so little privacy nowadays.'

'Of course. I forget. Will you write to me?'

'That would be unwise.'

'Oh well,' he said, making nothing of it, 'it will be a short war.'

It was a short war. In October the French won the Battle of Ulm in Germany. There Charles was wounded and decorated for conspicuous gallantry. Two days later the English smashed the French fleet at Trafalgar. In December on the first anniversary of his Coronation, the Emperor won, at Austerlitz, the battle of which he was most proud, and to which he most often referred, remembering every detail, even down to the weather. Before the end of the year he was in Vienna, dictating new peace terms. As soon as the Treaty of Pressburg was signed he turned his attention to the rearrangement of Europe.

16

During the war I had hardly seen Louis at all. He had been put in charge of the defences of the Dutch and Belgian coasts, appeared to have thrown off his physical frailties and acquitted himself well. It was plain that away from me he did better. It was also plain that with Europe at his feet, simply waiting to be rearranged, the Emperor would have many high-sounding posts and appointments in his gift. I hoped, as intensely as I had ever hoped for anything, that he would offer Louis something in a far place, too attractive to be resisted and at the same time order the children – still his putative heirs – to stay in Paris. Their extreme youth would be my excuse for remaining with them and Louis and I would be virtually separated.

Things did not work out that way.

One of the Emperor's first arrangements was to make a marriage between my brother Eugène and the daughter of the King of Bavaria, the Princess Augusta.

How Eugène felt about this we never knew. He was twenty-five, good-looking, popular, but although his name had naturally been linked by rumour with that of several eligible ladies he had given no sign of preferring one above the others; nor had he, for some reason, ever been the object of scandal, even in foreign papers. Perhaps it was because he regarded the Emperor's wish as law, or because he had never been in love, Eugène agreed to marry a woman of whom he knew nothing, of whom he had only seen a very bad portrait – painted on a tea cup! The Princess Augusta was equally malleable; merely saying that she disliked hairy men and wished Eugène to shave off his moustache, that veteran soldier's hallmark. It was her father who proved intransigent; his daughter was of royal blood, reared and trained for a royal marriage. What, he asked, were Eugène's prospects? Oh yes, Viceroy of Italy *now*, but a viceroyalty was, after all, only an *appointment*; before he could agree to the marriage he wanted his daughter to have a more assured future.

Then, after all the nagging about who should be his legal heir, the Emperor swung about and named Eugène. He should be Prince Eugène Napoleon of France adopted by the Emperor, one day Napoleon II. The prospect of his daughter being Empress of the French satisfied the King of Bavaria and the wedding was arranged to take place in Munich.

I was glad that Eugène was settled for life, but it meant that Non-Non and Lou became of less importance to the Emperor who would no longer be so eager to keep them under his eye in Paris. So if Louis were given some important post in a far place, they and I would have to go with him. After this interval of freedom from watchfulness and surliness, the prospect appalled me; as also did the prospect of leaving Paris and all my friends, Mother and the Emperor himself.

The beginning of our resumed conjugal life began badly. I wanted to attend Eugène's wedding. Mother was already in Munich, Caroline was about to join Murat there; I could have travelled with her. Louis forbade it. I was not strong enough, he said, to travel in mid-winter. So I was absent from Eugène's wedding, as he had been absent from mine. I hoped his marriage would be happier, and Mother, when she returned, said that it promised well, the bride seemed amiable, was young and pretty enough without being beautiful. Eugène had taken to her from the start.

Envy of Eugène took various forms. Murat was so infuriated that he broke his sword across his knee. Louis was very sulky. With typical perversity he, who had been so resistant to the idea of allowing Non-Non to be adopted, now chose to regard Eugène's adoption as a deliberate slight to our sons as well as to Joseph and himself. He said some cutting things about the Beauharnais's luck and the advantage of being a step-relative.

But it was Caroline who planned a possible, most subtle and far-sighted revenge.

Soon after her return to Paris, Mother, having contrived for us to be alone, suddenly said, 'Do you know Eleanore Denuelle de la Plaigne?'

My stomach lurched. I knew all about it. One of my ladies, Madame de Mollien, was very friendly with one of Caroline's. The scheme was supposed to be secret and I did feel that it might have been kept from Mother at least until it had borne some result. How much did she know? I said, cautiously, 'Yes. She was at Madame Campan's. Younger than I. She made a hopeless marriage and Caroline has been very good to her.'

'Not without reason. Do you know what Caroline is planning?'

'Tell me.'

'An experiment. Darling, this is rather coarse, but between ourselves … The child is one of those plump, pink and white creatures who appeal to men who are getting … To men no longer quite young. Bonaparte took some little notice of her. Now she is to live in a pavilion in Caroline's garden and no man, no man at all, is to go near her except Bonaparte. If she becomes pregnant the blame for this barren marriage will be laid squarely upon *me* and talk of divorce will begin again.'

That was precisely what I had been told. It seemed to me that Mother was taking this latest move to oust her with the most remarkable calm.

'It sounds just like Caroline,' I said.

'The result may disappoint her. I think Madame de la Plaigne will tire of being locked away long before she is pregnant.' She leaned forward and gave me a little tap on the knee. 'I know more than I say. I am not ignorant of that little secret room at The Tuileries where pretty young actresses come and go – sometimes within ten minutes. His infidelities mean nothing – he always comes back to me. But not one of his mistresses has ever conceived, or we should have heard about it. I have you and Eugène to prove that I am not barren. The fault lies with him.

I thought about that supposed pregnancy and miscarriage so soon after their marriage. Another man? Barras? Was that why she had accepted, so hastily, the first offer of marriage to come along? Perhaps the question and shock showed on my face.

'When I thought I was pregnant I was mistaken, I think now,' Mother said. 'The anxiety and the indecision, just being married again, after so long could upset the rhythm. I never was very regular. And the next time certainly made up … I don't say that he is an inadequate lover, but I think he lacks whatever it is that makes children. After all I was only thirty-three – at least I had not had my birthday – thirty-two. Old for a first child perhaps, but not for a third. And I tried everything.'

It sounded reasonable enough and I was glad that she was not perturbed. But I had another horrid thought. Caroline was tricky. If she had set herself to produce evidence, evidence there would be. Could Murat be forbidden access to his own garden pavilion? I kept that thought to myself.

Changes came thick and fast. Joseph was made King of Naples and Louis jibed, 'Promotion for the good civil servant.'

Murat and Caroline were given the Duchy of Berg and Cleves. Louis said, 'Give a dog a bone. And the quicker the better if the dog is angry.' Caroline said that the income from the Duchy would be welcome, but that she had no intention of going to live in some gimcrack German castle, pretending to be somebody like Elisa in Piombino.

What happened to me and Louis, when we became King and Queen of Holland, was rather different, the whole business conducted under the pretence that we were the choice of the Dutch people; chosen, not imposed. And it was true that deputations of sober Dutch citizens had forestalled being given a master and had requested that Holland should become part of the Empire, with Louis as their King.

I had a faint hope that Louis, from sheer perversity, would refuse. I thought of Holland as a dreary, flat country, half of it dredged up from the sea; a country with no long tradition of monarchy, full of dull, fat burghers, Protestant trades-men in dull grey cities so independent that they almost amounted to separate states. I must confess that the mere fact that Louis, during the brief war, had seemed to like the place and the people, made me think that I should not.

He accepted the throne of Holland, choosing to regard it, not as a gift from the Emperor but as an offer from the Dutch which he felt it his duty to accept. He managed to convey the impression that he was bravely shoulder-ing a very heavy burden indeed.

As usual, Caroline was infuriated. 'Joseph got a kingdom for seeing to buckles and kegs of salt beef. Now Louis has a kingdom for inspecting dykes and learning ten words of some barbarous language. And you will be Queen.' She gave me one of those diminishing looks, from the top of my head to my feet and back again, a look that said clearly, *And a fine Queen you will make!* 'Joachim shed his blood at Austerlitz.'

I said, coldly, 'Perhaps the Emperor is keeping you in reserve, Caroline. Nelson is dead, the King of England is going mad, they say. You could be Queen of England.'

What they all lacked, every single Bonaparte, was a sense of humour as it applied to themselves. It was their strength and their weakness. Caroline took this quite seriously and said, 'It could be. Then my Achille would be … what is it exactly? Prince of Wales?'

Mother said, 'I shall miss you and the children. And so will he, though he does not realise it. Though he did say that you must make frequent visits. Long visits, because Paris is now the centre of Europe. The one real capital.'

But in order to return to a place one must leave it and leaving Paris was a wrench to me. It was my home. My reluctance to leave it and go into exile had nothing to do with Charles de Flahaut who had been left on garrison duty in Germany.

I was to leave behind Adèle and the rest of my ladies. Louis, from the moment that he was proclaimed King of Holland, had become very Dutch indeed. We must, he said, avoid at all costs the impression that Holland was being invaded by the French. All posts of honour or significance must be occupied by natives of our new kingdom. The single exception to this rule was Madame de Boubers; she and I must learn the language quickly. 'My kingdom,' Louis said, 'is not going to be a mere appendage to his Empire, whatever he may think.'

But on the whole Louis seemed happy and invigorated, busy with this and that, fulfilled, with far less time and attention to spare for me, for being watchful and suspicious and waspish.

We were to leave for Holland on 16th June, formally from Saint-Leu. On the 15th, a day of heavy, warm summer rain, I went into Paris to say goodbye to Mother and to look in upon our town house to see that everything was in order there.

Except for our drive to the border, where our French entourage would be dismissed and replaced by Dutch appointees, this was the last drive I should take with Adèle. That was a choking thought. Taking leave of Mother broke down my resolution not to cry. I cried, she cried. The Emperor came in and said impatiently, 'One would think that you were both going to the guillotine.'

'I could hardly feel worse,' I sobbed.

He took me by the upper arm and shook me, quite roughly.

'You ungrateful little slut. Don't you realise that I have given you the pick of the basket? A clean, prosperous country, full of level-headed people. Different from that stinking Naples where fever breeds. And I have done you an honour quite unprecedented. Written into the constitution, specially. If Louis is absent for any length of time, or if anything happens to him, you will be Regent. Think of that!'

Gratifying, I suppose, to one with ambitions; to me no comfort at all.

'I would far, far sooner stay here, in my own country, with those I love. With my friends.'

'A fine way to talk. You have your husband, your children. You will not lack friends.'

I then said what I should have said much earlier.

'Even now, on the verge of departure, I wish I need not go. It was all so hurried, and you have been so often away and so busy when you were here … Couldn't Louis go alone and leave me and the children here?'

'I credited you with some sense. Think how that would look! High position calls for some sense of responsibility, and some self-control.'

'Nobody knows that better than Hortense,' Mother said. 'It was just that she feels the parting. I am to blame, I cried first.'

'Then be the first to stop. She is not going to Senegal!'

When it came to saying goodbye, however, he softened, embraced and kissed me fondly and spoke again about visits.

In the Rue Taitbout the house was already shuttered, the chandeliers encased in linen bags, the furniture that we were leaving, covered with dust-sheets. Louis intended to sell it eventually, while retaining Saint-Leu, but he wished first to see what accommodation and what furnishings awaited us in Holland. The house already had a dead and deserted air. The hamper, which contained a few completely personal things which I wished to take with me, was packed and stood in the entrance hall, left open in case I should wish to add something at the last minute. The caretaker who, with his wife, was to remain in charge, stood by, ready to fasten the hamper and carry it to the carriage.

At the last minute I remembered something – a little watercolour of Non-Non which Adèle had painted and thought the best thing she had ever done. I did not like it much, it was so like and yet so unlike the child. Every feature, every shade of colouring was correct, but the expression was one which Non-Non seldom wore, so grave as to be sad, an almost fated look. I had hung it close beside my bed, in a place where it did not catch my eye. As is sometimes the way with things one does not wish to remember, I had forgotten it when I made my list. Now with Adèle standing by and our first real parting imminent ...

I said, 'Now there remains only one thing. Your picture of Non-Non. I wanted to put that in with my own hands.'

Adèle went to fetch it; the caretaker went to fetch paper and came back immediately, without it.

'Your Majesty, a gentleman wishes to see you. He has a message.'

It was Charles; plain civilian hat pulled low, completely sodden; cloak collar turned high against the rain.

I said, 'How did you get here?' – meaning by what accident of chance, good or bad, had he come to the place at which I had arrived ten minutes earlier and from which, in another ten, I should be gone. He took the question literally and said, 'I rode. I've been in the saddle ever since I had a letter from my mother.' He had taken off his hat, spikes of wet hair framed a face grey and hollowed out by fatigue.

I could hear the caretaker coming back with the paper, and Adèle at the head of the stairs.

I said, 'If you have a message for me, monsieur, you had better come in here.'

I led the way to a little waiting room just off the entry. He closed the door behind him, loosed his cloak and let it and the hat fall, held out his arms. Impelled by the zombie I fell into them and we kissed.

Hortense knew that this was crazy behaviour, a titillation of a hunger that could never be appeased; the zombie went into what was almost a swoon, dizzy, weak-kneed.

When Hortense had breath again she asked, 'But how did you find me here?'

'The natural place to look. Your home?'

'I left it ten days ago and came back this afternoon for a quarter of an hour.'

'Fate ... I told you, we were meant ...' We kissed again. Then Hortense said, 'We must not think that way. This must be goodbye. You must forget me.'

'Will you forget me?'

The zombie said, violently, 'No. Never. I shall love you and remember you till I die.'

'Then listen,' Charles said. 'Murat and I have been at loggerheads for a long time. We have fallen out, finally now. The Dutch army will need French officers. I'll come to Holland.'

Hortense said, 'Please! No! That would be cruel to us both. There is nothing to hope for. Nothing more to be said. I must go.'

The zombie screamed, but Hortense moved to the door and opened it.

The hamper was strapped down and Adèle was sitting upon it waiting patiently. Near the hamper stood a square wooden box.

Charles said, 'They meant well, Your Majesty, and it is certainly the prettiest piece they have yet produced. It is a small, young factory, hopeful for patronage, of course. May I wish Your Majesty every happiness in Holland.'

The caretaker said he could carry both hamper and box. He set the box on the hamper, lifted them together and put his chin on the box to hold it steady. Adèle and I went out to the carriage. Behind us there was a crash and Adèle said, 'I offered to carry it. I do hope nothing is broken.'

Only my heart, and my integrity.

And a little venal present from a small, new factory near Dresden.

It must have been so beautiful when Charles snatched it up and decided to use it as an excuse to bring me a gift and a message of goodwill; a lidded bowl rimmed with tiny china flowers closely massed, rosebuds, forget-me-nots, convolvulus. Out of the wreckage I took a pink rose and Adèle chose a forget-me-not.

I found that I had misjudged Holland. In June it was green and pretty, full of fields as neat and well-tended as gardens, intersected with ditches, straight as a ruler, in which the water shone blue or silvery at this season. From the elevation of the carriage it seemed that one could look for miles, so far that houses and churches and grazing animals were made small by distance, a toy countryside.

I had also misjudged the people in thinking them dull and stolid; only imaginative and fundamentally gay people could have devised the decorations and spectacles which greeted us all along the road, even in quite tiny villages.

Perhaps the welcome extended to us was particularly warm because for twelve years the Dutch had been without any real focal point of government and hungered for the unity and authority that Louis represented. He had shown tact and wisdom in abandoning our French retinue, and was himself affable, pleased with everything, until we arrived at a prettily-named place, The House in the Woods, just outside The Hague where we were to stay and rest for three days before we made our official entry into the city which had been chosen to be our capital.

There his mood changed and he began to complain that The House in the Woods was damp and that one night there had exacerbated his rheumatism. He was also annoyed because Admiral Verhuell who up to the moment of our arrival had been head of state, active in the establishment of the new monarchy and responsible for all the arrangements for our welcome, had said that he spoke and understood French and suggested that His Majesty should use that language until he had mastered Dutch.

'Pompous ass,' Louis said. 'He wanted to show off his French.'

Then the food displeased him. With what I came to know as typical Dutch thoughtfulness, The House in the Woods had been provided with a French-trained chef and Louis, longing to identify fully with his new country, demanded real Dutch food, some national dishes.

I remember two. Raw herring, preserved in a mixture of oil and vinegar, each fillet rolled around two cloves, and a very solid, salty cheese. The Dutch are a seafaring nation and it was not surprising that two of their typical national dishes should be food that neither time nor climate could affect much. Louis ate both with a determination worthy of a better cause, and suffered the predictable upset of the digestion. When we moved into The Hague and took up residence in the Binnenhof, which, if it was not quite a palace in the accepted sense, was a very old and beautiful building, he was yellowish and irritable.

Four hundred of the most prominent Dutch citizens had come there, to be received, to extend the really official welcome. Louis, aping Bonaparte, began to circulate, acknowledging curtsies and bows and making remarks in Dutch. I, aping Mother, followed, saying, I realised, stilted little sentences which I had practised with one of my new ladies-in-waiting who was equally fluent in Dutch, German, French and English. I said things like, 'I am happy to see you', 'I am happy to be here', 'I hope you are well', 'What a pleasant evening'. (When Louis had said that Madame de Boubers and I must learn Dutch, dear Adèle had gone out and bought a phrase-book, the only one she could find in French, German, Dutch and English. It must have been composed for unfortunate travellers; it contained such useless sentences – in all four languages – as, 'I beg your attention. Our postillion has been struck by lightning. Advise us what to do.')

We were perhaps a third of the way round when Louis stopped, turned, offered me his arm and led me towards the two enormous chairs, heavily carved and gilded, that stood like miniature thrones on a little dais covered in red cloth.

'I am exhausted,' he said. 'And half of them don't understand their own language!' The four hundred had been gathered from every province and there were dialects; also Louis's Dutch was not as embracing as he would have liked it to be. He vented some of his displeasure on me. 'You sounded just like a parrot.'

'I felt like one, too.'

In a way this, our first official appearance, had in it the beginning of two things which were to affect our reign. Louis's disillusionment with the Dutch and his determination not to share his position with me. Not even in church.

Quite late on the evening of our first Saturday in The Hague, Admiral Verhuell requested a private audience with me and entered looking unlike himself. His good-natured, honest face wore an expression of distress, his buoyant confidence had given way to embarrassment.

'I trust Your Majesty will forgive me. I felt obliged to break this news myself and it's a job little to my liking.'

He then told me that from the moment when Louis was proclaimed King of Holland, prayers for the King and Queen and the Royal Family had been included in the liturgy. Now Louis had ordered my name to be omitted. Even I was shocked for a moment, used as I was to Louis. I recovered and said, lightly, 'Then it seems that I must manage without prayers.'

The Admiral thought this flippant.

'If I may say so ma'am, I think you should protest, in the strongest possible terms. I can assure you, you would have the support of all reasonable men.'

'I hardly think it worth making a fuss about. His Majesty probably has some good reason for his action. It may be that he wishes not to imitate the custom of other countries, notably England.'

Admiral Verhuell said, 'But ...' closed his mouth and opened it again to say, 'As Your Majesty wishes.' I reflected upon this advantage of being royal; one need not become involved in arguments or give lengthy explanations in private interviews. One could end a conversation at will.

I said, 'Thank you for informing me. Good evening Admiral.'

He said, roughly, 'You will be prayed for, none the less. I myself shall do it.'

17

The love-affair between Louis and the Dutch people was very brief. He seemed to go out of his way to make himself unpopular. Having come with the avowed intention of keeping French influence to the minimum, he veered about and sent to France for men to occupy all the highest and best-paid posts. I could not help noticing that the French he imported were seldom first-class men because he so often chose those whom the Emperor disliked and had passed over. Louis's right hand must always work against his left and his wish to spite both the Dutch – pig-headed, stubborn, intractable as he now called them – and the Emperor – arrogant and domineering – resulted in an influx of inferior officials. One of Louis's appointments was particularly offensive. He sent for Monsieur de Senegra, an odious oaf, of whom the Emperor disapproved so strongly that he had never allowed him to set foot in Court, and made him Head of the Navy Department. And that in a country renowned for its sailors and their seamanship.

When that appointment was made the shock of it made an impact even upon my intensely private life.

My life in Holland so far had been very private because Louis so decreed it and because I was not disposed to fight. I was allowed to perform a few purely feminine functions, visits to hospitals, schools, orphanages, even asylums, but the Keep-Hortense-In-The-Background policy that had begun with my omission from the liturgy had grown steadily and I welcomed it. I liked my Dutch ladies, particularly Madame Vosmar who was multilingual and under whose tuition I was becoming, if not very grammatical or perfect in accent in Dutch, at least fluent and colloquial, a thing Louis never was.

One day she said to me, 'Could you not hint that to appoint this Monsieur de Senegra is an insult to us all. Perhaps most of all to Admiral Verhuell, who will now be asked to take orders from a man who has never commanded so much as a fishing trawler.'

I said, 'You know, as well as I do, that I am not concerned with politics.'

'*I* am not much concerned with the army. But if my husband proposed to promote a deaf-mute idiot, over the heads of worthy and experienced men, I should feel it my duty to speak.'

'That I do not doubt. But I think, Gertruda, that if your husband were king you might feel differently.'

She said, very thoughtfully, 'No, ma'am. I think I should feel even more responsibility. A king is, after all, only a man in a crown.'

And there I recognised the authentic note of the voice of the Dutch people. They had, in a feverish moment, asked for a king, welcomed him, been disposed to like him. But they had no tradition of belief that a king was something special, almost holy, immune from criticism. Louis had no rooted tradition to fall back upon; he was only a man in a crown.

I said to Madame Vosmar, 'And a queen is even less. I must not interfere. We can only hope that when Monsieur de Senegra has given open proof that he cannot tell port from starboard his activities will be restricted.'

My seeming inertia and my light remarks, made for defence in a trying situation, gained me a reputation for frivolity. In Holland women did wield influence. An exceptional number of them were heiresses, relatives of men who had gone abroad to unhealthy places to make fortunes and died. There was also the fact that the majority of the Dutch were extremely middle class, so that their women escaped the work-animal status of the very poor and the pretty-idle-pet status of the very rich. The wife of a prosperous burgher thought nothing of going, clad in silk or furs and much bejewelled, into the family office or warehouse and checking accounts or stores. They expected me to take interest in affairs, and to interfere if necessary. I could hardly explain, even to the ladies with whom I was most intimate, that the one sure way to make Louis certain that he was right would be for me to hint that he was wrong.

Having added ungrateful to the list of derogatory adjectives which he now applied to the Dutch, Louis decided that Holland did not suit him and that his health demanded a visit to a spa, one he had not formerly tried, Wiesbaden. He insisted that I should accompany him. I ventured one mild protest, in the form of a question.

'You think it wise for us both to be absent at the same time? And so soon?'

He replied with another question, 'Would you say that if I were suggesting a visit to Paris?'

Neatly countered!

I had, of course, written to Mother, and although I had tried to write cheerfully, I must have allowed more of my fundamental loneliness to show than I had intended. Much as I liked Madame Vosmar, I could never be 'Hortense' to her and neither she nor anyone else could ever fill the gap left in my life by Adèle's absence. I did write to Mother – 'I miss you and all my friends, especially Adèle, there is no friend quite like a school-friend.'

It was a simple statement of fact. I had not expected, or wished, that Mother should take it very seriously or do anything about it and I had the biggest surprise of my life when, arriving at the small, pretty palace in

Mayence, which had been lent to Louis for the duration of his cure, I found Adèle, already installed.

We fell into one another's arms and laughed and cried from sheer joy.

I said presently, 'What are you doing here?'

'Obeying orders, like the good citizen that I am! Darling, how I refrained from writing and telling you, I shall never know. But the Emperor planned it as a surprise. And, Hortense, not just a visit. I am to stay, go back to Holland when you go.'

'How? I'm afraid that Louis ...' Oh, the sheer joy of being able to say *Louis*, not *His Majesty*, or *The King* or in moments of deliberately unbuttoned informality, *my husband*. It always sounded false.

'I brought a letter for him,' Adèle said, her grey-green eyes taking on a spark of malice. 'Letters for you, too. And presents for Non-Non and Lou.'

Mother's letter simply said that she had spoken to Bonaparte about Adèle.

> When Louis was being so very Dutch I thought it best not to interfere, but with all this talk about a man called Senegra, I mean if Louis can have him, surely you can have Adèle. I said so and Bonaparte agreed ...

Reading that rather ingenuous statement I had another flash of belief in the thing that I did not wish to believe in. There it was, very stark; if I had listened to Madame Vosmar, argued, protested, put myself at the head of the anti-Senegra opposition, I should not now have Adèle.

How the Emperor had expressed his wish that Adèle and I should be reunited, I never knew. Louis contented himself by making acidulous remarks – 'Now that you have Adèle to hold your hand ...' He vented his general displeasure upon the Emperor's choice of present for Non-Non; two perfect miniature uniforms, one a replica of his own studiously plain outfit, the other a Hussar's full dress.

'Had I known what was in that parcel,' Louis said, 'I should never have let the child see the stuff. There's time enough, before he needs to think about soldiering.' Or, more sarcastically, 'I realised that the recruiting age had been lowered; what I did not know was that four-year-olds were being conscripted.'

Then he said that the waters at Weisbaden were useless, he had given them a fair trial and had no benefit and intended to go to Aix-la-Chapelle and try the sulphur baths there. He had lunched with the Prince of Nassau who had greatly benefited from the sulphur baths, and who had suggested that I, my ladies, the children, should go, leisurely, in the yacht he would loan, down the Rhine as far as Cologne where Louis could join us.

Mayence, with Louis leaving every morning quite early in his carriage for Weisbaden, had been a pleasant respite. The new plan promised a prolongation of it. I was in a mood to snatch a moment of happiness, however fleeting.

The weather was good, a succession of warm sunny days. Non-Non wore his uniforms and strutted about giving orders to mythical troops, Lou made what Madame de Boubers called 'great strides', strong enough now in the legs to imitate Non-Non's marching; able to say 'No', when Non-Non demanded of him more than he wanted to give or do. The relationship between them was very touching to see and although Lou was less naturally precocious than Non-Non, he made up for it by earnest imitation of whatever his brother said or did. Even his tastes in food were governed by Non-Non's.

At Cologne another surprise awaited me. There was a heavy concentration of French troops there and Joachim Murat was not only in command, he was near his own ducal territory. For some reason of his own he had decided to give me a military reception. Troops lined the quayside where the yacht moored, and the streets along which we drove with a mounted escort. The houses were decorated with bunting and flowers and evergreens and the house, which had been 'borrowed' for what at most would be a stay of three days, was staffed and stored as though it were to be a permanent residence. Joachim had always been amiable to me, no more, and Louis he disliked, so I was amazed at the effort he had made to show us honour and ensure our comfort. I decided that he had simply wanted to put on a show to impress the citizens of Cologne and had snatched at the handiest excuse to do so.

There was the old, jibing note in his voice when he asked, 'And when may we expect His Majesty of Holland?'

'Tomorrow or the next day,' I said. 'It was a little difficult to time a river journey and one over land exactly.'

'Splendid. Then you will be able to dance at the Ball tonight.' I was astounded at the way information leaked. So far as I know I had not told anyone that one of the first rules laid down by Louis upon our arrival in Holland, was that I was to dance only with visiting Royalty; so far none had arrived so I had not danced. But now I was a little cautious; it did not seem to me to be quite dignified to connive behind Louis's back; it smacked too much of when the cat's away ...

'I am afraid that is impossible. I have no ball dress, no jewels.'

His face fell. 'You have what you took to Mayence.'

'Very simple clothes only. Louis was there for his health and I lived as a private person, taking an opportunity to spend most of the time with the children.'

Then the truth came out. 'I was counting upon you. Caroline still refuses to visit the Duchy and there are important people whom I need to entertain. It is very difficult without a chief lady. Couldn't you makeshift for once and be my chief lady?' Absurd as it was I felt sorry for him or at least for the situation in which he found himself.

'Adèle may have something that I can borrow,' I said. 'I shall not cut much of a figure.' Not only was Adèle shorter than I, her colouring was different; she was dark enough to look well in red or tawny colours which made me look anaemic just as my favourite blues and sea-greens made her look sallow.

However, I need not have worried. At about four o'clock in the afternoon a stout, matronly-looking woman, two drooping girls and a boy carrying a large box presented themselves. They spoke no French, so Madame Vosmar acted as interpreter. The stout woman introduced herself as the best dressmaker in Cologne. By a stroke of good fortune she had in her workroom a dress which lacked only the finishing touches. It had been designed and made as part of the trousseau of a very wealthy, wilful young woman who, when it was almost finished, had taken a dislike to the colour. If Her Majesty of Holland would accept it and perhaps wear it to show that pretty things could be made outside Paris, she would fit it and the girls could finish it in less than two hours.

It seemed rather too much of a coincidence; the more so when the box was opened to disclose a dress of my very favourite colour, a muted blue-green. On the other hand it could not have been made for me. Murat had had only very short notice of my plans, and he had expected me to arrive fully equipped. Also, when the dress was taken out of the box it substantiated the story of the German girl's trousseau; it was the very reverse of fashionable. The waist was lower than was the vogue, close-fitting, the skirt very full, edged with three flounces of beautiful lace. A similar flounce edged the bodice which was cut deeper than the Emperor would have approved. But pretty? Yes, it was pretty, one of the prettiest dresses I had ever seen. The girl who had scorned it – if that story were true – was slightly shorter and plumper than I. The hem and the lowest flounce needed to be lowered, the waist taken in, and I insisted that the neck line should be adjusted. The two young women, with grave patient faces, set to work, the boy took the box away.

'Jewels,' Adèle said, 'would spoil it. It's so simple, really. I mean unsophisticated. Darling, you look about sixteen. And how fortunate that hair is longer. The Titus style would not have looked well with this.' My curls were drawn back and pinned so that they made a little cascade.

Madame Vosmar said, 'But there should be *something*,' and eyed me, her head slightly on one side. 'As Mademoiselle Anguié says, the style is simple and very, very becoming. But for a Queen perhaps …'We compromised by threading a string of pearls around and among the bunched up curls.

It was a most extraordinary evening. Again I had to remind myself that Murat could not have counted upon my presence. Given a contrary wind and that enforcement of delaying current that could happen on the Rhine as the tide from the sea impeded its outward flow, I might not have been in Cologne for two, three days. Louis, coming overland, might have arrived before me, or on the same day, and he would certainly have forbidden me to participate, in a borrowed dress!

The reception before the ball followed the usual pattern. My German was quite as limited and stilted as my Dutch had been when I arrived in Holland, but Joachim did not say that I sounded like a parrot. He said I had charmed everybody, just as he had known I should.

From the room in which I had received people and smiled, we went through a temporary passageway, all silk-hung, into a supper room. Half-way through the meal, fortified by two glasses of wine, I said, vaguely, innocently, 'Wasn't Madame de Souza's son on your staff?' I knew the answer, of course, but I thought Murat would know where Charles was now; might mention him by name.

His face darkened. 'Young de Flahaut? Yes, he was, but I had to get rid of him. After Ulm he got far too big for his boots. He had the cheek to criticise a new uniform I introduced. He's on the Emperor's staff now …' The scowl became more ferocious, then lifted and Murat laughed. 'I was a bit annoyed. Then I saw that we had both saved face. And at least *there* the question of uniform can't arise. The Emperor won his first battle with fellows whose feet were either bare or tied up in sacking and that affected his thinking. There I differ. I believe that to look splendid is half-way to being splendid.' He took out his watch – an English one of the kind known as a hunter, snapped it open, glanced at the time, put it back and said, 'Take this affair, for example. When we move – as we may at any moment – we leave behind us an impression of power. And, thanks to you, of goodwill.'

After that, through another makeshift passage to the ballroom, a vast place. Coveted market? Drill halt? Riding school? All transformed by hangings of silk or tapestry and hundreds of candles into a kind of fairytale place of which, for the moment, I was Queen.

Men – as in any place where soldiers gather – outnumbered the women; Adèle, Gertruda, I and all the other females present, some of them rather old and rather heavy for the exercise, danced and danced. I was out of practice and tired too soon; the chalk that had been rubbed or stamped on to the rough floor to make it smooth and slippery began to rise, haloing the lights. I could feel my cough, so long quiescent, stir and threaten.

Somewhere, not far away, there was a clock in a church or some other public building. I had heard it strike twelve. Its next single boom, drowned by the music, I missed. It now struck two.

Time to go.

Murat said, 'Bless you. That is enough. More than enough. Come and catch your breath.'

The same passage? No another, shorter, a few stairs. At the top a door opening upon a small room, hung with pale rose, softly lighted. The inside of a sea-shell. A wide velvet-covered sofa, a low table, some glasses and a wine cooler, the lid lifted, two bottle necks protruding. Here, too, there were mirrors and I faced my own reflection with a second of non-recognition. Who is that blowsy creature? Me. Me! Flushed and bright-eyed from dancing, hair loose and tumbling, and the décolletage of the dress, about which I had been so careful, not at all what it should have been, so loose now that the uppermost curves of my breasts were revealed. I pulled it up with one hand while with the other I pushed back my hair.

Joachim said, 'Ah, don't! You look beautiful …' I turned, ready to make light of what was, after all, just a complimentary remark. The desire, the sheer lust in his eyes, hit me like the heat from a furnace. It was not quite *the* look, but it was enough akin to wake the zombie, so that for what seemed quite a long time I had it to deal with too. Handsome, said the zombie, a strong handsome *man*; you never had one, did you? Even Louis you have not had since Lou was conceived; you need say nothing; simply smile …

Hortense kept her gaze cool and steady. Hortense said, with a chilling lightness, 'why thank you, Joachim. A compliment from a brother-in-law is a compliment indeed!' Hortense indicated the wine and said, 'If that is the same local wine as was served at supper I will drink a glass while my ladies are warned and my carriage ordered.'

He understood. Perhaps he had a zombie, too, and was glad of help in beating it down. He went out, roared some orders, came back, poured wine, looked at his watch and said that he had expected a courier all evening.

The open space in front of the building in which we had danced was well-lighted. Adèle and Madame Vosmar were waiting, accompanied by General de Broc, who throughout the evening had paid Adèle marked attention. Joachim handed me into the carriage and our escort, with a creak of leather and chink of metal, moved into position. I heard Joachim say to de Broc, 'It looks as though we shall get to bed after all.' Then there was a little confusion;

a man on what was plainly a very tired horse swung into the lighted area, called, 'Make way there,' and reined in.

As the carriage moved forward I looked back, thinking – the expected courier. I saw Charles de Flahaut, unmistakable in the light that streamed from the doorway, dismount and straighten himself.

I could have, halted the carriage, gone back, pretending interest in the news. But to what end? No time; no privacy. If you cannot buy bread it is better to stay away from bakers' shops.

I was still awake when the darkness paled around the window, between the curtains. A door creaked and Non-Non's voice said, 'Mamma. Soldiers. Listen.'

'I know.' It had begun within an hour, the steady rhythmical sound of marching men, hoof-beats, rattling wheels.

'I was very quiet,' Non-Non said. 'I didn't wake Lou or Madame. Can we go and see them? Please, Mamma. I want to see them go.'

Our borrowed house stood high above and well back from the main road, shielded from it by shrubbery and a wall.

'We shouldn't see much, darling. It's hardly light.'

'They can see,' Non-Non said reasonably. 'Please, Mamma.' Had it been lighter he would have gone alone; very brave about most things, he had a curious fear of being alone in dusk or dark. 'We could see if we stood on the wall.'

So we went down and I sat on the wall, with Non-Non standing beside me and we watched them go, the soldiers of the Empire, on their way to war in Prussia and in Poland. They marched towards the sunrise, opal-grey, rose-pink, blood-red; and behind them a failing waning moon lost its silver as the light brightened.

'How soon shall I be old enough?'

I tightened the arm with which I held him but I gave an acceptable, not a maternal answer, 'Oh, a few years. You need to grow a little more.'

'Would they like it if we waved? They could see us now.'

We waved as they went.

18

Charles had carried, beside Murat's orders, a long letter for Louis. It was brought to the house by a soldier and Louis opened it when he arrived at midday. He read it, frowning, and then because he had no one else to complain to, talked to me with an unwonted freedom.

'He asks the impossible. How can I raise a year's taxes *in advance?* Isn't it difficult to collect taxes when they are due? Then, listen to this! I am to get together an army of Dutchmen – French officers, of course – and lead them against Wesel on the Rhine. Wesel is about as heavily fortified as any place in Europe. It could hold out over winter. My health simply couldn't stand a winter campaign.'

The sulphur baths had been no more beneficial than any of the others.

My step-father was, without any doubt, the most intelligent man alive. Where war was concerned he had genius, equalled only by his genius in administration. He was perceptive, too. But though he had few blind spots those he had were very blind. He still thought that Louis had the makings of a soldier. He believed this because he wished to believe it; it was part of his natural attitude – If I will something, so it is. And it was hard on Louis who lacked almost every quality that makes even a mediocre soldier, but, at the same time, had his full share of Bonaparte ambition.

'He is simply exploiting me. I should have listened to Lucien! Well, I suppose we must get back as soon as we can to begin to work miracles.'

I remembered what the Emperor had said about my being Regent should Louis be absent from Holland. I knew so little, had no experience and at the prospect my heart, my stomach seemed to shift. But I held on to the thought that I would be guided by those who had knowledge and experience, I would exercise common sense.

'Orders for you, too,' Louis said, fumbling the papers. 'Because of the danger of the English invading Holland, you and the children are to return to Mayence. Your mother will be there. You can sit out the war in comfort.'

I could not help noticing the note, almost of envy, and thinking – There is something a little wrong with a man who envies the supine role that women must play in war …

Not that Mother and I were inactive in Mayence. In early September there were two sharp battles, at Jena and at Auerstadt, both French victories and soon prisoners of war began to arrive, long files of them, dispiritedly shuffling their way to prison camps. Mother thought they looked hungry. 'If it had gone the other way we should wish our men to be fed,' she said. Beginning almost casually, mugs of coffee or tea and planks of bread topped with slices of ham or sausage, this charitable enterprise developed and became very expensive. There were our own wounded, too, better provided for but greatly appreciating visits and little gifts and such small services as the writing of a letter too personal and intimate to be entrusted to a fellow soldier who happened to be able to write and had the use of his hands.

Writing letters for wounded soldiers was in itself an education, they made so light of wounds that to me seemed terrible.

'Say I got a lucky one and am having a nice rest ...' A leg roughly amputated, the stump dipped in hot tar, a future of hopping about on a wooden peg.

And the brave deceitful letters that I wrote, who would read them? If a young boy of nineteen could not write, could his mother read? I asked once and had my answer.

'*He* made the law, everybody to go to school. Too late for me, but my young brother, Jean his name is, he can read and write like a proper scholar.' Pride there and gratitude.

I learned a lot about courage, about human adaptability. And about self-ishness, too. There were the casualty lists. The Emperor? Eugène? Charles? All well so far. Louis?

Even had I been in love with Louis I should have found his conduct difficult to defend. He went to Wesel with about half the force he had been told to take and when the Emperor's victories had made all resistance collapse he had gone about from place to place and as each Prussian flag came down, had raised the Dutch. He sent arrogant messages to his brother – he had conquered Westphalia which in future must be regarded as part of Holland. He had a terrible row with Marshal Mortier, his chief officer, appointed by the Emperor, because Mother said that a Dutch advance, made under cover of a French victory, warranted the hoisting of the French flag. Louis asked whom did he serve, Mother said the Emperor, and Louis told him to go to Hell. Then as Mother was about to leave, Louis said he must stay and take charge because he himself was not well enough to continue the campaign.

However, Prussia lay defeated, and by the beginning of the year 1807 the Emperor and his victorious army were in Warsaw, being welcomed by the Poles as liberators who had come to set them free from Russian rule.

There was news from Paris, too. Caroline's experiment had borne result; Eleanore Denuelle de la Plaigne had given birth to a boy.

The state of mind into which this threw Mother was proof of her basic simplicity; not until that moment had she seemed to suspect Caroline of trickery. Now she did, and was shocked; stunned that anyone could possibly be so false.

'I am afraid that Bonaparte will believe it. It flatters him. Anything could happen now. For one thing he has changed. His sense of judgment is not what it was. They'll talk him round, yet.'

I was sorry for her; and for the Emperor who was, I thought, being either duped or manoeuvred; but I had my own troubles. Louis had written me a long letter as soon as he was back in Holland. It was full of maudlin senti-ment expressed in clichés. We had both made mistakes, we must forgive and forget, make a fresh start, set a good example. He also said that since all danger of invasion was past the children and I must return to Holland at once. The prospect of a resumption of conjugal life at which the letter seemed to hint, held no appeal at all for me and the brightest spot that the New Year held was Adèle's marriage to General de Broc whom Louis had met and to whom he had taken a liking, and offered a post as Palace Governor.

The new start – made at an apt time of the year – held its impetus for about a week. Then it halted and the policy of inflicting petty slights on me was resumed. Louis would go to the theatre without me, explaining to anyone who cared to listen that my grasp of the Dutch language was not sufficient to enable me to enjoy a play. I ought not to attend one function, because of the cold, from another I must retire early because I was so easily fatigued. In a dozen ways, too silly to recount, he made sure that I should not share his new burst of popularity which stemmed from the fact that though Holland was not allowed to keep Westphalia, it had been given part of Friesland as compensation. Westphalia was to be given to Jerome who had, under pres-sure, agreed to divorce his American wife. The Dutch were pleased to own part of Friesland and attributed the acquisition to Louis's efforts in the war.

The worst thing about our situation was that Non-Non was now old enough and observant enough to take notice.

'Papa, are you angry with Mamma?' he asked one day, half way through luncheon.

Louis, who was having a glum, dumb day, looked startled. 'No. Why do you ask that?'

'When madame my governess is angry with me,' Non-Non explained, 'she will not speak to me and she puts on her sewing face. You have a sewing face.' He pressed his lips together; a good imitation of a woman threading a needle, or a man in a bad mood.

In April Louis decided that, contrary to popular belief, the Dutch were a musical people. He organised a series of small concerts in his private apartments – 'Too bucolic for your taste,' he said as an excuse for not including me.

Then Non-Non said, 'Why didn't Mamma sing last night? She sings a lot better than that lady.'

'What lady? How do you know?'

'I could hear. She sounded like vinegar tastes.'

'Oh come,' Louis said, 'that lady is supposed to be the best soprano in Holland.'

'What is a soprano?'

'A lady who can sing high notes.'

'Mamma sings better. All furry. Why didn't she sing?'

'Because your Mamma is a queen. Singers are people who are paid to sing.'

'Mamma sings to us. We like it, don't we, Lou.'

'Yes. We like it,' Lou said dutifully.

Once Louis accused me of alienating Non-Non's affection and I knew a moment of despair. A mind so twisted…

Then it was May, warm and sunny. Non-Non seemed slightly unwell.

Madame de Boubers said, 'It's just a snuffle, but a summer cold sometimes lasts longer than a winter one. He must stay in bed.'

He must stay in bed.

He must eat a boiled onion.

He must have a linseed plaster on his chest.

Madame de Boubers knew how to deal with a cold, even a stubborn, summer one.

Madame de Boubers thought that perhaps a doctor …

They came. Good, learned, solemn men and said, 'Croup'. A childish ailment for which no cure was known; only palliatives; the open window to ensure plenty of air, a kettle steaming night and day, to ensure humidity, more pillows …

The pillows were hardly needed because I sat on the bed, holding him as I had held him on the wall to see the soldiers pass. I sang, I told his favourite stories, I shared his broth-making gluttonous noises, 'Oh, yum-yum, this is so good, you must have a sip. Your turn now.' Strength must be kept up, the flicker of life fanned and fed.

But he died without me. He seemed to be better, all day everybody said he was better, all day he had not made that terrible crowing noise as he fought for breath. I sang him to sleep, heavy head on my shoulder, laid him against the pillows and hurried away on a necessary errand, long delayed.

Five minutes? No more. I hurried back. In that last choking attack he had turned towards the door. Looking for me?

Of what happened next I have no knowledge at all, except what was told me. They say I gave a great scream and fell on the floor. They said they thought I was dead, too.

When I did come to my senses I was aware that everybody was being very kind and that their kindness meant nothing. I could not share my misery. I could not even cry. I felt as though I were made of wood. I could think, hard spiked thoughts, so cruel that I would sooner have been dead than think them. Of how I had undervalued what I had, my healthy, happy, loving child, and yearned for what was forbidden. Every moment's thought that I had given Charles now seemed to my morbid mind to have been stolen from Non-Non. When I thought that I felt as guilty as though I had slain my own child.

Every now and then, before this bar of self-judgment, the most cruel court of all, I would think – I did get up that morning and go with him to see the soldiers.

I still had Lou, but he was as meaningless and as hurtful in my sight as Non-Non's other toys. There was even that deadly thought – Why should you be alive and Non-Non dead, lapped in lead, awaiting burial with a lot of dead stupid old Kings of France in Paris? Motherhood could not sink lower than that.

My own thoughts were sharp and clear, what came to me from outside myself was muffled and blurred. 'If she could only cry,' said Dr Corvisart, sent for in a hurry and arriving two days too late. Not that he could have done anything. Trying now though, saying, 'I think she should visit her mother ...'

For almost a year I had looked forward to seeing France and Paris again, but neither the distraction of the journey nor the sight of familiar things eased my grief. When Mother wept I envied her the healing tears and when she said would-be comforting things I despised them, was even irritated by them. His short life had been very happy; I still had Lou; I could have other babies; many people believed in a future life and reunions after death. I simply thought – Rubbish! Beliefs invented out of human need in the face of intolerable fact.

My step-father, who had written me a most stricken letter immediately after Non-Non's death, now wrote me another, urging me to show more courage, to think more of Louis-Napoleon; had I had room in my heart only for one?

I suppose courage, like everything else, is expendable and mine had been used up in secret, paltry ways.

I had many letters, all kind and sympathetic, many deeply mystical. Charles wrote from Poland, a formal rather stilted letter that could be read by anyone. All it did was to quicken my sense of guilt at not having been satisfied with what I had.

Eating so little, sleeping hardly at all, I grew very thin and my cough returned. Dr Corvisart recommended travel and finally Adèle and I, with the minimum of attendants, found ourselves in the French Pyrenees.

I had never before been in mountainous country, and despite myself or because Time had already begun its Lethe-like work – I began to notice scenery again. One day, seeing a gorge, dropping down blackish green to a stream the colour of pewter, I said, 'I should like to paint that.' Perhaps Adèle had hoped for some such remark, materials were instantly available, and after that we painted every day, walking miles to find some particular view, losing our way, sometimes buying food at tiny, remote farmhouses, set in stony, almost vertical fields. Once we visited a tiny market town where nothing had changed since the Middle Ages, trade was still being conducted largely by barter. It was a very hot sunny day and we bought, and wore, two huge straw hats. The purchase seemed to cause a good deal of politely-concealed amusement, and when we came face to face with a mule wearing an identical one, we saw the joke and laughed. I had not expected to laugh ever again and at once felt guilty and ashamed; but bit by bit and day by day I was becoming resigned, not to the fact of Non-Non's death, but – a very different thing – to the fact that beloved people do die and that those who loved them live on. They even laugh.

In August Louis joined us, looking old and haggard. I realised that from the moment when I saw Non-Non dead to the time I left Holland I had not seen him in the real sense of the word; and at no time had I given much thought to how he was feeling. I now felt a slight pang about that, remembering how he also had loved the child.

He was in a soft, amicable mood, saying that he had been anxious about me, and was pleased to see me looking better. It was almost impossible to believe that he was the same man who had made my life so miserable. With Non-Non still in the forefront of my mind I could not help remembering the circumstances of his birth, the counting of days in order to give the lie the lie. But though part of me held off, remembering old grudges, and was mildly revulsed when Louis said things like – We have shared a great sorrow and must comfort one another, I was really in no state to cherish any real resentment. I told myself that inside Louis Bonaparte's skin five or six different men, none of them quite complete, fought for mastery. Now one of them had come to me, it seemed for comfort. And what I had to give, I gave. By the time that we were back in Paris – *en fête* for the Emperor's return and the glory, both military and diplomatic, that he trailed with him – I was pregnant for the third time.

What I had hoped for, tightening my arm around Non-Non when he asked how soon he could be a soldier – Let it be peace long before that! – seemed now to have come about. The ease with which the Emperor had taken Poland and shown the Czar of Russia that it was better to have France as a friend than as an enemy. The Czar and the Emperor had met to talk in a carefully chosen neutral place, a raft in the middle of the River Nemen, and had instantly taken a prodigious liking for one another. The treaty talks had gone without a hitch. Except for Spain and her little neighbour, Portugal, and England, all Europe was now either subject to or allied with the Empire.

And the Emperor was free to turn his thoughts to such things as the making of sugar from a root that could be grown in Europe, the offering of a reward to anyone who could find a cure for croup and a thousand other non-military concerns.

Our stay in Paris was intended to be brief, but Dr Corvisart advised me not to travel for at least two months. Louis said he must get back, and would take Madame de Boubers and Louis-Napoleon with him. The Emperor then remembered Non-Non and, speaking of Holland as an unhealthy place for children, expressed a wish that Lou should spend winter in Paris. 'You must understand that at the moment this is the most important child in the world; my heir having as yet no heir.'

Louis, already annoyed by some of the instructions he had received about how to run his kingdom in future, took this further exercise of authority with ill-humour, but he went off alone.

Adèle left, too, thinking it her duty to join her husband and believing that I should be back in Holland in October. In fact, when the time came I was not well enough to travel and it was decided that I should stay in Paris until the child was born. I was out of favour with Louis again, for when I wrote to tell him this I received an official letter in return, written by a secretary: His Majesty had received my letter but had no time to reply to it.

I settled down in a house in the Rue Curetti and to the almost private life which suited me so well. My semi-invalid state excused me from doing anything I didn't wish to do, at the same time it was acknowledged that company and diversion were necessary. I had many faithful visitors – Madame de Souza among them – and lying on my sofa I caught up with all the gossip.

Charles was in Dresden. 'Of course mothers are told very little, but it sounds to me as though he is leading a rather *wild* life,' Madame de Souza said. 'I wish he would marry and make me a grandmother. Before I look like one!'

Well, I had told him to forget me; and zombies do not bother the pregnant body much.

None of my callers had seen – or admitted to having seen – the child called Leon Denuelle, but several of them knew someone who knew someone who had and this unnamed person had reported that in appearance, especially in profile, he bore a resemblance to the Emperor. Naturally, to me, Mother's daughter, the Emperor's step-daughter, these rumours were reported with every protestation of incredulity; as indeed were others – That in Warsaw the Emperor had indulged in his first open love-affair with a lovely young Polish countess named Marie Walewska: that one of the things discussed on that raft at Tilsit was the possibility of the Emperor marrying one of the Czar's sisters. It seemed to me that though nobody admitted to believing these things, everyone was saying them.

I never mentioned such matters to Mother, uncertain how much she knew and she never spoke of them to me, perhaps out of consideration for my condition. She *seemed* calm and happy enough and delighted at the prospect of accompanying the Emperor to Bayonne where he was going to settle a quarrel between the King of Spain and his son, a quarrel which was leading to civil war. The clothes she must have, the presents she must provide occupied half her mind, while the other half concerned itself with the worry that she might not be back in time for my confinement.

Mother's present-giving had got out of hand, no longer confined to the formal gifts, usually dull, impersonal things which all royal people bestow. One day, at a school or an orphanage where she was presenting prizes, there was one prize short and Mother had slipped off a bracelet and given it to a child who immediately became the envy of all the others. So nowadays, when fully dressed for an occasion, Mother wore a number of supernumerary trinkets which must be expensive enough to have seemed to belong to her. When people said she was extravagant, when the Emperor grumbled about her bills, such things were not taken into account.

When she came, softly rustling, sweetly scented, to say goodbye to me, she repeated her regret that she would not be with me. Then she said, 'Darling, I don't know how much you have *heard*.'

I said, 'Oh, this and that ...'

'You are not to believe any of it. You are not to worry about it. If Bonaparte intended to do what they say, would he be taking me to Bayonne? Oh, I know about the Walewska, nobody needed to tell me that! I knew by the way he wrote to me – far more loving than since the time he was in Italy. But that is over. And if he believed that pug-faced girl had borne his hawk-faced child, he'd have wanted to adopt it under some pretence or another …'

I was glad to see her so happy, so confident; for even if happiness is a fleeting thing, not to be counted upon, it is all the more precious for that.

The Emperor also came to take leave of me. He seemed happy, too.

'We need another boy, remember that, Hortense. There'll be a crown for him. You know what will happen down there,' he nodded his head towards the south. 'When two sparrows quarrel over a crust and invite a cat to arbitrate, who gets away with the crust? I shall take Spain without firing a shot or losing a man.'

(In Martinique the Negroes said, 'Look out when you get all you want. Fattening hogs ain't in luck.' In France nurses said, 'Laugh before seven, cry before eleven,' and there was something called 'hubris' about which I only knew because Madame Campan was such a devotee to Latin. Hubris, as I remembered, was that state of self-admiration that invited the anger of the gods.)

19

Early in March Louis wrote that he wished Lou to go to Holland. I sent back a careful letter pointing out that the winter was not yet ended and that it hardly seemed worth making the separation, since I expected to be confined in April, and hoped to be able to travel within a fortnight.

I had now become extremely attached to Lou and my way of life had enabled me to wake up for the neglect I had shown him immediately after Non-Non's death. He had missed his brother sharply for a while, and then with the adaptability of the very young, appeared to forget him. But the minds of children work curiously; when I told Lou that he would one day have a little brother or sister he looked thoughtful and then said, 'Will he be Baby? Can I tell him what to do?' Perhaps he had secretly resented Non-Non's ascendancy.

Louis replied to my letter by saying that he was despatching Dr Stok to fetch Louis-Napoleon.

Dr Stok arrived, a pleasant, kindly man who took some pains to explain that the climate of Holland was not unfavourable to children. Consider the number of healthy youngsters growing up there.

'Native to the place,' I said. 'They were born there.'

'Ma'am, that could also argue in favour of letting our young prince become acclimatised as soon as possible.'

He then remembered that he had brought me a letter, and a parcel from Madame de Broc. I had heard from Adèle regularly and often, loving but not very informative letters, and the last I had received only two days earlier. I was touched by her obvious wish to miss no chance to communicate. I wondered what the sizeable parcel could contain.

This was a terse letter.

Dearest, I have found a man who makes most comfortable shoes and am sending you a pair. Please try them on at once so that Dr Stok can bring me word that they fit.

When, presently, I did try them, putting on the left first, as was my habit, it was a perfect fit; in the right one my toes seemed to meet an obstruction. This, with some difficulty, I pried out and found it to be a piece of very thin paper covered with minute writing. I might have thrown it away thinking it merely a bit of stuffing to hold the shoe in shape, but I remembered that at Madame Campan's economy in paper had been encouraged by praise for anyone who wrote a small legible hand, and Adèle often won such praise. Screwing up my eyes, I read:

> Posts are no longer to be trusted. This errand is two-fold. Do you remember dancing in August? Some old stories never die! Whatever one's feelings, private audiences are useful. The Corner position would be advisable.

How Adèle must have racked her brain to produce so cryptic and useful a screed.

I had allowed Dr Stok to leave me with the impression that Lou would go with him two days later and I had already thought about what I should tell the child – A lovely holiday with Papa; Mamma and Baby soon coming to share it. I now sent for the man and received him standing; the Corner position of schooldays when to stand in the corner was the direst disgrace. I moved about the room, stood between him and the window as I told him that the Emperor having decreed that the Prince should winter in France, I could hardly let him leave before the first day of spring without express permission. Dr Stok accepted this with a bow and said he would inform His Majesty. I then added, 'I should be grateful if you take a message for me to Madame de Broc. Say I thank her for the shoes, and that they fitted very well, if anything the left more perfectly than the right.'

Holding on to Lou was a poor, possibly temporary revenge on Louis for this latest insult. Nothing but the sheer determination to believe himself a cuckold could account for this. Whom could he possibly suspect this time?

Anger was bad for me, so I tried to control it. When I thought the thing over I wondered whether the rumour might not have its origin with Caroline who had called upon me rather often and whom I had several times excused myself from seeing, pleading that my cough was bad at the moment. I found it so difficult to forgive her; that experiment, whether honestly or falsely conducted, had been such an open move against Mother, that her presence, even the sound of her name exacerbated my cough which I had ceased to regard as an ordinary, physical ailment; it was a kind of enemy, something that had no part in me, but pounced from outside whenever I was weak from some other cause. I made up my mind that next time Caroline called, I would receive her, in the Corner position, even if the effort to be civil to Mother's enemy made me cough myself sick.

Before I could implement this determination several things happened and among the rearrangements was one which explained to me why, if Caroline *had* re-started ugly stories about me, she had done so. (I had, of course, no positive proof that she had; my thoughts were all concerned with the possible, the probable, the likely.)

Down there, in the south, everything had gone exactly as the Emperor had foretold. King Charles of Spain wished to abdicate, Prince Ferdinand, having rebelled against his father, wished not to fight against those still faithful to the King. At Bayonne they both handed over their rights and their responsibilities to the Emperor of France, who did a chessboard move. Joseph was to be King of Spain; Caroline and Murat were to have Naples. The Duchy of Berg and Cleves was to go not, as might have been expected, to Achille Murat, but to my Louis-Napoleon.

In April 1808, when Caroline invited Lou and me to a children's party, in the Elysée Palace, none of the necessary proclamations had been made. But with words spoken and with words written down in preliminary drafts, the thing had been already decided, and in holding the party in a palace, instead of in her own spacious house, Caroline gave notice that she was now a queen. Which was true in essence. Also true was the fact that in Madrid, those who supported the King and those who supported the Crown Prince had for a moment forgotten their differences, united against the French arrangement and raised a riot. They were so ill-armed, sticks and stones, the tools of their trade, a few old firearms, long out-dated, that Joachim Murat, sent to see that the shift of power was made in a peaceable way, in one cavalry charge, could quell all opposition. Caroline was justly proud of him and what with that and the knowledge that she would be proclaimed Queen of Naples as soon as she reached Bayonne, she was in no mood to take criticism from me.

I thought and I said that the tight-rope, stretched crosswise from corner to corner of the room, looked dangerous. When I watch performers on a tight-rope I like to see a net below, and a clear space, under the net.

Caroline said, 'Oh you! You see danger everywhere. Except where it exists.' I had no time to think what that might mean. As the only crowned mother present, leading a young prince by the hand, I had time to seat myself first and I chose a place well away from the central area of the room.

Lou watched with rapture as the two young men and the two girls did their tricks, their feet in soft kid shoes seeming to curve and cling to the rope, prehensile as monkeys' paws or human hands. I wished not to watch, but found myself compelled to do so, thinking in an insane way that if I watched intently and *willed* that there should be no mishap … The antics were incredible; they ran, they danced, turned somersaults, played leapfrog, all on a rope high above the heads of gaping children, applauding mothers. I sat, admiring, but tense and apprehensive and waited for the entertainment to end. The final show was a kind of pyramid, the girls standing on the men's shoulders, jumping up from the rope to reach them. One girl just missed her footing; the living pyramid swayed as the man whose shoulder had just been missed used his arm to hoist her into position. I closed my eyes and felt the vertigo which they certainly did not feel. I heard the applause. The feeling in my stomach which at the missed step had said – This is it! now said the same thing in a different way.

This *was* it. My third son slipped into the world almost as soon as I was in my house; alive, premature enough to be an unnatural purplish colour and have to be wrapped in cotton wool and bathed not in water but in olive oil.

The Emperor wrote to congratulate me; he was, he said, delighted by the birth of another prince and had ordered a salute of guns to be fired all along the border between France and Spain. In Holland there was also an expenditure of gunpowder to mark the birth of the child whose father would never fully acknowledge him. Charles Louis-Napoleon was only a few days old when Louis found a way of referring to both children without calling them 'my sons'; he always said and wrote, 'my son and his brother'.

Mother and the Emperor came back from Bayonne and I took the first opportunity of telling him how Louis had sent for Lou and been disobeyed. He said, 'I cannot deny Louis the possession of his own children.' Then he gave me a peculiar look and added, 'Making the boy Duke of Berg and Cleves demands some ceremony. Also I have to go to Erfurt for another meeting with Alexander; I should like you to be in Paris to keep your mother company. I will write to Louis.'

I wrote, too, and my letter was returned unopened. The next communication to come from Holland was a letter addressed to Lou reproaching him for not sending greetings to Papa on his birthday. 'It is Mamma's fault; she does not encourage you to write to me.' Lou would be four in October! Shortly after that I heard by roundabout means that Louis was explaining my absence by saying that I hated Holland and was amusing myself in Paris, sometimes in an unbecoming manner.

This seemed to me to indicate the final breakdown of our marriage and I began to steel myself for the parting with Lou which must surely follow. I had no more right than the Emperor to deny a father the possession of his son – or a country the possession of its Crown Prince. I looked back on my own childhood and saw that life with one loving parent was happier than with two bickering ones; and I was sure that once he was in complete control, Louis would be a loving and conscientious father.

To say that I was enjoying myself in Paris, in ways unbecoming or otherwise, was untrue. Mother was at last facing the fact that divorce was pending, now merely a matter of time and of finding a suitable bride.

'At Erfurt he will make another bid for the Czar's sister, and failing her it will be that Austrian girl. She comes of a very prolific family!'

She was resigned, but melancholy, restricting her social activities to the minimum and spending much of her time with me in harking back to the past, which, as was I supposed natural, in retrospect she regarded as unclouded-edly happy. Now and again she made reference to having ruined my life and to that I replied, 'Only six years of it. Lou will have to go to Holland, I'm afraid. But you and I and Charles can all live at Malmaison and be quite happy.'

'Quite is not the same.'

However, the divorce she dreaded and the separation that I did, were both delayed. Fierce fighting broke out in Spain, and the Emperor had actually to leave Erfurt and make one of his lightning journeys to take charge and save Joseph's throne. Austria joined the war against us, and the English, who had never been at peace with us since 1803, landed troops in Portugal and again threatened to invade Holland. They did take a Dutch island, Walcheren, and but for the fact that they were incompetently led, could, from there, have invaded the mainland. In such circumstances even Louis did not wish Lou to be in Holland, and the Emperor was too busy to bother about divorce and re-marriage.

By summer of 1809, however, the Emperor had won another war and dictated his peace terms. Back in Paris he began to reorder his personal life.

I think that I may have been the first person to whom he spoke in a direct and intimate way about the coming changes. And those who thought that he divorced Mother callously, because he was tired of her, or because he was ambitious, should have seen him that evening.

He began with the words he often used, 'I want to talk to you. You know what about.' He would not sit down but walked up and down with less than his usual vigour. I had watched him pace about so often, and always with the pent-up energy of a caged animal; now he plodded, rather like those old horses who from habit, or fear of punishment, go on and on, turning mill-wheels, dragging carts.

It struck me suddenly that he was old – as much older for his forty years, as he had always, being so spare and active, seemed younger. He had put on flesh, around the waist, under the chin, below the eyes; and his complexion had a yellowish tinge.

'Yes,' I said, 'I think I know.'

'What you don't know, and must, is that it will make no difference. No difference at all. I shall still look on you and Eugène as my children. My affection for your mother is undiminished. I don't want to divorce her. I hate the word, I hate the idea … No man who has not been married to her …' He made a turn and plodded back. 'I haven't been faithful to her, I doubt whether she has always been faithful to me. But that has nothing to do with it. Nor the little rows over the debts, or her always being late. Counting sous, watching a clock she wouldn't have been the woman she is. All woman. Sweet and soft … *I* never held it against her that we had no child. You know, Hortense, the Turks manage things better, a wife to enjoy, a wife to breed, a wife to cook or sew or sing. But that is neither here nor there. What I wanted you to know, before the thing became public, was that it will make no difference.'

'It must make some difference. Eugène and I will cease to be your family once Mother is put away.'

'Put away! What an expression. Anyone would think that I was sending her, like an old horse, to the knacker's. And here I am planning that she shall lack nothing, retain her title, yield precedence to no one except the Empress. I'll pay all she owes, down to the last sou, and make her an allowance that should make it difficult even for her to get into debt again. She'll have Malmaison and the Elysée when she wishes to be in Paris. Why should you and Eugène be against me over a mere formality? Something I have to do for the sake of expediency?'

'I did not say that we should be against you. I only said that we should no longer be related.'

'Eugène is my adopted son. I'll adopt you, too, if I have to. I'm not having any changes except the one I have to make.'

'Have to?'

'Yes! What do you think I have been trying to tell you! I need a boy of my own, a direct heir. I need lasting peace with Austria … I should have thought that you had been misunderstood often enough to have some sympathy with me.'

'I do,' I said. 'I do sympathise with you. I think you are still in love with Mother. Also …' I wondered whether I dare say it; took the risk, 'it might come to nothing. Marie Louise might have no child, or a girl and I cannot think of one instance where a state marriage ensured peace.'

'No,' he said, 'nor can I, offhand. But I'll take the chance. Once a man can't take a chance he might as well be dead,' I could see him thinking of all the chances he had taken, successfully. For a second the aged, troubled look receded and something of the old buoyancy rose to the challenge. Then his shoulders slumped again and he shook his head slightly.

'I need Eugène and you. Joseph and Louis are being very ... wilful. And the English aren't wintering in Portugal for their health.' The last word brought something to mind and again he brightened.

'One good thing about being forty, Hortense. I've outlived that silly little trouble.'

The divorce, like most other Bonaparte transactions, must appear to have family sanction. Eugène was sent for to join the clan, mustering in Paris. He was summoned by a means invented for war, but useful in peace, something called the semaphore or visual telegraph; according to a pre-arranged code messages were sent by flashing mirrors or flag movements. The one calling Eugène to Paris was started on its way on 26th November and reached him in Milan four days later – far more quickly than any courier could have carried it.

I had not seen my brother for four years but we had written to one another and exchanged presents. One of his little girls was named for me, and had I had any say in the choice of my last son's name, 'Eugène' would have been included in it. I was very proud of him; in the latest war against Austria he and the Italian troops he had trained had acquitted themselves splendidly, noticeably at the victory of Raab. He was as good a Viceroy as he was soldier, an able administrator and completely incorruptible, something new in Italy.

'Four years had changed him very little; perhaps happiness is a preservative. He looked serious, and his first words to me after he had kissed and greeted me were, 'This is a bad business,' but he wore the air of a man who, sure of his place, sure of himself, and with a happy, contented background, is prepared to deal even with a bad business to the best of his ability and not tear himself to pieces in the process.

We had ample time for talk because I had arranged it. I drove out of Paris to meet him as he came in from Nemours and he left his carriage and got into mine.

'How is Mother taking it?'

'I think she is resigned now. Just wanting it to be over and done with.'

'She is greatly to be pitied. But he is going to make himself the laughing stock of Europe. Mother was his defence. I don't think he is capable of getting any woman with child.'

'Why?'

'Not properly equipped,' Eugène said, rather as though speaking of a man on parade with his boots on the wrong feet. 'The Denuelle affair was rigged from the start. Now the Walewska woman is said to be pregnant. Think what it would mean to the Poles to have a boy, wrong side of the blanket, but *his*, ready for the crown of Poland as soon as his nurse could hold his head up. I've never known a case of a man suddenly becoming potent in middle-age.'

'I always suspected the Denuelle affair. About the other I know nothing – except talk. I did pluck up courage once to mention that Marie Louise might not have a baby.'

'And what did he say to that?'

'That he must take the chance.'

'Yes. That is what bothers me most. The change in him.'

'Loss of judgment?' I asked, quoting Mother.

The look Eugène gave me, the way he said, 'Exactly!' made me think that his beloved Augusta might be a trifle slow of comprehension. 'Five years ago, he'd have seen for himself. To my mind, he has done so many seemingly impossible things that he can no longer distinguish between what, for him, anyway, is possible and what is impossible. You know, I always had the idea – it may seem fanciful to you – that the, er, disability accounted for the genius. Or the other way round. Energy that we ordinary fellows expend, and interest, too, all channelled in the one direction. That,' Eugène said, very gravely, 'and the fact that genius, real genius is so rare … As though Nature couldn't manage to make genius hereditary and at the same time didn't want to give a genius a lot of booby children.'

We spoke of other things: then Eugène said, 'I made my disapproval plain from the start. I shall let him know that I'm still against it, but I shall do no good. The devil of it is, this has lost me a kingdom.'

'Oh. Which one? How?'

'He offered to make me a brand new kingdom, all of southern Austria. I had to refuse, much as Augusta would have been delighted. It would've looked too much like being bought off.'

'You goat!' I said. 'If anybody ever deserved a crown …'

'What did Augusta say?'

'I didn't tell her,' Eugène said with a grin. 'I like peace in my home.'

20

Until the last weeks of 1809 there had been no open breach between Louis and me, but it came then, when, coming to the family gathering, he elected to stay in his mother's house rather than ours. Madame Mere was delighted until she discovered that he intended to bring a retinue of twenty people, then her parsimony came uppermost and she said she could accommodate Louis, his valet and one equerry. The rest must go elsewhere. She was already aggrieved because Nablione, having at last decided upon the divorce that she had advised thirteen years before, had refused to consider her candidate for the Empress's crown – his niece, Lucien's daughter, Charlotte, now fifteen years old.

Louis's refusal to share a roof with me was another public humiliation which, I felt, was completely undeserved, but I welcomed it, regarding it as the first step towards an accepted separation. Even had I minded I should have had Mother's example to fortify me. She was being discarded by a man whom she loved; she was in an unprecedented situation, the Bonapartes coming in like vultures, and she had never been more delightful, more gracious, or outwardly serene. Or indeed more beautiful, rather like one of her own roses at that moment of full-flowering just before the first petal drops. The date of the family gathering at which she was to be repudiated was fixed for 15th December and in the intervening time she entertained, was entertained, smiled and in general behaved as though nothing untoward had happened or was about to happen.

In order that the divorce might have some legal basis in the eyes of the Church, there was dragged up the fact that at the marriage just before the Coronation, no parish priest had been present. Uncle Fesch, a Cardinal, did not qualify as parish priest. So, in addition to other things, Mother had to face the fact that after all, in the eyes of the Church, she had still never been married.

One day I said, 'Really you are *wonderful*. No other woman …'

'It is just that I know now about Fate. Darling, I think we spoke about this once before and I said I would tell you. I never did. It always seemed so silly, even then, even to *me*. But lately … I think I will tell you.'

To her, not usually regarded as a very sensible woman, it may have seemed silly. To me it sounded a most romantic story, and something more; at once chilling and comforting, as difficult to define as to explain.

In Martinique, when she was thirteen, Mother had stolen out with her cousin Aimée to consult a negress fortune-teller whom they had been forbidden to visit. 'The trouble was,' Mother said, 'that we had so little money. We had to ask her to tell two fortunes for the price of one and that angered her; and so when she said what she did we thought she was mocking us. She looked in my hand first and said I should be more than a queen and know sorrow. Then she said that Aimée would rule from behind a throne in a far distant place. You can imagine how we felt. Twelve, thirteen … wanting to know whom we should marry and how many children we should have. We were so cross; we nearly asked for our money back. But there it is. I have been more than a queen. The old woman was right about the sorrow, too. And to think of it helps. Can you understand that … To think that all those years ago *she saw*, so that what has happened is not because of anything I have done or said or been …'

I said, 'Yes, that must help … What happened to Aimée?'

'That is very curious too. Her parents could afford to send her to France to be educated. She was on her way back to Martinique, and the ship she was in just vanished. It is possible that it was taken by the Barbary pirates. She was very pretty, very fair. And clever. And masterful. She'd rule wherever … Well, there you are, darling, my silly little story … Put away, almost forgotten. But it helps me now. I mean to think that what is to be *must* be.'

I said, 'It helps me, too.'

But it did not help me much when the Emperor cornered me and said, 'What is all this? I have been talking to Louis. He wants a legal separation.'

'I should welcome it.'

'Well, you're not going to have it. I've made Louis see sense. You must see it, too. We can't have two family disruptions at the same time.' He gave me that stern, over-bearing stare. 'And what purpose would it serve?'

That was not an easy question to answer. I thought for a moment.

'It would at least enable me to live apart from Louis without making excuses. And without having my absence from Holland attributed to false motives.'

'I know you have not been happy lately.'

'Lately! We were never happy. We began our married life under the shadow of a filthy slander which Louis chose to believe. He was threatening to leave me within a few weeks of our wedding. He has humiliated and insulted me in every possible way …'

'And you, of course, have always behaved perfectly?'

'Nobody behaves perfectly. I have been faithful to him if that is what you mean. I have sometimes, under provocation, lost my temper. Never in public, though. I have borne his children and, so far as he would allow me, identified his interests with my own and been rewarded by snubs and calumnies. I am heartily sick of it all.'

'Many virtues. No patience.'

'Yes, I can also claim to have been patient. For six years. But even patience comes to an end.'

'I am going to ask you, for my sake, to be patient just a little longer. Say a year. Make a partial reconciliation. *Now* while all eyes are on us. Nobody expected you to go to bed with him again. It would not be his wish, either. If you will do this for a year you shall have your separation on the best possible terms. And I will make things easy for you. You need not spend much time in Holland. Just enough to show a united front.'

'Against what? Or whom? In what way can our marriage matter to anyone except ourselves?'

'You're just like your mother – no political head at all. But she had something you lack. Instinct. I'll try to explain in simple terms. If you leave Louis now it will look as though Bonaparte and Beauharnais are breaking up; that I do not wish. That is one thing. Another is that it does not help when a man cannot get on with his ministers and officials, for them to be able to say, "Look, even his wife cannot live with him." Also, and this is very important, there is a very strong feeling in Holland that you have been ill-done-by. There is an anti-King- pro-Queen-and-Prince faction, headed by this Admiral Verhuell. Disgruntled people like to adopt some sentimental cause; valid or not they don't care. And when Louis goes back to Holland he will take with him some orders that will make him unpopular, not for his personality, for his policy. Your being there would ease things if only by disarming the sentimentalists. Is that plain enough?'

'It is plain, but I am not convinced. For one thing it was an incident when I was there, during our very first week in Holland, that gained me Admiral Verhuell's sympathy. It could happen again. Also I fail to see how the situation can alter much in a year.'

'In a year,' he said, 'I shall have things in hand and the Dutch can be pro the Sultan of Turkey if they so wish.'

The outward reconciliation was facilitated by Louis having one of his feverish attacks. I went to see him one day; on the next I took both children. We concocted an explanation for his not having come to the Rue Curetti – and for not coming now – by saying that on the 15th, immediately after the repudiation ceremony, I was going to stay at Malmaison with Mother.

The ceremony was horrible. Even the Bonapartes – they were all present except Joseph and Julie who had thought it unwise to leave Madrid at this point, and Lucien, still in disgrace – were made uncomfortable when the

Emperor, reading his declaration, choked and broke down as he said, 'She has adorned my life for thirteen years; the remembrance of those years will remain engraved upon my heart.' Mother then began to weep; some of those beautiful tears which rapidly got beyond control and turned into real ones. When her turn came she said a few quite indistinguishable words and her speech was read by the Grand Chamberlain. Then every member of the clan signed the papers; the Emperor kissed Mother's hand and led her away, came back and said to me, 'Go to your mother.' We went to Malmaison that afternoon, in driving December rain. Nothing could have been drearier, but Mother had regained her serenity. She said, 'If only he can be happy, I shall be content,' and with that seemed to put the whole thing away.

She had always loved rearranging furniture, pictures, mirrors, and faced with a long empty evening before us I thought of this as a distraction. One of those dark old Italian pictures hung immediately opposite the hearth in the main salon and I said, with casualness, with cunning, 'You know, a glass there would reflect the fire; then that picture could go there, where those small ones are, and they could go ...'

Mother who had so often said, 'Let's change things around,' now said, 'No. When he comes I want him to find everything exactly as it was.'

I thought that was pitiable; a whistle in the dark. But I was wrong. He came the very next day and he found everything, including Mother, exactly the same.

I thought of what Eugène had said about his having so often done the impossible. I thought of his own words about nothing being different. I thought about the nature of genius ... an infinite capacity for manipulating other people.

I also thought, distantly, about Marie Louise; young, about to be married to a man old enough to be her father, the man from whom she had twice fled – after each French conquest of Austria the royal Hapsburg children had been removed to safety. How would she feel about being married to the Corsican Ogre, the Bogeyman who was still in love with his first wife?

Bonaparte had never seen her, but he had been told that she had the height, the build, the colouring of the Queen of Holland, but was quite unlike.

Marie Louise was to come in April, and the weather being bad, the Family clinging together and the Emperor having much to discuss with Louis it was ordained that we should not return to Holland until after the wedding. So through the first three months of the new year Louis and I went through motions, like fish in a pond, meeting, passing, moving on; we stood together at receptions, King and Queen of Holland, we exchanged a few trivial remarks when a show of amicability seemed called for. Louis appeared to me to grow more glum as the weeks went on and at family gatherings was markedly disrespectful to the Emperor.

Marie Louise's reception, even her route, had been planned to follow as exactly as possible that of her aunt, Marie Antoinette, when she came to France in 1770. Mother said that this invited misfortune and laughed when I pointed out that superstition and fatalism were inconsistent. The curious relationship between her and the Emperor had continued; he went to Malmaison as often as he could, when he could not he sent letters, short but affectionate; he never went hunting without dispatching a gift of game to Malmaison. He gave Mother another estate, Evreux in Navarre, and she took with good grace the suggestion that she should go to visit it and stay there until the wedding had been celebrated. 'It is much better that I should be well out of reach. For all our sakes.'

It was to be a wedding to surpass all weddings; the world seemed to converge on Paris. I met Eugène's wife at last and liked her, though I understood what Eugène had said about liking peace in his home. She was one of those very feminine, demure women who can on occasions make surprisingly caustic comments.

We all went out as far as Compiegne to await the bride. It was a pouring wet day, but the Emperor left us there and rode to meet her, accompanied only by a couple of his staff. Soaked and muddy as he was, he climbed into her carriage while we, at Compiegne, put on full Court dress and stood in the prescribed formation. We hardly had time to curtsy, or bow, and no time at all to stare. He whisked her straight off to bed – as he was legally entitled to do, since they had been married by proxy in Vienna – but it was a breaking through of the strict protocol that he had himself ordered.

Paris next day, when the official entry was made, was gaily decorated. The Arc de Triomphe which was being built to commemorate the Emperor's victories had not been completed in time, but it had been made to look as though it were, timber masquerading as stone. There were flags and flowers, everything that could be ordered was there, but it seemed to me that the crowds were thin, though the weather had cleared. In fact the new marriage was not popular at the level which makes people crowd out, perch on insecure places, hoist their children on their shoulders. Mother had been greatly loved and had been superstitiously associated with good fortune. And Marie Louise's origin counted against her – Spend your lifeblood fighting the Austrians and then go and marry one! And the memory of Marie Antoinette was lively not only in palaces … Less than fifty years ago another young Austrian archduchess had come into France and been enthusiastically welcomed, had become the most popular woman in the world, been accused of unmentionable crimes and gone to the guillotine with a dignity and composure which had categorically denied the new-born theory of equality.

In that she was not alone. But I always thought that the French people felt a bit guilty about that execution, and because guilty, resentful.

But perhaps I was alone in thinking the crowds thin. Nobody remarked on it.

Marie Louise went to her official wedding with four queens carrying her mantle. I was one.

Having carried my quarter of it I made ready to go back to Holland to live out the one year sentence to which I had committed myself; a year of which, with the coming of April, three months had already sped.

21

Louis had finally, after much vacillation, decided that Amsterdam should be his new capital. There was nothing remotely resembling a palace there, so he took over a Town Hall with an imposing façade. The apartments assigned to me were horrible. There is a proportion about places, as about people, that defied this way or that, as with giants or dwarfs, becomes an offence, an enormity. My rooms, because they had been made out of what had once been the criminal court, were immensely too high for their size, the timber partitions rearing up like cliffs, and the old tiled frieze, designed to impress, all skulls, black and white, running across the top of each original walk. Outside the windows ran a canal which stank of sulphur, of a tanyard effluent and other things.

The one thing I had hoped for – reunion with Adèle – did not come about, and for a reason so chancy and involved that Mother's theory about Fate seemed the only explanation. All the Emperor's talks with Louis had apparently borne upon the subject of Frenchifying Holland, repairing all the forts, manning them with French soldiers, looking strictly to the customs where Dutch officials dealt very leniently with Dutch smugglers who were defeating all the rules about not trading with England. But if all the official posts were to be given to Frenchmen, there must, Louis said, be some compensation on the personal side. So Adèle's husband had been dismissed, had written to Eugène and been given a post – comparatively humble beside the one he had held in Holland – in Milan. So Adèle and I met like stars, in transit. But it was a cheerful meeting; I told her about the year's sentence, at the end of which I should be free and should certainly visit Eugène at the first opportunity. She said that apart from prolonging our separation she was happy to be leaving Holland and at the thought of getting her husband out of Louis's employ. 'He is such a worrier and the constant changes over even trivialities were very wearing. His health was suffering.'

So in Holland my ladies were all new and apparently chosen from the pro-King faction, for though civil enough they seemed to be embarrassed when I made tentative efforts towards friendliness. I saw little of Louis-Napoleon whose nursery days had ended and tutelage for princedom had begun, and Charles-Louis had, at the last minute, been ordered to remain in Paris with Madame de Boubers to look after him. Perhaps the Emperor had remembered that Non-Non died in May.

I was seldom alone, but I was lonely; I was also isolated, for only on a few most formal occasions was I allowed to appear in public. My best friend during this curious period was a woman I had never seen and should never see, an Englishwoman named Ann Radcliffe who wrote gruesome, spine-chilling novels which, had Madame Campan ever seen, she would have condemned as absolute rubbish. At the moment they perfect for me; deep in *The Mysteries of Udulpho* I could forget everything, even my cough which had returned with such force that I sometimes wondered whether my ladies kept their distance because they thought me consumptive and feared contagion.

Besides reading I had another hobby, a rediscovered one. It was years since I had exercised my small talent for making rhymes, flippant or romantic according to my mood. My verses were now all romantic, and sometimes sad, not exactly the outpourings of my own heart, or rather my own feelings disguised and transposed. One, about parted lovers, appeared to concern itself with a knight going on Crusade and leaving the lady who loved him. I could not bear to give that the unhappy ending which in real life would have been likely. I was superstitious, too, in a way, and I felt that to let the knight die might augur ill for Charles, who was now in Spain where the most horrible kind of war, civil war, guerilla war, was going on.

Apart from that one fleeting glance at Cologne I had not seen him for four years, but I still thought of him a great deal, my thoughts tending to bear as much resemblance to once vivid feelings as a dry, pressed flower bears to one freshly cut. Madame de Souza still mourned the fact that he had not married; she mourned even more vigorously his posting direct from Dresden to Spain without a visit to Paris. Did soldiers not have leave any more, she demanded, or had he had leave and spent it elsewhere. She declared that she doubted whether she would recognise him in the street.

One evening in mid-May Louis came to my room and said abruptly, 'You were always a favourite of his. He reads your letters, mine he ignores. You must write a letter for me. I told him, until I was hoarse, and he goes on doing it.'

I had now taken what seemed an inevitable step forward and was trying to compose music to fit the words of my verses, to make them into songs. I had my pen in my hand, and pushing the score sheet aside I said, coldly, resenting both the interruption and the being made use of, 'What do you wish me to write?'

'Tell him to stop sending French soldiers and officials into Holland. He is undermining my authority. Of course the Dutch smuggle, everybody smuggles. Those stupid Berlin Decrees of his were an open invitation to smuggle. How the devil does he think that I can have the whole Dutch coast watched? A small boat can land anywhere along it. The Dutch are a trading nation, what else have they got? If I deal strictly with the smugglers I shall have a rebellion on my hands. And if he makes one more threat, tell him …'

'Is this letter supposed to be from you or from me?'

'From you. I said so, didn't I? Your writing, your signature, your seal. Then he'll read it, and when he knows how you feel about the situation, maybe he'll take notice … Well, go on, begin. Remember it is supposed to be from you, but I will tell you what to say. Tell him he's making my position untenable …'

It really was a very funny letter in every way. Louis, excited to begin with, became more and more vehement, denunciatory and incoherent as he dictated – 'Say *I* feel, no, *you* feel …' And as I wrote down these supposed feelings of mine I could imagine the Emperor reading them and thinking that I must have gone mad. Lacking all political sense, as he himself had told me and now writing so heatedly, and confusedly about political issues. At the final sentence even Louis jibbed and halted. 'Tell him that I, I mean you, will abdicate if this goes on …' I laughed a little, but to myself, at this absurdity and the smothered laugh provoked the cough which was not quite as usual. My mouth filled with something warm and salty. I used my handkerchief. Blood!

'Say – Louis threatens to abdicate unless things alter. End as you usually do.'

I just managed that, hand unsteady, mind running to and fro like a frightened mouse. About to die? This ridiculous letter the last I should ever write? Life, however unsatisfactory, so much to be preferred to the told darkness of death.

Louis said, 'Be quick. I want to send it off tonight.'

Anyone could fold and seal it with my seal. I said, 'I need a doctor,' and held out the bloodied rag that had been my handkerchief as proof of my need.

Perhaps Plombières, they said; wishing to sound fashionable, French-favouring; wishing to get me away so that no one could say that Holland had killed me as it was said to have killed my son. Or wishing simply to get me away …

Plombières had worked no miracle for Mother, but the dear crystalline air had as curative effect on my cough as the Pyrenees had had on my spirit three years earlier. I was making a rapid recovery when I heard that Louis had in fact abdicated, in a manner so typical of him. He had simply left Amsterdam in the middle of the night and nobody knew for a time where he had gone. When he was next heard of he was in Bohemia at a place called Toplitz where there were mineral springs.

The Emperor wrote to me:

Louis has now committed his final act of folly. I have sent for Louis-Napoleon. He and Napoleon Charles will await you in your Paris house. There you can live tranquilly. All I need to know is that you are restored to health and have now no cause for unhappiness.

Well-behaved prisoners have their sentences shortened. Mine had been halved. Early in July I was back in my own house in the Rue Curetti, with both my children, with Madame de Boubers and with Adèle. Perhaps her husband's health had been more undermined than even she had thought; very soon after his arrival in Milan he had taken a local fever, the kind of affliction which those who live in Italian cities expected as the weather warms. Summer fever; for most a little, rather nasty two-day indisposition, for one in a thousand, fatal. For General de Broc, fatal, and so there was Adèle, widowed, terribly, terribly sad … no children of her own, reaching out to mine, comforting herself as I had once comforted myself with the memory of how in a grey dawn I had gone with Non-Non to watch the soldiers pass. 'I did what I could to make him happy. We never had a cross word … And he died so easily, took his medicine and said, "I shall be better tomorrow" and just fell asleep. I sat there, holding his hand, and it wasn't until it began to turn cold that I realised … He seemed so peaceful …'

I tried to comfort her as she had comforted me and for her, presently, life mended itself and went on.

Mother was now back from Evreux and I spent a great deal of time with her at Malmaison. She never came into the city and the Elysée Palace seemed to have become the Paris headquarters of Caroline and Murat. I often had, at this time, the curious experience of spending part of the day with Mother and part with Marie Louise who had taken a fancy to me. I soon discovered that she was very shy. Secure behind the barrier of protocol and formality she could play her part fairly well, though she lacked entirely Mother's ease and grace and spontaneity, brought face to face with people on more intimate terms she became so tongue-tied and stiff of manner that she gave the impression of being hostile or too proud to unbend. I believe that at heart she was scared of the Emperor though his manner towards her was extremely indulgent. She could keep him waiting and not be scolded. Generally he behaved towards her as a man would to a well-loved daughter, then he would seem to remember the gap between their ages and try to bridge it by being boisterous. When this happened her nervousness and uncertainty showed in her eyes.

He showed lack of tact, too, in suggesting that they should go together to make a visit to Mother; he should have waited until Marie Louise made some sign of wishing to meet her predecessor. As it was she agreed and then, in the carriage, began to cry. It took some time for him to discover what was the matter; when he did, he had the carriage turned. So they never met.

The great question for Mother was would this girl succeed where she had failed and by late summer we knew the answer to that. Marie Louise was pregnant and hoping for a baby in March.

'Then I was wrong,' Mother said, when I told her. 'I am glad. Yes, I am *glad*!' She turned away and cried a little. 'This does at least make it all worthwhile.'

For the Emperor, too, the news seemed to have resolved any lingering doubt as to the wisdom of his action. He looked happier, healthier, younger, and he abandoned the boisterous behaviour.

I had made up my mind when I came back to Paris that I would live as privately as possible. I could not avoid certain Court functions and Marie Louise's fondness for me involved me far more than would otherwise have been the case, but on the whole I was now leading the kind of life that suited me best. My entertainment was almost entirely informal. I kept open house for my friends; we played cards, had musical evenings, other evenings when we sewed or knitted garments for the poor; we had amateur theatricals and sometimes for Lou's sake charades, guessing games and wild romps of hide-and-seek. He had had his sixth birthday and to be allowed to 'stay up' occasionally was at once a bribe and a spur to make him attend to his lessons. His education was a matter of concern to me; perhaps the more so because his future might be uncertain. Louis had abdicated *in favour of his son, Louis-Napoleon*, and as the constitution of the Dutch monarchy read, Lou was now Louis II of Holland and I Regent during his minority. And we should have been in Holland. If I had been ambitious for myself, or for Lou, I suppose I should have taken a stand. As it was the whole thing seemed to have lapsed; the Emperor had ordered Lou to Paris, Holland was now so full of French that it was really no more than an appendage; and perhaps the Dutch had had enough of monarchy.

So when I engaged tutors for Lou and tried to coax him to learn, it was not of his future as a king that I was thinking; it was of the blessing of education in itself. To be able to speak and understand languages other than one's own; to have some knowledge of history, geography, mathematics. I was aware that I had been singularly fortunate in receiving more education than most girls in France could hope for; I wanted Lou to have more and to enjoy having it. But he was one of those children born to be led and already in six years he had lost two leaders, his brother and his father. There had been a day when Non-Non was there issuing orders, and shortly afterwards a day when Non-Non had vanished and Mamma had gone too ... Then, when he had just begun to look to Papa as the one who had taken him out of the nursery, replaced Madame de Boubers by a series of tutors, made Lou feel grown-up, Papa had vanished much as Non-Non had done. A lot of experience crammed into six years ... And it had resulted not in an inability to concentrate, but an unwillingness ... a kind of mental inattention of which all his tutors now complained.

So I used 'staying up' as a bribe and 'Lou's evenings' meant charades – good for the vocabulary – and other things which I invented – a map for example, tacked out on a table and its counterpart, in small pieces, cut up by a jigsaw, distributed in haphazard fashion among the players. Each in turn while the others counted, quietly up to twenty, tried to fit in one of his pieces which must accord, either with a piece already laid and credited, or with some definite mark on the map, coastline, river, town. Even adult people could become quite excited.

Caroline once described my evenings as *too bourgeoise*. And that did not annoy me. They were. Whatever we had been doing the tea-trays came in at ten o'clock and we all drank tea, ate little cakes, talked for a bit and parted. Nobody came to my house in the evening to seek preferment, augment his or her own income or take a step upward socially. Nobody talked politics or did any back-biting.

Once Marie Louise said to me, 'I hear you have such *merry* parties, Hortense.' She sounded wistful. It must have been well on into October and she had been told to live very quietly, standing for any length of time made her legs swell. I said, 'They are really very ... homely. We play rather silly games.'

'So I am told. Next year you must invite me to come and participate.'

The Emperor said, 'I hear you have riotous times. One evening I shall look in and see for myself.'

I said, 'Sire, you would be very welcome. But if it were known that you were to be found, playing childish games, in my house, I should soon have company not much to my taste.'

He made one of his wordless assents, a kind of grunt.

'Umph. Umph. Those who can't get through the front, trying the back. Eh?'

It was in the middle of one such evening that I turned from whatever I was doing to greet a latecomer and found myself face to face with Charles.

I had seen Madame de Souza quite recently and she had made no mention of his coming; seeing him walk in like that took me so much by surprise that I was literally speechless. The four long intervening years fell away and the memory of how we had parted on the eve of my departure for Holland was there, as vivid and disturbing as though it had happened only yesterday. I felt my face change colour and my heart begin to jump. Fortunately it is not every day that a soldier comes back from the wars after an absence of four years, and other people came forward to greet him so that my dumb discomfiture went unremarked, except by him.

All evening I had to fight the tendency of my eyes to look in his direction. I must not stare. I was unable to give my attention to anything that was done, or said. The zombie was in full charge.

I had met Eugène after a similar interval and found him little changed. Charles had not altered so much that his mother's remark about passing him in the street was justified, but there were changes. The lines of his face were harsher and there were more of them. He looked well over thirty, weathered and tough, the jaunty self-assurance increased rather than diminished. He seemed very gay. Once or twice our eyes met and there was the look, more confident and powerful now.

The tea was brought in, poured and drunk; soon the party would break up. Would he leave with the others, remain behind and be conspicuous? Hortense and the zombie began to grapple.

My marital status was ill-defined. I was still married to Louis, but we were so completely alienated that I was never sure, at any given time, of his whereabouts. When he abandoned Holland he had abandoned me, too. You were ill, the zombie reminded me, and he did not care whether you lived or died; you owe him no allegiance. It had another argument, too. I was twenty-seven and so far as simple sex was concerned (the zombie never minced words!), my experience had been calamitous. Most women after eight years of marriage had either come to terms with their husbands, taken a lover or done both. Why not take what was now offered, the love or – to put it at its lowest – the desire which seemed to have survived rebuff, long absence and, I was certain, much experience on his side. Why not? There was no reason.

But Hortense knew that she must be very cautious because of the children. By some freak of fortune Louis had made the final break in such a way that the children had been left to me. But one breath of scandal – and scandal very easily attaches itself to women in my position, neither married nor unmarried – and Louis would claim his son, if not 'his brother'. And by giving rise to that breath of scandal I should lose my best ally, the Emperor who, while allowing himself a certain licence in these matters, was a Puritan at heart.

Adèle said, 'General de Flahaut is in my sitting room.'

I gaped and the zombie, who had seen him leave with the others and suffered disappointment, a feeling of deprivation and defeat, was lively again.

I looked at Adèle and remembered that I had seen her, during the tea-drinking, talking to Charles.

And I thought that Mother was right in saying that what was to be must be. Even a dog counted. Even a dog.

Adèle, bereaved and sad, hurrying back to me, anxious to share my life, my home, my children, had brought with her a little dog of no known breed or age, which she had rescued in Milan from a bunch of children who were stoning it. It was devoted to her and hated everyone else, more single-minded than Mother's Fortuné and its sanitary needs, since it refused to be let out, or in, by anyone except Adèle, and since it was cheerfully incontinent, had constituted a bit of a problem until Adèle had moved down, relinquishing the good sunny spacious rooms that I had assigned to her into much inferior quarters on the ground floor. The narrowness and the sunlessness of the rooms she chose were in her opinion amply compensated for by a door opening into the garden. First thing in the morning, last thing at night, if necessary in the middle of the night, she had only to open a door and stand there, assuring Peppi of her presence.

So there, as though designed for the purpose, was the place of assignation; and here, in Adèle, the perfect collaborator.

I said, 'Adèle, I do not know what to do.'

'Be happy. I was. Not for long. But long enough to know … To wish it for you, too.'

And so began the time, the joy for which there were no words.

It did not last long. Two weeks in the old year; two in the new. A month. Not merely the happiest month in my life. A month of happiness apart, out of this life, out of this world.

❧ 22 ❧

To end in such squalor: that was what seemed so incredible, so horrible.

Adèle said, 'Perhaps the cold weather ... Perhaps parting upset you more than you realised. One must not anticipate.'

But I knew. I was hopeless from the first. Everything must be paid for. I had been reckless and thoughtless and must now pay, not by being blown upon by the breath of scandal, but scorched, shamed, ended, by the full furnace blast.

Adèle said, 'I believe there are pills ...' She veiled her face and went to one of those shops under the arches of the Palais Royal; a shop that openly sold cosmetics and scents and false hair and trinkets, but also, less openly, other things.

The first lot were flat and sugar-coated. Two every night and morning. I looked at them, lying so innocently in my palm. That which love begot ... Think that way and you are undone. Think of Mother, of the Emperor, of the children. Swallow the murderous dose, and wait to see murder done. Wait. Wait. Seven days and seven nights.

The next lot were smaller, uncoated, pinkish, not so safe. One at night, one in the morning; never more than the two in one twenty-four hours, Adèle said.

No sentimental thoughts now about love and infanticide; desperation and fear harden one quickly. There were twenty of them. If the first ten do not work; if in five days' time I am not out of this trap, I'll swallow the other ten in one go and die. Better be dead than disgraced. The children? Better for them to grow up motherless than to learn the truth; and perhaps, who knew? Link it with suspicions about their own beginnings. I could just imagine Louis, merciless and gloating, 'I always knew she was no good ...' So I thought when Adèle warned me that the pills were dangerous. Five days later when the moment came for taking the lethal dose, I thought differently. To commit suicide demanded more courage and determination than I possessed. In that seemingly hopeless moment even hope revived.

Something would happen. Some way out be found. One of those fairytale plans about which Charles and I had whispered in the secret darkness would be found to be possible. And alongside these thoughts ran one that was practical – I had not yet completed the course of the corrective treatment; why should Madame Thérèse have sent twenty pills if ten would do the job?

I struggled on. The pink pills seemed to have every effect except the one desired and of course these effects must be concealed as far as possible. In The Tuileries Marie Louise was nearing the end of her pregnancy and seemed to cling to me more and more. She loved stories, but did not care for reading them and one day, to divert her mind from the coming of which she had an almost hysterical dread, I told her one of the stories which had offered me a means of escape from Amsterdam – cutting out some of the more blood-curdling details, adding episodes of my own invention, and after that she was insatiable as a child.

Early in March, however, on a bright blustery morning, when I rose from bed the whole room started to spin. Then I was sick. Adèle, who was now in almost constant attendance, said quickly, 'It must be the fish. I thought at the time … And *I* do not feel very well this morning.'

The other of my ladies who was present, Louise Cacholet, said she had had a squeamish spell in the night, but added that she had eaten no fish yesterday. In the animated search for some scapegoat dish, something we had all eaten, the bad moment passed. I lay back in bed and knew that I should not be able to go to the Palace that morning. Louise went away to pen and dispatch my excuses and when we were alone Adèle said, 'This must stop. You cannot go on poisoning yourself. We must face it and think of some scheme to get away where nobody knows us by sight. And change places, so that it seems like *my* baby.'

She had lived a life of unblemished virtue, been briefly but happily married and was, I knew, absolutely devoted to the memory of her husband. Now, for my sake, she was offering to sacrifice her good name. I asked myself what I had ever done to deserve such a friend.

'You see, I do blame myself. I … I encouraged you. I did so want you to have a little happiness.'

I should have liked to be able to say that the happiness had been great enough to make even this worthwhile; but the lie would not be said. The zombie had fled, taking with it things to which it was not entitled, all tenderness, all sentiment: Hortense was left capable of feeling nothing except apprehension and self-disgust. And, of course, amazement that I could ever have been such a reckless fool. The truth is that I had never for an instant thought of the risk. When Charles and I came together at last it was so different from the dutiful, pedestrian performance that had resulted in children that there seemed no connection at all.

I said, 'You must not blame yourself, Adèle. Leave that to me. I mean blame myself, not you.'

'When we took that holiday in the Pyrenees,' she went on, pursuing her idea, 'there were places where had I said I was Queen of Holland, I should have been believed.'

I said, 'But, darling, this is going to take months. By June … Could such a pretence be kept up?'

Somebody then tapped on the door that led to my sitting room and Adèle said loudly, 'No!' and went to the door and said with a fury of which I should not have thought her capable, 'Did I not say Her Majesty was not to be disturbed!' Then she went out, closing the door gently behind her and I thought – Marie Louise has sent to ask about me: or the Emperor has sent to tell me to make an effort to go at once. He was inclined to be a bit callous about minor physical ills.

Adèle came back and said, 'Madame de Souza. She seemed disinclined to go away and won't give me a message.'

I thought – Charles! Killed. The thought brought none of the pain that it would have done any time in the past four years; merely a kind of remorse that he should be dead just when I had no feeling for him. For a moment I had the crazy thought that by not feeling I had in some mysterious way damaged him, rendered him vulnerable …

I said, 'I'll see her, Adèle. But not here, not like this.'

The room was still a little unsteady as I put on a loose wrap. I tottered to my dressing table and saw the pale, sick face, the limp, lustreless hair. A few strokes of the brush, a flick of the powder puff.

'I do hope it is not bad news,' Adèle said as she helped me through to the sitting room and on to a sofa.

I knew it was bad the moment I saw Madame de Souza. She was one of those women who need no rouge; this morning, under the powder her natural colour had gone patchy, and her eyes, still bright, perhaps over-bright, had that indefinable look of strain that follows a sleepless night. Then I did feel something – Poor woman! Poor, poor woman!

But she said very quickly, far too quickly, 'Charles is safe and well. I had a letter yesterday.'

I thought – Yes, and what else did that letter say. That you should come here, looking like that and hot-foot to reassure me? A vast resentment stirred in me. In some clumsy, possibly well intentioned way he had betrayed me. I thought – I shall deny it, absolutely.

I said, 'I am happy to hear it, Madame de Souza. Please take that chair.'

Then I had another thought. I might be the victim of my own self-centredness. That too prompt statement might have another meaning. It could be saying – My son is in Spain, safe and well, busy in bolstering Joseph Bonaparte on his throne … and therefore I, a Frenchwoman born, as the mother of a French soldier, deserve better treatment than I have lately received. You must intercede for me.

She could, with some justification, have said that. Portugal, the base from which the English were giving support to those Spaniards who would not accept Joseph Bonaparte as King of Spain, could no longer be regarded by the Emperor as a neutral country. That old phrase about diplomatic relationships being broken off had applied to the Portuguese Ambassador and Madame de Souza had lost those many small privileges that she had formerly enjoyed.

Had she come here, this morning, when I felt so ill, to complain about not having her reserved box at the Opera?

She sat down in the chair I had indicated.

She said, 'Your Majesty …' stopped, got up and moving like a cat went to the outer door, opened it, looked out and repeated the performance at the inner one, the one which led to my bedroom. Then, instead of resuming her seat in the chair she pulled forward a little footstool and squatted upon it, her legs bent so that she seemed to be kneeling. Close up, the red in her face seemed darker, the white more livid. She said, in a low, hurried voice, 'Your Majesty, if I am wrong I am about to commit an irretrievable offence. I beg your forgiveness in advance and ask you to believe that I am *compelled* to it. Not least by the regard in which I have always held you …' She halted. Under my eyes the marbling in her red and white face shifted. She said, 'I came to say it and it must be said. With one's own one does not need to be told. He was so *happy*. And his bed hardly ever slept in. And then …' she paused again. 'Twice, at Madame Thérèse's … Madame de Broc, veiled and furtive, coming from that inner room …'

If she were wrong it was such a deadly insult that I could have her banished for life. If she were wrong, or if I wished to make her think that she was, I must now rise in my wrath, ring the bell, order her out. She waited in that humble posture but with her gaze steady. I thought – What courage! And with that the moment for indignation, righteous or feigned, was gone. Nausea engulfed me. Cold sweat broke out on my face and the evil-tasting fluid rose in my throat.

She went swiftly, but without noise or bustle into my bedroom, brought a bowl and a towel, held me while I vomited, wiped my face, laid me back on the cushions. She said, as though to a child, 'You will be better now,' and went to dispose of the bowl and the towel. When she came back the colour in her face was smooth again. She said, 'I have known some bad moments, but that was the worst.'

She spoke in a manner so intimate and sincere that it sounded as though she and I had been together, and emerged together, through some horrifying ordeal. As indeed we had. But her worst moment was over and done with; mine could have prolonged itself into an almost endless embarrassment and doubt as to whether I had behaved wisely; but it did not because she would not allow it. She took charge.

First she asked if I felt well enough to talk. Well then, who knew? Only Adèle. How far gone? Over two months.

'You poor darling. It must have been Hell. But I'm with you now. Trust me. I will arrange everything. With God's help. Oh, I have known doubts but every now and then I see His finger. And never more clearly than in that seemingly God-forsaken place … One must acknowledge a sign when it is given. I visit that shop, of course, as a customer, but Thérèse Fontain and I have another connection – she is not all bad, or at least, if bad, useful. That kind of errand takes me there perhaps four times in a year; in the last six weeks I have been obliged to go twice and on both occasions, as I said, I saw Madame de Broc. I asked myself, On whose behalf? I went through an agony of indecision. But now here I am.'

She spoke as though her knowing, and her presence altered everything. I thought – How does it help? I also thought about those two chance, coincidental visits in which she saw the finger of God. Pointing where? Did she, mature, worldly-wise, know a trick that would work where the pills had failed? I waited, committing myself into her hands.

'And does it not seem strange,' she went on, 'that you, the cause of Charles not marrying, should be the one to bear the child I have longed for. That has been such a grievous thought – that he might die without having stamped his pattern. This could be a remarkable child.'

And this, I thought, is a remarkable conversation. It sounded as though I were married to Charles, and she, all motherly, grandmotherly, was looking forward over seven months with no more to bother about than the provision of a layette and the choosing of a name.

Then she said, 'May at the very latest you must leave Paris. How and where, leave to me. I have a very *inventive* mind …'

When she had gone I felt better; perhaps simply talking; perhaps her confidence; perhaps because now for the first time the child seemed real, not just an unpleasant symptom. In the afternoon I was well enough to go to The Tuileries and cheer Marie Louise with those worn, feminine lies about childbirth being nothing to dread, nothing much, soon over, and then, more effectually, with the latest instalment of our verbal serial.

The Emperor came in and seeing her moderately happy, looked at me with approval, said some complimentary things and I thought the inevitable thought – If you only knew!

Marie Louise's fears were more than justified. Despite being young and healthy, and having had a welcome and cherished pregnancy, she had a long, hard labour. The longed-for child upon whom so much depended, presented itself wrongly. To add to her misery she was denied all privacy, even in the birth chamber itself. All the old dusty rules about royal births had been dug up and strictly applied. I suppose they had once served some purpose, in barbarous times when a desperate woman might substitute a living boy for a dead one, or for a girl – there was some story of a King of England being a newborn peasant smuggled into the Queen's bed in a warming pan – but now it simply meant that all the family and a horde of officials milled about at one end of the bedchamber and in the anterooms. As the hours of the night went on the close-pressed bodies heated the exhausted air. The Emperor went restlessly in and out, white-faced, wild-eyed, shuddering visibly each time the Empress screamed. As a member of the family I was bound to stay though it was like being present at a torture scene, the woman on the rack, the man in the thumbscrews. At one point the screams lessened and we all hoped it was over; but a doctor, looking like a drowned man, elbowed his way to Bonaparte and gasped, 'Sire, it is a question of mother or child.'

It took him less than a second to make this, one of the most momentous decisions of his life. He said, 'The Empress!' And I thought what it must have cost him. The child, his first to be born in wedlock and if a boy the indisputable heir; the woman a toy, easily replaced. I had never admired him more than at that moment. Then Marie Louise began to scream again; the child, dragged into the world by forceps, was a boy, uninjured. France had an heir.

Paris and France went crazy with joy; the satellite countries put up a good pretence. Messages of congratulation and gifts poured in. The little boy was immediately given the Emperor's secondary title and became King of Rome.

In the Rue Curetti Adèle and I set about the surreptitious letting out of seams, just an inch here, an inch there. My cough returned and gave me an excuse for seeming to coddle myself, guarding against the vagrant draught by wearing scarves of gauze or lace, sitting down whenever I could and retiring early.

'So long as you are *seen*,' Madame de Souza said. 'And the cough is a Godsend; a perfect excuse for coming to Aix-en-Savoy in May.'

She had repudiated the idea of my going to some remote village in the Pyrenees. 'You cannot simply vanish for three months. Aix is a wateringplace, becoming fashionable, a stay there will cause no comment. Also there is the question of comfort.'

In April she travelled to Aix and hired two houses, one for her, in the town itself, very near to the centre where people went to drink the waters and to take baths, the other, rather more grand on the outskirts, half-way up a hill and very difficult of access. The latter was hired 'with staff' down to bedchamber maids. 'If you took your own, they might wonder why they were left when we made our little – er – trip. As it is, hired with the villa they will stay there unquestioning.'

The whole thing was planned with the precision of a military exercise and so far as the plan was concerned everything fell into place like one of those jigsaw puzzles. Even Mother had contributed, all unwittingly. She had bought a house at a place called Pregny in Switzerland, near the lake of Geneva. Her choice of place may not have been very rational but her decision to buy a new house was. She hated Evreux, she said the château there was the coldest place she had ever been in and it was forever associated in her mind with her exile from Paris and its neighbourhood during the wedding celebrations in 1810. She had herself ruled that no changes should be made at Malmaison – though the Emperor's visits had become rarer and rarer, so her home-making talent, that wish to rearrange and experiment, suffered frustration. Explaining the purchase of Pregny to me, earlier in the year, she said, 'I feel I could make something of it. And there would be another advantage, too. Foreigners seem not to understand, or are too *curious*. People will visit me, even at Evreux. French people realise that I now receive only a few faithful, intimate friends. The others don't, and, darling, it is a little difficult to turn away a caller – in his own country a person of importance – who has made such a journey.'

So this piece and that piece fell into place. The Queen of Holland with her horrible cough would go to Aix-en-Savoy in May. In September, making a little detour to see her mother's new property, she would visit Pregny.

'All but a few days accounted for,' Madame de Souza said. Her inventive mind had seized avidly on Adèle's idea about a change of identity. 'Perfect,' she said, 'for those three or four vital days.'

She thought of everything; even of the fact that we should not appear to be too intimate. Not here, in Paris. In Aix it would be different; in a strange place people who had lived in the same street for twenty years and never exchanged more than civil greetings, meet as friends.

A week before Adèle and I were due to leave – Madame de Souza had already left – I was officially informed that at the christening of the King of Rome the Queen of Holland would stand proxy godmother for the Queen of Naples who was unable to attend.

I stared at this communication with dismay. The christening was to be on 9th June, almost exactly a month ahead, and between being five months pregnant and six months there is a considerable difference.

'You must get out of it somehow,' Adèle said. 'For one thing it would mean a new gown being measured. Impossible.'

The Emperor was already annoyed by Caroline's defection and when I made my stumbling excuses roared that he wanted no more nonsense.

'Caroline could have come had she wished. She can come from Naples for a ball or a parade. It's jealousy that makes her not wish to take part. Is it the same with you?'

I said, 'Indeed no. Of what should I be jealous? It is my health, this wretched cough.'

'Corvisart can give you something to quieten that for a couple of hours.'

'But I don't feel well enough to stand for two hours.'

'Then sit. We'll have a chair handy and a man doing nothing but watch you. Make a sign and he'll bring it forward.'

'That would be most improper on such an occasion. Sire, I really must beg …'

'I agree. It would be improper. So make up your mind to stand. Think of Madame Mere – in her sixties!' She was to be the other godmother and when I thought of her I thought of standing, in a month's time, under that eagle eye.

'You take this cough altogether too seriously,' the Emperor said. 'If you were consumptive you'd lose flesh and you look to me to be gaining …'

Dangerous ground!

'The approach of middle age,' I said as lightly as I could.

'Erumph,' he said. 'Well it comes to us all. How old are you, exactly? Wait! Twenty-eight last month. Well, I suppose for a woman … It's time we did something about your situation. No hope, I suppose, of your patching it up with Louis.'

'None at all. I don't even know where he is.'

'I know where he *was*, a week or two back, Gratz, in Styria. He wrote me one of his muddied letters accusing me of having robbed him of his throne, his personal property in Holland and his son. A very inimical letter. Then he switched round and said he was homesick and wanted to come back to France on his own conditions, of course asked me to arrange for Louis-Napoleon to go to him. I wrote back that it would be time enough to think about that when he had a settled home to offer the child. So that fobbed him off for a while. We have to face it, though, say "divorce" and he'll say "custody of the child" and get it.'

'I suppose so … And yet he abandoned him when he left Amsterdam. Having done his best for months to make Lou depend on him, *only* on him, he ran away in the middle of the night … And if he claims him now it will be to spite me and for no other reason.'

'Well, we'll deal with that when the moment comes … Now, presents for godmothers. Caroline was to have had rubies. She won't get them now. And you never wear them, do you?'

'They are my least favourite stone,' I said, wondering that he should have noticed.

'Diamonds, then? They go with any colour. Your mother ...' he snapped off that sentence and tried to cover the slip, 'My mother said she wanted no trinkets, she would sooner have the money, safe in the bank, or well-invested. And nobody, *nobody* can make her see that the value of money fluctuates while a good diamond retains its value and can be carried around ...'

Working like moles in the night Adèle and I reconstructed a dress that had never been seen in France. It had been made for me in Holland during Louis's most 'Dutch' period, when local industry must be supported and local talent encouraged. I had worn it once, on one of those unhappy evenings that had ended in a row which now seemed to have been about nothing; then I had put it away and like a faithful but unloved dog, it had followed me and arrived somehow in the Rue Curetti, and was now to have its little day. 'What will Your Majesty wear?' 'Ah, that is a secret.' 'Who has the honour of designing it?' In every workshop there was a paid spy. 'Ah, that is a secret, too.'

Ironically on the day everybody looked at the dress and had I stood there by the front and broken out into a measle rash hardly anyone would have noticed. The stuff was so stiff and bright – the nearest thing I have ever seen to the 'cloth of gold' of medieval times – and so new-fangled, with two floating panels, made out of the original train, falling from shoulder to toe that inside it Hortense stood as little noticed as a dressmaker's dummy. Also, of course, when I held the little King of Rome, his christening gown was so ruffled and laced that it would have disguised a far more advanced pregnancy than mine.

And the Emperor was just. I had done my duty by his son, he would do his by my boys. While I sought a cure for my cough in Aix they should live in St Cloud where he could keep an eye on them and they could lunch with him and the Empress every day.

Once again all seemed to be working well; but, when I actually said goodbye to the children I had one of those piercing pangs quite as destructive as months of passive misery. I thought, in a few minutes, all those things I should have thought when I went down to Adèle's room on that winter night to embrace joy. Only a *bad* mother would have acted as I had done. Walking down a few stairs, leaving them asleep, I had deserted them quite as fully as Louis had deserted Lou in Amsterdam. More so, because this might well be goodbye for ever. This time I should not be in the hands of a skilled obstetrician; in some remote place between Aix-en-Savoy and Pregny some village midwife would deal with me – and Madame de Souza, with her resourceful and inventive mind, would stage a carriage accident or some other good reason for my demise … My darling boys would be motherless because I, not content with what I had, must reach out and grab at what was forbidden. Tears filled my eyes, and I felt no better when Lou said solicitously, 'Don't cry, Mamma. It always makes you cough.'

23

If the house outside Aix had been specifically designed to shelter me for three months it could not better have served its purpose. Whoever built it must have been a determined recluse. The drive that led up to it was at least half a mile long with five sharp hairpin bends, extremely difficult for a carriage to negotiate. The surface was abominable, partly cobblestones, unevenly laid and partly the bedrock of the hillside laid bare by rain rushing down the steep slopes. Here again Madame de Souza had doubtless seen the finger of God, for one of our problems was to be rid of my own carriage and my coachman. It was the easiest thing in the world to say that my nerves would not stand making that ascent – and worse still, the descent – every day and that I must find some other conveyance, probably a little donkey-cart. I said that very positively while in the carriage and again when I alighted. Then my man 'discovered' for himself that whoever had lived here previously had kept no carriage. There was no coach-house, no accommodation for a coachman and stabling only for one horse. These facts he related to me with great distress and an undertone of reproach that implied that I really should have managed better. 'And not a bit of pasture, Your Majesty,' he said.

Feigning concern and deep thought I said, 'Really, Bonnet, I think the best plan would be for you to take the carriage away – if you can get it down – and go and find some proper accommodation. Madame de Broc will give you some money. Let me know where you are and if I need you I will send word.'

While two hired maids, very shy, unpacked, Adèle and I explored the house which had few rooms, but those very spacious and well furnished. Then, having had tea, we went into the garden which lay on the side of the house opposite the unsatisfactory approach. This, too, was on a slope and consisted of many little terraces connected by short flights of narrow steps. The roofs of the town were immediately below us. 'I do believe,' Adèle said, 'that it would lead straight down into a street. Wait here, I'll go and see.' I sat on a stone seat surrounded by oleander bushes, pink and white flowered. Presently from the terrace below the one on which I sat I heard voices, Adèle's and Madame de Souza's. Madame de Souza was flushed and breathless.

She curtsied. Throughout, her manner had remained entirely correct. On that March morning she had called me 'darling' and once she had said 'my dear', but as she herself had explained when I had suggested less formality it would be a mistake to become familiar in private as it might lead to a slip in public.

She said, 'I hope Your Majesty approves of the place.'

'It could not have been better if you had built it,' I said. She looked gratified. 'How did you get here?'

'By the gate that connects my garden with yours. At least it did while both properties belonged to one man. Then it was locked; but I have had it opened. So I can come and go as I wish.'

Everything went as planned. Aix-en-Savoy, not yet as fashionable and crowded as Plombières, Montpellier or Baden, was ambitious and growing. The arrival of Her Majesty the Queen of Holland was fully publicised. Her Majesty duly made her appearance in the vast marble hall – the nearest thing to a Roman palace that modern man could devise – and watched, and for a while shared in the morning parade at which the drinking of rather strange-tasting water was made into a kind of social gathering. Her Majesty took no baths, was inclined to sit, rather than stand, in the echoing, palm-decorated place, was gracious and agreeable to those who wished to be presented. (Was a little frightened by the number of French people who appeared as the season advanced.) And she was occasionally called upon, but less as time went on, and it was discovered how difficult and vertigious was the drive up to her house, and that she was not entertaining.

I went down into the town in a little wicker cart, hardly bigger than an armchair, drawn by an almost white donkey with a string of blue beads round its neck – to keep off the evil eye. Presently I made another use of the conveyance, and sat in it, outside the bath house, and sipped my daily doses and held a kind of court. My cough did not improve, but of that there was no public mention. It was enough that Her Majesty should be there.

Madame de Souza came up through the garden almost every evening. Half-way through July she arrived slightly more flushed and breathless than usual and said, 'I have a little surprise for you.' She had been overwhelmingly kind, sensing my lowness of spirit and had planned many little chance pleasures, a new book or song, a young man who played the guitar and sang local peasant songs …

I said, 'How kind you are! What is it today?'

'Promise not to be too much surprised. It is Charles.'

My first feeling was of consternation. In the ordinary way a husband becomes accustomed to the day by day changes, the thickening figure, the heavier step. In addition to these I had the horrible cough and an almost translucent pallor which seemed to consume the rouge I so carefully applied. I felt ugly, sickly, far removed from the companion in joy that I had been during that winter month.

'Does he know?'

'Of course. That is why he is here.'

She called him in and went out, closing the door.

And so began the second and far more serious time of thraldom. Something in which the zombie played no part at all. Now, when he kissed me, I felt the kindness and the reassurance. When he spoke I could listen to what he said and not to the wild thunder of my own blood. This was a kind of belonging, every bit as important as, more important than, the physical possession on a bed.

He said, 'My darling. I blame myself utterly. When I heard I was appalled. You must have been so lonely. I would have come if you'd let me know. Why didn't you let me know? I'm selfish; I'm thoughtless; a brute in human form, but I would have come.'

'You could have done nothing.'

'I could have taken you away.'

We were back where we had been towards the end of the happy time when he had suggested America, Turkey, Russia and the zombie had cried, 'Go! Go!' and Hortense had argued that she did not wish to lose her children, give Louis a case against her, infuriate the Emperor, scandalise Europe. Hortense had wanted illicit love, a blameless reputation, her family and security. For though Charles had spoken bravely about soldiers being welcome in Turkey or even Russia, the Emperor's arm was long and the man who had run away with the Emperor's step-daughter was not likely to prosper. Hortense had wanted altogether too much; and she had been punished.

I said, 'Let's not talk about that. Tell me, when did you learn; and how?'

'Mother wrote. About a month ago. Oh, carefully. Trust Mother. She invented a cousin for me. Called Sophie. My cousin Sophie of whom I was so very fond, who danced so well, who had two little boys, one with my name … I read that signal and as I say, I was appalled. Do you hate me?'

There had been bad moments when I was lonely and afraid. But now I said, 'It takes two, you know.' His face brightened.

'There's nobody like you in the world,' he said.

'How did you get away?'

'I talked the Marshals into the belief that their quarrel with King Joseph could proceed without me for a month, or even two.' I knew what he meant. Joseph Bonaparte, in many ways so different from Louis, was behaving in Spain almost exactly as Louis had done in Holland – working against French influence, against the Emperor's controlling hand.

Charles had a perfectly adequate reason for being in Aix, apart from his mother being there. The wound that he had received at Ulm, four ribs and a collar-bone broken, had seemed relatively trivial, leaving only a puckered scar and a slight bumpiness where the bones had knit. In those winter nights, in the secret happy time, I had often laid my cheek, my lips against the bumpiness. Lately he had suffered some pain and stiffness. 'And the right arm is the sword arm, so when horse-linament failed ...'

He took the baths and drank the waters conscientiously, sometimes joined the little group around my donkey-cart in a civil, inconspicuous way and then at evening climbed the steps through the garden. Madame de Souza always came too. Once, feeling better, and venturesome, I went down to visit them and was shocked to see the house in which they were living. It had originally been the gardener's cottage. Someone had bought it as a speculation, counting upon the town's growing popularity and the likely demand for rented houses. It had been made gay with fresh paint and furnished with new, cheap stuff and a certain picturesqueness, but it was basically a cottage and a small one at that, with stairs going up like a ladder against one wall of the single sitting room. Above were two tiny rooms which I did not inspect, but could guess were too low for comfort. There was a lean-to kitchen in which the one servant spent the night as well as the day. The whole place was dark and airless and smelt damp. That Madame de Souza should for one moment have considered living in it, simply because of its extreme convenience of situation, I took as further proof of her devotion.

'But do not people wonder to see you living in such a very humble place?'

Her eyes sparkled. 'Did you not know that I am an inveterate unlucky gambler? During my first trip in Aix I had a very fine hired house in the Place Savoy. Three long sessions in the Casino so nearly ruined me that everyone considers me very fortunate to have found this cheap place to fall back upon. And, if anybody is interested, my state of penury explains why, when Your Majesty returns to Paris by way of Pregny, you will be kind enough to offer me accommodation in your carriage and I shall be glad to accept.'

I thought – She is *enjoying* this. And that is why she does it so well. I remembered that she had once written a novel and it seemed to me that she was now writing another with living characters and real situations. The thought did not make me less grateful to her, or for her.

Time moved on and it was August, very hot. On two successive mornings I felt too languid and heavy to clamber into the little cart and sit shrouded in a rug however light and lacy. Adèle went down and fetched my water ration in a little covered jug.

'And everyone I spoke to,' she said, 'says that one sure sign of the cure being effective is that one should wish to do nothing but sleep.'

I lay sprawled at ease on a sofa, just inside the open window that gave upon the first terrace of the garden; and I was thinking about Charles. This interlude, with the zombie banished, with our meeting every day in a set-ting more or less domestic had enabled us to get to know one another in a way hitherto impossible. And one thing had struck me, not disillusioning, but enlightening, that made me glad in a deep, crooked kind of way, that I had not agreed to run away with him, when, spent with loving, we had lain on Adèle's bed and talked of plans for the future. Once, I remember, when I spoke of losing my children, he had said, 'There could be others. Ours.' And that had sounded romantic, enticing, then. Now I knew better …

Never once, even by accident, had he ever referred to the child inside me, lively and kicking, in any paternal terms. He had come to be with me, loving and kind – but all as though I had broken a leg. He said things like 'When this is over', and 'When you are well again'. He never said 'the child' or 'our child'. His attitude implied that I was suffering from, say, an aching tooth, which must be drawn, and that he felt in some way responsible for my affliction and had come, because he loved me, to see me through the ordeal. I had, I knew, no right to criticise this attitude – I had done worse; I had tried to rid myself of the child with little more human feeling than a woman might feel over the unblocking of a drain. So I must not mind when I said, of the child who was now so very real to me, 'I do wonder about its future', and he replied, 'Mother will see to it', I thought – Just not cut out to be a family man.

There was the other side, too; he never once queried the paternity which meant so little to him. And that he could so easily have done. It would not have taken an unduly suspicious mind to think that a rendezvous so easy of access, a waiting lady so willing to connive and quick of understanding might have served others: also this pregnancy, like all my others, had been extremely prompt. But Charles accepted what he called the blame for my condition though he brushed off all responsibility for the child.

I was thinking these things when from the front of the house came the sound of someone arriving.

'Some lady has come to enquire for you and to tell you how the cure affected herself,' Adèle said.

I composed myself more elegantly on the sofa and pulled over me the flimsy cover which always lay handy on the sofa's foot.

I was hardly ready when she darted back and said, 'It is Eugène.'

Apart from Mother no one could have been more unwelcome. And that was a horrible thought.

He came in, his honest face beaming, changed to concern when he saw me and said, 'I hoped to find you better. I was told that you were …'

'I am. I am. It is just the heat. It makes me lazy.'

I carefully raised myself a little and held out my arms. 'What a lovely surprise.' Hugging me, he said, 'It seemed to me as near to Italy as you'd ever been. I came on impulse, no time to let you know.'

We hugged, we kissed. 'My dearest sister. I am so glad to see you, but I wish you looked better.'

'My dear Eugène. It is lovely to see you. And I am very well really, much better than …'

He straightened up and the lacy shawl, caught in his coat buttons, rose too. I lay exposed.

Eugène said, 'Oh! So that … Nobody told me. I thought you and Louis …' In a second, recovered from his surprise, he would be congratulating me. I said in a quick, harsh voice, 'It isn't Louis's.'

Eugène said, 'God!'

I had seen wounded men, but never at the moment when the steel or the bullet went home. No man, taking a mortal blow, could have looked worse than Eugène did then, the colour drained from his face, his eyes wide and dark. He took a blundering step backwards, hit the back of his knees against a chair and fell into it.

I said hastily, 'It is all right, Eugène. Everything is all right.'

'All right,' he mocked me savagely. 'How can you lie there …? How can it be all right?' His mind thrashed round, seized upon the one thing that for him would make it all right and blundered on, 'But you've seen Louis. He believes …' Say *Yes* to that and understanding would begin, tolerance take over.

'I have not seen Louis since I left Holland in May last year.'

Poor Eugène then fell back upon the only other explanation of my use of the phrase, *all right*.

'The Emperor knows?'

'No. Only three people. The man, his mother and Adèle. Now you.'

'God!' Eugène said again. He gave me a look of great hostility, the first in all our lives.

I said, 'I'm sorry, Eugène. I'd have given anything rather than you should know. And now you do, by the sheerest accident. I never had any luck. Hundreds of women have lovers by the dozen … I had one, for a very short time and this happened.'

'Who is he?' I saw a murderous glint in his eyes.

'It would be better for you not to know.'

'I'll find out; and I'll kill him.'

'That would be very helpful!'

He retaliated for the sarcasm with reproach.

'I always thought so … so highly of you. I knew that your marriage …
But I thought you were above … that kind of thing. I thought … dignity,
taste. I've always admired you …'

'And now you find I'm only human.'

The hostility vanished.

He said, 'Well, I suppose … You must have had a hideous time. And not
over yet. What about servants? They always know everything.'

I thought of the endless tricks and subterfuges that had kept even my bedchamber maids in ignorance. One was worthy of Madame de Souza herself.

I said, 'Not even those closest to me. In. fact those I left behind in Paris,
the two I have here, I mean bedchamber maids, if you went and told them
that I am as I am would flatly contradict you, quoting the evidence of their
own eyes.'

Amazement, incredulity and some distaste showed on his open face. But
he was recovering; the wound perhaps not so vital as it seemed.

'And you think you can manage it to the end?'

'I hope so. If not it will not be for lack of planning.'

'I must hear about that. And if I can help …'

'Your presence alone will do that. If you can bear to share a roof with such
a disreputable …'

'Hortense *please*. It was such a shock. I hardly knew what I was saying. Try
to forgive me.'

'If *you* can forgive *me*.' I used the phrase that had ended our few childish
squabbles. 'Friends again?'

'Friends again,' he said.

Few people ever thought Adèle clever, but when I asked her to run down
through the garden and warn Madame de Souza and Charles, I found that
she had already done so, the moment Eugène arrived. I could not yet trust
Eugène fully; a gentleman with a grudge against another can always find
some excuse, if necessarily far removed from the original offence, to justify a
calling-out and although the Emperor strongly disapproved of duels – 'Save
your steel for the enemy!' – they did still occur.

Eugène's coming and his presence served me well by shifting the focus of
attention. What, after all, was a queen without a throne, in poor health and not
given to hospitality, compared with the Viceroy of Italy who had paid Aix the
compliment of preferring it to a famous watering-place in his own domain?

And his own good sense had come uppermost once he had accepted the
situation. He asked my plans, and when I told him, seemed to approve of
all but one detail and that concerned the business of sending Bonnet with

my own carriage and horses on to Pregny, several days in advance, and then buying another equipage in which to travel myself.

'What reason could you give the man?'

'That I want him to go ahead and warn the caretaker at Pregny to have all ready; and that by sending on a good deal of baggage in advance we lighten the load. There will be four of us in the new carriage.'

'I see. I've no doubt you'd get something that seemed roadworthy, but a lick of varnish on a carriage can hide faults and you might all too easily get bad horses – the tricks horse-dealers get up to stagger the imagination … I'll leave you mine, that will be best. It is good and sound, so are the horses.'

'And quite as noticeable as my own, Eugène. That would defeat our purpose.'

He said, 'No. There you are wrong. Genuine escutcheons I tolerate – if a fellow's remote ancestor went on Crusade with three boars' heads or some such on his banner, on his breastplate, and he still wants the symbol all over his possessions who's to blame him? As for me I keep state when I must, but when I ride for pleasure I use a plain carriage. So you can have it. I'll buy a horse and ride back. Do me good.' Having settled that he said, 'And now, what about the fifteenth? The Emperor's birthday, goose. Had you forgotten?'

'I cannot possibly entertain, Eugène.'

'Oh yes you can. And you must. When I came in, only four days ago, I should never have suspected.

He surveyed me as though I were enemy terrain likely to be ambushed.

'You'll do,' he said. 'But watch for buttons! We must invite every French person of consequence in Aix and give them something to remember. And something must be done about that road.'

Now that he was so whole-heartedly on my side I told him about Charles and his reception of that piece of information chilled me a little.

'De Flahaut? My God, Hortense, what could you see …? Oh, he's a pretty good soldier, but a bit of a nit-wit I always thought. What in the world did you ever find to talk about?'

I said, 'Nothing. There was no need.'

Eugène was now accustomed to exercising authority. By the day of the Emperor's birthday the hairpin bends had been widened and eased, the road resurfaced, waxed sailcloth stretched taut over the two upper terraces of the garden, strings of little coloured glasses, each containing a slow-burning candle, decorating the trees.

All over the Empire the day was being celebrated, but nowhere more merrily or lavishly than in the place where the Emperor's step-son moved about, the perfect host, and his step-daughter lay on a sofa, watching the dancers on the terraces and presently the fireworks set off from a lower level. And – Oh yes, how kind! My cough is much better. Oh yes, how kind! By the time my cure is completed I shall be dancing again.

When Eugène left, having outstayed what he meant to be a flying visit by some days, he held my hands and said, 'If anything should go wrong, come to me. I mean that, Hortense. Even if the worst happens, and the plans fail, come to me.'

Nothing went wrong. Madame de Souza had spied out the land. Not a village, she said, in villages everybody knew everybody else's business; a small town, near the Swiss-French-Italian border, with a decent inn accustomed to guests, and a doctor who could be called upon if needed.

Pont St Pierre, as the little town was called, was not unlike the one in the Pyrenees where Adèle and I had bought the mule hats. It was a little, only a little, less primitive. Money was more used here, and there was an inn, because the place was the centre of a wide sheep-rearing area and so much frequented by wool-buyers and stock breeders. It was now September, the sunny days still warm, the evenings cool with a hint of autumn about them. It was the time when the flocks were culled and the town was full of sheep, brought down from the upland meadows and offered for sale in pens under the dusty plane trees. My fourth confinement is inseparately associated with the smell of sheep and with their plaintive cries.

We had changed drivers three times and our own identities twice, and were now a party of the utmost respectability; a French lady, Madame Tournelle, with her son, Charles, her two daughters, Adèle and me. I was Madame Cavalcanti, on the way home to join my Italian husband, anxious that my child should be born in its father's country.

This pious wish was not to be granted. Travel over rough roads, Madame Tournelle explained, with well-stimulated distress, had precipitated the birth; she apologised for the inconvenience.

Actually luck, was with us; the timing could not have been better, we might have been obliged to linger here for several days, concocting excuses: and the people at the inn could not have been kinder. The midwife, they said, was 'better than any doctor', and it was a well-known fact that any child who drew his first breath in the wonderful air of Pont St Pierre, would be healthy and live long.

It was a very easy birth; the child was another boy. Madame de Souza was beside herself with joy. 'The living image of Charles,' she said; and it was a blessing that it should be a boy. 'The world in any case is kinder to men; and placed as he will be …' I looked down upon the little sleeping face, wondered how he would be placed, and was overwhelmed again by guilt and remorse. Madame de Souza would, I knew, see that he was well cared for and I intended to practise the most stringent economy so that he should be provided for, but he would never know a mother, or a father, and even to his grandmother would be nothing more officially than a protégé.

However, it was too late now to consider these things and moping did no good. Also there were practical problems.

Ironically, this child I could have fed and the midwife was extremely annoyed with me for not doing so.

'Oh,' she said with a sniff, 'it may not be the *fashion* in some places; but it's best for the child, and for the mother, too.'

I could see her good opinion of me waning.

'It is not on account of fashion.' That I could truly say. My next statement was a lie. 'I tried to feed my other baby and had a terrible abscess in my breast. I have no wish to go through that again.'

'Then we must find a wet-nurse.'

'That would be a mistake, too. You see my mother knows how very anxious my husband is to see the child, and proposes to take him to Italy in a day or two. A wet-nurse, even if she were willing to go so far, would need a passport to cross the frontier, and there is not time enough to procure one.' I smiled but she still regarded me with stony displeasure.

'It's the wrong time of year for ewe's milk. That's the next best thing. It'll have to be goat's. And if he doesn't flourish as he should, you'll have only yourself to blame.'

It was a region where cows were very few.

I could only hope that my love child would continue to be, throughout his life, as tough and adaptable as he was in the first few days. He sucked the warm goat-milk from a piece of clean linen wadded into the shape of a teat, went to sleep and digested it.

On the fourth day we parted company; Madame de Souza, Charles and the baby ostensibly bound for Italy; actually she going post-haste to Paris and he to Spain, where Spanish patriots blew up bridges, poisoned wells and set fire to houses where the French were billeted. And with the exception of the one small flaw – his indifference to the child – he had from the moment of his arrival in Aix behaved perfectly to me, kind, considerate, attentive and cheerful. But his relief that the whole thing was over could not be concealed, nor, since I shared it, could it be criticised. Once, in a moment of deep melancholy, looking at the baby, so soon to be removed, I said, 'Perhaps I was wrong. Louis-Napoleon will soon be seven, Charles-Napoleon nearly three, they're over the worst. This one is so very small and helpless … Perhaps we should have gone to America …'

He said, 'Darling, you didn't think so last January and you won't think it once you are back in Paris. Look ahead. Louis will divorce you, without any scandal. Then we can be married, properly. And if you like we'll adopt this little fellow.'

It was the right, the sensible view, but there are moments when sense seems cold …

So they went, and three days later, since time must be considered, Adèle and I went to Pregny.

24

Madame de Souza said, 'But of course you shall see him, as often as you like – or as often as is discreet. I assure you, he is very well cared for. He has been properly registered, the son of Auguste Dumorny and his wife. He has been named Charles Auguste. Auguste Dumorny is a veteran soldier with a small pension which he is willing to augment by any legitimate means; his wife is younger, but unable to have a child of her own. I have known and used them for twelve years. They are the best foster parents in the business.'

The business! Used!

I said, 'You have used them before?'

She said, hastily, and in an embarrassed way, 'Well, that happens to be my pet, private charity. It also happens to be what took me ... takes me ... to Madame Thérèse's, not as a customer and not at the usual time. She feels for them, too, the least wanted of all unwanted children, the children of prostitutes. Who ever thinks about them? The girls, women, have cut themselves off from their families, never go near a church. And as I said, she is not all evil. The women constitute the bulk of her customers, both in front of the counter and behind, and when she fails, she ... feels a certain responsibility and does not like to hear of a new-born baby put on a rubbish dump, or into the Seine. I am sorry if I have shocked you, but it does happen ... We have saved quite a few. Not enough of course.' She made a hopeless gesture and then smiled. 'Fortunately I am very handy with my needle and so my dress allowance stretches out. And I am not always so unlucky when I gamble as I was at Aix.'

I said, 'I cannot tell you how much I ...' Was I going to say *love* or *admire*? I hesitated and she said quickly, 'It is so little. I have always been so fortunate, and one owes ... The great thing about Coralie Dumorny is that she loves children while they are *very* small and then seems to tire. When Auguste is two I shall begin to think of other arrangements. If you and Charles are not by that time in a position to make your own. In the meantime he is in safe hands and I will request Coralie Dumorny to bring him for inspection on any afternoon next week that is more convenient to you.'

All my other children had been fed at other breasts, their physical needs met by other hands than mine so there was really no reason why the sight of Auguste, in his foster-mother's arms, should be so hurtful. But it was, on that first contrived meeting and on each subsequent one. He was clearly well looked after, but very poorly dressed, his flannel clothes felted and yellowed from much washing, his linen patched.

'But of course,' Madame de Souza said when I commented upon this. 'Neither Thérèse nor I have money to waste upon fripperies. We have a clothing pool and manage as best we can. It would be not only invidious, but unwise to make distinctions and give one baby a new outfit. And he does not know what he is wearing.'

One day he would, though! And suppose Charles was killed and I died, or some other unforeseen thing prevented our marriage ... I began to wrestle with the problem of how to make long-term provision for Auguste Dumorny, not only in terms of money but of guardianship. The obvious choice was Eugène, but the subject was one which I dared not write about with the posts as they were. So I waited and watched Lou and Charles-Napoleon, with their ponies, more toys than they could use, more food than they could eat, wearing silk, wearing velvet, welcome and pampered visitors to palaces and I understood the full meaning of illegitimacy.

On the surface life was very gay as 1811 slipped into 1812. And 22nd April of that new year had been for me an ordinary, busy day. Breakfast with the children, an informal call at The Tuileries where Marie Louise and I talked about tooth-cutting, a process then troubling the King of Rome, then on to Malmaison to lunch with Mother and to admire the daffodils, at the very peak of their glory. I was home again, changed into easy house-clothes, prepared for one of my domestic evenings, actually arguing with Lou, who was to stay up, about Charles-Napoleon staying up too.

I said, 'Darling, he really is too young. Only just four. You never stayed up until you were five.'

'But we like to do things together.' And that was something that I had encouraged in a way, offering Charles-Napoleon to Lou as a substitute for Non-Non.

I said, 'Of course you do, and there are many things that you can do together. I'm afraid staying up late is not one of them.'

'Then I think I will go to bed when he does?'

He looked at his brother, and I looked, too, and saw on the face of a four-year-old a most unchildlike expression – triumph. I had a flash of thought; Lou had been dominated by Non-Non and when Charles-Napoleon was born he had hoped to dominate him. But the boot was on the other leg. Charles-Napoleon had not said a word about staying up – or indeed anything else – and he had no need to, Lou was his spokesman ... I had a funny feeling of being up against something more significant than it seemed, something secret and cunning, out of place.

I said, 'As to that, Lou, you may please yourself. I think it would be rather a pity, but ...'

And then the footman came in, holding the little silver salver with a piece of paper, folded once, not sealed, on it.

'The messenger said it was urgent, Your Majesty.'

I took it up and read in Mother's writing, 'Eugène has just arrived. Do come. Let us have *one* evening together.'

One evening together. That was Mother's strength, perhaps her weakness, too; the reduction of everything into terms that she understood and could handle. So far as she could make it that momentous evening was as much like one of those long ago when Eugène and I had coincidental leaves from school as it possibly could be. The blazing fire on the hearth, the folding table extended and drawn close so that all three could enjoy the warmth and a helter-skelter of dishes.

But we had all come a long way from the little house in what had been the Rue Chantereine ...

'... will not listen,' Eugène said. 'He told me to sound out opinion. I did it. This afternoon I told him, honestly, how people felt, how I felt, what I thought. But he simply will not *listen*. And he need not listen, twenty minutes' serious thought and he'd know, without listening to anybody. By the time an army of six hundred thousand men are on the move we shall be well into May and if nobody raised a finger, if we just took a walk, it'd be September ... The Russian winter sets in in October and sets in hard ... I begged, I pleaded, I went on my knees. He simply would not listen. It must be done this year... and that, I think, is impossible.'

Who had said, a while ago, and in some other context, that Bonaparte could no longer distinguish between what was possible and impossible – for him?

Now I knew what had graved the lines which passing years, battles, responsibilities had failed to mark on Eugène's face. Tonight he looked old, and defeated and anxious. I tried to find some comforting thing to say and could think only of one, 'He has taken risks before, Eugène.'

'Yes. But, never one like this. Imagine what it takes to feed six hundred thousand men, Hortense. Even one meal a day. And not living off the country. Prussia may be quiet but she's no friend and the Poles are disappointed in him for not giving them a king. Feelings count when it comes to supplies and supply waggons slow down the march.' He ran his hand over his hair. 'There's no point in saying all this to you. But it was on my mind.'

Mother said, 'Yes, it must be a worry. But now you have unloaded your mind, darling, try to eat your supper.'

Eugène ate two mouthfuls, not knowing what he was eating, and spoke again.

'There's another thing, too. He wanted me to stay behind and act as Regent for him, here in France.'

Mother's face brightened.

'That is a great honour. And you would not be in danger.'

'Mother, eighty thousand of those men are mine and I have spent eight years knocking them into shape. Besides … I went to war with him in '96, and just because he's taking such a risk and won't listen to reason makes it all the more imperative … Let's talk of something else.'

We tried to, but somehow the talk would drift back and presently I asked, 'What will happen in Spain?'

Eugène shot me an understanding look.

'I can tell you that to the last detail. The pick of the troops there will go to Russia and the English will make mincemeat of fat Joseph. Serve him right.'

My chance to have a private word with Eugène came when he walked out with me to my carriage.

'Come in and sit with me a moment,' I said. 'I'm sorry, Eugène, to bother you with this at such a time, but I have a worry, too.' I explained it briefly and as always he was sensible and kind. He would certainly take the best of my diamonds, see that they were sold and the money invested in a trust for Charles Auguste Dumorny, but the guardianship was another matter. 'I'd keep a discreet eye on him, of course, but it wouldn't be wise for me … Somebody, somewhere, might see the connection. We must think of the future. Besides, why should anything happen to *you*? It's far more …' He bit off that truth.

'Oh, Eugène,' I said, and hugged him.

He said, 'But I'll see to it. There are good lawyers in Milan. One or two of them honest …'

'When do you go back to Italy?'

'When the war is over. I shall meet my own troops at Mayence and go on from there. There's so little time …'

That was the theme of the next few weeks; so little time in which to prepare for the great venture. The idea was that the Russians would be surprised, not even, in that vast country, fully mobilised by the time the French Grand Army marched in. Surprised even that war should have been declared at all over such a seemingly trivial thing as continuing to trade with England. That was the forefront of the Czar's offences; he could not, or would not, close Russian ports to English shipping. And ignorant as we were of that great sprawling country it was not difficult to see why. Until very lately Russia had been living in the Middle Ages, a completely agricultural and feudal country. She had no industries, no factories of her own. She had no craftsmen, even; just landowners living on unbelievably vast estates and serfs tilling those acres by primitive means. She needed to sell timber and hides and furs in order to buy the materials and the skills that go to make up a modern country. So she had traded with the enemy and was now to be punished.

Paris seethed with soldiers. Danes, Swiss, Dutch, as well as French. I did not know whether to hope that Charles would come up from Spain — where so far no harm had come to him — or that he should stay there. Russia, because it was so huge and unknown, and because Eugène had spoken so gloomily, seemed worse in a way; ominous. Yet I wanted to see him; nothing more; I had learned my lesson and it would have taken wild horses to get me into bed with a man again until I was certain that nine months later I could take a child in my arms and say, 'This is mine.'

We had communicated, but cautiously, through Madame de Souza. 'I enclose a letter from Sophie', she would write and he would write, 'Please give the enclosed to Sophie'. It was better than nothing, but it was rather like gesturing through a pane of smoked glass. At this game I did better than he, I could write, 'The other day I made a poem, here it is, it is called *Thinking of You*: I hope you like it.' He was less resourceful and his letters, even to Sophie, cousinly, were stilted. But his hand had written 'I hope you are well. I am well', and similar trite phrases, and his hand had touched, folded the paper.

Caution was still necessary. The Emperor had been as good as his word and written to Louis saying that he now considered a divorce advisable. Louis replied that he would think about it — 'You hurried yours through, but you wished to remarry. I don't.' So my position was still uncertain.

Madame de Souza came and told me that she had heard from Charles; he was going to Russia, but not via Paris. She cried a little.

'I know ... I know. If you have a son and he is a soldier ... this is different. Men can fight men, and the brave fare best. But cold and hunger make no distinction ...'

About the possible hunger we could do nothing; about the cold perhaps we could. I reached back into the past and remembered my apprenticeship days with Madame Lannoy. We had worn mittens in that unheated work-room, mittens which left our fingers free, but warmed our wrists and our hands, the lower joints of our fingers, so that we had never even had chilblains. Those mittens were made of raw sheep wool, the natural oil left in it.

That kind of wool is very coarsely spun and a whole garment of it would be bulky and heavy. So I unravelled it, inch by inch, and using two strands of the eight, knitted a very curious garment, the first of its kind ever seen, a sleeved tunic and close fitting trousers, all in one piece. It would – if he ever received it – keep him warm from neck to ankle. I added a scarf and a pair of mittens.

Charles's knitted things, all that love could devise, went trundling eastwards on a blazing hot June day. And we knew that he received it for he wrote, thanking his mother 'and dear Sophie' for the gift. 'Six of my men are dead of sunstroke,' the letter added. 'But the garment in its neat little bag makes a splendid pillow.'

So then we were all knitting. A similar 'combination suit' for the Emperor, for Eugène, for all those who were dear. We knitted until the supply of untreated wool – never in great demand – was exhausted; and until the great silence came down.

It was not a complete silence. Perhaps one out of every ten couriers got through. The French Army advanced, as planned, and met little opposition; there were skirmishes, mainly at river crossings, then the Russians retreated and the French advanced again. But scattered groups of rough-riders, called Cossacks, closed in behind them, and any courier carrying dispatches to Paris was likely to be set upon by the Cossacks, and then, by wolves.

(That lent a peculiarly macabre touch. In the Europe we knew a few wolves remained in mountainous, forested country, but it was unthinkable that a man on a horse should be set upon in the open road and torn to pieces. That this happened to a dispatch rider bringing news to Paris we knew because another rider found his remains and the letters in a leather case that had been partially chewed.)

What news came in was, on the whole, good. The Grand Army reached Moscow by mid-September and from that city Charles wrote to his mother on 2nd October. It was a light-hearted epistle.

Will you tell my dear cousin that if I did not already love her as much as possible I should love her more because her gift has made me the best-dressed man in the army. There is not much competition. The Emperor is wearing a peasant woman's shawl and Murat, always the dandy, has a sack over his head. The cold is intense and today it has begun to snow …

Everybody thought that with Moscow in French hands the Czar would make overtures for peace: but no news about that came through. Instead, in December, came the rumour that the Emperor was dead.

I drove straight to The Tuileries. Marie Louise had already heard and was either unmoved or giving a display of the famous Habsburg stolidity. 'It is only rumour, Hortense. Until it is confirmed it would be wrong to be affected by it.' There was a little rebuke in the last words. I was not actually crying but I was affected, feeling again, but more powerfully, as I had when his death was rumoured in the Egyptian campaign, a cataclysmic loss.

I went to Malmaison, hoping that Mother had not already heard, meaning to break it to her gently, emphasising that it was only a rumour. But news had outraced me and although she had been crying she was calm by the time that I arrived and had already applied her talent for comforting to herself.

She said, 'I have been thinking. We all must die and that is how he would have chosen. And there is another thing … I don't know what you have heard. But we were told that the army was cut to pieces and in full retreat. If that is true, he would … he would rather be dead.'

I thought – How strange! I was prepared to comfort and support the two women closest to him and neither was in need!

When I went back to Paris it was like an occupied city. The soldiers were French, the young boys, the old men, the veterans not fit for full active service who made up the National Guard. I was obliged to stop and identify myself several times and my own carriage entrance was guarded. 'General Malet's orders, ma'am. And curfew at six o'clock.' I had never heard of General Malet until that moment, but he sounded official and in order to have turned out the National Guard and imposed a curfew he must have some authority. So I stayed indoors and worried and grieved and wondered about tomorrow.

Next day all Paris was laughing, a little shakily and self derisively. General Malet was a lunatic and a forger. He had for twenty-four hours deceived everybody, even the Legislature, by producing some orders purporting to give him complete control in the event of the Emperor's death. He had complete control for twenty-four hours and then he was back in the asylum from which he had escaped.

The next thing we heard was that the Emperor, so far from being dead, was coming back to Paris as fast as sledge and carriage could carry him. That was authentic news. Equally true was that the Grand Army had been cut to pieces. Charles? Eugène?

25

We had expected to welcome home a broken man, a man who had never suffered defeat until this, and this such a defeat as was unprecedented. Of the five hundred thousand men, the biggest army that had ever marched under one command, no more than fifty thousand came back. And that they returned disciplined and in order was entirely due to one man – my brother Eugène.

But with the greatest military disaster ever known behind him the Emperor came home far from broken; hardened. It was not that he underestimated the extent of the disaster, or ignored it or had not suffered. As far as Vilna in Lithuania he had come, step by step with his men and had left them only when news of General Malet's plot reached him. 'I realised then,' he said grimly, 'that I should be more use in Paris than staying there. Another mouth to feed.'

Some of his enemies, regarding the defeat as final, were emboldened to say that he had 'deserted' the remnant of his army, limping, maimed, snow-blinded, frost-bitten men who were eating their skeleton horses, the harness, their boots. Bonaparte bore this ugly accusation with the same fortitude as he bore the defeat. 'If I had done that would the Senate have voted me another three hundred and fifty thousand men so that I could desert *them*?'

He took calmly, too, Murat's treachery. He had left him, not Eugène, in command, with orders to bring the army home. Murat deserted immediately and rushed to Naples, intent upon saving his own throne from the wreck of the Empire that he seemed to foresee. From Naples he wrote urging the Emperor to make peace, immediately and at any price. Bonaparte sent him back a caustic message: 'Surely you are not one of those who think the lion is dead!'

Possibly Murat's behaviour did not come as a surprise; the behaviour of the Austrians did. In all this troubled time I saw him visibly shaken only once, and that was when he heard that his father-in-law had joined the latest alliance against him. Despite then fact that he had once admitted to me that he could not think of an instance of a state marriage being of any political use, he had obviously not expected that a man would make war upon a country of which his daughter was Empress and his grandson the heir.

Even so he was considerate for Marie Louise's feelings and after that, at our private gatherings, the preparations for war, the negotiations for a last-minute peace on terms, acceptable to everybody, were scarcely referred to and I ceased to be a witness behind the scenes and relied, as others did, upon was what reported in the papers, or spread by word of mouth. Or visible to anyone – the extreme youth of latest conscripts whom the Senate had voted into the army; the dearth of tough veterans who had fought all over Europe and had one god – Bonaparte.

Charles was one of the fifty thousand who came home; thin, ragged and subtly changed. Like so many of those who had survived, he had, at moments when he was not animated and thought himself to be unobserved, a haunted look. Like them he had very little to say about that long ordeal. Once he did say, 'People who think Hell is hot are mistaken …' He had been wounded during the advance at one of those river crossings. 'A mere graze,' he said. 'And lightning *can* strike twice in the same place no matter what people say. That bullet glanced off my right shoulder and did it the world of good. The old wound has never troubled me since.'

He was not in Paris long, and in public we were careful to preserve appearances. In private I at least was careful, too. Caution? Fear? Hope?

There was definite hope now. In the midst of all the myriad things that he had to think about and to deal with, the Emperor had had time to tell me that Louis intended to return to Paris and had agreed to think about divorce. But, even with that hope ahead, it was very difficult not to resume love-making. Everything was so uncertain in that spring of 1813; one could count upon nothing. The summer might bring peace to France, bring Louis to Paris, bring freedom to remarry to me and the chance of a happy, normal life ahead; it might see the war renewed, Charles far away again, dead … So far luck had been with him, it *must* be third time unlucky, and how should I feel having denied him what, as soon as he was even partially recovered in health and spirit, he seemed to desire more than anything?

He said, 'Then you don't love me.'

I wailed, 'I do! I do!' And it was true. The zombie a little less in control, perhaps, though troublesome enough at times; but all the other things that go to make up love increased rather than diminished.

I should have given in but for Adèle's absolute refusal to cooperate.

'*You* may have forgotten in two years,' she said. '*I* never shall. I blamed myself so much … You must please yourself, of course, but you must make other arrangements. I tell you frankly, my door will be locked and so will my little wicket gate in the garden.'

Other arrangements. How was it possible? It had, in that happy, thought-less time, been just possible, just because of Adèle's connivance. I had been still in my house and if the very worst imaginable thing had happened and one of the children had been taken ill, she, on guard in her sitting room, drowsing, waiting, would have heard the disturbance and nobody could have queried my right to have gone down in a sleepless midnight to chat with my senior lady-in-waiting, my oldest friend.

Without the services of such a friend it is very difficult indeed for a queen to commit adultery. And, strange as it may seem, the sheer difficulty, a plan half-formed and discarded, another born dead, weakened my determination whereas perhaps two years earlier it might have strengthened it. All through April, which is such a lovers' month, a time when zombies grow strong, I havered, put him off, said, 'I will think of something. Darling, I will. Failing all else, I will *beg* Adèle …'

And there was a day and another day and a month gone in indecision; and then he was gone, too, with the Emperor to Dresden. To another war! Immediately I felt as guilty about not having given in as I had two years earlier because I had. And Adèle said, 'Perhaps I was wrong,' in a wavering voice, and then, 'but I think not,' in a firmer one. We were both mopish. After a day or two Adèle suggested a holiday.

The time was opportune; Marie Louise had gone with the Emperor to Dresden and Mother had already spoken about having Lou and Charles-Napoleon to stay at Malmaison. 'She had seen less of them lately than she would have liked because children at the ages of five and eight cannot be relied upon to be tactful. They both loved Mother and after a visit to Malmaison would talk about her in the presence of Marie Louise, thus upsetting her determined theory that Mother did not exist. Yet one could not tell them not to mention Grandmamma or Malmaison. Lou would have asked 'why not?' and if he failed to get a satisfactory answer from me would probably repeat the question at The Tuileries or St Cloud. He was at an age for awkward questions and would say things like, 'If Grandmamma was once your wife, why aren't you our Grandpapa, Uncle Bonaparte?' Questions of that kind were natural and could be neither forestalled nor, justly, corrected. So they had gone to Malmaison less often, and to make up were now asked to stay. Provided there was a little gap between Malmaison and Marie Louise's presence it would be all right, Mother and I had decided. So Adèle and I were free to take one of our private holidays and walk and sketch or simply be idle.

Adèle chose to make another visit to Aix-en-Savoy. The open reasons for her choice were that it was a healthy place, and that on our former visit we had not been able to do any sightseeing. I think she had another reason, too; in Aix I should be sharply reminded of how love-making could end and perhaps cease to regret that I had refrained from it.

We did not, this time, stay in the inaccessible house, but in the Place Savoy, perhaps the very house which Madame de Souza had so briefly occupied.

Everything combined to make that holiday most enjoyable; the country was in the full flood of its May-time beauty, the weather warm but not hot; and the news from the front was good. The Emperor had won two short sharp battles against the Prussians and there was a lull in the fighting. Madame de Souza had promised to write to me and pass on any news she had of Charles. I received a letter from her on 10th June. I noted the date because of making allowances for anything having happened during the inevitable interval. I scanned the letter quickly and said to Adèle, 'He was all right when the fighting stopped, she says.'

'I am so glad. Now if only it has stopped for good, and Louis will set you free … I want you to be married, and happy ever after.' Adèle gave me one of her rather rare kisses. She was not a very demonstrative person and the kiss, the wish, coming as I knew, from the heart, seemed to promise that all would be well.

I said, 'Thank you, darling. Somehow I feel now that everything might come right. And what are we doing today?'

We were going to visit a waterfall of which she had heard. It was called the Rainbow, because it threw up a spray which in the sun caught all the colours of a prism.

It was out of walking range and directions as to how to reach it were rather vague because many people who said how beautiful it was had never seen it but were speaking from hearsay. However, we drove in the general direction, and our coachman made enquiries and was finally told to take a certain turning and drive on until he reached the mill.

The road, because it served the mill, was well kept up and when it ended we could understand why so few people had actually seen the Rainbow Falls. We were in a cul-de-sac, to our left a mountainous outcrop of stone, to our right a gentler slope, terraced and cultivated, directly ahead the river, narrow but swift, turning the great wheel and then dropping out of sight, and some buildings, including a neat little house. The waterfall could be heard, roaring away to our left, beyond and below the mountain's shoulder.

Adèle said, 'How very disappointing! Nobody told me.'

I said, 'Never mind, it was a lovely drive.' For much of the way it had been under arches of chestnut trees, in full flower, and with leaves still freshly spread and green.

Then the miller came out and said words which had perhaps deterred many people. His manner implied that; it was anxious to be helpful and at the same time slightly bored. The Falls, he said, were visible only from the other side; if the ladies wished to see them, he would place a plank … Most ladies, one felt, declined this kind offer. But Adèle looked at me and I looked at her. I could see she wanted to; she had said, 'How very disappointing.' She had suggested this excursion and would feel that she had dragged me out on a fool's errand. So I said, 'Shall we?'

'Having heard so much, and come so far …'

We alighted and the miller fetched out his plank.

I crossed first – so accustomed to taking precedence of all but a very few women that I never gave the matter a thought. It was a good, wide plank, firmly lodged on both banks and though it ran across water, just below the mill, where the stream began to drop into the gorge, to walk across was no more than to go directly across a room. On the other side I could see the coloured halo and feel the spray of the falls. I took one look and said to Adèle who was in the centre of the makeshift bridge, 'I'm so glad …' As I spoke the plank tilted and threw her into the water.

The rocky bank on which I stood was not high, no more than six or seven feet above the water. She was, she seemed to be, within arm's reach as she fell. I dropped prone on the spray slippery rocks and held out my arm, screaming, saying, 'Adèle! Adèle …' The water turned her over, and quickened as it did so. If she could have reached upwards as I reached down …

I was wearing a light silk shawl, I got to my feet and tore off the shawl in one movement, and ran, dangling it, screaming to her to catch. It actually touched her as, turning over again, she swept past to where the gorge deepened and the water speeded towards the fall.

There was the fall, glassy smooth, green, and at its foot the foam and the spray and beyond a quiet stretch where the little river, after its headlong descent, gathered itself together before continuing its journey to the sea.

My screams were heard. The miller and a younger man and coachman righted the plank, crossed and came to me. There was nothing they could do. They tried to take me away. Come up to the house; have some brandy; be driven home; better not to see …

I was not senseless as I had been when Non-Non died. I was capable of speech. To every suggestion I said, 'No. I must stay until she is found.' Only the younger man could swim: he dived into the placid pool again and again. My coachman said, 'Your Majesty is wet through.' The miller gave me a sharp look and urged the young man to try again. I sat, soaked with spray on a wet rock, and shivered and waited. Until at last she was dredged up, dead. She wore an expression of such profound peace that it was startling.

I had always been first with her – except for that brief time of her marriage, and even then she had remembered me and cared enough to devise ways of communicating. I thought of that and was stricken because she had not been first with me; I had had Mother, the children, Charles. Had she realised how much I loved her? She had known that she was my dearest friend, but had she known how dear? I suffered all the morbid thoughts that bereavement brings; not loving, not appreciative enough, taking her love and loyalty and complete devotion too much for granted.

Alongside these wretched thoughts ran the sense of loss. Nobody could ever take her place in my life. One can have other children, other husbands, other lovers, but a friend from childhood is irreplaceable. I had lost what few women ever know.

Before I left Aix I gave orders that a stone bridge should be built to span the river at the fatal spot and that one of the stones should bear the words, 'As you cross, remember those you love'. I also set on foot some plans for buying and endowing a house in Aix for the benefit of people who might benefit from a stay there and could not afford it. I would sell some more of my diamonds, those pretty stones which Adèle had so often handled and admired, and never once envied. I then took her body back to Paris, for burial in the private chapel at Saint-Leu.

And is it unduly fanciful to say that from the moment of her internment there, the place for me was changed? It had always seemed inimical to me, associated with Louis's gloom and suspicion and in itself gloomy with the ruins of the original château and the encroaching forest. But once Adèle was laid there it seemed to change; it was the place where she was.

I had another fancy, too, a very strange one for a revolutionary-bred agnostic. It was based on a dream sequence that began in Aix while I was suffering from the shock and the chill. In that first dream and in every other that followed I was in a frantic muddle. Things I had completely forgotten, trivial, silly things would crop up again, much more important in the dreams than they had ever been in actual life, and an astonishing number of them concerned with my short apprenticeship to Mademoiselle Lannoy, the dressmaker ...

I had been sent out to buy bread for supper and on the way lost the money; the baker would give no credit, claimed that he did not know me and I thought – What will Mademoiselle Lannoy say? What will the girls say? (In real life, when this happened, I had gone back to Mademoiselle Lannoy and she scolded me, but had been more angry with the baker, had given me some more money and sent me to another shop with orders to run all the way.) In the dream I was more deeply distressed and afraid to face Mademoiselle Lannoy; and then there was Adèle, smiling and saying, 'Everything will be all right ...' How it was right I never learned, because I woke then with a curious feeling of having been looked after, of having someone on my side. And even when I was fully awake, knew that I had been dreaming and that Adèle was gone forever, some faint sense of comfort remained.

The dreams continued, sometimes based on actual experience, some sheer fantasy, such as turning up at The Tuileries, late and stark naked. Adèle was always there, smiling, assuring me that everything would be all right. And what, waking, I always remembered was that in the dream Adèle was neither old nor young, neither the young girl of schooldays, nor the woman of later time. Just Adèle, as though the whole essence of a personality could be condensed into a smile and a tone of voice.

26

Men who survive battles can never give a lucid account of them. The same is true of those who witness the collapse of an empire, the fall of a capital city.

The hope of peace which had brightened our early summer holiday had failed and in October 1813 the Emperor fought and lost the Battle of Leipzig. It was called The Battle of All the Nations, because ranged against the French were Russians, Prussians, Austrians and Swedes. It was a decisive defeat.

The Emperor made one flying visit to Paris, frenziedly trying to rally the remains of the National Guard, and the representatives of the Government to the defence, not of France, but of Paris. I saw him then, broken, distraught, ill. I was one of the extraordinarily silent crowd who watched him hold up the King of Rome, that pretty, lovable child, just two and a half years old, and remind people that this was his heir and taking Marie Louise by the hand, present her as Regent. I was also later that day in The Tuileries when he burned hundreds of papers, throwing them on to the fire in the hearth until the fire died under the weight.

To me he said, 'Look after them for me. All I can do now is to make the best possible terms. I will see that you and the boys are taken care of.'

Then he was gone and all that we could do was to wait.

There came a day when we could hear the guns. With slight intermissions France had been at war since I was nine years old, twenty-one years, but it had always been other cities that had shuddered to that sound of man-made thunder. Now it was Paris, the one city in Europe that had never known an invader – and if the little boys in uniforms too large and with guns too heavy to be properly shouldered and the old men, the very old men, veterans of battles whose very names were forgotten, could prevent it, Paris never would be. Paris was being very valiantly defended.

But, even in the most momentous and shattering circumstances ordinary people can only take a narrowed view of what goes on around them. I did not believe as many people did, that the Russians were cannibals who ate roast baby for supper, or that the Prussians used babies as living targets for bayonet practice. I was spared that much. I had other worries. The Emperor had said, 'Look after them for me,' nodding towards Marie Louise and her son; and then, before leaving Paris he had been activated by his old family feeling and left his wife and his son in the charge of Louis, and Joseph, his brothers, both newly arrived in Paris. They had both failed him, ungrateful, recalcitrant, using the throne he had given them as mounting blocks from which to defy him and both, as a consequence, had lost their thrones, the one by the wilful act of abdication, the other ignominiously driven out as the English advanced into Spain. And yet, in this critical moment because they were his brothers, because they were men, he trusted them again.

I had managed to avoid meeting Louis and he had made no attempt to get in touch with me, or to see the children. I saw Marie Louise at least twice a day and gathered from things she said that Joseph and Louis were urging her to leave Paris. At first she had scoffed at the idea, but as the days went on and it became plain that, however doggedly defended, the city could not hold out forever, she began to waver. Once she asked me point-blank what did I think.

I had been told to 'look after', which meant be companionable, be as cheerful as possible, try to distract and amuse. It was not for me to advise upon such a momentous matter; there was a special Regency Council for that. While I hesitated she asked, 'In my place what would you do?'

'Stay in Paris. You have nothing to fear from the Allies and if you run away you may lose your crown. And endanger your son's. Whatever happens the French will always remember that you stood by them when they were desperate.'

'And if I leave – they will remember that, too?'

'Yes.' Having said that much I quailed a little; suppose something, some unbelievable mischance happened ... Not only wounded men, but very sick men were coming in from the fortifications. Suppose one of those very contagious diseases swept the city. Or a fire ... 'Truly I cannot advise. There is the Regency Council. What do they say? What does Monsieur Talleyrand say?'

For once I saw that Hapsburg impassivity disturbed. Speaking about staying in Paris, or leaving it, her firm-fleshed young face had betrayed no emotion. Now something flicked across it like a whip-lash. Fear? Hatred? Her pink, rather thick lips parted, then closed and when she spoke her voice was cool, judicial.

'I should not care to take his advice on any matter. Openly he ridicules the idea that the Allies will ever enter Paris. But I have private information. He has written to Alexander of Russia saying that Paris is waiting to welcome him; and to the Bourbon in England that the throne will be his in a few days.'

I said, 'Incredible! Was your ... Was the source of this information reliable?'

'Yes. You should know, Hortense, that I take no notice of rumour.'

I thought quickly and said, 'If that is true then it is the best reason you could have for staying here. The throne is not vacant while the Empress, the Regent, is here with her son, the heir, in her lap.'

She said, 'You are right. I shall stay. I shall stay until the Emperor orders me to leave.'

I went home through streets crowded with people who did believe the atrocity stories and were on the move; in the main poor, but not the poorest people. Paris had grown enormously in the last twenty years and there was a whole class of citizens who still had their real roots in the country, who had come away because the family farm was too small to support them. Now they were going home. They had never felt at home in Paris, never really safe, so now they were going back to their village sanctuaries, carrying their babies and their few poor possessions, dragging older children, little carts, overladen donkeys.

On the whole people who had any real stake in the city, a house, however small, of their own, a business, however humble to tend, did not join this exodus. Nor did the very poor who had nowhere to flee to, nothing to salvage.

When I reached home the Commandant of the National Guard waited upon me and begged leave to ask whether I intended to leave Paris. He was an old man – or a young one prematurely aged – and I spoke as sturdily as I could, to cheer him. I said that I intended to stay.

'That, Your Majesty, will hearten us all. We will defend you. To the last bullet, the last drop of blood.'

He then said something about if it came to fighting in the streets I must take to the cellars and I went to bed worrying a little about how Charles-Napoleon would act if it came to that; he had a horror of anything that gave him a feeling of being closed in. But I thought we would deal with that when the moment came, if it came; and make it a game.

I dreamed that I was in a cellar, very dark and cold and growing smaller. I was cowering away from some nameless thing that threatened and as I went into corner after corner walls near me, beams above, collapsed. And then somebody began banging on the door and I thought – If this goes on the whole place will come down over my head and I shall be lost in the ruins. I screamed, 'Stop that,' and woke myself. I woke, but the knocking went on.

It was my nightwatchman, woollen bonnet and lantern in one hand, a piece of paper in the other. He was apologetic and agitated.

'He said give it to you straightaway. He said not a minute to lose.'

I thought of a thousand possible catastrophes as I took the paper and unfolded it, held it to the lantern's beam.

'The Empress is preparing to leave. I command you to bring the children and come with us. Louis.'

I had fumbled my way through darkness to the door. I was in my nightgown.

'Is the bearer of this waiting?'

'Yes, Your Majesty.'

I said, 'Lend me your lantern.' From its candle I lit the one by the bed, gave it back to him and said, 'Wait.' I then closed the door and sat down, trying to think calmly.

Marie Louise had changed her mind; and she might have good reason. Perhaps a direct order from the Emperor. I had been told to look after her, and perhaps it was my duty to accompany her. But Joseph and Louis were going with her and I saw clearly that a woman, separated in all but legal terms from her husband, who in a crisis obeys his orders, appears even to be seeking his protection, puts herself in an ambiguous position. Until the war took this disastrous turn I had still cherished the hope that the Emperor would somehow manage things so that I might have a divorce and retain the custody of my children. Once they were in Louis's hands there would be much less hope.

I wrote on the back of the paper, 'I intend to remain here until the Emperor orders me to leave.'

Having dispatched that message I thought again about the possibility of Marie Louise having received orders from his Headquarters, in which case, whether I were specifically mentioned or not, perhaps I should regard myself as included. I should soon hear.

I roused Madame de Boubers and Louise Cacholet – no maids clumsy with panic – and we began to pack the minimum of necessities for ourselves and the children. Louise took my jewels out of their cases and tipped them into a linen bag.

While we were moving softly about, the old watchman came again, not to hand me the note I expected but with a querulous complaint. Two fellows were outside the house and refused either to tell him their business or move away.

'National Guardsmen,' I said.

'They are *not*,' he said flatly.

My heart gave a thud. The enemy, already?

'Ask one of them to come to me.'

He came back and said that they were forbidden to leave their post. I was now dressed, so I ran downstairs, anxious to see which enemy, if enemy it were, had arrived first. I was too flustered to remember that few Russians, Prussians or Austrians would have been able to communicate with an old French nightwatchman.

I stood on the top step of the main entrance and told the watchman to hold his lantern higher. Even in that imperfect light I could see that the man below was not a soldier; he wore servants' clothes and was lounging.

'What are you doing there?' I asked sharply.

'Obeying orders.' There was a covert insolence about the answer. I said, even more sharply, 'Whose orders?'

'The Count's.'

Louis had taken to calling himself Count de Saint-Leu. 'And what were they?'

'To see that nobody left this house.'

I thought how typical of Louis to send one man to order me to The Tuileries and two to see that I remained in the house. I glanced aside and could just see the dark build of another man outside the carriage entrance.

I was hardly upstairs again when the second message came. This one was threatening. 'We leave in an hour. Unless you are here I shall come and take the children by force. Louis.'

There had been no order from the Emperor or Louis would have mentioned it.

I began to write on the back of that note, too, and then thought better of it. On another paper I wrote, 'I shall be ready to leave in half an hour.'

It took ten minutes to rouse and dress the children and have the horses put to the carriage.

It would have taken more than those two lounging fellows to have stopped the carriage but I knew that unless we turned in the direction of The Tuileries they would run and report. They might know some shortcuts. Louis might have me followed. So I showed Louis's second message to the nearest man and then told my coachman to turn towards The Tuileries, take the left hand road at the fork and then I would direct him.

The boys were by this time fully awake and Lou asked, 'Where are we going?'

'To Grandmamma's.'

'Malmaison,' Charles-Napoleon said in a pleased voice.

'No. To Grandmamma's other house in Evreux. It is a long way and time would pass quicker if you went back to sleep.'

Mother had been forced to leave Malmaison because she had been so greatly pestered, ever since things began to go wrong. The pesterers ranged from the apparently rational to the obviously demented. They all credited her with far more influence over Bonaparte, over Eugène, over Fate, than she had. It was put to her, seriously – and perhaps truly – that the Austrians were only in this latest war because they hoped to regain their Italian provinces; so if she would use her influence on Eugène and persuade him to stop fighting and make a separate peace, the Austrians would withdraw from the war. At the other end of the scale it was put to her seriously and with all the force of superstition which can be stronger than reason, that she had been the Emperor's lucky talisman, that nothing had gone well with him since the divorce and that she must get into close touch with him again, even if it meant joining the army as a camp-follower, a *vivandière*, one of those who trudge in the army and brew coffee or soup on smoky little fires and carry little casks of brandy. When this extraordinary suggestion was made to her – and it was made more than once – Mother said, 'And honestly, darling, if I thought it would do the slight bit of good and that he would not know, I would do it. But … but I am not the right shape, and Bonaparte will go around the campfires. He'd recognise me. And think what people would say!'

I understood what she was bearing because I, in much, much lesser degree, had also been subject to pressure. I had been asked to put it to Eugène that if he made a separate peace Austria might withdraw, and that he might even be made Provincial Governor. I had also been asked to use influence on Marie Louise, urge her to use her powers as Regent and declare that the Emperor was mad.

Mother had also had to bear being *looked* at, which sounds a slight thing for a woman who has always attracted attention, but a kind of cult had grown up. Veterans recalled to the colours would trudge out to Malmaison and beg her to see them, to look at them, to wish them luck. Then the young conscripts, copying their elders, began to do it too. 'Darling, they look younger than Eugène did when he first went to Italy,' Mother said. 'I cannot bear much more.'

So she had retreated to Evreux and we were going to join her there.

For me and Lou and Charles-Napoleon it looked as though it might be the first stage of a long road into exile. I had been willing to stay in Paris and take my chance, but when I heard that the Bourbons were certain to be restored and that the brother of the one who was now Louis XVII was with the Allies, ready to move in with them, I realised that nobody named Bonaparte would have a very bright future in France. I seriously contemplated selling the rest of my jewels and going to Martinique. I talked this over with Mother and with Louise Cacholet and Louise pointed out that I had other assets which it would be folly to abandon; my house in the Rue Curetti and all its contents, some of them valuable. She offered to go back and take charge of it for me. She was not Adèle – nobody could ever be that – but she was a staunch friend.

Then one day a state official, a Monsieur de Maussion, arrived and was closeted with Mother for half an hour. He left rather hurriedly, I thought, and I went in to find her crying as even I had never seen her cry before. To my questions as to what was wrong, she said, 'Oh how could they …?' and then cried harder. She said, 'How cruel …' She said, 'I never dreamed …'

I thought – They have shot him! It was not such an illogical thought. To the Bourbons he was a usurper, near enough to a traitor. Heady with victory, anxious to have him out of the way … I tightened the arm that I had put around her and said, 'Dead?'

'No. Better a thousand times … You can't mock the dead.'

For some reason I thought of Christ and the Crown of Thorns.

I said, 'Mother, please. Do try to tell me. I care for him, too.'

She said, 'The very cruellest thing …', broke down again and finally gulped out, 'Elba. It's a rock somewhere, twenty miles long and six miles wide and he is to be allowed to call himself Emperor of it.'

I said, 'Yes. It would have been kinder to shoot him.'

I sat beside her, with my arm around her and I shared her feeling. Not the tears. Somewhere along the years I had lost my ability to cry. Presently I felt her stiffen. She straightened up, blew her nose on her handkerchief and drew her sleeve across her eyes.

She said, 'I shall go, too. I've had a silly title for four years. I'm the only person in the world who can truly sympathise.'

My mind sprang into action.

'You might not be permitted.'

'I'll *get* permission,' she said with all the confidence of a woman accustomed to getting her way. 'Unless …' – confidence ebbed. 'Of course, if Marie Louise goes, I cannot. Do you think she is likely to?' I thought – Not if she is given any choice! But I had no real reason for thinking that, and I was anxious not to delude Mother with false hope. So I said, 'I really do not know. I rather think that she would do whatever she was told to do.'

'Yes,' Mother said and brooded. 'And the person who does the telling will be the Czar. This all began in Russia …'

She threw off my arm and stood up and went towards a long mirror on the wall, faced it, studied her reflection, turned and looking over her shoulder gave her side view, left and right, a kind of deadly scrutiny. In any other woman who had just been crying her heart out the action would have seemed a denial of the emotion that had evoked the tears, but to Mother looking into mirrors was as natural as breathing. Every place she had ever occupied had been full of mirrors and even this bleak, unloved château at Evreux had its share of them.

She turned from this self-inspection and said, 'My looks have gone, Hortense. No man will ever again do what I ask simply because … Of course what I ask is not much … Just to be allowed to share this ridiculous … But you are young and pretty. You must help me.'

I went and stood beside her and I said, 'Mother, look! Really look. In the glass. As though you were seeing me for the first time.'

Thirty-one in any case is not young and I had missed, through grief, worry, ill-health, anxiety, that gentle mellowing process that carries women over into middle-age and even beyond. Adèle had taken the last of my youth; the cough which had resulted from the chill I had taken on the day of her death had had its usual effect of stripping my bones and my hair was no longer golden, it was silver gilt.

I imagined that I knew what I looked like and I had challenged Mother to look and see for herself; but I was, none the less, a little surprised to see that, standing side by side, reflected in the glass we were so much alike; rather like two drawings made from the same model, one in warm soft colours, the other in cool ones.

Mother said, 'Of course that is a very unbecoming dress.' Then she said, 'And after all, Alexander of Russia is no boy. Let me think … I always found sums so difficult to do in my head. He is … at least thirty-six. All we have to do is *charm* him …' She swung round and gripped my arm. 'Not simply to get his consent for me to go to Elba, if *she* does not go, but for your own sake. You have the boys to consider. They need a powerful friend. Life in Martinique is not what it was in the old days … If we handle Alexander properly … We must leave for Malmaison tomorrow. Bonaparte himself often said how *lonely* a conqueror feels in a conquered city. We must see to it that Alexander does not feel lonely.' The faintest glint of mischief shone in her reddened, swollen eyes.

I was glad that the thought of some positive action had come to help her through this bad hour, but I dared not let her hope too much.

'Bonaparte never had an ally in the cities he conquered,' I pointed out. 'Alexander has helped to restore the Bourbons. He is not likely to need or to seek the company of people called Bonaparte.'

'But, darling, we are not Bonapartes. Or only by marriage, and even that does not apply to me.' Then she added, with one of those startling touches of shrewdness, 'Besides, Allies always quarrel. He'll be lonely and we should be within reach.'

Even so I should have felt dubious about going to Paris had I not received a letter from Louise Cacholet. My house was occupied by Swedish troops who did not use the main rooms; everything was exactly as it had been left. She had been visited by various officials who had told her that Allies did not regard Mother and me as Bonapartes and that we should be welcome back in Paris whenever we cared to return. In fact the Czar had expressed a wish to make our acquaintance. All the born Bonapartes had fled to Italy.

27

The Czar of Russia was a strange man. He was tall and stalwart, soldierly in appearance, until one looked closely at his face and saw the dreamy, mystic eyes, the melancholy, dissatisfied droop of the mouth. His manner varied between absolute authoritarianism and a disarming diffidence. Here was the Czar of all the Russians, complete despot of a country whose furthest frontiers had never been properly defined, and of a people whose numbers had never been accurately reckoned, a people to whom he was god. And here was Alexander Pavlovitch, eager to ingratiate himself, wanting beyond all things to be liked and admired, but uncertain of his ability to command liking or admiration. At our first meeting I could see exactly why he and my step-father had taken to one another so quickly and completely when they met on that raft on the river. They were almost exact opposites; my step-father, self-made, rocky with confidence, full of drive and ambition, his dignity prone to be the prey of his rough sense of humour, practical and tough; the Czar who had inherited so much that he had never been obliged to make an effort or cherish an ambition, who had no real confidence, no sense of humour, effortless dignity and an almost feminine sensitivity.

Mother had been right about Allies falling out as soon as they had achieved their goal. The Prussians would have looted Paris as victorious armies had always looted taken cities. The Czar thought Paris a beautiful place to be pre-served, just as it was, so we witnessed the irony of public buildings, bridges, some private houses being guarded by the very Cossacks who had done so much to bring about the defeat of the Grand Army and by even stranger men with inscrutable, yellowish faces and slit, tip-tilted eyes. They would have looted, one felt, most thoroughly, but God had forbidden it.

Mother had been right, too, about Lou and Charles-Napoleon. I took them out to Malmaison to meet Alexander and under the threat of unname-able punishments, they behaved well. He looked at them with the wistfulness of a man who has no legitimate son and said, 'They are fine boys. I hope you will allow me to take charge of their affairs.' They soon forgot my threats, lost their awe of him and Lou, who must have heard and remembered some story about the wolves, was asking if Alexander had ever seen one, and had he killed it and Charles-Napoleon, who had inherited the Bonaparte pos-sessive strain, produced his less simple question – 'Do all the horses belong to you?'

Alexander said, 'All the *Russian* horses, yes.'

'There's a little one, not white but nearly, with a very long tail. I want it.'

Mother was much less direct in her approach. Elba was not mentioned, not to be mentioned until the right moment and that would be when Alexander had been assured that he was welcome to Malmaison and regarded as a friend for his own sake. She had summed him up swiftly and thoroughly. 'Darling, he is very chivalrous and very selfish. If he thought he was being used he would be offended and … and upset in himself. I shall wait and slip in a word when I think the time is ripe. And then depend upon you to support me.'

Apparently she thought the time was ripe on a day early in May, for Malmaison a month second only to June for sheer beauty. In Mother's garden the daffodils had shrivelled, but the tulips stood straight and tall and the lilies-of-the-valley were a white, scented tide under the lilacs. Alexander had lunched with us, one of those deceptively simple meals which he professed to enjoy so much and which Mother contrived so cunningly. He had arrived before me and as Mother welcomed me she whispered, 'I have spoken about Elba at last. I rely upon you to say that I am not mad or impulsive. Offer to show him the magnolias and do the best you can.'

I said, 'It may sound almost unbelievable, but some of these were brought as seedlings in English ships, by English seamen and sent to Mother.'

'Why should that be unbelievable?'

'Well – most of the time we were at war.'

'War is for men. Not for beautiful women. Or flowers. And even the English seamen are human.'

We were sitting on one of those marble seats, looted from Italy, over the placing of which Hippolyte Charles had taken so much care. Alexander studied the vista before him and then said abruptly, 'How could she be happy in Elba? I'm told nothing grows there except pines and aloes.'

'Mother could make a garden on bare rock. She once made one on a warehouse roof.'

'On a warehouse roof?'

'Yes. It was flat and just outside the window of our apartment. In one of our penurious periods. She and I and Eugène carried up soil from the Bois de Boulogne. In baskets. It was a flimsy roof and the weight was too much for it. It caved in and the owner was very angry. We always thought …'

'What?'

'That he may have been the one who denounced her. In those days it didn't do to fall out with one's neighbours.'

'What is it like to be poor?'

'Horrible. At least, not so much the being poor. It was the debts that were a nuisance.'

He laughed. His laugh was high-pitched and thin for a man of his size.

'Your mother's capacity for running into debt was notorious. Even in Russia men would scold their wives for being like Josephine.'

'She loves pretty things. Even so she has always given away almost as much as she spent on herself.'

'Speaking of money,' he said, 'I suppose you know the conditions which the Emperor wrote into his instrument of abdication. No? He wished you to be known as Queen Hortense and to have an assured income of four hundred thousand francs a year. Will that be sufficient? That is for you and the children. Louis Bonaparte was mentioned separately.'

I was grateful to him for not saying *your husband*.

'The Emperor understood our situation. Our marriage was not happy and we have lived apart for four years.'

'So I understand. And I sympathise. My own marriage was a failure from the start …' He stared ahead and the melancholy look deepened. I thought – We have come a long way from Elba; I must get back to it! But by this time I knew him well enough to know that under the deliberate informality and genuine goodwill there was a touchy autocrat who might resent any attempt on my part to direct the conversation on any important issue. I had always to remember his background: he had once told me that his education was faulty because in Russia tutors were forbidden ever to put a direct question to any royal pupil.

Presently he said, 'There will be no difficulty about the allowances for the Empress Josephine or for you. I am a little troubled about the stipulation regarding your brother.' Eugène had fought to the end, not only against the Austrians but against the Neopolitan troops treacherously put into the field by Murat and Caroline. I listened with interest to know what provision had been made for him. 'The Emperor wished Prince Eugène to be given a suitable domain, outside the boundaries of France. Now that is, to begin with, very vague. One asks what would be suitable for the man who has been Viceroy of Italy? That question could be answered. More difficult is the question, What ruler in Europe would be willing to give up part of his dominion to be ruled over by a man whom even his enemies admire, but who is French?' He paused again and then said with a rueful, half-apologetic look. 'I could, of course. And I willingly would, but it would be resented by those who are not willing. And I am already more out of step with them than is desirable. I am considering an alternative which I think might slip through without arousing too much opposition. I hope I am not boring you … Your brother owns an estate in

France and various properties in Italy. The Allies intend to confiscate all property owned by any Bonaparte anywhere; but it is arguable that your brother is not a Bonaparte. I think that if he were allowed to retain his property and assume some title such as Duke of Leuchtenberg ... What do you think?'

I said, 'I know that Eugène would prefer it. He would not want a domain carved out of another domain. He once refused a kingdom of that kind when the Emperor himself offered it to him.'

I did not think it necessary to explain why Eugène had done so.

'And now,' Alexander said, 'I wish to ask a favour of you. I should like to visit Saint-Leu. Will you invite me to lunch there on the 14th?'

'But course. With the greatest pleasure. It is nothing like this,' I indicated the wealth of flowers, the smooth green lawns, the glass of the cool and hot greenhouses, just visible from where we sat.

'I know it is very short notice. But you need make no preparation. Simply invite me and then I shall have an excuse for not attending the Requiem Mass for Louis XVI and Marie Antoinette which is to be held that day.'

Louis XVIII had now arrived from England and one of the first things he had done was to arrange this Mass in Notre Dame. Why did the Czar wish to avoid it? Very dimly I knew that there was a difference between the Roman Catholic Church and the Russian Orthodox, but he seemed to me to be a man who strove so hard to be liberal and tolerant that I should hardly have thought that sufficient reason for absenting himself.

'I hate hypocrisy,' he said. 'When Louis XVI was alive that fat brother of his was one of his worst enemies. He always wanted the crown for himself. Now he has it. This belated show of grief is humbug. Bad taste, and bad policy. I want no part in it.'

He jumped up and offered me his arm. We walked in silence for a moment and then I said, as lightly as possible, 'I think Mother is serious in her desire to go to Elba.'

Mistake! Mistake!

'I must first assure myself that she would be happy there. And the Empress Marie Louise must be considered. Her father feels that she should join her husband. The Hapsburg set great store on the marriage bond. As well they should; they have done better out of marriage than by war! It is not a matter to be decided in a moment.'

I said, 'Of course not,' and we went into the house.

On 14th May I had an unexpected guest at my table – my brother Eugène who having seen Augusta and children safely to Bavaria had come to settle his affairs in Paris and to discuss his own future with the conquerors.

Eugène had inner resources that most people lack, one of them the fortitude which most people can only derive from religion; one of them what I can only call a kind of defiance. Eighteen years earlier he had chosen his hero, set up his idol, served to the utmost, seen his advice and argument disregarded, seen catastrophe, seen collapse and remained, in the core of himself, unshaken. Having done what he could he was prepared to bear what he must. This may have been his Beauharnais heritage. Our father, sent to the guillotine by the very Revolution that he had supported, had gone gaily.

Eugène had spent the night at Malmaison with Mother and she must have told him that the Czar was disposed to be friendly. I had told her the gist of our conversation and Eugène must have known that to a great extent his fate lay in Alexander's hands. But Eugène did not make one effort or say one word that would have ingratiated himself. As the man in the family he was a civil host and no more. It was not until the Emperor was directly mentioned and Alexander said, 'What I fear is that Elba was actually a sentence to death by boredom,' that Eugène warmed.

'With all due respect … with *him* that is impossible. His love of detail alone would prevent his ever being bored. Nobody realises. Everything, anything is of interest to him, from the shoeing of a horse to the arrangements of sheets in the linen cupboard of a hospital. I once heard him say it – I hope you take sheets from the bottom of the pile; it equalises the wear. I'll guarantee that within a week of his arrival on Elba he will be busy making the iron mines produce more and more easily, improving the harbour and the roads, looking into fishing boats …'

'But my dear man, you cannot seriously contend that a mind of that calibre could be content with such trivialities.'

'He wouldn't think they were trivialities while he was busy with them,' Eugène said with an air of explaining something.

From there they went into competitive talk, which one had most admired Bonaparte, understood him best, seen something in him that the other had missed. In the circumstances – between the stepson who had been faithful to the last and the friend-turned-enemy – the talk had a fantastic note. It tended, too, to slip into the past tense and Mother said, plaintively, 'Please! Don't talk about him as if he were dead.'

We had planned that after lunch we would take a drive around the boundaries of Saint-Leu but Mother at the last moment excused herself. She had a slight cold, she said; so slight that it was nothing at all, but she thought she would go back to Malmaison, perhaps even to bed. As she made these excuses she held Eugène by the arm and gave me an eloquent look. We were her children, we understood her; I had no doubt at all that Eugène read into that gentle pressure on his arm her desire that he should go with her, just as I read into her glance a plea to make the most of this being left alone with the Czar to charm him, to bring up the subject of Elba again.

I should have taken her excuse more seriously had she said she had a headache. So far as I could remember she had never had a cold in her life, a fact that she attributed to her fondness for warmth, heaped fires, heavy silk underwear in winter, furs. Headaches, rare but quite incapacitating, she had suffered from, and more often of late.

So she and Eugène went away and Alexander said to me, 'Of what does this estate consist?'

'Mainly of trees.'

'Trees I can see in Russia. I would like to investigate the ruins, if they are genuine … I mean not part of what is called landscape gardening.'

I was able to assure him that my ruins were genuine, the visible remains of a remote past. The original château had been moated once.

I had never really explored that little area of broken walls and humps of ground covered with weeds, known as 'The Old Place'. I had never thought even the relatively new château a cheerful residence. To me it was a place that Louis had chosen to buy, which I had visited occasionally and which the Emperor, after Louis abdicated and vanished, had said should be my country residence. I had never liked it, never taken enough interest in it as it was now to care for what it had been. It was in fact Adèle who had told me about the moat now reduced to a few little ponds on which ducks swam and water lilies grew.

Bright May days can wear three faces; straightforward, mild, sunny, full of promise; a backward look to March – I have known snow in May; a forward look to sultry summer. This one, as Alexander and I crossed the garden, tidy and well-kept but so different from Malmaison that I felt bound to make apologies, looked forward and it might well have been high summer with a hot spell ending in a thunderstorm. The sky took on a purple colour against which the broken walls and a tower looked pale, just as, against a pale sky, they looked dark. When they looked dark they were a little sinister, now, looking pale they were ghostly against the lowering sky.

As a form of entertainment for a Russian, a soldier and an imaginative man, nothing better than this neglected ruin could possibly have been devised. The fortified château of western Europe was new to him; in Russia quarrels had been settled and invasions repelled by much the same methods as had been used two years ago against the French; mounted men meeting head-on in open spaces, ambushes in forests, contests at river crossings; war of movement. But he had read about sieges and when in the very centre of my ruins we found what was quite indisputably a well, he was delighted and dropped a stone into it and listened to the resulting *plop*, far, far down, with an enjoyment that Lou could not have outmatched. (Actually on the few visits we had made as a family to Saint-Leu the children had been strictly forbidden to go near the ruins because of the pools and the risk of falling stones.)

As though catching my thought, Alexander said, 'I expect your boys have wonderful games here.' I explained and he looked at me dubiously.

'It does not always do …' he broke off diffidently and began again. 'It is customary with mothers to think of danger as something to be avoided but for boys it should be faced and understood. And handled.'

No man in their lives! Poor little things!

None of the ruins was now of any height except for one small tower with a flight of worn stone steps circling up around its inner wall. He seemed to wish to climb these and with the implied rebuke of being over-cautious still in my ears, I went too. The sultry, oppressive atmosphere of the afternoon had increased and when we reached the top I was glad to sit down on the ledge of stone that ran like a shelf about five feet below the top of the crenellated wall. Alexander stood up on it and peered over.

'From here they shot arrows or arquebuses. Every inch of the outer wall would be covered. What a pity that nothing remains of the drawbridge.'

He was back in the past again and I was worried about the present. Unless I brought up the subject of Elba Mother would feel I had failed her.

So, diffident in my turn, I said, 'I know it has not been long and that you have many things to think about but have you thought about Mother's request concerning her future?'

'Yes. But far more about yours.' He jumped down and sat beside me.

I said, 'Oh. Well, mine is a little uncertain so far as the divorce and the children are concerned. But I am still hopeful. And I understand that I am to be allowed to live in France.'

'And you think you will be happy here?'

'I shall be very unhappy if I lose Lou – or worse still both children.' It was a thing I could hardly bear to contemplate; there were even times when I wished that Louis had taken Lou with him when he ran away to Toplitz; it would have proved his genuine attachment to the child, and it would have spared me four years of growing to know and love Lou more and more. If that had happened Lou would now be as lost to me as Non-Non, still loved and thought of but irretrievably out of reach. Also, perhaps with Lou in his keeping Louis might have forgotten about Charles-Napoleon. But once divorced I should marry Charles and I was still young enough to have the other children of whom he had once spoken.

I said, 'I expect I shall manage. I have learned not to expect too much.'

He said, in a cool, judicial voice, 'I do not think that you will be welcome at The Tuileries. The King's niece is unyielding and embittered. Only the most devout Royalists will be at her Court.'

'I should prefer not to go. Too many memories … Besides I always had a hankering for private life.'

'A private life,' he repeated the words thoughtfully. 'I can offer you that. In Russia. I would give you a beautiful estate in the country and a new house in Moscow. It is being rebuilt fast. I would look after the boys and give them either appointments at Court or high rank in the army as they preferred. I would spare no effort to make you happy.'

He spoke as though making some purely business proposition, but his eyes gave him away.

I have known many women who imagine, and say, that almost every man with whom they come in contact has fallen in love with them. No attitude is more tedious. But only a blind woman, or one of the utmost stupidity, could have looked at Alexander then and missed the real meaning of what he had just proposed.

My first feeling was one of intense surprise. I was indeed so aware of having lost my looks that I was rather dreading the moment when Charles and I would come face to face again. I had not seen him for a year; an incredibly swift-moving year; he at Leipzig and in every other of the lesser fight-and-fall-back engagements and had finally arrived with the Emperor Fontainebleau where the instrument of abdication had been signed. He had then been one of those sent to escort Bonaparte to the ship that was to take him to Elba. He should be back any day and I had been cramming myself with food in an attempt to banish that all-eyes-and-mouth-and-bones look. I had bought some of Madame Thérèse's age-defying preparations. I had thought about dyeing my hair. I did not want him to come back to an old woman.

Now Alexander was looking at me – not as ardently as Charles had looked across the ballroom, not as hotly lustful as Joachim Murat had once done, but in a way that assured me that to him I seemed desirable.

I was surprised, and confused, too. It was not an offer to be lightly rejected, coming as it did from the man who for the moment was the most powerful in the world. A rebuff might injure us all.

'That is a most kind offer.' I hoped that my face did not look as hot as it felt. I tried to speak as though the offer was simply of a home. 'It would mean a tearing up of roots. I should have to think about it.'

'But of course. There is plenty of time … I have to go to this Congress in Vienna. That will drag on. But think about it. You would be safe with me.'

An echo? All those years ago at the Luxembourg; the same words dropping straight into the heart of a child whose experience of safety had been scant. They still had an appeal, for the intervening years had brought me many experiences, but never yet the feeling of being safe *with* anyone.

And to be honest, had I not still been in love with Charles and still cherished the hope of marrying him, I should probably have accepted the offer made to me that afternoon. The zombie would never leap up and hunger for Alexander, but Hortense liked him well enough to have managed. I *liked* him far, far more than I had expected to do when I came back to Paris prepared to make some pretence at consorting with the enemy for Mother's sake. He was companionable, kind and, I thought, trustworthy. Mother had used the word 'selfish' about him but I think she meant aware of himself rather than self-centred, and that made him vulnerable – to other people's feelings as well as to rebuffs. He had, for instance, immediately accepted and joined in with my pretence that there was nothing more in his offer than the words implied.

And again we had come a long way from Elba. I wondered what to do. Twice he had evaded the question; to revert to it might seem like nagging.

He said, 'Your brother seemed to welcome the arrangements I hope to make. He spoke of making his home in Bavaria. That would please his wife – though she did not relish returning to her father as a pauper. There is of course no question of that. I think it would be politic for your mother and Eugène to receive the King of Prussia and the princes. They are anxious to meet her and she will charm them as she has charmed me and that will make things easier. As regards Elba there is one small thing. Does she know that Pauline Bonaparte intends to go to her brother there?' He gave that half-apologetic look again. 'Rumour held that there was no love lost between the two ladies.'

'That is true. But I don't think it would deter Mother.'

'So long as she is not making an impulsive gesture which she will regret …'

As a matter of fact I thought that hearing of Pauline's intention would harden Mother's determination. And the fact that Pauline was going was an almost certain indication that Marie Louise would not; Marie Louise would not have allowed it, detesting Pauline as she did.

I began seriously to contemplate what life would be like with Mother permanently absent.

❧ 28 ❧

I had opened Saint-Leu solely for the purpose of entertaining Alexander there and as soon as he had gone drove back to the Rue Curetti. There I found Charles awaiting me; a very joyful surprise. He was alone in the salon, but one never knew, so we met as acquaintances and he gave me his reason for coming – he had brought me a letter from the Emperor. I was then able to ring the bell and announce that General de Flahaut had brought me an important letter which I intended to read in the library where I was on no account to be disturbed.

There we could meet properly and for some moments everything was forgotten; and when I could think it was that *now* the war was really over, he would not be obliged to leave and go into danger again. We could see one another almost every day and as soon as legal procedure had ground its slow course, be together always.

I had forgotten about my looks but, as we drew apart at last I saw that the swift, eventful year had aged him even more than it had done me. He had fewer silver hairs, but they showed up in sharper contrast against that brown hair and the lines in his face were now so deep that I had the idiotic thought – How difficult it must be for him to shave!

I said, 'Darling, was the end terrible?'

'Not at the time. Like being wounded. When it happens one does not feel much. Only afterwards … I suppose,' he said, in a voice I had never heard him use before, 'I always lived in a fool's paradise. Hortense, I did not know till lately that the world was so vile. Moscow and the retreat were bad, but nothing to Fontainebleau …'

I said, stupidly, 'Was there fighting at Fontainebleau? I didn't know. You see, for a reason of my own I left Paris and …'

'No. No fighting. Only two men know what happened at Fontainebleau and I am one of them … Just back from Lusigny, where I had done my best while all the time my father, God damn him … Forgive me, darling, you may now even know. Did you know that Talleyrand was my father, if my mother is to be believed. She must have told ten million lies in her time, but somehow I believe … So while I … It's the most grotesque thing that ever happened; and the worst …'

I tried to comfort him as I would have comforted Lou or Charles-Napoleon. I put my arm around his neck and drew his head down on my shoulder and I said, 'Tell me. Tell me everything. Darling, you can tell me anything. You will feel better ...'

As the sorry tale unfolded I could dimly see why Eugène had survived, unbroken, and was able to speak of Bonaparte, busy on Elba, and plan for his own future in Bavaria, whereas Charles, never so far as I knew a really besotted Bonaparte worshipper, was now so completely shattered.

Out it all came. How the Allies had halted and offered, for the second time, to call a truce if the Emperor would agree to France being reduced to the boundaries of 1792; the first time he had rejected them; then with Paris close-pressed he had sent Charles to negotiate. But Talleyrand had outmanoeuvred him – Marie Louise's private information had been correct.

'Faced with abdication, he tried to kill himself,' Charles said. 'Ever since Moscow – he was so afraid of being taken prisoner – he had carried poison in a little bag round his neck. It didn't work; it was too old. It simply made him sick. And he took that as a sign that he was meant to live. Live! Like a caged bird. When I think ... I was so near a settlement. But I failed him. Even Death failed him.'

I said, 'You must not blame yourself. Eugène said, only this morning ...' I told him what Eugène had said and he retorted that Eugène had no imagination. Charles would not be consoled; nor diverted. He went on and on. Among other things, he said, 'I never idolised him. Splendid soldier, yes; but as a person. I suppose it was my upbringing, very Royalist. I always thought, a bit of an upstart ... But since Moscow, since Leipzig ... When a man is broken he shows what he's made of. I must have been very blind.'

It was a little like the remorse I had felt after bereavement and I could tell him, with truth, that time would restore a sense of proportion. He scorned that consolation too, but it made him think of the future.

'And Mother,' he said bitterly, 'now wants me to sign the act of submission. The only way to stay in the army. I loathe the very thought. But outside the army what prospects have I? I know nothing but soldiering, I have no property. And begging in the streets won't be very profitable. There'll be hundreds of us at it.

'Darling, I shall always have enough. Not great wealth; but enough.' Perhaps I said it too quickly, or in the wrong way. Perhaps I should not have said it at all just then. He looked, if anything, even more gloomy and said, 'Oh yes, one of Mother's arguments was that if you could strike up such a friendship with the arch-enemy, I should be able to accept the Bourbons.'

'I don't consider the Czar to be the arch-enemy. But for him Paris would have been sacked. And the money is nothing to do with him, except that all the Emperor's conditions have to be ratified at the Congress, and there

Alexander's word will carry weight. And Heaven knows, darling, I need somebody's goodwill if I am to get a divorce and keep the children.'

'Oh that!' he said as though it were of no importance. 'If you still hope for that, you will be disappointed. It might have been possible while the Emperor was in charge. Now, it will be a matter of law, pure and simple. Even Alexander,' he spoke the name with a faintly satirical note, 'can hardly interfere with French law.'

'He can use influence.' A thought so cunning as to be disgraceful occurred to me. Alexander wanted me to be happy in Russia. And he knew that I should only be happy with both my boys. I must deceive him a little, so that when Lou's future was being decided he would visualise him with me in Russia.

'Oh, I agree. A little influence goes a long way.'

Except for those few moments at the very beginning, this had not been a happy meeting and when Charles had left, after saying sourly that he had no wish to meet the Czar either in my house or anywhere else, I opened Bonaparte's letter and found that oddly unsatisfactory, too. It was a brief note of thanks for all I had done for Marie Louise. And although from the moment he married Mother, in every letter he had sent me he had signed himself as my loving, or very affectionate *father*, this time he wrote, *your brother*. A sharp reminder that he now regarded me as his sister-in-law. As Louis's wife.

There was not much time for brooding. Mother's cold proved to be genuine enough, a very bad cold indeed. But she must entertain the King of Prussia and his princes, Eugène's future was at stake. The children must be seen. Following the trend set by Alexander they all declared themselves to be uncles and Lou said with delight, 'I didn't know I had so many uncles!' Charles-Napoleon said, with just the right touch of childish naivety, 'Uncle Alexander gave me a horse. White with a very long tail.' The new uncles went into sharp competition.

That evening, presiding over her dinner table, charming as ever, though with a gentle melancholy instead of the old gaiety, Mother sounded hoarse to me, but the condition was probably not noticeable to those meeting her for the first time. Her voice had always been low-pitched.

Eugène noticed and said, 'She must go to bed and stay there. I shall send for her doctor.'

Soon she had four; her own and two others whose help he had in dealing with this extraordinarily stubborn cold, and the Czar's own personal physician. His diagnosis was at least different – 'For a broken heart there is no cure.' The others went on with their doses, their bleedings, their purgings. She bore everything with the utmost fortitude.

I said to Alexander, 'I cannot understand about the broken heart. Why now? Why not when Bonaparte divorced her? Or when his visits ceased? Or when the son denied to her had been born to the new wife?'

He put his arm around my shoulders, brotherly as Eugène, and said, 'My dear, that was his Russian way of saying that she is going to die.'

She died as beautifully as she had lived. She had never occupied a place, from a cheap, hired apartment to a royal palace, from a prison to a derelict leper-house without embellishing it, giving it something of the beauty she loved and which she personified. In the rose-pink bed, in the rose-pink room she seemed to fall asleep, long enough asleep to be called a coma, and deep enough to be death.

Eugène and I were there, but when, around midday on the 29th May she opened her eyes, she did not look at us, but beyond. And a most astonishing expression transformed her ravaged face. Joyful recognition. In her own voice she said, 'Bonaparte! Elba! The King of Rome!' A young woman, coming unexpectedly upon husband and child, in a pleasant place.

Eugène and I planned a simple funeral, interment in the village church of Rueil-Malmaison, again a place which her charity had beautified. But we had reckoned without the ordinary people. Twenty thousand of them came out from Paris, most on foot, a great many of them old soldiers who remembered her as their Lady of Victories. But these old veterans followed the coffin along a path lined, from the door of Malmaison to the door of the church, by Russian soldiers and National Guardsmen, and as they walked they rubbed shoulders with Royalists whom Mother had helped as soon as she had a sou to spare ...

No sign of royalty on the coffin or its drapings, nor on the plain marble slab under which she was laid to rest. But she went to her grave like a queen – or, as the old soothsayer in Martinique had said, 'More than a queen.'

Eugène and I, stricken with grief as we were, had to turn our attention to practical things. He was anxious to get back to his wife and children, but we were joint heirs in Mother's estate and these were things to be sorted out. Bonaparte had said, at the time of the divorce, that Mother's settlements would make it difficult for her to get into debt again. She died owing three million francs, not counting the dowries she had promised to her waiting-ladies, and the pensions to her servants and the donations to the orphanages, the old soldiers' homes.

There were assets of course. A shrewd businessman came out to Malmaison and told us that everything, down to a shawl which the Empress Josephine had ever owned, had what he called 'souvenir value'. But all she had owned she had chosen with care and loved and the idea of an auction repelled us both. Most of her pretty, personal belongings we gave away to her friends and protégées. We paid her debts. When all was settled Eugène and I each owned a half share of Malmaison, some jewels, some pictures. Malmaison still seemed so much *her* place that we could not bear to sell it. Since Eugène had daughters and jewels are more portable than pictures I argued him into taking the jewels and leaving me the pictures. A few of these were valuable, but many more Mother had bought for the best reason in the world – she had liked them, thought them pretty. These were in the main worthless, and so were many that she had bought because she was sorry for the painter.

I was still in mourning for Mother when a Monsieur Decazes called upon me. He had once been one of Louis's secretaries and was now, he said, his man of affairs. He had, he said, instructions to enquire how I felt about a divorce.

'I should welcome it. On condition that the children remain with me.'

He said, quite kindly, 'But madame, that is not feasible. The younger, just possibly … Prince Louis-Napoleon, no.'

Alexander had been most sympathetic and understanding about Mother and had one day come along with something which I suppose he thought would cheer me – like giving a child with a grazed knee a sweetmeat. It was the news that I had been given another title, a less tenuous one than 'Queen Hortense', I was to be made Duchesse de Saint-Leu, in my own right, and when I died Lou would be Duke of Saint-Leu. Even in my deep misery I was grateful, not least because it augured that in the eyes of authority Lou was associated with me rather than with his father. So now I had that to lean upon and I said, very firmly, that I should not hand over my son without a fight. I asked where Louis was. In Lausanne, temporarily …

I said, 'You see, he has no settled home to offer a child. He has not seen him for four years; when he was in Paris in the spring he made no move to see him …'

'Then I am misinformed. I was given to understand that in a moment of grave danger His Highness made some attempt …'

'I had already made arrangements for the children's safety …'

He said 'Yes,' in a long-drawn-out dubious way that informed me that that headlong flight would, in court, count against me.

Decazes did not come again. Louis's next emissary was a professional lawyer, a Monsieur Briatte, who told me in a cold, legal voice that his client was willing to compromise. Hand over Lou and I could keep his brother. That invidious term again! And then the divorce could be obtained with the minimum of publicity and scandal. I told Monsieur Briatte what I had told Decazes. I wanted both boys, I was prepared to fight …

Charles was very critical of this decision. In his opinion Louis had offered the best solution to our problem and I should have accepted it. He went so far as to accuse me of loving Lou better than I did him. I replied that that was an absurd thing to say; one might as well say that one preferred bread to water.

He had recovered some of his buoyancy of spirit and with it the desire to make love and my decision had made it necessary for me to remain cautious. A woman about to fight for the custody of her child must present a front of impeccable virtue to the world. Not only would I not go to bed with him, I begged him not to come to my house too often, and when he did, to come in company.

'With us,' he said, 'it is always tomorrow.'

'But at least now we are sure of tomorrow,' I pointed out. 'Whichever way the court decides we can be married as soon as the decision is given.'

I did not tell him that I must also be careful not to alienate Alexander who had gone, first on a visit to England and then on to Vienna. From both places he wrote to me, long, affectionate, entertaining letters to which I replied rather as though I were writing to Adèle, in that I was certain that whatever I wrote would be understood and appreciated. He was the only man I ever knew who could follow a flight of fancy. So far as the contents of the letters I wrote were concerned I gave my pen free rein, but I was careful never to say anything which he might misconstrue into a promise for the future.

As soon as I was out of mourning I resumed my informal evenings. Some of my guests were new to me, brought along by Adèle's sister Eglé who had married Marshal Ney, others were old acquaintances from my days at Compiegne, ex-officers and their wives who in the intervening years had been posted all over Europe. Many of them were now greatly reduced in circumstances. Charles's words about ex-officers begging in the street had contained some truth. I noticed that whereas, in the old days, tiny sweet cakes had been nibbled daintily and the dishes never completely emptied, they were now consumed quickly and completely. I began to provide rather more substantial comestibles, making Lou and Charles-Napoleon the excuse – 'growing boys are always hungry' – and for the same reason having the trays brought in at an earlier hour.

My evenings were almost as gay as ever, but elsewhere social life in Paris was more dull than it had ever been within my memory. Rightly or wrongly the Court sets the pace, and Louis XVIII's Court was deadly. He was oldish, obese and gouty; his niece, the Duchess D'Angoulême, who acted as his chief lady was pious in a Puritanic way, frugal, low-spirited. She never wore any jewels, wishing to point the contrast between the Restoration Court and the Empire's glittering one. To her Paris was the place where she had been imprisoned as a child, and the Parisians, all save a few staunch Royalists, were the people who had beheaded her father and mother. Her coachman had orders never to drive past the two prisons, the Conciergerie and the Temple, or across the now renamed square where the guillotine had stood.

All these details I heard from Madame de Souza who, alone of the Royalist set, still visited me. The defection of the others was understandable, though there were those who might have remembered that Mother had befriended them.

One day Madame de Souza came in the morning. She looked grave and after an exchange of casual sentences, said, 'I felt I must tell you that I have adopted little Auguste.'

It was as though she had punched me.

'But I .... we ... intended to do that as soon as my affairs were settled.'

'And that may take a considerable time. I have given this a great deal of thought. A great deal. He is three years old ... Up to the age of two, so long as a child is fed and clothed and cared for that is enough. After that background is important. I could not contemplate with equanimity my grandson acquiring plebian habits of eating, of speech, of thinking. He is no longer a baby for Coralie Dumorny to treat like a doll. Very soon he would be pushed out to play in the streets, in the gutter.'

I had been neglectful. What with one thing and another I had not, for some months, asked Madame de Souza to invite me to her house at a time when the child and his foster-mother would be there. Nor, since things had settled down again, had she suggested a meeting. When I did think about it, usually in the middle of the night, I had taken comfort in the thought that momentarily I had done what I could and that one day ... Now Madame de Souza had forestalled me.

I said, 'I think I should have been consulted.'

She said, 'Possibly. That would have meant more delay. You were, forgive me, not in a position to take immediate action. I was. And I did. Coralie Dumorny now has another baby to cuddle and I have Auguste.' And although she did not say so in words, voice and manner said, *And there is nothing you can do about it.*

I said, 'Does Charles know?'

'Of course. And he fully approves. With everything so uncertain ... what better place for an illegitimate child than with his grandmother? Even if she cannot acknowledge him *as so many are able to do.*' Rebuke there, too. If Charles had seduced a peasant girl and his mother had 'adopted' the child everybody would have understood. And eagerly studied features anxious to reassure her that she had not been cheated!

And of course I was helpless. She knew everything.

I said, feebly, falsely, 'Oh yes, I am sure … And I hope he will be a joy to you. I hope you will allow me to see him, often.'

'But of course, my dear. As to being a joy. Without a doubt. He is exceptionally intelligent – that was why prompt action was so necessary. Genius often skips a generation you know.'

Talleyrand's genius for intrigue, coat-turning …

'And now, with that settled,' she said, 'there is something else that I feel bound to mention. I know you are already rather displeased with me, but when you think it over …. Believe now that I speak as a friend. Did you know that your house is now called The Bonapartist Club?'

I jumped from frustrated maternalism to political awareness.

'But that is nonsense – as you must know. Have you ever heard a political sentiment expressed in this house?'

'I space my visits cautiously … And you are so *innocent.* Did you never realise that political affiliations need not be spoken. Look at that.' She pointed to a wide, shallow bowl of violets that stood in the centre of my round table. They were forced in one of the hot houses at Malmaison. All the gardeners there were so pathetically grateful for being kept on that my house in Paris was always full of flowers, fruit and vegetables. '*And* you give them away!' Madame de Souza said. 'Are you out of this world that you do not know what is being said? *He will come back with the violets.* This is the thought that keeps old soldiers alive.'

I looked at the innocent flowers. I thought of the one, the only time when anything verging upon politics had been mentioned in my house – an occasion when Charles and his cousin, another Charles, Charles de la Bedoyère had come in, so much annoyed because the medal of the Legion of Honour, which they had won in battle, was being so indiscriminately given to completely untried men, returned emigrées of the baser and poorer sort, that as a gesture they had hung their medals on their horses' tails.

'I thought I should warn you,' Madame de Souza said.

I said, 'I am warned. And I am grateful. If a few flowers …' When I had so many … 'I shall go to Saint-Leu,' I said. 'And stay there …'

She said, 'That would be very wise.'

In that sad place, in winter, in loneliness I devoted myself to preparing both my boys to face, if they must, separation from me, exile from France, being handed over to Louis. My case was due to come before the court in January 1815. My own lawyer had said that he felt it his duty to warn me that the most I could hope for was to retain my younger son. And just before I left Paris I had received two letters, one from Eugène, one from Alexander. Both in their way disheartening. Eugène, like Charles, thought my decision unwise – 'You have taken an indefensible position; a man has a right to his son.' He now had a son and wrote from the heart. Alexander's letter made no reference at all to my action, but he did say that Vienna was very gay. Previously he had called it frivolous and complained that too much time was spent in dancing. He also made mention of weather. How less severe the cold in Vienna than in Russia. Evasive, elliptical, but I understood, or thought I did. In his 'Russian way', like that which his physician had used, he was telling me that his vagrant fancy had transferred itself and that the Russian climate would not suit me. The tacit withdrawal pleased me; it would make things easier eventually, but I felt that I had lost, not a friend, but someone with a vested interest in my future.

I must learn to be alone.

My case was bedevilled from the first by considerations which were really irrelevant. They varied from the sloppy-emotional – How horrid of me to wish to shuffle off Louis when he had no position, no settled home, no real title; to the strictly practical – Would not a Bonaparte born, ten years old, be better out of France with the rest of them?

There were undercurrents, too. Why did Louis make no claim to Charles-Napoleon? Any stick, however crooked and dirty, will do to beat a dog with and in France, early in 1815, nothing that could be said about a Bonaparte, born, or by marriage, was too bad to be believed.

I was obliged to move back into my Paris house in order to be accessible to my lawyers, but I could not bring myself to face the court sessions. All those people who had once crowded to entertainments at The Tuileries or St Cloud, or Malmaison now crowded in to hear the arguments of what the *Journal de Paris* called 'The Great Trial between a King and a Queen for the possession of a little Duke.' There were worse headlines in less reputable papers. 'Whose son?' The question might appear to apply to the future, but the innuendo was plain. As the case dragged on, through February and into the first week of March, there were moments when I almost regretted that I had not settled with Monsieur Decazes and accepted a simple divorce. Then I would look at Lou and feel otherwise. Reputation well lost if the battle could be won. Charles-Napoleon's future was never in doubt, Louis laid no claim to him, and this, naturally, spurred on the gossip.

However much, at this time, I wished to shun company there was one duty which I could not avoid. After Austerlitz the Emperor had founded a school for soldiers' orphaned daughters. The fathers had fallen on many battlefields, but the girls were always known as the Daughters of Austerlitz. He had done me the great honour of making me the school's patron and had chosen Madame Campan to be its Head. No longer restricted by limited funds she was able to put in practice all her theories about education, and to experiment, even in matters of diet. She was intensely happy and the school was famous.

I usually visited it at least once every two months and I always pretended to assist Madame Campan in the selection of new pupils from the plethora of candidates. My last visit had been to attend a concert given by the girls in mid-December.

In February Madame Campan wrote to me asking me to give a date convenient to me in the near future to help her decide which ten girls out of nineteen applicants should be admitted. There had been many more anxious to enter, but she had already done the preliminary sieving. In fact the final choice was always hers, so, without giving the matter much thought, I wrote back telling her that no date was convenient at the moment and that I had entire faith in her judgement.

She saw through that, of course, and wrote me a typical Madame Campan's rebuke, very brisk and direct. Neglecting one's duty had never yet helped a difficult situation! For her to make the selection unaided would place too much onus upon her already burdened shoulders and would be a direct contradiction of the Emperor's wish. She gave me four dates from which to choose.

One of these was 5th March, and I chose that because it was the most distant and it was just possible that by that time the Court would have announced its decision, just possible that I should be vindicated. This did not happen. Yet the visit was just like former ones, except that Madame Campan spared a moment to tell me that in standing up for my rights I had shown the correct spirit and she very much hoped that I should be rewarded. We then chose the ten girls whom she would have selected had she been alone and I took my routine walk around the school.

On my way home, at the Pont Royale, a horseman drew in alongside my carriage. As he swept off his hat I recognised him, an Englishman, Lord Kinnaird. He had once visited me, brought by Madame de Souza who, from her exile in England, had retained many friendships, interrupted, but not ended, by the war years.

'Madame,' he said in a voice of excitement. 'Have you heard the great news? The Emperor Napoleon has landed in Cannes.'

When I could speak, I said, 'Lord Kinnaird, is it *true*?'

'Absolutely true, upon my soul.' He sounded pleased, English though he was, and presumably Royalist. But the English have a reputation for loving their enemies, once they are beaten, and they are a romantic race, susceptible to lost causes and the kind of half mystical legend that was growing up around Bonaparte's name.

In a different voice Lord Kinnaird said, 'You should get your boys away at once!'

'Why? What possible danger …?'

'They'd make very useful hostages.'

It was a thought that would not have occurred to me in a thousand years, but I could see that he was right.

'Thank you! Thank you!' I called to my driver, 'Home. As quickly as possible.'

As we rocked along I thought – Where? With whom? It must be some place that nobody would think of.

My brain suffered from that paralysis that descends in emergencies, but it was struggling. Wherever they went it must not be in this carriage, it told me.

I ran into the house. Where? With whom? And by the time I had given the news and explained the danger to Louise Cacholet and been assured that anything, anything at all that she could do to help would be done, I had a *just* feasible answer.

Five miles to the north of Paris there lived one of the Austerlitz widows whose daughter had been given a place in the Ecouen school – one of the first, a genuine Daughter of Austerlitz. The mother, Marie Planche, had been supporting them both by doing washing, scrubbing and seasonal work in fields. She was quite illiterate and like many of her kind wanted something better for her child and looked upon education as the magic door to opportunity. The younger Marie had seemed, at the age of eight, to be what Madame Campan called 'promising material'. Untaught as yet, unable to read, but with a lively look, a likeable manner and – which was not always the case – a desire to come to school. She had proved to be uneducable. She had defeated even Madame Campan. After six months of coaxing, exhortation, punishments, tears, she had not mastered the alphabet. With a worried frown Madame Campan said, 'Anything she *hears* she can remember. And there is nothing wrong with her sight. I have considered that and the possibility that she might need spectacles. She does not but it seems that she cannot see letters, or at least the connection. After six months she cannot spell C A T cat and thirty children who could, or might, have been turned away. She must give her place to one of them.'

I urged another trial period, setting a close time, three months. Almost nine years old Marie Planche could still not spell 'cat'. And the inability, the repeated failure, the pressure was changing a very pleasant and in a way intelligent little girl into something different, resentful, sullen. She must leave. At that moment I had the Emperor's ear and it was not difficult to persuade him that the money which would have been spent on educating Marie Planche, had she been able to read, might as well be expended on two acres of ground and perhaps a cow, so that the elder Marie, who had never learned to read, could at least labour in her own interest and the younger who could not learn to read might be usefully employed, making butter, making cheese, supplying something for the ever hungry, ever proliferating mouths of Paris.

The elder Marie, once the thing was arranged, had come and professed everlasting gratitude to me. And it had taken practical form: several times a year she handed in her touching offerings, a dozen large brown eggs, some special cheese, a home-made terrine, honey.

I asked Louise whether her willingness to do anything would extend to living in some discomfort in a primitive place for a day or two and she assured me again that she would do *anything*. She went out herself to find a hired cab and bring it back to the garden entrance, and I prepared the boys. It was a game, I said, a game of pretend; they were going to have a short holiday, in the country, and pretend that they were country boys and that Louise was their aunt. I said they must be very good and do exactly what they were told.

Lou was too old to be duped by what was not, I admit, a very subtle story, just the best I could think of on the spur of the moment with my mind occupied by the need for haste and also with the question as to whether Marie Planche's everlasting gratitude could be counted upon so largely.

'This isn't really a game, is it?' Lou asked. 'We are hiding from Papa.'

I almost said – Yes, but I thought just in time how fatal, if the court decided against me, to have given a child the idea that his unknown father was something to hide from. So I said, 'No, darling, not from Papa. From ... from being hungry. Paris may be short of food again. You remember last year, before we went to Evreux. In the country there is always plenty of food.'

He said, 'But ...' and I said, 'Lou, please. Don't argue.' I had just remembered that I had forgotten the name of the village in which Marie Planche had her small farm. I had never seen it and it was nine years since I had seen its name on paper. I stood completely confounded and I suppose looking distressed. Lou said, 'We will be good, Mamma.'

Good!

Good children! My mind struggled back. Madame Campan saying something, one of her quips about the younger Marie Planche's birthplace, some story attached. I had it. *Remblai des Bons Enfants*. The Embankment of the Good Children; so named because children had either mended the embankment that kept the fields from being flooded, or given warning about its collapse.

Louise came back. 'The best I could find,' she said, preparing me for the sight of a vehicle, a horse, a man, all so old and decrepit that five miles there and back seemed too much to ask. Three times where the road sloped uphill we all got out and walked. But the decrepitude had an advantage; in the old man curiosity was dead. He was only too pleased to stop and wait on the verge of the village.

It was not dusk, but the beginning of the lingering spring twilight and slightly misty. At this end of the village street was a forge. I said to the others, 'Walk on.' I turned in and asked directions to Madame Planche's house; the smith gave it without lifting his head. It was not far. Low, neat, whitewashed dwelling-place and cowshed under the one roof. A strong smell of pigs.

The kitchen was lighted and the door stood half open. The elder Marie was busy at the stove, the younger sewing at the table. I rapped on the door and called.

Had I been a visitant from another world they could not have been more astounded.

I had intended to say as little as possible, simply to ask if my children and a friend could stay with them for a few days as I thought it advisable for them to be out of Paris. I did not mention hostages lest they should be anxious. But Madame Planche was abreast of the news and jumped to the same conclusion as Lou had done, so I had to explain a little about the Emperor's return, the possibility of some fighting in Paris. My mind had not yet taken in the full meaning of what his return would mean. The two women's tears and expressions of joy made the news seem real for the first time. Marie Planche said she had prayed for the Emperor every morning and evening. 'And for Your Majesty, too,' she said, wiping her eyes on her apron. Then she twisted back to my personal predicament. 'You'll be all right now, thank God. There was no talk of your losing the young Prince while the Emperor was on the throne.' There was a certain truth there; but, however swiftly he came up from Cannes, and whatever the outcome might be, if the verdict went against me it would be difficult for even Bonaparte to reverse it without making mock of the law. So I must hope on. In the midst of all the instructions – to Madame Planche to forget about titles and treat the children as though they were young relatives; to Louise not to get in touch with me unless one of them should be ill;

to the boys to remember the game, pretend to be country boys, even help about the place if they could, the thought kept recurring that this parting with Lou might be the one before the last.

Back in Paris I paid and dismissed the old man at some distance from my house and set off on foot. As I neared home I could see light streaming from almost all the windows, hazed by the mist. It was Monday, not one of my evenings – and even had it been, so many windows, on every level, lighted and uncurtained would have been unusual. I crossed the road, took a few stealthy steps and watched. Both my carriage entry, and my main door were under guard and inside the lighted rooms men were moving about. Soldiers of the King! I recognised the smart new uniform. Louis XVIII had been known to say that his brother's fate had befallen him because he had not, until too late, taken steps to surround himself with a personal, military guard. So he had formed what was called the Maison de Roi, Members of this immensely privileged body were guarding and searching my house. It occurred to me, somewhat belatedly, that in default of Louis and Charles I might be regarded as a useful hostage.

I turned and walked swiftly away again asking myself – Where? With whom? And again there was an answer. Mother's mulatto maid, Marian.

She had married a man considerably younger than herself and her generous dowry had enabled him to set up in business for himself, as a saddler. They lived not over his workshop but apartment house no more than ten minutes' walk away. Marion's marriage had worried Mother a little. 'I have inspected Jean Lefebvre and he did not impress me favourably. I feel that he is marrying Marion for her *dot*. But I dare not even hint. It would injure her self-esteem. *And* she would think that I do not wish to lose her. There she would be right.'

However, Marion seemed happy. Mother and I had gone to visit her in her new home, and she had been a proud hostess and a proud wife, bringing 'my husband' into almost every sentence. I now felt that Marion would shelter me for a few crucial days, as willingly as Marie Planche had agreed to take the children; and perhaps her husband would remember that I had been his first substantial patron; from the moment that he set up in business he had had my custom.

Marion welcomed me effusively; her husband with more reserve. Very civil *but* … The neighbouring apartment was occupied by known Royalists and the partition walls were thin. I must not be heard moving about, or speaking. I must not look out of the window. Marion must be very careful when marketing never to buy more than usual in any usual place. He was in his own home and plainly enjoyed laying down the law, as was his indisputable right.

Marion out of his presence was different, was wonderful. In a hired cab she went out to the farm and told Louise where I was. She went and joined a group of idlers in the Rue Curetti and learned that my house was guarded because Bonaparte was expected to go there, should he reach Paris. She shopped for me, discreetly.

That was a very curious time. I spent most of it in a kind of cupboard, quite large, but windowless. Marion had several friends who came in to drink coffee and talk; her husband had friends who came to drink a thin sour wine and talk, and at such times I must be out of sight. But the cupboard door was flimsy. I could hear everything and often thought how very embarrassing it must be for Marion when I was the subject of the women's gossip, as I often was. She always did her best to change the subject, or to stick up for me, saying she'd known me since I was so high and didn't believe nothing, not nothing of what was being said. But she was outnumbered.

The men's talk was political. All Jean Lefebvre's friends, with one exception, were Republicans, and professed themselves perfectly willing to have Bonaparte back, not as Emperor, as President, in the American fashion; they wanted to see a vote for every man, and the abolition of all titles. The odd man out was a veteran of Austerlitz who said that he'd known this would happen; the cage wasn't built that would keep the Emperor in. 'Just waited to get his breath back. Winter quarters as we used to say.'

They teased him good-naturedly.

'He had your one leg, Francis, looks as if he's coming back for the other.'

'And welcome. I shall hobble out to meet him as soon as he's a bit nearer. And I shan't be alone! Any of you been across the Place Vendôme this evening? No, well I did. Talk about laugh. Bloody great notice. Message from Bonaparte to Fat Louis telling him not to send him any more soldiers, he'd got enough. Joke of course.'

Even the Republicans laughed and one of them said, 'True enough. Ney went against him, saying he'd bring him back in chains. When he saw him he cried on his shoulder and fell in behind. And as I say, I never minded *Bonaparte*, it was that Emperor tomfoolery …'

'And it wasn't only Ney,' the one-legged man said. 'Before that, when he hadn't more than a handful. Right at the start and he didn't know which way the cat'd jump. When he met the Fifth of the Line and walked out alone and told anybody who wanted to kill him to go ahead. That took guts.'

'Nobody never said he hadn't got guts. All we ever said was he did away with the Republic.'

Crouched, immobile on my makeshift bed, desperately smothering my occasional cough, I heard it all.

I was steeled to hearing my name during the morning or afternoon sessions. To hear it in the evening was a jolt.

At Grenoble the whole garrison – a large one – had gone over to the Emperor and in that city he had made a speech, promising peace to France and to every man the vote which Lefebvre and his friends so much desired. When this was being discussed, some cynic in the outer room said, 'I'll believe that when get it. Sounds to me like a bribe; a bit like the money all the soldiers got at Grenoble.'

'What money?'

'Money Queen Hortense took him. In bags.'

Jean Lefebvre was not the most agreeable of men, but there was a streak of justice in him and he said, 'She couldn't have …' Then I suppose he remembered, or Marion gave him a glance. He stopped abruptly.

'Well, she was seen there, handing over the money. And she ain't been in her house since he landed. So why couldn't she have?'

Marion said, ''Cos she couldn't get back there in the time is why. Not less she took wings. Grenoble mighty far away.'

Nobody contradicted that. Jean Lefebvre, anxious to cover his slip said, 'Yes. It'd have taken wings. Or a witch's broomstick.'

Somebody said, 'Well, I wouldn't put it past her. Sounds like she could be in two beds at once; why not two places?'

Marion's voice again. 'Jean, this bottle empty as a promise. You open next one or your frens go 'way thinking you very mean man or can't afford …'

In the midst of so much excitement the question of whether a child should live with his father or his mother lost importance. Virtually unremarked the verdict was given against me. Lou was to be handed over to Louis within three months.

It was a blow, for to the very end I had hoped. It was also a smear. My counsel had made so much of Louis's undesirability as custodian of a child, a man without a country, without a home, in bad health that the only inference was that I must be even more undesirable for other reasons, less precisely stated.

Marion, bringing the news back from the morning market, said, 'Now, you doan go fretting. Lot can happen in three month. Emperor, he on his way back. He put things right for you …'

29

Two days later, with the Emperor said to be within a day's march of Paris, Marion, who had passed by my house every day, reported that the guards had been withdrawn and the place looked just ordinary. Her husband, coming home for his midday meal, said that the King had left, driving fast towards the Belgian frontier, and all over Paris the white flags and lilies of the Bourbons were coming down.

I went home.

I remembered his fondness for taking people by surprise, sudden comings and goings. If he was supposed to be a day's march away in all likelihood he would arrive in the night. To an empty palace, as I had arrived to an empty house. Empty, that is, of loved ones.

I took a long, long bath, dressed in my best, the Court dress with a train, most of my jewels that remained. I wished that I could have gone to welcome him with a child on either side but I was being cautious. Remblai des Bons Enfants might, just possibly, be called into service as sanctuary again; better that no one should know.

I was not alone, I was not even first at The Tuileries. There was a crowd, many people who, like me, had never been there during the Monarchy and quite as many who had for the second time in a year changed coats. Of the real old Royalists, not one. The mood was hilarious. Somebody had discovered that on curtains and carpets the Bouro lilies had only been *tacked* over the Imperial bees and men who had never in their lives bent their backs or busied their fingers with a menial task were ripping off the symbols.

The welcome accorded me was astounding. All forgotten my months of private life when only the most faithful made visits, all forgotten the filth flung, indirectly. Remembered was the thing that Madame de Souza had warned me about – that my house had been a Bonapartist Club. I was even supposed to have *financed* this return. My best diamonds had gone to ensure little Auguste's future – and were missed by some sharp female eye. And what about Mother's? Nobody knew about her debts. 'Never were diamonds sacrificed to better purpose,' some woman, rising from a curtsy, said with tears in her eyes.

Bonaparte came back at nine o'clock that evening, carried in, shoulder high, up the stairs, through the crowd of weeping women and men crying, 'Long live the Emperor'. He wore the shabby grey overcoat and the battered hat which he had always spoken of, sardonically, 'my working clothes', he was very pale, fatter and quite impassive, very much like the of those images, gods, which Dutch ships' captains were bringing home from the farthest east. General Lavalette, who had married my cousin Emilie, walked backwards before him, clearing a way with thrusts of his shoulders and heavy arms. By this time I was standing with Julie, Joseph's wife, who had come timidly and been surprised and pleased to find me already there. 'I felt I should come,' she said. 'Joseph would have wished me to. Family you know ...' Joseph for the past year had been in Switzerland, like Louis banned from France. Julie, like myself, had been allowed to stay – not a Bonaparte by birth. Maybe she had her own reasons for not joining Joseph. I could not know; in all the months since the Empire's fall, she had not visited me, or I her. But on this evening we stood together; his family ...

Lavalette cleared the way and, borne aloft, Bonaparte went into his study. The door slammed and two soldiers as though conjured up by magic came and took guard positions. The crowd waited, either silent or speaking in lowered voices. After about fifteen minutes Julie and I were admitted.

Emotional atmosphere is not fancy. I had taken only two steps into the room, prepared to curtsy, kiss his hand, be embraced, when I knew that he was displeased with me and that he wished me to keep my distance. Julie may have felt the same, or was basing her behaviour on mine; we both curtsied and then stood.

He attacked her first. 'What are you doing here?' How she had offended was not difficult to decide: she should have been with Joseph! In the Emperor the Corsican liking for marital solidarity had been reinforced by resentment that *his* wife had not followed him to Elba. Julie blushed and looked confused, but before she could give any answer he swung round on me.

'So you lost your lawsuit! I could have told you you would. You should have known better than to have brought it.' In other words – You should have let the divorce go through quietly and not stirred up old mud.

Julie and I stood silent, like scolded children.

'Where are the children?' the Emperor asked.

'I thought it advisable to send them out of Paris for a little while.'

He gave me a sharp look.

'You won't get away with that! Paternal rights are paramount.' There again his had been denied. The little King of Rome was now in Vienna, being brought up as an Austrian prince. 'I shall expect you to bring them to see me tomorrow.'

'I had intended to do so.'

'That will do then,' he said.

As early as was reasonable next morning I took my carriage and went to Madame de Souza's house in the Rue Verte, and from there sent my coachman home. I hoped to see Auguste, I hoped to see Charles, and I needed to cover my tracks. Ushered into Madame de Souza's boudoir I apologised for calling so early, explained my position and asked if she would do me the favour of sending a servant to hire a cab for me. She did so. Then she said, 'Auguste has gone out for an airing with his nurse.' I thought I detected a slight defensiveness about her manner.

'It is a fine morning. And I came unexpectedly. I did not really expect …'

'Where have you *been*?' she asked. 'Vanishing like that without a word to anyone. Poor Charles was quite distraught. He went to your house that Monday evening. He had been in court all day and wanted to break it to you gently that he thought the summing up would go against you. He was sure that you had been arrested. He went to the Chief of Police. *Were* you arrested?'

'No. I went into hiding. As I told you, Lord Kinnaird said … And I had no time.'

'A week. Surely in that time you could have sent a message to allay our anxiety. Did it not occur to you that we should be anxious?'

'But of course.' That was untrue. Incredible as it now sounded my sole concern was that nobody should know anything about our hiding-places. 'I am very sorry. It was extremely thoughtless of me. But … well my position was difficult. The … the friend with whom I lived had her ordinary life to pursue. She went on one long errand for me, and went past my house every day … And of course every day I hoped to be free to return …' The excuses sounded very feeble.

Madame de Souza said, 'We were forced to conclude that you had gone on some errand so secret that even Charles, even I could not be trusted to know.'

'What kind of errand?'

'Taking money to Bonaparte.'

'Oh.'

'Somebody did. Heaven knows how many thousands of men he collected. They weren't fed on air.'

'Nor on anything I provided, I swear to you.' I remembered that she was, always had been, an ardent Royalist. 'I saw the Emperor for the first time last evening at The Tuileries – and a very cool reception he gave me. He is very cross with me. About the case.'

Her face changed.

'Yes. Yes, of course. I am very sorry. I should have said so sooner. Very sorry. I know how fond of him you are. It will be a wrench.'

In this milder climate I could say, 'Where is Charles?'

She spread her hands, 'How should I know? Back with his regiment, wherever that may be.'

The servant said he had found a cab.

Madame de Souza embraced me.

'My dear … These are troubled times. Forgive me if I sounded sharp. This cannot last, you know. It is a gambler's last throw. Invariably fatal. Within three months the King will be back in Paris and Bonaparte back on Elba.'

I took the cab as far as the forge, collected Louise and the children, chose the right moment to say, 'We can walk from here,' and so went home. The boys were greatly excited at the idea of seeing Uncle Bonaparte again.

It was at this interview, after the fond greetings – in Charles-Napoleon's life a year loomed larger than it did in Lou's and he did not, I think, remember the Emperor so vividly, but based his actions on his brother's – that I learned that I had not offended only in the matter of the lawsuit. I was in the absurd position of being outside The Tuileries, credited with being the most ardent Bonaparte, plotting and in part financing the Emperor's return, inside being accused of consorting with the enemy.

'You should not even have stayed in France,' Bonaparte said angrily. 'You should have left with the rest of us. I should have thought that you … you of all people, would have preferred a bit of black bread in a ditch to hobnobbing with the enemy. I thought of *you*. At that worst moment. At Fontainebleau. I wrote it in, an assured income and a title. Was that not enough for you? Licking that fickle fellow's feet to get yourself made Duchesse of Saint-Leu! I would never have believed that you would so completely have deserted me.'

I said, 'I was civil to Alexander because Mother wished me to be. She wanted permission to join you in Elba and he was the one with the most influence at the time …'

'Josephine wished to come?'

'From the moment when she was informed of where you were.'

'Nobody thought to tell me that.'

'Nobody knew. Before anything could be arranged she was …'

'Dead! And nobody thought to tell me that, either. Do you know how I learned? Some wretched servant went to the mainland to visit his family and saw a paper and came back and told me. You could have written.'

'I did. The very day after. I wrote how beautifully …. and what she said, with her last breath. Eugène wrote too … about the funeral. And he asked if there was anything at Malmaison that we could send. For you to remember her by. We had no answer.'

'I never had any letter. That will show you ... And she lies where?'

'In the village church.'

'That will not do. She was Empress of France. She must be taken to St Denis, where when my time comes I can lie beside her; I shall see to that, later. At the moment ...'

At the moment he had other things to see to.

In Grenoble he had promised peace. But as soon as the news of his landing reached Vienna the Allies had ceased their bickering over trifles and declared that they would never make peace with Bonaparte. The English Duke of Wellington, the one who had driven the French out of Spain and thus earned his place at the Congress of Vienna, had already left and was posting up to Brussels, a convenient centre for the rallying of English, Prussian, Russian forces.

At the moment the Emperor had something other to think about than Mother's final resting-place: but he did make time on another day, shortly after this reconciliatory scene, to come out to Malmaison with me.

I had never been there since Mother's death, now almost eleven months ago. April was too early for roses, but all the spring flowers were in full beauty under the young, just spreading leaves. The Emperor and I walked the paths in silence, remembering many things. One memory I did not share with him was Hippolyte Charles posturing and gesticulating as he planned vistas upon which one would come suddenly with a sense of surprise. I was thinking of that and how successful the plans had been when the Emperor said, 'At every turn of this path I expect to see her. My poor dear Josephine. I still cannot believe ...'

We had just turned on to a grass path bordered with hyacinths, closely set, almost overbearingly scented. Sorrow ached in my throat. We walked on, again in silence, until he said, 'A future life. Do you have any thoughts about that?'

'Thoughts sometimes. No views. And yet, when she died ...'

'Tell me.'

I did so, ending with the comment, 'It seemed more like a beginning than an end.'

He said, without looking at me, 'That would be a comforting thought. There's the danger ... And yet what about ghosts? I've known men, hard-headed fellows who claim ... Wait for me here.' He left me and went into the shuttered house alone. I sat on one of those marble seats that had come from Italy and breathed the scented air and thought of Mother and of Adèle and of Non-Non. I would have welcomed any assurance that they had life outside my own mind; but none came.

When he joined me I could see that he had been weeping. But he took out his watch, that strict timepiece that Mother had dreaded and always said was at least fifteen minutes fast, and said, 'We must get back. I'm glad you held on to this place. Later on, when I'm less busy, we must open it properly and come often.'

Two days after that Charles came to see me.

Like his mother, like the Emperor, he began by scolding me. 'How do you imagine I felt? The house full of the King's men and you vanished without a trace. They damn near arrested me. So did the Police when I went to ask them about you. And there was no time. I had to get south to meet *him*.'

'I know. I lost my head completely. I'm sorry. Sorry. Sorry.' I wished I could cry, some of those beautiful tears that had served Mother so often and so well. I could only pretend, bowing my head, brushing my eyes with my fingers.

Then he said, 'Don't cry, darling,' and took me in his arms and kissed me and I knew why people in love *invent* quarrels.

Presently I said, 'What you doing now?'

'Kissing the girl I love. You should have noticed.'

'I meant officially.'

'Oh. Well, as I was saying, I went south. Not with the mob. I was an early bird and was rewarded with a worm – an appointment at the War Office.'

'So you will be in Paris?'

'Very little. He can see to Paris. And my job is not counting soldiers on paper; I count the real ones – at various assembly points; comfort the home-sick, kick the laggards, see that they're all fed and equipped and trained not to shoot one another. It may not sound much, but I assure you; I now have a lot of authority. I am doing what *he* would do, what he used to do, when he was younger and could ride without discomfort. Darling, forget that. I should not have said it.'

I said, 'But you did say it, darling. So tell me, what ails him? I knew some-thing was wrong, physically, from the moment I saw him, carried into The Tuileries. And when he went to that great parade in the Place du Carousel … he took Lou and Charles-Napoleon and they were so disappointed to go in a carriage and not to ride all the way … What is it?'

'Let's say Elba water. It has some quality which makes for good vines, good wine. But taken as he took it – he was always abstemious, as you must know – well, it's hardly a subject but between us, he has an inflammation on the bladder – very painful, not serious. He cannot ride far or fast. I can. So I act for him and sample recruits' fodder and look out for flat feet and squint eyes. But now I am in Paris, for two nights.'

There was that tone in the voice, that look in the eyes.

I said, 'Could you go to Malmaison? Tomorrow? About nine o'clock?'

The Emperor's mandate was once again all sufficient, covering even apparently eccentric behaviour. Next day I went early in the evening to Malmaison and explained to the caretaking couple that the Emperor wished the house to be used again; not immediately, but at some not too far distant time. I had come, I said, to take stock; later on I should hire staff. I told them to ignore me. I might decide to spend the night, but had come prepared with everything I needed. If I did stay the night perhaps they could manage to give the coachman a bite of supper. This suggestion was very welcome since the coachman and the caretaker's wife were related in some complicated way.

This time Charles and I were ghosts in a ghostly place. So much had happened since that month in winter, almost four years ago, and we had both changed so much that sometimes even the joy had a curious echoing quality about it. Not less, just different.

For one thing we could not contemplate marriage and years of life ahead – always with the *if*, if Charles survived. He was sure that he would. 'Don't worry, darling. I am a professional survivor,' he would say. He also said that there might be no war at all. 'When the Allies, especially the English, see how solidly France is behind the Emperor they may decide against making an unprovoked attack. Last time they could pretend that they were liberating France from a tyrant. They can't say that now; he has, you might say, been re-elected.'

And that was virtually true. Apart from a few Royalists who had either run away or retired into locked and shuttered houses, all France was now Bonapartist; even Republicans, like Lefebvre's cronies, preferred Bonaparte to Louis XVIII. The war weariness of 1814 had vanished; defeats were forgotten, victories remembered, and the recent humiliations only thought of as something to be avenged. This was the moment for which the veterans had waited; and boys too young last year were old enough now, and they had been crammed with stories of gallantry and stirring action and near escapes which, it seems, are all that men ever bring back from a war.

In Aix Eugène had called Charles a nit-wit and asked what we had found to talk about, and I had replied that there was no need for talk.

Now we talked about many things, marriage foremost. Tomorrow, the day after, a week from today? To say that there was never the apt time sounds like a confession of lack of will, but the truth is the time was never right. We agreed that the Emperor must be told and invited to be present. Otherwise we should give offence and I felt rather like a debtor whose debts have been forgiven, but whose credit is no longer good; and Charles was very anxious not to do anything that would put him out of favour. Also, although Bonaparte could no longer ride far or fast, he was capable of travelling in a carriage and at the journey's end mounting a horse and showing himself to those soldiers who remembered him and the young to whom he was only a name, so he was not often in Paris and Charles, working a far wider orbit, was there even less often.

In fact, between April, when at Malmaison the last hyacinths sweetened the air, and late May, when some of Mother's earliest roses were just showing colour, we managed only six nights together. Once he rode forty miles, arriving about midnight and leaving at first light. There was something peculiarly eerie about that morning – we had not slept at all – creeping down through a dusk quite different from that of evening, to the gateway of the paddock where his horse was. It was a most unpromising-looking horse, very angular with a huge head and after Ulm useless as a cavalry mount, because its nerve had been broken. But Charles had not sold it into slavery, to drag an overladen cart, the fate of so many old cavalry horses, because it had speed and endurance and would come at a whistle. In the grey distorting light by the paddock gate he whistled. The horse came up, tame as a dog, and for a minute or two Charles busied himself with the bridle and the saddle that had lain for the few short night hours just inside the paddock gate. Then he turned, lifted me and held me and said, 'It may be a fortnight this time. Till then remember that I love you and shall love you forever.'

It was in fact just a little over a fortnight. A scribbled line, anonymous, non-committal: '11th June; ten in the evening', sent time into a spinning whirl. For 11th June was a Sunday and now the old routine of Family gatherings around the dinner table in the private apartments at The Tuileries had been resumed. I could only hope that the Emperor would not be in Paris on that Sunday; but he was.

Lucien had at last been forgiven, made a Prince of France and given a place in the Government; Joseph's less open rebellion had also been condoned. Louis had been invited to return to France and was, I understood, on his way. One had the sense of the Family closing ranks in time of crisis. Jerome was not present at this particular gathering because he was with the army mustering on the Belgian frontier; and Caroline was in Trieste, prisoner of the Austrians. Murat had made his last fatal throw. Without waiting for the outbreak of general war he had made a bid to recapture his throne by taking independent action against Austria and been soundly defeated early in May – a fact not to be wondered at since the majority of the men he led had really no notion whom or for what they were fighting. Murat's lost battle cast no gloom on the French and Caroline's fate seemed not to affect the Family much; it was reported that she was being given royal-prisoner treatment.

If Madame Mare, behind her inscrutable face, missed some of her brood, she could see the gaps being filled by the young; my two sons, Joseph's two daughters.

We all knew now that war was imminent. Those stout believers in free choice – the English – had either wavered or been overruled. There was to be no free choice for the French. But we had not been told anything positive until half-way through this dinner when the Emperor said, quite casually, 'Next Sunday at this time, I shall be in Brussels.' In a way he spoke for the whole of France, resurrected and confident; the general feeling was that there would be one battle, not on French soil, and that one a victory.

When he said that, I understood, or thought I understood the change I had detected in his manner. Ever since his return from Elba there had been something heavy about all his moods, angry, sad, gay, official, informal. But on this evening he was genuinely gay, laughing and joking with the younger members of the Family. Whatever had weighed him down was gone; he looked and seemed younger, less ponderous. I remembered, almost guiltily, what Charles had told me and hoped that the weeks away from Elba and its water had cured his ailment.

At nine o'clock I made Charles-Napoleon's youth an excuse to leave. It was not well-received. The Emperor said, 'Another half hour won't hurt him.'

'Eight o'clock is his bedtime,' I said. 'He is only six.'

Lou said politely, 'And a half, Mamma. I always think that after the half age should go, I mean for counting, the other way. Forward I mean, not backward.'

The Emperor said, 'Bravo. Up to thirty, Lou, up to thirty. After that you go the other way.'

Charles-Napoleon put in his well-considered word.

'Lots of boys, smaller than I am, stay up late. Lou and I hear them playing in the street when we are in bed.'

I said, 'Yes, but they do not …' I was about to say, 'grow tall'. One of Madame de Boubers's many theories; she believed that children grew in bed and could quote a case of a boy who had had some kind of fever which kept him in bed six weeks; when he got out of bed he was a foot taller than when he had taken to it. I remembered, just in time, that Bonaparte was the reverse of tall. It was something that nobody noticed really because his dominating personality made up for the lack of inches. I ended my sentence – 'have mothers who care whether they are in bed or not.'

Madame Mere said something in her swift Italian. The Emperor laughed and translated for my benefit.

'My mother says that she attributes my ability to go without sleep and to take a cat-nap at any time to early training. When we were on the run in the *maquis*.'

The *maquis* was the rough thyme-scented scrub of Corsica and the Family had once taken refuge in it long ago, from some enemy, a political party long inoperative.

Joseph said, 'Ah. The *maquis*. I can smell it now; and that simple statement sparked off an argument. Had Joseph taken part in that headlong flight or was he already at school in France? Given nothing of more importance to argue about the Bonapartes could run such a hare to ground, and did, for a quarter of an hour. I began to sweat slightly. I had to take the boys home and say goodnight unhurriedly; for this was June and my time with Lou was if anything more precisely limited than my time with my lover. And then I must get to Malmaison. Charles would wait, but not patiently … and this might be our last night, for a time. That it might be the last in fact, the last forever, I simply dared not think about. Hurry, hurry, hurry!

But there was the other side to it, too. I suspected that the Emperor would not go to bed tonight, he was preparing for one of his sudden pouncing moves. If he meant to leave at midnight he now wished for company and distraction. And at any other time …

And then there was the leave-taking, for the Emperor exceptionally long-drawn-out. He said to Lou, 'You must not be unhappy about leaving your mother, Louis-Napoleon. I had to leave mine when I was just your age, but here we are you see, happy and together.'

Lou, as always, looked distressed at this mention of his future: Charles-Napoleon, already over-tired and over-excited by the Emperor's teasing and joking, threw himself at his brother and burst into sobs.

Madame Mere recalled sufficient French to remark, 'Come! Come! Boys should not cry.'

Lou threw her a look of pure hatred and said, 'Oh yes they can. Till they're seven.'

Undeterred she said, 'Nor should they answer back.'

The Emperor said, 'Madame Mere never allowed us to answer back. *And look at us now!*'

At last we got away. I should be late. I should be very late. My coachman, forewarned that I must go to Malmaison – I had told him that I must be there first thing in the morning to arrange for some trivial repairs to be begun – did not drive into the carriage entry but drew up outside the street door. I almost did not go in with the children, but changed my mind; so late already ten minutes would make little difference.

'I shall just say good night and you must go straight to bed,' I said.

As we entered the lighted hall I glanced at the marble side table on which letters and messages were always laid out. Ever since the news of the Emperor's landing at Cannes I had been receiving letters and notes from enthusiasts and cranks. A number had awaited me when I came out of hiding and several of those had warned me that attempts to assassinate him would be made if he ever reached Paris. There had been messages of commiseration, or abuse, concerning the lawsuit; and many more praising me for the supposed part I had played in the return. Tonight there was only a single piece of paper on the table, not sealed, folded so carelessly that the edges were not in line. I almost ignored it; but as Lou put his arm around his brother who was still emitting a gulp at intervals and drew him towards the stairs I took up the paper which had been handled by somebody with very dirty fingers and in their bedroom I read it.

It said, 'Sudden orders. Moving immediately. Don't worry. Remember the gateway. C.'

In the grey dawn. 'I shall love you forever.'

30

This time the agony of waiting was not prolonged. In our hearts we had all known that while, given the Emperor's genius and the great upsurge of national spirit, the French might win a single decisive battle, they could not sustain a long war. The Allies outnumbered them two to one; and the French army was made up of too few tried veterans and too many boys.

The Emperor left Paris at the midnight between 11th and 12th June and on the 16th won a battle against the Prussians at Lusigny. All the bells in Paris rang to celebrate this victory, but it was not the single decisive battle that was needed. That came two days later at a place named Waterloo. A day-long battle: the Duke of Wellington called it a damned close run; but we lost.

Alongside news of this disaster came the information that the Emperor was on his way back to Paris, only just ahead of the advancing Allies. I found out that he was heading for the Elysée and I went there.

This time there were no welcoming crowds. One might almost say no Bonaparte, just an old man, broken in spirit, sick in body and sunk in torpor – perhaps a merciful torpor. There seemed to be a gap between his sight and his perception, between his mind and his tongue. For a moment he seemed not to recognise me. Then he said, 'Ah, Hortense.' A little lapse. 'Spare me your pity.'

'I wanted only to say that I am sorry for your misfortune, Sire.'

'Come back … in an hour. I must see …' Joseph and Lucien were there, several harassed-looking ministers, some generals. Walking in the same unco-ordinated way as he spoke he went into a room with them. I was too restless to sit down and wait so I went out into the street. Groups of people stood about, for the most part stunned, for Parisians oddly quiet. Nobody noticed me. Here and there a voice would be raised. That old ugly story was on its rounds again. Bonaparte had deserted his beaten army; but this was denied as often as it was said. I learned that the Prussians, of all enemies the most dreaded, would be in Paris within twenty-four hours. But there was no visible panic and I saw nothing of the exodus to the country that had taken place last year. All but a few people seemed to share the Emperor's inertia. One of the audible, positive statements I heard was, 'They won't make peace while *he* is in France.'

I thought – And he should not be here. He must get away. Last time Elba …

I almost ran back to where my carriage waited and said to Bonnet, 'Home. Quickly.' Then I ran upstairs, and tipped the best of my remaining diamonds into a stocking. Then I drove back to Elysée. There was a National Guard on either side of the gateway and we were halted, as we had been rather less than an hour earlier to identify ourselves. While the one guard inspected me, and apologised for doing so, a woman, young, garishly dressed, said to the other, 'Why stand there like a dummy? Come and have a good time with me. Bring a friend.'

'Can't leave my post.'

'He left his. Come on.'

Then she either recognised me or heard my name. She screamed at me. 'Queen! It's queens like you make it hard for honest whores like me to get a living. Go ahead boys, get it free inside!'

Bonnet hit out at her with his whip, but missed.

I saw that the very lowest elements of Paris, the people who had made the time of the Terror possible, were emerging from their hidden holes.

I said, 'Sire, you must get away. This time it will be something worse than Elba. My carriage is waiting.' I had even, with that prostitute's words ringing in my ears, told Bonnet to take up a position from which it would be possible to move in the least possible time. 'My horses are good and fresh. You must get to the coast. Go to America.'

There was that lapse, as though I had spoken in a foreign language and his mind must translate it before he could understand and answer.

'My brothers ... and some of my generals ... think that Paris could be defended.'

'Do you think so?'

He said, 'I don't know.' And I thought – He was always the one to know; he even knew what other people should know. What they should do, how act, how think.

I said, 'You must listen to me. You must get away while there is time. Do you want to spend the rest of your life in a *real* prison?'

There was the pause, the lapse. Then he said, 'My dear, it no longer matters.'

Nothing mattered any longer; not Lucien standing up in the Chamber of Deputies and saying that to fail Bonaparte now was to fail France. Nor the retort of that old Republican, Lafayette, that it was Bonaparte who had failed France. Frenchmen had followed him through the sands of Egypt and the snows of Russia and as a result three million of them were dead. A telling point.

He was dead, too. Nothing stirred in him when I urged escape, nor when mobs of soldiers gathered outside the Elysée shouting 'Long live the Emperor', and sent in deputations begging him to lead them again. I stayed with him because he clung to me. 'Don't leave me, Hortense.' That, at least, was positive. So I stayed.

Now and then I thought of that attempt at suicide at Fontainebleau – but the truth is that in order to commit suicide a man must be alive, with something to kill. Self-destruction is a positive act, demanding decision, action. Dead men do not commit suicide, and he was as dead as if he had fallen at Waterloo. I do not believe he could have roused himself even if the Government had decided to make a last-minute stand and called upon him to organise the defence. He showed no interest in his future and when that was hastily decided, a lifelong sentence of exile on an English-owned island in the South Atlantic, St Helena, he was unmoved.

The date for his leaving was fixed, the 29th, and when he heard that he did again say a positive thing, 'I should like to spend the last days at Malmaison.'

I went with him and stayed until the end.

The garden was at its best, roses in bud, roses fully open scenting the air from dawn until dusk. The weather was wonderful and although the Prussians had reached the village and set fire to a bridge, in Malmaison there was a curious air of peace, except for people coming to say goodbye to him. His family, my boys for whom I sent, the Countess Walewska and her beautiful child, a few officers, one of whom told me that Charles was alive and well, but where he did not know.

I spent my time while he was engaged with his goodbyes making a belt to hold the diamonds, so that he could wear them hidden around his waist. I offered it to him on the evening of the day before he left, and he did push aside apathy long enough to protest.

'No, no. I must not rob you of your trinkets. What do I need?'

'Money, or its worth, is always useful. Please, I wish you to have them. Most of them you gave me and the rest came to me because of you.' Young Hortense Beauharnais in the Rue Chantereine had owned no diamonds nor any prospect of ever doing so. I did not feel that I was making any sacrifice.

'As a loan then. I have no notion of what my circumstances will be. On Elba I was supposed to have an allowance, but it was not paid. Are you sure you can spare these?'

'I have others.' A surface truth. For sentiment's sake I had retained a ring of which Mother had been especially fond and I had left at home a few things of small value.

He took the belt and then, looking around the garden, said, 'How pleasant it would be if we could stay here, Hortense.' Even that was said without any great feeling; merely an expression of opinion. I was glad; glad that he had lost his abilty to feel as I had lost my ability to weep. In the rose-crowded, rose-scented garden we made, I thought, a peculiarly well-matched pair, except that I had a future and he had none. But I suited him *then* as I think few women could have done; about Madame Mere there had been the unspoken but unmistakable air of 'This I expected'. Marie Walewska had cried until she could hardly see.

He said, 'Josephine would have been very unhappy now.'

In the morning they sent a most unworthy vehicle to take him on the first stage of his journey to St Rochelle where the English frigate waited. Beside it we said goodbye, without tears, without a wasted word. Just 'Goodbye', which says it all. Then I went back to Paris.

And it was very different from last year when my house was guarded with everything as I had left it, waiting for me. It was now occupied; Prince Schwarzenberg had decided to take it as his headquarters and it was full of soldiers. My children, Louise de Cacholet, Madame de Boubers and one maid were housed in part of the servants' quarters. The maid, nobody else, was allowed access to the kitchen at such time as the cook-orderlies permitted; nobody was allowed to go into the garden, or the street.

Prince Schwarzenberg was not unknown to me; he had come out with others to Malmaison in the spring of last year and seemed affable. I was reasonably sure that when I went to tell him that I was here and to plead for some mitigation of circumstances – there was not, for instance, a bed for me; in my own house! – he would listen.

He did listen; and he said, 'I am sorry that you have been inconvenienced. So have I. I need the whole house and hope that you will arrange to leave as soon as possible.'

I said, 'Leave?'

Up to that moment the thought had not occurred to me. Last year, married to a Bonaparte I had not been counted as one. This year, with that horrible lawsuit behind me, surely … Oh, granted I had gone to The Tuileries to welcome Bonaparte back, I had lived out the Hundred Days in the Paris he held, attended his Court, hoped for his victory. But so had thousands and thousands of other people.

'Perhaps you have not seen this morning's *Moniteur*,' the Prince said. He fumbled among the papers on my big round table and found the *Moniteur*, folded it small and held it to me. 'Enemies of France', I read. And a long list, headed by my name.

'You see,' the Prince said, cold and cruel, 'France itself denounces you. Perhaps I should tell you that in the last two days there have been demonstrations outside this house. By French Royalists, and very ugly. One took ten of my men to control. Had you been here and we had not, the consequences could have been unpleasant.'

I thought of the woman outside the Elysée; people like her, not Royalist or anything else, just ready for any excuse for rowdyism.

I also thought of the Czar. True I had not heard from him recently, but there had been war. True I had sensed his withdrawal of that offer of special protection, but we had remained friends. True the lawsuit had damaged my reputation, but I looked upon it as a stroke of luck that he had ceased to want me as a mistress before the mud was flung; a friend would be more tolerant than a would-be lover.

Perhaps my face looked less anxious, my posture less tense as I thought of my powerful friend. The Prince said, 'I think you should know that you now have no friend among the Allies. The Czar is particularly incensed. Only yesterday when there was a question of a pension for Madame Mere, he said he would do nothing for any Bonaparte. He mentioned you by name, saying that he had befriended you last year yet you had been largely responsible for the recent upheavals.'

I said, 'I know ridiculous stories are told about me. Only very foolish, credulous people believe them.'

'Then foolish, credulous people constitute the vast majority,' he said.

Alexander might be credulous over some things, but he had never struck me as foolish. I made up my mind to write to him immediately and trust to his understanding. Meanwhile ...

'I am obliged to ask you one favour,' I said, again regretting that I had not inherited Mother's charming pliancy of manner. 'It concerns the children. Could they be permitted to use the garden?'

He hesitated so long that I thought he was going to refuse. Then he said, grudgingly, 'Very well. And I would ask you to make arrangements to leave as soon as possible. I need the whole house.'

I went straight and wrote to Alexander, a letter as brief and simple as possible. I denied that I had ever plotted, ever taken political action. I mentioned the story of my having been seen carrying money in Grenoble; that was demonstrably false and typical of the rest. As I wrote it seemed to me that the forefront of my offence, the thing that singled me out from all others, was that I had stayed with the Emperor *after* his defeat, when almost everyone had deserted. I excused this as due to natural affection and filial duty; he had been a very kind step-father to me.

Louise Cacholet – granted permission to leave the house – delivered this letter herself. I waited for an answer for two days. None came, except indirectly. On the evening of the second day the Czar came to dine with Prince Schwarzenberg. I did not see him. Next morning the busy-body press reported that the Czar had visited the Duchess of Saint-Leu, and on the following day Russian Headquarters published a categorical denial that there had been any communication between us.

I then made a package of all the letters he had ever sent me and attached a brief message. I wrote that I no longer wished to keep letters which contained expression of friendship if the friendship no longer existed. I thought that he might glance at some of the things he had written from Vienna before he found it so gay, and relent a little. But he did not. Then I realised that I must take stock of my assets and begin to convert what I could into ready money.

It was the worst moment for selling anything. A shattered community, unsure of the future, means a bad market, except for speculators who will invest a little in the hope of huge profits presently. Also there is a kind of superstition about material things. Mother, despite her ultimate misfortune, was associated in most people's minds with luck, that mysterious, invisible yet potent thing which *might* be transmitted by contact. Of me the reverse was true. Nobody much wanted even my spare horses, so well-matched, so well-fed, so well-treated as to be easily manageable. Nobody much wanted even the best of my pictures. Nobody at all wanted my house, now full of enemy soldiers whose term of occupancy was uncertain and who would, when they left, leave damage behind them.

In all these negotiations Louise Cacholet acted as my agent – and true friend.

I was obliged to seek another interview with Prince Schwarzenberg and explain that I could not move until I had sold some things and that I could not, marooned as I was, take any action. He forbade me to leave the house. If I went anywhere and were recognised there was likely to be a public disturbance, he said. But he did agree that Louise should come and go as she wished.

She came and went, and she brought back stories of public disturbances not of my making. This occupation of Paris and its environs was quite different from the former one. This time there was no pretence that the Allies had come in as liberators, deserving and expecting friendship from the French. There were many cases of robbery, murder, rape. And the consequent acts of revenge, often upon men not guilty of the original offence. The English were seldom involved in horrid incidents, their Duke of Wellington was a very stern disciplinarian – and the English had never been invaded by the French. Prussia had been and of the occupying armies the Prussians behaved worst. Their Marshal Blucher wanted to blow up the most beautiful bridge in Paris and was dissuaded, not by Alexander – last year the protector of beautiful things – but by Louis XVIII, now back on his throne. The Russians were not much better. Listening to the tales Louis brought back I sometimes thought that Alexander had lost his power, or had no longer the wish to exercise it. Bonaparte had called him fickle …

My arrangements to move were under way by early July. I had decided to go to Pregny, Mother's house near Geneva. It still belonged to Eugène and me though, immediately after her death, with all those debts, we had tried to dispose of it. We almost had, but at the last moment there had been some hitch and Eugène had been so anxious to get back to his family that we had temporarily abandoned the business. Now that I was regarded as a Bonaparte and must share their exile I was glad to have a house to go to.

I had heard nothing from Charles, or about him. All I knew was that so far he had not been listed among the high-ranking officers whose loyalty to the Emperor was regarded as treason to the King. Marshal Ney was one who had been, and was in gaol, awaiting trial. As July moved into its second week I was divided in my mind, hoping that Charles was safe somewhere far from Paris, wishing to see him before I left. I wondered why Madame de Souza had not written to me, and even as I wondered realised that she might have done so and that I had not received the letter. There was now little communication between the main part of my house and the rooms where we lived on sufferance. Letters addressed to me might easily have been confiscated, or even thrown away.

So far no actual date had been set for our departure but I hoped to leave at the end of July. On the 14th Louise had arranged to go out to Malmaison to meet a dealer who was mildly interested in some of the pictures there and just as she was about to leave I scribbled a hasty note to Madame de Souza, asking for news and telling her that I expected to leave in about a fortnight. I asked Louise to deliver it. She always nowadays hired cabs for journeys of any length and I did not think an anonymous vehicle pausing outside Madame de Souza's house could possibly embarrass her.

One of the trivial inconveniences of our present way of life was the restricted use of the kitchen. On the evening when the Czar dined with Prince Schwarzenberg, for instance, we were unable to have access at all and could not even boil a kettle for our evening tea. Fortunately the weather was warm so hot food was not a necessity.

The soldiers, even the humblest, were very lordly – had the French been so arrogant and pretentious in Prussia, in Poland, in Austria? Those who now occupied my house had their boots and equipment cleaned and their errands run by three or four shuffling old Frenchmen, glad to earn any sum however pitiable. Attitudes work downwards and are very contagious. All but one of the old men treated us with veiled insolence.

It was the one civil one who on this morning, with the boys playing in the garden, Louise on her way to Malmaison and the maid in the kitchen with the lunch, two hours ahead of time, shuffled in and said, 'There's a Madame Dumorny to see you, ma'am. They were for sending her off, but I tipped a wink at the one on the door and got her in. She's in the passage.'

My heart gave a great thud. The truth was that nowadays everything was so sordid, so hateful, that my first thought was that Coralie Dumorny had somehow found out the truth about Auguste's parentage and had come to extort blackmail. I rebuked myself almost instantly. Madame de Souza, that good Royalist, dared not visit me herself, so had chosen an inconspicuous, trustworthy messenger.

But the woman in the passage which connected the front and rear portions of my house, seen over the old man's shoulder, was not the Coralie Dumorny that I knew. As I said, 'Thank you, Jules. That was kind, I thought – Who? Who? The woman moved forward from the dim light of the passage into the room that now served us for all purposes, sitting room, dining room, playroom and I thought – Like … No, it is!

Madame de Souza in what amounted to disguise. Her plump but still shapely body was hidden under one of those timeless, shapeless black dresses, not even quite black, faded, dusty, that are part of the decent working-woman's uniform. Without any cosmetic, not even powder, her face was dark red, without any salve, her lips almost purple. Her hair was hidden, her face shaded by one of those vast linen caps worn by women who worked in fields or had stalls in markets.

I said, on impulse, 'Adelaide!' We had been, I suppose, as close as two women could be, back in that long-drawn-out masquerade at Aix-in-Savoy, and the more intimate hours at Pont St Pierre; but she herself had deemed familiarity unwise, and habit sticks. Even in my mind I had thought of her as Madame de Souza. Now because she had taken such a risk and come in such clothes, such shoes, I said, 'Adelaide' and reached out both hands, and she took them and said, 'My dear.'

Among the plants that Mother cherished were her fuchsias, tender half-tropical plants with pendulous bells of colours that would be thought disagreeable if combined in anything but a flower. Now, looking at Madame de Souza, crimson-cheeked, purple-lipped, I thought of fuchsias – there was even one which had a white frill. Like her cap.

I said, 'It was good of you to come.'

She said, 'Charles is safe. I must get my breath. I walked.'

She sank down into a chair near the open window and drew out a delicate, lace-edged handkerchief which gave the lie to her disguise and delicately dabbed her forehead, her upper lip, her neck.

She took some deep breaths.

'How I managed it, God alone knows, but I did. I got his name removed from that court-martial list and I got him away. To England.'

'England?' I said the word in astonishment.

'Yes. I have friends there. Good friends.' I thought – Good friends indeed; better than mine if they can be so regardless of politics as to welcome a refugee who had been one of Bonaparte's right-hand men.

She said, 'One in particular; Lord Keith. Very influential.'

The inference was plain. The unsaid thing as distinct as an odour. For a moment I saw her as she had been a quarter of a century ago, pretty, vivacious, brave, resourceful, young in years but very worldly wise. I knew exactly in what way that friendship had been particular.

I said, 'I am so glad. I have been anxious.'

By this time she had recovered from her walk, the crimson of her cheeks and the purple of her lips had both lost sharpness and were merging into a general rubicon colour not unsuitable to her peasant clothes.

She said, 'How anxious? This is something that I must ask you, and you must ask yourself. Honestly answered it will make easier what I have come to say. You know me, I know you. We are both, I think, reasonable women – as women go. If you have indeed been anxious you have concealed your anxiety very well. You neither came to enquire, nor write. Oh yes, yes,' she said, bringing into her voice the gesture of brushing away a fly, 'Malmaison, those five days I understand. Better than you think. But you have now been back in Paris for two weeks.'

I said, 'I know. I know. But I think you do not understand how I have been living lately. I have been, I still am, under house-arrest. I have been waiting to hear from you. Hoping every day … As a matter of fact Louise Cacholet, when she went out this morning, carried a note, asking for news.'

'After a fortnight,' she said, as though reminding herself. 'Not that I had news until three days ago and when I had it I still waited. Deliberately.'

'Why?'

'To settle something in my own mind. I wished to be reasonably sure …' Her manner was calmly confident, but the colour in her face was growing patchy, as on that other never-to-be-forgotten occasion. I braced myself for her next words, guessing that they would be disturbing. She said, 'I want you to give him up.'

It was as though something had exploded so noisily that it had made us both deaf and dumb and paralysed. We just sat and looked at one another. Her expression was defiant; what mine was I did not know but I felt my face shrivel and stiffen.

Speech came back and I said, 'I cannot do that. I love him.'

She said, 'You think you do. You are in love with the *idea* of loving him – a very different thing. But, even if you loved him as much as any woman ever loved any man, I should still ask you to give him up. *For his own sake.* Believe me I am sorry for you, very sorry, and I know it is brutal to speak like this when everything has gone so wrong for you. But he is my son. With me he must come first.'

I said, 'But Charles loves me.'

She shook her head slightly. 'Charles, just at an impressionable age fell in love with a dream. It lasted longer than such dreams usually do because it remained a dream. It was never subjected to the rub of ordinary life. But there again, if he loved you as much as a man ever loved a woman, you must see that there can be no future for you together.'

'But there is now,' I said quickly. 'For the first time. All through these *hideous* days that has been my one comfort. I have been borne up by the thought that now, at last, we could be together.'

'Where?' She sounded like that inexorable old god of the Jews, speaking from a mountain top.

'In Pregny.'

She looked blankly astonished, and then pitying.

'My poor child! Do you seriously believe that you will be allowed to stay there?'

'Why not? Switzerland is a neutral country.'

'Neutrality consists of not taking sides, of keeping on good terms with everybody. You will find no permanent home there, nor anywhere else until Napoleon Bonaparte is dead and buried. Wherever you go you will be a centre of suspicion. So will any Frenchman who speaks to you. For a man with Charles's record to be seen in your company would be positively dangerous. Even on your own you will be harried about from pillar to post. You really must face the fact that for some years you will be compelled to live like a … like a gypsy.'

I faced, perhaps not the fact, but the possibility, and was appalled.

'But not in complete discomfort,' she said, in a different voice. Those black peasant dresses had capacious pockets; she fumbled in hers and pulled out a lumpy little parcel, wrapped in paper and tied with string. She held it towards me but I could make no move to take it.

'I beg you,' she said. 'Not from me, from God. For once I was lucky. I bet on a certainty – that the King would be back by the end of July. Look!'

She slipped the string from one end of the parcel and leaning forward tipped into my lap a shimmering tangle of diamonds. I stared at them stupidly, able only to think of Eugène who had refused a kingdom for fear he should have seemed to have been bribed.

I said, 'Are you trying to *buy* me?'

Tears leaped into her eyes and just brimmed over; her plump chin quivered. In the sunlight the tears hanging on her lower lids sparkled as brightly as the stones in my lap.

'How unkind! How could you even *think* …' Her voice was unsteady, but she mastered it. 'Could I bear to think of you in penury? You gave me Auguste.' She added in a more practical way, 'And I know you have not received a proper price for anything you have sold so far.'

I said, 'I should not have said that. I apologise. What with one thing and another, I hardly know what I am saying or doing. I will take these, more gratefully, and hope to repay you, when my affairs right themselves. About Charles I can promise you nothing. In the end the decision must be his.'

Her face mottled again and she said, 'You must forgive me. I do not wish to hurt you … Lord Keith has one child, a daughter, unmarried. She will be a considerable heiress. Charles can be irresistible when he chooses. And recent events have shown him where dreams end.'

By a paddock gateway in the grey dawn, saying I shall love you forever.

'I think you wrong him.'

'I hope not. I know a little about men. And about women. I know that you would make things easier for yourself if you would accept the truth. You loved Charles, with your body. And with your mind. But your heart was never his. You gave that long ago, to Napoleon Bonaparte.'

A second, even more shattering explosion.

And before I could speak, old Jules shuffled in again. He looked frightened. 'The Prefect of Police,' he gulped out.

I thought of arrest, imprisonment, leaving the children. I prayed to the God I had never believed in – Give me strength to bear it and to behave well. I looked into the passage and recognised Monsieur Decazes, once Louis's man of affairs, dismissed because he had not been able to make me give up Lou without a struggle. Prefect of Police now. What an odd world!

Then I looked at Madame de Souza who had jumped to her feet and turned so pale that her lips looked startlingly blue. She bent over slightly, the posture of a peasant asking a favour, she spoke with a whine.

'Anything, madame, in the way of household stuff that you don't want to take with you. No matter how old or shabby. I'll give you a fair price, madame. I'm known as a fair dealer. Don't forget, Dumorny's the name.'

I managed to say, 'I shall remember.' Knowing that we should never meet again I tried to inject the words with meaning – I shall remember all that you have done for me.

Humbly hunched, face averted, she sidled past Monsieur Decazes, whose first words as he entered did nothing to reassure me.

'I could have sent, madame, but having regard for your rank I came myself.'

From the garden came the sound of the children playing at their interminable game of soldiers. Would he allow me to say goodbye to them?

To Decazes I said, 'Yes, Monsieur?' and indicated the chair Madame de Souza had vacated.

'I have first to inform you that you must leave Paris on the 17th; first thing in the morning. Your passport is being prepared and will be delivered tomorrow.'

The relief was so enormous that I turned dizzy.

I said, 'Thank you. We shall be ready.' And glad to go! For the first time in my life, glad to leave my beloved France.

He went on, 'You will be given a guard to see you safely out of Paris. And Count Woyna – he is an Austrian – will escort you to the Swiss Frontier. I trust that you will find him congenial.'

Was there, in that last sentence, a kind of tilt, and in this sober, pompous middle-aged man's manner just a flash of something nasty, an echo of what had been hinted at during the lawsuit, a hint that to me any man not decrepit from senility would be congenial?

Probably another unworthy thought and I put it away.

I said, 'Thank you. Monsieur Decazes, shall I be permitted to reside in Switzerland?'

'That I cannot answer, madame. It will be a question for the Swiss authorities.'

'Would the French authorities object to my making my home in the house at Pregny which belonged to my mother?'

'That again I cannot answer. The most I can say is that so far as I myself am concerned, I hope not.'

I said, 'Thank you,' again. But his attention had left me and he was looking at the diamonds which I had laid on the table. There the sun did not strike them and they seemed to have lost brilliance.

'There is another thing,' he said. 'You would be well-advised not to take anything of value with you. In *certain* places feelings run high against you, madame, and there are those only too ready to make political issues an excuse for lawlessness. You might be robbed.'

Louise had already decided that if I left at the end of the month, she would not come with me; she intended to stay in Paris and squeeze out the last sou. I could safely leave the diamonds with her as I should leave a good deal of unfinished business. Louise, who had always lived a very sheltered life and was at heart less practical than Adèle, had proved during these last weeks that she was as capable of driving the best possible bargain as any woman who had spent her life haggling. She had indeed resorted to something I had never heard of. On this flabby, uncompetitive market if a man said, for instance, that he must consult his wife before he could decide to buy a piece of silver, a picture, some china or glass, Louise would say, 'we cannot await your wife's decision, should another buyer make an offer. Unless you care to take an option.' The amounts she fixed for options were trivial, but they mounted up.

Louise would bring me the diamonds with the money, now trickling in, from sales to be made, options not taken up in the last days of July.

So now I said, 'I will take nothing. Mademoiselle Cacholet will bring these, and some money to me presently.' Then a thought struck me. 'If she is given a passport.'

He said, 'There at least I can be helpful. She shall have it, I promise you.' He rose, rather ponderously to his feet. Through the open window came the boys' voices, amicably squabbling. Charles-Napoleon no longer accepted Lou's orders quite as meekly as Lou had once accepted Non-Non's and there was also the problem that in this soldier game neither of them wanted to be English, Prussian, Russian. Their disputes were not serious because they were so fond of one another, and they tended to move within earshot of me so that I could arbitrate and say, 'Who's turn?' or even suggest some other game. The boys were playing that trick now, coming close to the window.

Decazes looked out and said, 'You have them, at least.' When he said that something struck me for the first time. In March the French court had given me a three months' lease on Lou; it had run out a fortnight ago and here he was, still with me. I thought – 'live like a gypsy'. Gypsies were notoriously difficult to nail down: they stole fowls, horses, linen from drying lines, they would stop in hidden places and make charcoal from other people's trees and move on. Hardly ever were they called to account.

I thought – Yes, I will live like a gypsy and if Louis tries to nail me down, he will have his work cut out.

To Decazes I said, 'Yes, I have my boys.'

He said, 'I hope you will have a pleasant, uneventful journey.'

Not an ill-meaning man.

When he had gone I sat down and put my head between my hands … Everything was very quiet. The boys, realising that I was not for once going to intervene, had settled their squabble and moved away. I was alone in the quietude.

Once, driving in the Bois du Bologne, I saw a carriage wheel come off. The carriage lurched, the axle of the wheel digging a jagged groove. The wheel went spinning away on its uncontrolled, erratic course and now my mind did much the same. It wobbled.

Face the future; face the truth. What future? What truth?

A future quite possibly without a settled home, without much money and without friends. Well, I must face that and be cheerful, make the little hardships seem like a game. I also would plant gardens on warehouse roofs if necessary.

The truth. I must take nothing of value; simply myself, my thirty-two years of experience, my children and my memories. I felt hope transfer itself from Charles coming to me to Lou staying with me. Charles would not come, and who could blame him? What had I to offer now compared with that unknown English heiress, presumably young, perhaps pretty, and with an unblemished reputation.

Madame de Souza had said body, and mind and heart – heart always to be relied upon to take charge in a crisis.

Where did you run, Hortense, when you came out of hiding? Straight to The Tuileries, to welcome him.

Where did you run when the world crashed? Straight to the Elysée, to comfort him.

Face it. Swallow the brew. When you thought of men dead on battlefields far away, which came first? Not your lover, not your brother. In the same heartbeat perhaps, but not first. First was always the man whose given name, even in your thoughts, you dared not use. My step-father: Bonaparte: the Emperor. Never once Napoleon. You did not dare. Look upon the forbidden thing; speak the forbidden name and be struck dead!

How? And why? And when?

The sun shone and the children shouted in the garden. I sat and held my spinning head in my hands and my mind wobbled backwards: back to the moment when Mother said – And so I asked him to join us here this evening …

THE EPIC 'HOUSE' TRILOGY

THE TOWN HOUSE

£7.99

978-0-7524-4869-5

THE HOUSE AT OLD VINE

£7.99

978-0-7524-4868-8

THE HOUSE AT SUNSET

£7.99

978-0-7524-4870-1

MORE NORAH LOFTS TITLES FROM THE HISTORY PRESS

NETHERGATE

£7.99

978-0-7524-4879-4

HERE WAS A MAN

£7.99

978-0-7524-4824-4

If you are interested in purchasing other books published by The History Press, you can also place orders directly through our website

www.thehistorypress.co.uk